THE

W O M A N

**The item should be returned or renewed
by the last date stamped below.**

Dylid dychwelyd neu adnewyddu'r eitem erbyn
y dyddiad olaf sydd wedi'i stampio isod.

Newport
CITY COUNCIL
CYNGOR DINAS
Casnewydd

To renew visit / Adnewyddwch ar
www.newport.gov.uk/libraries

BOOKS BY ANNA-LOU WEATHERLEY

Chelsea Wives
Wicked Wives
Pleasure Island

THE DETECTIVE DANIEL RILEY SERIES
Black Heart
The Couple on Cedar Close
The Stranger's Wife

THE
WOMAN
INSIDE

ANNA-LOU WEATHERLEY

bookouture

Published by Bookouture in 2021

An imprint of Storyfire Ltd.
Carmelite House
50 Victoria Embankment
London EC4Y 0DZ

www.bookouture.com

ISBN: 978-1-80019-357-4
eBook ISBN: 978-1-80019-356-7

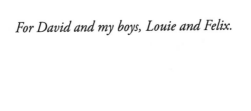

For David and my boys, Louie and Felix.

'We know what we are, but not what we may be.'
William Shakespeare – *Hamlet*

CHAPTER ONE

July

'Come on, Daisey, let me buy you a drink, eh? G & T, is it? Or are you more of a Porn Star Martini kinda girl? You look like you could do with a proper drink. Dunno about you, but this fizzy crap is giving me chronic gas.' He drains the dregs from his glass, pulls his lips over his teeth and belches. 'Tastes like gnat's piss.'

'I wouldn't know,' she retorts, pulling a face, but he doesn't hear her over the din.

'We need to get this party started… fancy a little livener?' He tugs at the sleeve of her shirt encouragingly – black and silky with a deep V-cut at the front, more daring than her usual attire – and stares at her cleavage lasciviously. 'A cheeky line, maybe?'

She feels a flush of self-consciousness prickle her skin; the shirt was a deliberate attempt to attract such attention after all, but now she wishes she hadn't worn it. The likes of Tommy White's sartorial approval is hardly a compliment. Less than five minutes ago she'd seen him sloping out of the Ladies loos with some dishevelled, shame-faced, middle-aged woman from Kitchenware shuffling awkwardly behind him.

'Haven't you grown out of all that crap by now, Tommy?' She attempts to squeeze past him, catching a waft of his aftershave – sweet and pungent – the sort that lingers on your bed sheets far longer than the memory of the sex.

'Aw, c'mon! I didn't have you down a such a basic bitch, Daisey.' His tone is playful, though she hears the disappointment in it. She doubts he even knows what 'basic bitch' really means – he's probably heard it used by the young trendies who work at Warwick's and thinks it sounds cool – he's so desperate to stay relevant even though, like her, he's hurtling towards middle age at a rate of knots. She looks out into the crowd in front of her – a hot sea of skin and sparkles, the warm scent of perfume and fake tan and cigarettes mixed with anticipation in the air. 'That blouse says anything but basic bitch.' She hates the word 'blouse' – it makes her think of schoolteachers.

Warwick's department store's annual summer party, the high-light of the season's social calendar – for some people anyway – free canapés and cava made to look more fancy than they actually are, thanks to the attractive young waiting staff serving them from giant platters and gold-rimmed champagne saucers. She imagines they are probably only being paid minimum wage as well.

An image of Luke suddenly flashes up inside her mind like a warning; he would hate it here tonight. '*Such vulgar corporate commercialism… so contrived… an exploitation of young, foreign students…*' She imagines the disdain in his eyes; his dark-rimmed glasses matching his well-cultivated beard as he scans the party with barely disguised disgust. He is probably at home now – his *new* home, with his *new* (or not-so-new as it had turned out) 'partner' Charlotte with her make-up-free flawless face, eating home-cooked vegan shepherd's pie between careful sips of organic wine. Maybe they're having an important discussion on the works of Dostoevsky, or debating some politically sensitive humanitarian case she was working on. Or maybe they're fucking each other senseless on the deep seaweed-green velvet sofa that they had purchased together, *her* sofa that *they* had chosen – and one he had taken with him when he'd left. She doubts it though; 'Cho' – as Luke likes to affectionately call her – is so painfully politically correct that she probably thinks having sex is against her feminist values or something. She wonders if he's mentioned to 'Cho' about the sex they'd had over the kitchen table yesterday morning when he'd called her and made an excuse to come over and collect the last of his things? Somehow she doubts that more.

Screw it.

'Oh, go on then, Tommy, why not?' she acquiesces. 'I will have that drink. Just a quick one though. Ros and the others are waiting for me...'

Tommy winks at her, a gesture that makes her inwardly cringe.

He hands her the cocktail and she gulps it back in one hit.

'Easy, tiger.' He shoots her a look that falls somewhere between impressed and shocked. 'I didn't mean to offend. It's just that I heard...'

'What did you hear, Tommy?' She doesn't want to have this conversation with him – or anyone – she just wants to walk away, go and rejoin the girls back at the table, but now part of her is invested in knowing what's been said and who by.

'Just that you and your bloke broke up... that's all... and judging by that blouse you're wearing tonight I'd say the rumour is true.'

She drains the dregs of the cocktail glass. It tastes strong and instantly she wants another.

'Ran off with another other bird, so I heard...'

Well, didn't good news travel fast!

'Can't believe anyone would dump you though. I mean, he must be mad! I wouldn't kick you out of bed!' His eyes wander back down to her cleavage. 'Weren't you engaged as well, the pair of you, just about to get hitched?'

'Cheers for the drink, Tommy.' She hands him her empty glass and pushes through the clock of sticky bodies jostling for space at the bar.

'Hey! Wait a sec… hold on… Daisey! Jesus, I was only having a laugh… let me buy you anoth…'

'You OK?' Ros mouths the words to her as she rejoins the others at the table. They both recognise the question as a rhetorical one.

'Daaaaiseeeeey!' Manjeet is already drunk. Then again she is – by her own admission – a shocking lightweight. She waves her arms above her head and then outwards as though to embrace her. 'C'm sit with meeee…'

Daisey laughs a little as she is pulled onto her colleague's lap. She really needs to get drunker, like Manjeet. She snatches a glass from a passing waiter, gulps it back and takes another, and one for Manjeet too. Ros starts chatting, animated, to Bex and a flamboyantly dressed guy with a purple quiff who she thinks might work in Leather Goods; anyway, he's newish and she doesn't know his name. She hovers next to them, hoping she doesn't look as wretched as she feels. It was a bad idea to come to the party tonight. She wasn't ready for it, but Ros had insisted, said it would do her 'the power of good'.

'I remember her… lovely she was, always smiling… gives me the bloody willies when I think about it, I mean, twenty-eight – it's no age, is it? And to go like that… her poor family…' Bex shakes her head and takes a sip of her drink almost simultaneously.

'My God, that's *awwwful…*' Purple Quiff's mouth has formed an exaggerated 'O' shape. 'When did they find her?'

'A few weeks ago – didn't you read about it in the papers? Found in her own bed apparently… throat slashed open, sick bastard…'

'What are you talking about?' Daisey interjects. She's not really invested in the conversation, not really taking any of it in. Right now, all she can think about is Luke and Cho who are maybe or maybe not having sex on her green velvet sofa.

'Fern.' Bex brings her back into the present.

'Fern?'

'Yeah, Fern Lever, she worked at Warwick's, a few years back in Junior Fashion before she moved away. I knew her… well, not knew her knew her, but we'd spoken a few times, sat together in the cafeteria once or twice. Terrible,' she says again with more gravitas.

'So they haven't caught him then.' Purple Quiff's face is animated in horror. 'The killer?'

Bex shakes her head. 'Nope, not yet. It's horrible to think he's still out there… on the loose…'

'*Stooop*, you're scaring me.' Purple Quiff is shrieking again. 'You don't reckon he was stalking her, do you? God, you don't think… I mean, do you think he *knew her*? Bloody Mary Mother of God, maybe he works at Warwick's!' His eyes dart around the crowded room in exaggerated panic.

'Yeah, in the Leather Goods department.' Bex giggles and Ros starts laughing too.

'Shut *uuuuup*! Oh my God! You're winding me up!'

Bex pushes him playfully. 'We shouldn't joke; it's not funny. Anyway, it was years ago when she worked here, so I doubt it, but well, you never know, do you?'

Purple Quiff clutches his chest dramatically. 'Well, if he's still out there, this nutter, I think it would be prudent if none of us goes home alone tonight – just in case.'

'With a bit of luck I wasn't planning to.' Bex eyes up a passing – and very attractive-looking – waiter and flashes Purple Quiff a conspiratorial eyebrow raise. They all start laughing. Daisey tries to join in but she hears how false and stilted she sounds and thinks the others probably can too.

'I'm going for a cigarette.' Daisey turns to Ros and squeezes back the tears that have formed in the outer corners of her eyes. She can't seem to shake off her maudlin thoughts, even with a bellyful of booze inside her. 'You coming?'

'I'll follow you out, love. Just got to use the little girls' room first.'

It feels better outside, away from the music and the merriment that she feels so detached from. Propping herself up against the corner of a wall away from the main exit of the venue, she takes a cigarette from the packet inside her bag and searches for a lighter. She has one somewhere, in among all the gubbins. A little unsteady on her heels – higher than she generally wears – she places a foot against the wall to steady herself and is slightly startled by the hiss of a bus as it suddenly passes by. The warm night air reminds her she's a little drunk, though not a lot drunk, not Manjeet drunk – at least not yet. Where's that bloody lighter…

'You looking for one of these?'

The click of a flame comes into her peripheral vision.

'Thanks,' she says, glancing at him briefly, leaning forward and placing her fingertips lightly on his as she steadies her hand and lights her cigarette. She notices something… something different, something odd about his… He quickly snatches his hand away, shoves the lighter back inside his pocket and keeps his hands in them even though it's a warm evening. She doesn't recognise him, though assumes he's just another Warwick's employee. Why would he be here otherwise?

'You don't look like a smoker,' he comments. His voice is soft, almost a whisper.

She blows blue smoke high into the air.

'No? And what exactly does a smoker look like?'

He pauses briefly, thoughtfully.

'I don't know. Just not like you, I suppose.'

She pulls on her cigarette. She's really not in the mood for small talk.

'Him over there, for example.' He nods in the direction of two men standing a few feet away from them, to the left. They're chatting and laughing; one of them looks like he's telling the other a funny story. They're drunk and happy and animated and she wishes she were too. 'Now he's definitely a smoker.'

'Yes, well, he's smoking a cigarette so that's pretty much a given.'

'You're missing the point…'

She looks at him properly then, although everything is a little fuzzy round the edges, like she's looking through a smeared windowpane. Perhaps she's drunker than she realises – anyway, he's smaller than her, and even in these heels she's only about five feet five inches. At six foot one, Luke had towered above her, but she'd kind of liked that, and so had he, once. *We're all the same height lying down!* She'd always laughed whenever he'd said that but now she thinks it is exactly the kind of thing Tommy White would say, followed by a sharp elbow and a cheeky wink. She'd been so blind. Luke had been no better than a womaniser, like Tommy only much cleverer at disguising it.

'Yes, well, *the point is* I couldn't give a fuck if I'm missing the point.' She's being rude but can't help it. She feels like being rude. She's never bloody rude. She's not rude enough. '*You need to step out of your comfort zone sometimes, Daisey. You're always so… safe, so eager to please everyone.*' Luke's voice rings loud like tinnitus in her ears. Yeah, well, she hadn't been 'safe' yesterday when he'd made some pathetic excuse to come over to get his 'things', had she? Self-loathing and shame burn inside her solar plexus as she thinks of their encounter on the kitchen table – she'll probably have to go and get the bloody morning-after pill now too.

'You see,' the stranger continues, unperturbed, 'even if that guy over there wasn't smoking, I'd guess he was a smoker, because he just looks like one. He's got that undefinable smoker's look about him.'

Her rudeness appears to have passed him by unnoticed, or certainly without offence. She's almost disappointed.

'Fascinating,' she replies, throwing her fag to the pavement and crushing it underfoot. 'Thanks for the light.'

He nods, makes brief eye contact with her and suddenly she's gripped by a strange sensation: fear? No. Not fear. Something like it, though, an odd feeling that causes her to fold her arms and grip herself tightly as though she's just been caught by a gust of icy wind.

'Enjoy the party, Daisey – make sure you get home safe,' he calls out to her but she doesn't turn back to look at him.

Cava. Lots more cava, two more cigarettes and dancing badly to Justin Bieber with Ros and Bex. She checks her phone to see if Luke's left a message. Has he got nothing to say about yesterday? She bets bloody Cho isn't the type to drop her drawers and bend over the kitchen table – even an artisan bespoke one. For a brief moment she almost feels smug that she can give him something Cho can't – or won't – and instinctively pulls her phone out of her handbag and starts compiling a text message:

I liked the way we said goodbye. Let's say goodbye again soon. XOXO She reads it back through blurred vision. *Let's say goodbye again soon?* No, that sounds pathetic… like she's desperate. God, what on earth is she doing? She's drunk and not thinking straight. She makes to delete the text but accidentally presses send instead.

FUCK! A wave of hopelessness mixed with nausea washes over her. She wants to go home, slink off unnoticed and avoid all those inevitable protracted goodbyes. This way she can pick up a bottle of wine on her way and drink and smoke and be as miserable as she likes without anyone asking her if she's all right, or worse, telling her to 'cheer up'.

'Daisey!' She hears someone calling her name. 'Hey! Daisey! You're not leaving already? It's only 11.30! The place hasn't even got going yet!' *Shit*. She'd collected her jacket from the cloakroom and was almost through the exit as well.

Tommy stares at her as though she is about to commit a mortal sin.

'Yes, Tommy, I'm going home.' Her voice is a little slurred maybe, she can't quite tell.

'Well, at least let me take you? You can't go home on your own in that state. I wouldn't be any kind of gent if I let you…'

They're in a cab together. She thinks she's given the driver the right address. 'Hounslow… other side of the river… yeah, you need a passport to get to it…' She thinks she must've fallen asleep as when Tommy gently shakes her awake, she's already outside her apartment – the apartment they bought together and one she now can't afford to live in, at least not alone.

'You can't come in,' she says as he helps her out of the cab. He's already paying the driver before she can object.

'It's OK… OK… I'm not going to ask to come up… though I could do with a piss.'

Charming! She's swaying on her aching feet and takes her shoes off. She doesn't know how these models do it, must have feet like a ship's rudder, all of them.

'I just want to make sure you get through the door safely yeah…? Did you see in the news about that girl who got killed – some lunatic broke into her flat and cut her throat? She worked at Warwick's, you know… few years back…'

'Yeah… so I heard…'

She's scrabbling around for her key. Why does everything fall into one great big clump at the bottom of her handbag? It's so irritating. She feels the heat of her frustration reach her earlobes. She can't wait to get her PJs on.

'Got it!' She opens the door, turns to look at him, his eyes wide and expectant like a puppy that's just peed on the carpet and doesn't want to be told off. She sighs heavily.

'Literally, you can use the bathroom then you've got to go, OK? I'm really tired, Tommy. I just want to go to bed.'

He holds his palms up.

'Just a quick shake of the snake and I'll be gone, promise.'

God, he is so uncouth. She drops her handbag and shoes as she steps inside and they clatter in a heap against the wooden floor. Padding barefoot, a touch unsteady, into the kitchen, she opens the fridge.

'Blimey, nice gaff.' He gives a little whistle. 'Bit posh, ain't it?'

Yes, she thinks miserably. It is; it was their dream apartment, their 'forever home, until we have lots of babies', as he'd once put it, only now the dream had become a nightmare.

'Warwick's must be paying you a shitload more than they're paying me, is all I can say!'

'Bingo!' She spies a bottle of opened Prosecco next to the milk – and there's more than half left – result. She'll polish it off once Tommy's gone. She hears the flush of the toilet from down the hallway and wills him out of the front door.

'Thanks for seeing me home, Tommy. Goodnight!' she calls out to him but he's already behind her and she jumps as she turns to see him standing there.

'What, not even a nightcap; a little one for the road? I've got to go all the way back to South London, you know.'

'I'll call you an Uber,' she says flatly. He looks crestfallen and suddenly she feels guilty. He has come all this way she supposes but… no! She hadn't asked him to and really she honestly just wants to be alone to wallow in her own misery and drink more wine.

'I'm sorry, Tommy. I really don't feel great tonight… Look' – she moves in a little closer towards him – 'maybe we can meet for drinks to make up for it. This Saturday, if you're free?'

'You asking me out?' He grins at her, eyes glassy in the light of her kitchen. She shrugs. He can call it what he likes as long as he just leaves.

'If you want, drinks… dinner even. But I need you to go now…'

He looks placated and she's relieved.

'I'm going to hold you to that,' he says, making his way towards the front door, finally. 'I know where you live now, remember? I'll book us somewhere nice… you like Japanese food?'

'Love it,' she says, practically pushing him out of the door. 'I'll see you at work. We'll go out afterwards, on Saturday, this Saturday.'

'I'll look forward to it. Night, babes,' he says, lurching forward and kissing her just shy of her mouth.

'Goodnight, Tommy,' she says, snapping the door shut behind him and wiping his residue from her skin with the back of her wrist. He is nothing if not persistent, she'll give him that. She laughs gently to herself. Maybe dinner and a few drinks won't really be so bad…

She slinks back into the kitchen, takes the wine from the fridge and pours the entire contents into a large glass before gulping back a few mouthfuls. Turning the speaker on, she plugs her phone in and searches through her playlists. Something upbeat. No, some Adele, more fitting of her current mood. 'Rolling in the Deep' rings out through her apartment and she begins to sing along to it badly through swigs of Prosecco. Her mind runs back through the night's events: Tommy and his clichéd one-liners, her conversation with Ros and that bloody text message she'd accidentally sent to Luke – one he hadn't even replied to – and that strange little man who'd given her a light, the one with the…

That unsettling feeling she'd experienced earlier returns. '*Enjoy the party, Daisey – get home safe…*' An odd thought suddenly strikes her. How had he known her name? She doesn't remember telling him though clearly she must've done.

The sound of the front door buzzing pops her thoughts like a bubble. She rolls her eyes. It buzzes again in succession, persistent.

'Jesus, Tommy, don't you take no for an answer…' He's pushing his bloody luck now. She's going to tell him to piss off.

'Don't tell me,' she says as she pulls the door open, 'you forgot something – oh!' she says, taking an unsteady step back in surprised confusion. 'It's… it's *you?*'

'Hello, Rosie,' he says smiling, his head cocked to one side.

Rosie? He means Daisey, surely? Or perhaps she's just heard him wrong. What on earth is *he* doing here? And how the hell does he know where she lives and…?

As she opens her mouth to speak she notices that he's holding something in his hand. It looks like… what is that? Oh God, is that… *is that a hammer?* Adrenalin spikes spitefully through her system but before she can react, everything is black.

CHAPTER TWO

A bolt of adrenalin mainlines straight through to my aorta like a shot of amphetamine. I can physically feel it, palpable, painful, *personal*, as I enter the bedroom. I'm overcome by a diabolical sense of déjà vu as dread drops down around me like a black curtain falling at the end of a theatre performance. *It's him*. I know it instantly as my eyes process the horror, the same horror they've witnessed twice before in the past two months – he's getting more prolific, less time passing between each murder. Instinctively I rub them; they're gritty and sore through lack of sleep, thanks in part to Juno – or Pip as I call her – my eight-month-old daughter – who seems to have her days and nights back to front – but mostly due to the monster responsible for the scene in front of me – and the two others that have preceded it.

The MO is exactly the same: she's youngish, like Jasmin Godden and Fern Lever were – late twenties early thirties, though I'm notoriously rubbish at guessing any woman's age, living or otherwise – and, like them, she's naked on the bed. Her throat looks like it's been slashed and I'd bet a good night's sleep – the rarest form of currency in my life right now – that she's suffered a blow or blows plural to the head first. Her body has been positioned identical to the other victims': arms folded across her chest, like he's laid her to rest, and chillingly he's left his calling card on her body – a single pink rose, fresh and fragrant with a few of the petals scattered loosely around the bed.

Only there's something different about this scene from the other two. Something, I don't know what yet, but I feel it instinctively like fear, and it grips me in the same way that fear does, stifling and choking, blocking out all the other senses.

'There's something different.' My thoughts make themselves public to my trusted colleague, DS Lucy Davis, who is standing just a little way behind me. 'Something's not right…'

I look around and see the blood juxtaposed against the neat femininity of the woman's bedroom. Her lightly patterned floral bedspread is splattered a dark crimson; there's a window to the left, the white wooden blind covering it is closed but the floor lamp, one of those trendy arch-shaped ones, is switched on, giving the room an unnatural orange glow. A few items of clothing have been neatly folded in a pile on the wooden floor, the same way in which Jasmin's and Fern's had been left. He's undressed her and put them there. Why does he do that? It doesn't make sense. Then again, none of it does.

Davis says nothing as she gets on the phone. Doesn't need to. For some moments there are no words – moments like this one. I take a step closer to the bed.

'Get SOCO here,' I say without taking my eyes off the body. 'I want video and photos of everything. And call Vic Leyton. I want her on this one, Davis.' Vic is the best pathologist out there.

The young PC who discovered her is saying something about the woman who made the call. 'Her name's Daisey Garrett, thirty-three, works at Warwick's department store on Bond Street. A colleague, Rosalind O'Donnell, came to pick her up in the morning and give her a lift to work like usual but got no response. They'd been to a work do the previous evening, and she got a bit worried, said she'd recently broken up with her fiancé and was feeling a bit depressed… so she let herself in – she has a key – and found her. As soon as I walked in I knew that it was…' His head drops slightly. 'I checked for a pulse, but nothing…'

I'm only half hearing him through the thumping bassline of my heart inside my head; it's pulsing so loudly in my ears I can barely make him out.

'Warwick's…?' Voices mushroom cloud in my mind, fracturing and splintering off in all directions like high impact on glass.

I hear Jasmin Godden's father's voice: 'Not another one, Riley… you couldn't save *my* girl but you could've saved this one.'

Fern Lever's mum too: 'She was just the most beautiful, precious girl, Detective Riley; please say you'll find out who did this to my princess.'

The reporters: 'Why do you think he leaves them a rose, Detective Riley? Will you get him before he kills again?'

I hear my new boss, Gwendoline Archer, Woods's better-looking replacement – not that this would've been too difficult – and visualise her almost standing over me, looking down at me in thinly veiled disappointment.

During the first few months of Juno's life I was a stay-at-home dad while Fi embarked upon a well-earned new position as senior news reporter on *The National Post*. She's avidly covering the Rose Petal Ripper's case – as the press has daubed him – and keeps badgering me for insider information, which she knows I can't give her even if I had any to give, which I don't. Depressingly, the press know as much as we do, and even with their help, even by releasing as much information as we already have to them, nothing has come of it, except spreading more fear and panic among the community and a waning confidence in the police, i.e. me.

Adding to the intense pressure I have put on myself to solve this case is the fact I was brought in especially for it.

'We need you on this one, Dan,' Archer said sagely in a tense telephone conversation while I was still on paternity leave. 'We need this bastard caught. The media are having a field day, people are scared, women are frightened in their own homes and they're not helping with all this sensationalism. We need the best we've got on this… so when can you come back?'

As if on cue, Juno, who was over my shoulder at the time, threw up her feed all down my back.

'As soon as I can sort out childcare,' I'd replied as the milky acid stench hit my nostrils.

Finally, I see Rachel, my beautiful dead girlfriend Rachel, who I lost over four years ago now in a tragic motorbike accident. She's holding Juno in her arms, my girl, mine and Fiona's baby – the happy result of our one-night stand – and she's rocking her to sleep as she looks up at me and says: 'This could be *your* daughter, Dan. This could be your own Pip…'

Davis touches my shoulder gently and I physically flinch as it brings me out of my thoughts.

'Warwick's,' I say again, though mostly to myself. 'Fern Lever… didn't she work there too once?'

'They're on their way, gov,' Davis says. 'Leyton's been notified and SOCO are minutes away.'

I attempt to gather myself, but I'm shaking. *You could have prevented this, Dan. You should have prevented this.*

'You know the drill, Davis.' I turn to her. 'Get the whole street sealed off, no one other than SOCO in or out. Don't touch anything. Start the door to door; get intelligence onto it. I want CCTV, potential witnesses, all of it… and whatever you do, make sure no bastard press slips through the net…' I'm swearing; I'm angry. I take a deep breath, maybe two.

'It's him, isn't it, gov?'

I understand why she's asked the question. She desperately wants me to tell her otherwise because she doesn't want it to be him as much as I don't. She knows what the implications will be; she knows what's coming as a result. 'For Christ's sake,' she says, exhaling deeply.

I imagine she's turning away from the body, from the horror of everything it represents to us and so many other people, but I can't know for sure because I can't keep my eyes from the bed, from the woman whose throat has been cut open. I think I see something, a flicker in my peripheral vision. Since Juno arrived and has more than halved the irregular, fitful sleep I've experienced since Rachel died, I've been seeing things out of the corner of my eye, things that aren't really there, like spiders and well, I don't know, just movement. They say this is common among the severely sleep-deprived, something to do with light playing tricks on the retina or something; anyway, they don't bloody tell you about it in all the self-help baby books, do they? There's no chapter on 'Seeing spiders' between 'Weaning' and 'Colic', is there?

I hear Davis leave the room and the PC outside comforting the colleague, who's crying loudly. That's the thing about murder; it's akin to dropping a boulder into a still pond from a great height. The ripple effect travels far and wide beyond any killer's warped and disturbed imagination ever could. Perhaps this is the whole agenda, not wanting to affect just one life, but many. I'm mindful of this as I get close to her; I kneel down beside the bed, unmade, like she'd been peacefully sleeping in it before her worst ever nightmare became real. I desperately want to take hold of her hand and…

I jump backwards, my knees almost giving way beneath me. Adrenalin explodes inside my guts like a sucker punch. She moved! Her finger, her finger flickered!

'Hello! Daisey! Oh Jesus Christ… Daisey, can you hear me?' I seize her hand – grip it. It's still warm! I feel her finger pulse against mine; it's twitching. Jesus Christ God!

'Davis,' I scream, 'DAVIS!' It feels like minutes pass before she bursts back into the room. 'An ambulance, Davis… get an ambulance! NOW!'

'What is it, gov?' She's breathless behind me, peering over the body as I feel for a pulse.

'I *knew* there was something different; I felt it,' I say, fighting back the tears that have almost freed themselves from the outer corners of my gritty eyes. I look up at Davis. 'She's still alive… God help us, she's STILL ALIVE!'

CHAPTER THREE

July 1987

She feels the sweat prickle her skin as it drips from her chin onto her bare chest. Jesus, she's so hot. Her thighs are covered in an oily sheen, her hands slipping as she attempts to grip them in a bid to gain some purchase on the pain. The starchy hospital sheets have softened with sweat – and other bodily fluids – like she's submerged in a sea of her own excretion. She's never felt such discomfort. She wants them to open a window but there isn't one in the room to open. *Why isn't there a bloody window?* Every time she takes a lungful of air it's like swallowing fire.

Another wave of pain sweeps through her lower abdomen and she groans, a low, animalistic moan, which she knows will gradually crescendo into a high-pitched scream, one that will make John wince and start apologising profusely again.

'Oh God, John, help me… oh God… argh… arghhhh!'

He grips her hand tightly, dabs at her forehead with a flannel. It's damp and warm with sweat and she flicks his hand irritably to take it away.

'You're doing great, babe… really great. It's OK… nearly there now, you're OK, Trace… keep going baby… keep going…'

This was not how Tracey Eggerton had imagined herself giving birth, not remotely. Throughout her pregnancy she'd read and studied all the birth sections in the books with excited anticipation and had compiled a precise birth plan, one that John had professionally printed up for her with embossed gold letters on the top that read *Tracey's Birth Plans for Rosie and Lillie* as a keepsake. It was here, on the bedside table next to her and she feels like reaching for it and ripping it into a thousand pieces – if only she had the strength.

The Eggertons had been ecstatic when they'd discovered they were having twins, shocked but elated – two girls, *two baby girls*! Tracey had always secretly hoped for a daughter, but to get two was like winning the lottery. 'Only special people are gifted twins,' her grandmother had said to her when she'd broken the happy news. And she'd been right; she had felt special throughout her relatively problem-free pregnancy, a little different from the other expectant mums. She got a buzz out of watching other people's expressions whenever she'd rubbed her swollen belly and proudly announced, 'There's two of them in here!'

Tracey made a noise she'd never heard herself make before as her baby passed through her pelvis and met the world, her euphoria only just usurping the relief that flooded through her like a natural analgesic.

'Let me see her,' she panted, breathless and wet with sweat as John kissed the top of her head and squeezed her. He was crying, blubbing in fact, just as they had both predicted he would – he was such a softie.

'You did it, Trace… you did it!'

The sound of their daughter opening her lungs for the first time causes them both to laugh and cry simultaneously.

'Don't get too comfy, young lady,' the midwife says stoically with the tone of someone who has witnessed such a scene a thousand times over. 'You haven't finished the job yet – her sister won't be far behind her; there's more work to be done, I'm afraid.'

Tracey doesn't care; she's high on endorphins and Entonox.

'Oh God, John, she's beautiful, she's so… so… beautiful,' she says, biting her lip as the midwife hands her daughter to her, wrapped in a pink receiving blanket – perhaps the only thing on her birth plan that had been adhered to. She looks down at the tiny, snuffling little creature in her arms and feels love flow through her body like a warm river, the pain almost a distant memory already. 'Hello, Rosie…' She looks down at her baby in her arms. 'I'm your mummy and this is your daddy.'

'So, this little one is Rosie, is she, eh?' John says, cuddling in close to the pair of them.

'Yes,' Tracey coos, 'she's definitely Rosie.'

'She's beautiful, like her mummy,' he says, kissing the tip of his daughter's button nose. She smells new, like pure joy wrapped in a blanket. 'Are you ready to meet your sister, Rosie?'

As if on cue, Tracey feels the beginnings of a contraction and noticing this, the experienced midwife gently takes the baby from her.

'Round two, my love,' she says in a no-nonsense tone. 'You'll have them both together in your arms before long… there's a good girl, that's it… lie back…'

Tracey moves for the gas and air but the sharp stab of pain reaches her lower abdomen before she can get a lungful of it – there's no gradual build up like before, the pain has gone through her in 0–90, revving like a Formula One car. It was excruciating, even worse than before, much worse, and she cries and lashes out with her arms as John makes futile attempts to soothe her with hand strokes and soft reassurances. Searing pain rips through her like razor-sharp teeth shredding her insides. Instinctively something feels wrong, different this time, she doesn't know what, she can't articulate it, she can only feel it – a strange and unwelcome sense of dread and fear mixed with agony, an agony that is somehow far more egregious than what she's just experienced.

'What's happening?' She manages to squeeze the words from her trembling lips. All of a sudden she feels cold, her body's shivering, like it's going into shock. The sheets, which moments ago were warm and damp with her sweat, now feel like ice beneath her, stinging and burning against her exposed skin. John and the midwife are animated in conversation, but she cannot make out their words exactly – the pain is so fierce it has muted her other senses, rendered her almost deaf and blind. Suddenly, there is a flurry of activity in the room; the midwives are checking the monitor and talking to each other. Their expressions have changed; they're no longer smiling.

'Call the consultant, Jeanie,' the older of the two midwives says. 'The heartbeat is slowing down. The baby's in distress.'

'Stop,' she screams. 'Make it stop. I want it to stop! No… No… NO!'

Tracey is overcome by a horrendous feeling that she doesn't want this baby to come, doesn't want to birth it, although she knows it's too late. The consultant has arrived and he has his hands inside her, pulling and rummaging around as though searching for something in the bottom of a suitcase. She screams out in pain and hears John exhale and turn away, unable to bear watching his wife in such distress.

'Jesus, can't you help her?' he says.

'We're going to use forceps, Tracey,' the consultant explains, as the midwife hands him the giant stainless-steel tongs. 'This one doesn't seem to want to come of their own accord. We'll need to perform an episiotomy first, OK?'

John doesn't know what this means but Tracey does and she starts wailing, juxtaposed somewhere between wanting this baby out of her and not wanting to give birth to it at all. It must be the drugs, the pain and the drugs that are making her feel like this.

A terrible thought flashes through Tracey's mind as the consultant takes a scalpel to her perineum. *It doesn't matter if the baby dies…* Confused and disturbed by her own thoughts, Tracey almost passes out as the midwives stand over her, pull her legs further apart and utter instructions she cannot comprehend through the agony. John stands back, pale-faced with worry. She can feel the baby move through her birth canal now, feels her perineum slice open further as it slides from her body, like someone has opened her up like a tin can. Neither the midwife nor the consultant is speaking and the silence in the room is palpable as they take the baby from her and usher it away.

Tracey doesn't feel the same rush of elation as she'd felt moments earlier; it's something else, something she can't describe, a feeling she has never experienced before and doesn't know how to place – a *bad feeling*.

'Is she OK?' John asks, watching as the consultant and mid-wives huddle around their second-born child. He hasn't heard the baby cry yet – why hasn't she cried? Fear suddenly grips him. 'Is the baby OK?'

They don't answer him and he turns, wide-eyed, to his wife. 'Oh, Trace… Oh God, love…'

But then it comes; a high-pitched yelp. More of a mew than a cry, but it's a sign of life.

'Oh thank God.' John is crying again, this time with relief. 'Oh thank God.' He almost collapses onto his wife's spent body and she feels the weight of him on her chest, smells the sweat on his hair as it sticks to her dry lips. 'They're here, darling… both of them. Our girls are here…'

'I'm cold,' Tracey says. 'Get me a blanket.' He does as she asks and drapes one over her shoulders though it does nothing to quell the shivers. She hears Rosie snuffling inside the Perspex cot at the end of the bed and wants to hold her in her arms so that she can experience that feeling again, that rush of oxytocin flowing through her, warming her bones like a hot bath on a cold February night. She tries to push back the other thoughts she has, thoughts of not wanting to hold her new baby, the one who has just been brutally torn from her body.

'Hey,' John calls out to the midwives again, slight concern marring his euphoric tone. 'Is everything OK over there? Is she OK, the baby; is it all OK?'

The midwife and the consultant are deep in conversation but eventually they come over to the bed, the midwife holding the baby in a blanket – white this time.

'There are a couple of complications, I'm afraid,' the consultant says, his tone laced with gravitas. 'Nothing life-threatening, nothing too much to worry about.'

John stands abruptly, the flannel he'd used to mop Tracey's sweat falling to the floor with the momentum.

'Complications? What complications? Jesus… is she OK, is our daughter OK?'

'Son, you mean,' the midwife says as she brings the baby closer. 'Congratulations both of you, it's a little boy.'

CHAPTER FOUR

Two weeks after the attack on Daisey

'Traumatic amnesia?' I blink at Mr Anderson, the consultant neurologist at The General, from behind his desk. He's a tall man, big in stature, but his gentle tone belies his cumbersome bulk. I've heard what he's said – I even understand what he's said, sort of – but I don't want to believe it. The call had come in from the hospital that morning to inform us that Daisey Garrett had regained consciousness from the medically induced coma the doctors had deemed necessary to keep her alive following her savage attack – a state she has been in for a little over a fortnight. According to the hospital – who were under strict instructions to alert me the moment she regained consciousness – she was awake and lucid and Ros – the colleague who had found her – was currently with her. Davis and I made the thirty-minute journey to The General in less than fifteen.

Finding Daisey Garrett alive had felt like a gift from the gods. That she was still breathing, just, when Davis and I arrived at her apartment that morning had felt like a lottery win for the whole team. I was – we all were – elated that she'd made it, that she'd just fallen short of becoming the third murder victim of a sadistic serial killer; one I'm convinced will kill again, and soon, if we don't get to him first. Daisey is the potential key that could open the door to our man's identity after nothing but dead ends.

She came face to face with him, looked him in the eyes; she may have heard him speak; she might even know his name… Only now I learn that while we still have the 'key', we have no idea of the address – a bit like winning the lottery only to discover that you've mislaid the ticket.

My dismay fills the consultant's room oppressively like noxious gas.

'Yes,' he replies, tentatively, apologetically. 'I'm afraid it's not completely uncommon in people who've suffered blows to the head, Detective. I'm very sorry.'

I shuffle from foot to foot, try to disguise my frustration, my anger – it's not his fault and I sense he feels personally responsible for having to break this news to me, which highlights the fact he's a decent human being, a man with integrity and a conscience.

'She's suffered damage to the prefrontal cortex.' He looks up at me for signs that I follow and taps the front right part of his forehead with an index finger. 'The part of the brain that governs emotions, memories, feelings…'

My heart drops so forcibly that I almost expect us both to look down at the floor and see it lying there, shattered in pieces. I start pacing the small office – an office I suspect has contained many an agonised cry courtesy of the delivery of unwanted news – massaging my temples with my thumb and forefinger. He's silent for a moment longer as he lets the words sink into my own prefrontal cortex. 'I realise this isn't what you want to hear, Detective Riley, but—'

'So, what does this mean *exactly*, Mr Anderson?' I cut him off. 'Is it a temporary thing? Is it a case of when she regains her memory and not if?' Perhaps naively I'd pinned a lot of hope on Daisey Garrett's recollection of her attack – and of her attacker. She's the only witness we have, pretty much the only solid lead.

He sighs gently, places a hand onto the desk. I notice that his nails are perfectly manicured and spotlessly clean and for some reason I imagine they are also warm to the touch.

'Yes, usually, but there are no 100 per cent guarantees, I'm afraid. Neurological injury can be a very complex matter, an unknown quantity and—'

'Yes, but in your experience, Mr Anderson, in all the years you've dealt with brain injuries… you must have some idea as to—'

'I've witnessed a couple of other similar cases in my career – possibly three in total,' he gently cuts me off. 'And in each case, yes, they all regained their memory in full, eventually.'

He's redeemed himself slightly but it's the 'eventually' part that bothers me. Time is not something we have plenty of.

'The brain is an extraordinary piece of machinery, Detective Riley,' he continues. 'When she – when Daisey – arrived here the prognosis wasn't looking too favourable. As you know there was sufficient swelling to her brain for us to make the decision to place her in a coma in a bid to prevent any further damage. The blunt trauma – the two blows that were inflicted upon her – could've killed her. And coupled with the asphyxia and the slash to her neck, it's really quite miraculous – and testament to her strength, both physical and mental – that she survived at all.'

He's going round the houses but I know what he's trying to say, that I should simply be thankful that she's still alive, that this should be enough, and I am, truly, and it is, yet still I cannot hide my palpable disappointment.

'So it's a case of when not if?' He's already qualified this but I'm compelled to ask the question again nonetheless.

His sigh is deeper this time, wearier.

'Yes, but I really can't be specific, Detective,' he reiterates. 'Her memory, up until the night of the attack, is in perfect working order. She knows who she is, where she lives, date of birth, the name of her first pet even… but the night in question is regrettably a blank, currently at least.'

I struggle to stop myself from cursing; physically swallowing the offending words back like a Tourette's tic.

'Can I see her?'

He nods but his demeanour is less apologetic now and he's straightened up.

'She's weak, Detective Riley, confused, and her voice has been damaged by the ventilation tube, though it will recover. I do feel it best that you should give her a day or two, allow her to regain a little strength in her voice – and elsewhere – before you begin questioning her.'

But I'm already halfway out of the door as he says it.

CHAPTER FIVE

Ros is sitting on the bed next to her and she feels the comforting warmth of her body close by; it's the next best thing to her mother being here. Leila Garrett lives in Australia now with her 'new' family and although she was distraught to learn what had happened to her daughter, she was unable to travel due to her epilepsy condition. Daisey had understood that it wasn't safe for her to fly during their tearful phone conversation – but right this moment she'd give anything to have her mother by her side. Sometimes, like now, it's all a girl needs.

'I'm Dan, Dan Riley. Detective Inspector Dan Riley.'

'I know,' she says. 'Ros has told me all about you.'

He smiles, displaying neat teeth and she thinks how his smile matches his eyes. 'I'm heading up the team who're working on finding your attacker, who we believe is also the murderer of two other women. I want you to know, Daisey, that we will get the man who did this to you, *I* will get him and I will make sure he stays behind bars where he can never hurt you, or anyone else again – I promise you that, OK?' He goes to shake her hand and she takes it, though her wrists feel limp, like her hands are detached from her arms. 'I just need to ask you a few questions if that's OK? I understand it's a lot for you to digest, a lot to take in but…'

Daisey is only half listening to the detective; her concentration feels impaired and her mind keeps wandering. The doctors said this was to be expected, that she may have trouble concentrating and that it will take time before her brain is functioning normally again. She'll need regular monitoring, hospital visits and psychotherapy. The idea of it all makes her feel exhausted. She just wants to go home and hide away until her mind feels straight again, until she can process what has happened to her, if that is possible.

The detective is speaking again, saying something about how strong she is, her physical and emotional resolve…

'… A lot of other people wouldn't have survived such an attack, Daisey,' he says, as though he's about to present her with an award. 'But you did. That makes you pretty special.'

'That's what I told her,' Ros agrees zealously, stroking her hand. 'Someone up there said it wasn't your time, love; they kept you here for a reason…'

Daisey feels overwhelmed with all the thoughts that are battering her broken mind. She rubs her temples with her fingers in a bid to get them to stop. Detective Riley continues to talk but his voice sounds like it's underwater. They've told her, the doctors, that she has something called 'traumatic amnesia, a result of blunt trauma to the skull'. Instinctively she rubs the stitches in her head, running the tips of her fingers over them. They feel ugly and wiry, the shaved hair around them prickly to touch. Her hair will come back, she reassures herself, just like her memory, or so the doctors say. Not that she's in any rush for it to. Why would she *want* to remember? It would be too much. It was all too much.

Earlier Luke had been in to see her, apparently for the first time since she's been in the hospital, according to Ros anyway. He'd brought flowers, gerberas and lilies and… *roses*… Not exactly appropriate, given the circumstances. He clearly hadn't been thinking right, or at all. But at least he had come.

'Jesus.' That was what he'd said as he'd walked into the hospital room, unable to hide the horror on his face. She knew she looked a fright, her head swollen and stitched, part of her hair shaved off, and she felt ugly and ashamed, much like she had after their encounter on the kitchen table the morning before the attack – miserably she'd had no difficulty remembering that.

'God, you look terrible.' He'd sat down on the bed next to her and for a moment she'd thought he was about to take hold of her hand. She'd wanted him to, wanted to feel the comfort of his familiar touch, but instead he gripped them tightly in his lap.

'Thanks,' she'd croaked hoarsely. 'You don't look so hot yourself.'

He'd managed a small smile, one that caused a twinge inside her chest. She'd fought back tears from wanting to embrace him, the man she had loved – still loved maybe. She'd felt safe in his arms once, but now she realises she had been fooling herself even more than he'd been fooling her. His familiarity – or the memory of it – had almost undone her completely and tears had slipped involuntarily from the outer corners of her eyes and onto her pillow. She'd hoped he wouldn't notice.

'You've become something of a celebrity,' he'd said brightly, as though she should be tickled pink. 'You made front-page news.'

'I know. Great, isn't it? They used our engagement party photo – Ros showed me. They must've got it from my Facebook page,' she'd said, wiping her eyes. They felt sore and swollen and she'd suddenly felt embarrassed that this had happened to her, that he had to see her this way – *a victim*.

'Yes, I recognised it,' he'd said, looking down at the bed sheets. He'd seemed unable to meet her eyes and suddenly she'd thought that maybe he wasn't just here to make sure she was OK, but for some other reason.

'Have the police been to see you?'

She'd sighed, the thought of it – of all those questions.

'Not yet, but they'll want to speak to me. Ros said that—'

'They came to see me,' he'd interjected. 'Came to my flat, a day or two after the…'

'Oh?'

He'd cleared his throat awkwardly.

'They wanted to know where I was that night… the night it happened.'

She'd paused for a second, her mind clunky, her reactions slow and laboured.

'They thought you… surely they didn't think you…?'

'Well, I'm the ex-boyfriend, aren't I? They always look to the spouse first in a murder…'

'But I'm not dead, in case you hadn't noticed. And you're not my spouse. You're not even my fiancé… anymore.'

'They wanted to know where I was that night, where Cho was too,' he'd continued. Instinctively she'd wanted to laugh but it was too much of an effort and she was scared she might burst her stitches if she did.

'We had solid alibis, obviously. I don't know why you're smiling; it wasn't remotely funny. I mean, I was shocked… horrified…'

She'd wondered what had been more shocking to him, her being left for dead or the fact that the police had the audacity to question him about it. 'I know we've had our differences, but I'd never… well, I'd never want you to come to any harm, Daisey, never.'

'That's good to know.'

There'd been a pause. *Here it comes*, she'd thought.

'Listen, Daisey, I'm really sorry about what's happened to you. I mean, it's terrible, just awful.'

He sounds genuine at least, she'd thought, but it had felt strange. There he was, the man she had spent seven years of her life with and had been six months shy of marrying – a man she had shared so much with, been so intimate with, and yet as he'd sat opposite her on the hospital bed he'd felt like a virtual stranger, like she'd never spent more than a day with him in her life. The cognitive dissonance unsettled her.

'So you don't remember anything? Nothing at all about the attack?'

She'd shaken her head. Her neck had felt stiff and sore, and her whole body had ached, like she'd been hit by a truck and dragged for ten miles.

'No. I only found out when the doctor and Ros told me. It's a blank, the whole thing. I know I'd been at the work party that night, but I don't remember being there, what I did, who I was with, what I wore or drank, or what happened after it... nothing...'

He'd shifted awkwardly on the bed.

'And the day before, do you remember the day before the attack?'

There it was.

She'd looked at him, her face surely giving her away.

Their eyes had met briefly, but long enough for them both to know why he was asking.

'Yes,' she replied. 'I do remember.'

His head had dropped a little.

'And have you... are you going to tell the police?'

'The police? Why would I tell them we had sex on the kitchen table?'

'Keep your voice down,' he'd hissed at her automatically then quickly checked himself, remembering the fact that she was in a hospital bed.

So, this was why he was really here, she'd thought. It wasn't out of concern for her; it was out of concern for himself.

'You see, I kind of told them... well, I told them I hadn't seen you for over a month. I didn't mention *that* morning, when I'd come to pick up the last of my things... I couldn't.'

'Couldn't? Because Cho was there when they asked you?'

He'd sighed heavily.

'Jesus, Daisey, what else could I do? I couldn't exactly come out with it like that…'

'Why? Because she'd leave you if she found out?'

'Well, yes, probably.' He'd looked at her. 'OK then yes, definitely. Anyway, we both know it was a mistake, it was just a quick…'

Her mouth had fallen open in shock.

'Look, I'm sorry, OK?'

'For what?' She had tried to raise her voice to match her anger but her vocal cords couldn't withstand such strain. 'Cheating on me with her for months behind my back, destroying our lives and the future I believed we had together, and then cheating on her with me and *then* asking me to cover up for you so you don't get found out – all while I've just come out of a coma following an attempt on my life? Sorry for *that,* you mean? Are you even for real, Luke? Really, are you?'

He at least had the good grace to look mildly ashamed.

'All of it… I'm sorry for all of it.' He'd buried his head in his palms, dragged them down his face. 'Look, I know it's a cheek to ask you not to say anything to the police, given all of this, and after what I've done. I know I haven't really got the right to ask anything of you…' He'd looked down at the floor again. A moment's silence had ensued. 'I wanted to talk to you about the flat too.'

'What about it?' Nerves danced around inside her guts. She didn't like the turn the conversation had suddenly taken. 'You said I could still live in it, that you'd continue to pay half the mortgage. We agreed this, Luke.'

'Yes, yes I know we did.'

'Is that why you're really here? First you ask me to lie to the police and now you want to turf me out of my own home?'

She'd felt the anger swelling inside her stomach like yeast. 'I bet you were disappointed that he didn't finish me off, weren't you? You and that prissy student of yours… would've solved a lot of problems for you both, wouldn't it? If I had died you'd get the apartment – and the life insurance we took out together when we got the mortgage. Which reminds me, I must change that.'

She'd felt like screaming and bursting into tears and punching him all at the same time. If only she'd had the strength.

'How can you even *say* that, Daisey!' But he'd sounded a little disingenuous, as though her words had been bang on the money and he could barely disguise it.

'Who are you? What did I ever do to you that you could possibly hate me so much?'

More tears had come but this time she hadn't bothered to hide them. She'd felt so pathetic she wasn't sure which one she hated more in that moment, herself or him.

'Don't be ridiculous, I don't hate you… and I'm not asking you to sell the flat, not yet anyway – even I'm not that cruel.'

'Well, that's up for discussion, isn't it?' she'd shot back. How could he do this to her, drop this shit show on her now?

'Look, Daisey… I'm sorry,' he'd apologised again, his voice an octave lower. 'I can't afford to pay my half of the mortgage plus the rent on mine and Ch—' He'd stopped short of saying her name. 'I'm haemorrhaging money every month and it's crippling me… I'm sorry, I really am.'

'This is Cho's idea, isn't it?' she'd said, barely able to disguise the hatred she'd felt in that moment. That bitch! Not content with taking her husband-to-be, she wanted her home as well.

'No, it's not her idea! It wasn't…' He'd leapt to her defence, making her feel even more miserable. 'But she does agree that it's a waste to pay for somewhere I no longer live and…'

A waste? *A waste*? He didn't know the meaning of the word! Seven years of her life – prime years too – spent with a shallow, heartless, duplicitous fake, a facsimile of a person, a cardboard cut-out phoney – now that was the *real* waste. 'So as a compromise we thought… rather than forcing a sale, you could continue to live at the flat – that's assuming you still even want to after everything but you'll need to come up with all the mortgage payment yourself each month.'

He'd said the last part of the sentence quickly, like ripping off a plaster, as if somehow this would lessen the blow. He knew this wouldn't be financially viable for her, not on her salary alone.

'And if you can't afford it, well, Cho and I thought we might… well, maybe *we* could live there instead and you could find somewhere else – we'd buy you out, of course, you'd have a bit of equity as well as what you initially put in… it's something to consider anyway, maybe think it over while you're recovering. You know, it might be good to have a fresh start, somewhere new, somewhere without the bad memories.'

'I don't have any bad memories,' she'd snapped back. 'I can't remember anything… oh! You mean with you? Yes, plenty of those Luke… plenty…'

Panic mixed with anger and adrenalin and emotion had made her feel a little dizzy and she'd lain back onto the pillow. Sensing her distress, he'd nervously shifted towards her on the bed.

'I don't want to upset you, Daisey, really I don't.… look, there was never going to be a good time to discuss this and I'm running out of money.'

'Get out,' she'd said, her head swimming. 'Leave. Now please, I don't feel very well.'

He'd looked at her, seemingly a little surprised by her abrupt dismissal.

'Like I said, I don't want to upset you… it's just an untenable situation, at least this way…'

'Fuck off!' she'd screamed at him as loudly as her damaged vocal cords would allow. 'Just fuck off, Luke. Get out, get out, GET OUT!'

He'd jumped from the bed in alarm. The look on his face had given her a shiver of satisfaction in among all the other emotions swilling around inside her. She'd never have dared spoken to him like that when they'd been together. She'd always been the more subservient one; he'd been the one in charge, the one in control, the clever one, the more capable one, the intellectual. But something in her in that moment felt changed, a new-found determination inside of her, something more defiant.

'OK! OK! I'm going.' He'd backed away from the bed. 'But this will be the last month I can pay my share of the mortgage, OK? I'm sorry.'

She'd turned her head away from him in utter disgust; his words – and the timing of them – had cut deep.

'I really do hope you get better soon; that you get the support you'll need to help you through it. You're stronger than you think, Daisey... you've always been quietly determined...'

'Fuck you, you patronising shit,' she'd croaked between tears, but she wasn't sure he'd heard her. Surreptitiously she'd watched him from beneath the hospital sheets as he'd walked out into the corridor, past the window of her room. He hadn't even turned back to look at her. Once he'd left she threw his pathetic cheap flowers in the bin and cried some more.

She'd decided in that moment that she would definitely return to the apartment now, just to piss him and Cho off – and the sick bastard who'd smashed her skull open and left her for dead. Together, the three of them had taken everything from her – her future, her love, her dignity, her memory and safety – but they weren't going to take her home.

CHAPTER SIX

'… But if there's anything from that night… anything at all that you can remember, however small, however insignificant you might think it is – someone you spoke to, someone you saw, anything unusual…'

Detective Riley's smooth voice comes back to her, dragging her from her thoughts of Luke's hospital visit. Someone else has joined them in the room now, a woman; more police, she assumes. Her mind begins to crackle and fizz, a loud noise like static in her head that is painful and causes her to wince, like someone trying to tune a faulty radio. It's happened a few times since she's been awake and it scares her.

'We know you went to the work party. Ros has given us an account of what happened, when you left and who with…'

'I left with someone?' The noise fades and she detects the surprise in her own voice, like she's outside of herself looking in.

'Yes,' the female detective speaks now; she doesn't know her name although she's probably been told it and forgotten. 'With a male colleague, Thomas White?'

'Thomas White?' It takes her a second to recall the name. 'I left the party with… *Tommy White*?' Her voice sounds scratchy and broken and she wonders if she will ever sound the same – if she will ever *be* the same – again.

'He took you home, love – remember I told you,' Ros says, coaxing her like a mother does a small child. 'In a cab, he came inside your apartment for a bit, to use the loo, do you remember?'

'No… no, I don't!' she says. 'Tell me I didn't sleep with… tell me *he* didn't do this… It wasn't Tommy White… was it?' She sits up again, or attempts to, aided by a flush of adrenalin. She doesn't even like Tommy White much – he's a prat, fancies himself as a bit of a player if she remembers rightly.

'He says he left your apartment at 12.45 a.m. and that he got into an Uber just shy of 1 a.m. The driver corroborated his story.'

'He voluntarily gave his DNA too,' the female says. 'No match to the DNA we found in your apartment. His story checks out.'

She blinks at Ros for affirmation.

'It wasn't Tommy, darling,' she says, her voice soothing. 'Tommy saw you home safe. He's been in pieces ever since, feels terrible about it, keeps saying, "if only I hadn't left her…" He blames himself.'

'The attack happened at approximately 1.05 a.m., moments after Tommy left, which is why we believe your attacker must've been watching your apartment and struck when he saw the coast was clear. Unfortunately, there's no CCTV footage, and Tommy says he didn't see anyone loitering – he saw no one, nothing.'

She blinks at the detective, tries to take in what he's saying, but it's as if she's grown a membrane inside her mind and the words keep bouncing off it like a trampoline.

'Perhaps someone followed you home from the party…' Detective Riley continues. 'Daisey, has anyone been stalking you? Can you remember, in the weeks, months – in the run-up to the night of the attack – if you've had any unwanted attention, any messages, any phone calls? Has anyone been harassing you?'

She shakes her head. 'No… no one… not that I can remember…'

But the question bothering her most is what on earth was she thinking, leaving a party with Tommy White? She must've been drunk, drunk and desperate. Suddenly, she's hit with the bizarre and horrific realisation that everyone in this room, everyone who's huddled around her bed and looking at her with a mix of pity and admiration and concern and God only knows what else, has seen her naked. That's what she's been told – that she'd been naked when they'd found her – though they assure her there was no signs of sexual assault. She doesn't know why she even cares about this – she knows that it hardly matters and isn't important in the grand scheme of things – but she does care, and a flush of humiliation heats her face as she thinks of it.

'We took your phone, Daisey,' Detective Riley says gently. 'Your phone and your laptop, for intelligence, see if we could find anything, any leads, anything that might point us in the direction of whoever did this to you. Do you remember sending a text message – a message to Luke the night of the party?'

They've gone through her phone, taken her laptop, all her private things?

She shakes her head. She remembers nothing. It's as though someone has taken a chalkboard eraser to her mind and rubbed half of it out. She thinks about her encounter with Luke in the kitchen and hopes they won't ask her about it. She feels humiliated enough already.

'Luke is your ex-partner, that's right, isn't it, Daisey?'

'Fiancé.' Her voice is a hoarse whisper, barely audible. 'He's my ex-*fiancé*.'

'And when was the last time you saw him?'

'I… I can't remember.' She doesn't want them to know about the kitchen-table sex – she doesn't want anyone to know.

'We've spoken to Luke and he says he last saw you on 12 June, a little over a month ago, is that correct?'

Questions, so many questions, they're hurting her head. Her eyes dart over to Ros in an attempt to silently translate her feelings. She's perched on the other side of her hospital bed, smiling encouragingly. Luke has lied; he's lied to the police about when he last saw her, just like he'd told her. He doesn't want them to know about their encounter in case precious Cho finds out. She feels disgusted by him – and herself, though for different reasons. Luke had cheated on her with Cho and then he'd cheated on Cho with her. Now he wanted it all covered up so that he could get away with it. If he'd never left her in the first place then none of this would ever have happened. She'd never have gone to the party in the first place and would've been at home with him, safe. Daisey wonders why she cares so much more about Luke than she does about the maniac who attacked her. It was probably because she has no recollection of him, or the attack itself. It feels like none of it has really happened. Isn't that what people say: 'If you can't remember something then it didn't really happen?'

She doesn't answer the detective and hopes he will simply put her lack of response down to confusion – it's not like she needs to try too hard to fake it.

'We found DNA on your body, Daisey,' Detective Riley continues gently. 'Three sets, yours and two others yet unknown. There were traces of semen present…'

She swallows dryly, feels sick. 'We can't rule sexual assault out entirely, although this doesn't appear to be part of his usual MO – he didn't sexually assault the other two women and there's no other physical evidence to suggest it, but it would help us if you could…' He clears his voice and she suspects that for a moment he feels as uncomfortable as she does. 'If you could tell us if you'd recently had sexual intercourse?'

Daisey realises that while she has been in a coma, she has been intimately examined, that samples have been taken from her body, that people have been digging around inside her vagina, searching for evidence and she feels so violated that she wants to scream again. *How can this nightmare be happening to me?*

She wants to tell the detective that the semen they found almost certainly belonged to Luke, that they'd had sex the morning before the party. She wants to expose him for the self-serving liar he is. So what if Cho finds out and dumps him – he'd only have himself to blame. She hears his words from earlier, 'It was a mistake…' It had all been a mistake. *She'd been a mistake.*

She makes to speak but can't do it. Even after everything, even knowing what a heartless, arrogant, selfish, hypocritical, cheating bastard he is, she can't bring herself to deliberately throw him under the bus.

'No,' she says eventually. 'I'm sorry, I really don't remember.'

CHAPTER SEVEN

Nothing. That's what we've got. Every lead, every avenue, every promising link has led us down a cul-de-sac, a dead end, a brick wall – one I feel like beating my head against repeatedly.

'Let's go through it again, Davis,' I say. We are sitting in my car outside a sandwich bar, and I'm picking at a cheese and pickle sub that looks about as appetising as my shoe – and almost cost as much.

She bites into her sandwich; the contents of which looks unidentifiable and equally as unappetising as my own, perhaps more so.

'So,' she says, swallowing it quickly – I assume before she can actually taste it, 'we have two different sets of DNA, which match all three of the DNA profiles found on our victims and at the crime scenes, and then a separate profile from the semen we found on Daisey, which doesn't. We know it's almost certainly a male, approximately between twenty and forty years old. We know that he surprises them, hits them over the head, presumably to incapacitate them before strangling them, cutting their throats and then stripping them. He folds their clothes neatly in a pile, arranges the body and then leaves a single fresh pink rose on their chests and scatters some petals around or near their bodies.'

I give in and take a mouthful of my cheese and pickle sub. It tastes much like I imagine my shoe does. 'Why a rose? Why not a lily or a daffodil or a carnation?'

Davis shrugs, throws her sandwich down onto the paper bag on her lap almost in surrender.

'He prefers roses. Anyway, daffodils aren't in season at the moment, harder to get hold of.' She sighs. 'I don't know, gov.'

I force back another mouthful, wash it down with the tepid remains of a flat white.

'There has to be some kind of significance to the rose. Have we got anywhere with the florists yet?'

There are even more florists and shops that sell roses within a twenty-mile radius of each of our victims than there are different species of the flower itself, which, I'm informed – as someone who could kill a cactus and could write what I know about gardening on the back of a postage stamp – is around 150, possibly even more. Our killer prefers hybrid tea roses, one of the most recognised and popular, of course. It's been a laborious task to say the least, compiling a list of anyone whose purchased roses around the times of the murders – and that's assuming the killer doesn't grow them himself, or pick them from parks or an unsuspecting neighbour's shrub.

Davis doesn't need to answer my question – we both know the answer already. Besides, she's got a mouthful of sandwich.

'Roses represent love, don't they?' she says, brushing crumbs from her shirt. 'You give them to someone you love.'

Years ago, when I first started out on homicide, I remember a seasoned and particularly brilliant detective – who I viewed as a mentor – told me something that has always stuck with me: 'Where there's murder, Riley, there's motive – one does not truly exist without the other. Find the motive, find the man.' And this is the head-scratcher: motive.

All three of our victims were – are – no disrespect meant to them, very ordinary, everyday, unremarkable women. Looking into their respective backgrounds it appears they were all extremely well-liked with no obvious enemies, no sketchy pasts, nothing especially colourful about their lifestyles that would raise any red flags. The only real lead we have so far is the connection between Daisey Garrett and Fern Lever, the killer's second victim. Both were – Daisey still is – an employee at Warwick's department store. Fern Lever worked at Warwick's for almost a year in 2017 as a sales advisor in the Children's Fashion department – a coincidence or something else?

It's possible, though not a given, that the killer worked there too. Approximately 230,000 people have been employed by Warwick's since 2010, over half of them men. That's somewhere in the region of around 115,000 names to sift through and cross reference, assuming that all the names on that list are legit – our killer could've used a pseudonym, or identities plural. It's taking good old-fashioned round-the-clock police work to plough through the list; painstakingly checking and confirming identities, ticking people off manually one by one… a bit like looking for one of Willy Wonka's golden tickets blindfolded.

'Why doesn't he rape them? He strips them naked, which suggests there's a sexual motivation, but doesn't assault them…'

'Perhaps with the exception of Daisey… semen was found on her,' Davis clarifies.

I'm not convinced, however. Forensic came back with three sets of DNA from Daisey Garrett's apartment: hers and two others unknown and unrelated. Daisey claims she cannot remember having recently had sex with anyone, which could suggest our killer has upped the ante and started raping his victims, only the DNA Forensic came back with doesn't match the other sets found on the other two victims. My guess is that Daisey did have sex near the time of her attack, but not with the man who tried to kill her, just to complicate things further. We've ruled out Tommy White, the man who took her home that evening, no DNA match there. So if he did sexually assault her, why not the others?

We've been through all of this so many times, over and over to the point of paralysis. I can almost taste my own frustration when I swallow – it's only slightly less palatable than my cheese and pickle sub. What we really need is for Daisey Garrett to regain her memory of that night and start talking. She's the key that will unlock this whole case and I was hopeful that something might have come back to her by now but when I spoke to her just yesterday our conversation was much the same as our first: 'I'm sorry, Dan... still nothing... you know you'll be the first to know when it does... *if* it does.' The consultant at the hospital has told me to 'stop pushing her' and to 'be patient'. But my patience is running out and my heart drops like a stone just thinking about it.

'He wants to humiliate them?' Davis says. 'Degrade them for his own gratification... that's why he strips them.'

'So he hates women; they've hurt him, let him down, cheated on him. He wants power over them, he's inadequate, a loser in love...'

'Aren't we all?' Davis sighs heavily again.

'Speak for yourself,' I say, but secretly I'm not entirely disagreeing with her. Fiona and I still haven't really got around to discussing 'us' since our Juno was born. I put this down to us both being occupied by the myriad demands of parenthood, although I realise this is a poor excuse, on my part anyway, because I sense Fi wants us to have the conversation, especially given the fact we've ended up being intimate a couple of times since Pip arrived. The truth is, I don't know what Fiona and I are. I despise the term 'friends with benefits'; it strikes me as the kind of phrase a commitment-phobic shallow player would use and I'd hate to think I'd ever fall into that category. Besides, she's more than that, much; she's the mother of my precious Pip.

'What do you think he does with the weapons?' We know our killer's choice of tools is a hammer and a knife, but we've never found them.

'Takes them with him,' Davis says with a mouthful. She has pink Marie Rose sauce on her chin, and I hand her a flimsy napkin and she wipes it, missing a bit.

I think about the killer, imagine him as he commits his hideous crimes, try to visualise what goes through his mind, which is nigh on impossible and probably a good thing, I suppose. Given that he cuts their throats, how come no one has seen a heavily blood-stained man walking down the road or on public transport? How come a flatmate or girlfriend or sister or mother hasn't noticed the claret-coloured clothes of their loved one in a washing basket?

'Perhaps…' I sigh, my mind wandering. 'What did you think of the ex-boyfriend, Luke somebody or other… Luke Bradley…?' We'd interviewed him a day or two after Daisey's attack. It's standard procedure to try to eliminate those closest to the victim first.

'Fiancé,' Davis corrects me, 'her ex-fiancé. Well, his alibi checks out. He was at home with the new girlfriend. They ordered a take-out, showed us the Uber Eats receipt.' She flicks through her notepad. 'Wagamama's, *vegan.*'

'I didn't like him,' I say. 'Something about him…'

'Well, he managed to drop into the conversation that he's an Oxford graduate no fewer than three times.' Davis rolls her eyes. 'Struck me as a bit arrogant.'

I nod sagely as I think of Daisey, cheated on by her fiancé then attacked and left for dead in her own home. I wonder why it is that some people seem to suffer so much more than others.

'He was holding something back.'

Davis turns to me. 'Like what, boss?'

'I'm not sure exactly. I just sensed that he was lying, or maybe not lying but not giving us the full picture. The way he appeared so affronted that we'd dared to even question him. And he refused to give us voluntary DNA, which is his right, of course, but still, you've got to ask yourself *why*, Davis. If it were me I'd want to be eliminated.'

She nods her agreement.

'Anyway, they know him,' I say. 'The victims knew him, or recognised him in some way. There wasn't any sign of a break-in in all three cases. He rings the bell; they open the door. Maybe they invite him in? They turn their backs and… wallop! Anyway, they don't feel threatened at first, which makes me believe they must've been familiar with him or expecting him.'

Davis gives up on her sandwich. She's eaten over half of it though, so I'm quite impressed by her determination. I've already abandoned mine.

'Well, we've checked everyone out in all three cases: boyfriends, ex-boyfriends, family, friends, associates, colleagues, followers, Facebook friends… there's no connection, no one in common to link any of them.'

'That we've found yet,' I add, because I'm convinced there's a link somewhere. There has to be. The answers are there in amongst the tangled mess of people's lives and pasts. It's like Daisey Garrett's memory – it's simply a case of when it comes to us, not if.

Davis sighs once more. We're silent for a moment, the sound of the wiper blades punctuating it – it's drizzling outside.

'Roses!' Davis proclaims, suddenly animated. 'Oh my God!'

'What? What about them?'

Her eyes are bulging. 'I can't believe we missed it, boss.'

'Missed what?' I ask, trying not to let my urgency turn to irritation.

Davis is shaking her head now. 'That's the connection!'

'Roses,' I interject. 'You said something about roses…'

'I did.' She grins smugly. She's enjoying this, knowing something she thinks I don't yet know, or haven't thought of. It's that hint of professional competitiveness, which is no bad thing really. It's good to be kept on your toes in this game.

'He leaves them a rose, right?'

'Yes. He leaves them a rose,' I repeat back to her.

'And the names of all of our victims?' She clasps her hands together, almost childlike and I feel a sudden wave of affection for her. *Good ol' Davis.*

'Jasmin Goddard, Fern Lever and... hang on, bloody hell Christ!'

Davis laughs as she watches the realisation dawn on me. 'Daisey Garrett! The victims, they've all got floral names, gov!'

I shake my head. 'My God, Davis,' I say. 'You're only bloody right!'

She claps her hands together in self-congratulation. 'But what do you think it means exactly?'

My sobering question kills her buzz instantly.

'Well... I don't know... he's a gardener? He likes flowers... his ex-girlfriend was called Poppy?' She exhales again, bubble burst. But it's ignited something in me. A thought has taken hold. Something Davis doesn't yet have in as much abundance, but that I know she will someday. *Intuition.*

'Good call, Lucy,' I say, nodding at her, and she smiles, looks pleased with herself. 'And by the way, you have sauce on your chin.'

CHAPTER EIGHT

'Mind if I join you?' The woman sits down opposite her before Daisey can answer, places her tall latte onto the table, spilling a little of the froth down the side of the glass. 'You look pretty much how I feel,' she remarks with something nearing over-familiarity as she throws her handbag down onto the adjacent empty chair. 'Like shit,' the woman says bluntly, though she's still smiling.

Daisey almost laughs at her directness, bordering on rudeness. *No, please, tell me what you really think!* 'Like you lost twenty quid and found a fiver,' she adds.

'Yeah.' She gives a gentle snort. 'Something like that.'

The woman blows at the foamed milk on top of the coffee in a bid to cool it, watching her from over the rim. She takes a sip, recoils.

'Jesus, this coffee is like lava.' She places a napkin against her lips. 'It should come with a warning.'

'Yeah, like some people,' Daisey quips sardonically, but she's not sure the woman has heard her. Clearly she works here – she's wearing a staff tag around her neck – but she doesn't think she knows her; doesn't think she's seen her until today. That said, she's been off for a while, out of the game, and people came and went at Warwick's all the time. For some people, like her, the infamous London department store becomes a second home, and for others it's simply a transit zone, just temporarily while they pass through.

'I'm Iris.' She smiles at her, the expression on her face changing to a slight furrow. 'Have we met before?' She licks the foam from her lips.

Daisey fiddles with her scarf, a scarf she has taken to wearing in a bid to disguise the angry red scar underneath. The doctors say it will fade in time anyway, but for now the scarf stops people from asking questions. Questions: that's largely what she feels her life has consisted of ever since the attack. Everything everyone ever asks her now is open-ended.

Iris blinks at her, waiting for a response. She thinks she's small, like her, though it's difficult to tell as she's sitting down, and her hair is a similar colour to her own, though shorter, cut into a neat long bob.

'I don't know… I don't think so,' she replies, trying to be friendly although it feels like a chore. Everything feels that way to her now. The only reason she's here, back at work, is because she has no choice. *She has to be here for financial reasons.*

The police had advised her to move house after she had been discharged from hospital. Her Family Liaison Officer – a robust Scottish woman called Maggie whose overly sweet perfume got up her nose and made her feel sick – had tried to suggest that a change would be 'a new start', just like Luke had said in the hospital. But instead she had, at her own insistence, stayed with Ros, temporarily until she felt confident enough to return to her apartment.

She supposed she should've felt fearful going back to the place where she had almost lost her life, but the truth was since she still couldn't remember anything of the attack she felt nothing. Ron, Ros's bloke, had gone round to the apartment to look at security and had fitted her with a panic alarm. He'd also put a spyhole in her internal door and added two new locks, one with a chain. The whole block now had CCTV cameras, apparently as a direct result of her attack, which she'd felt was a bit like shutting the stable door after the horse had bolted, but nonetheless seemed to reassure the neighbours.

It had felt strange, coming back. The apartment had looked the same, but it had felt different somehow, like it now had a filter on it, like the way you view a person at the end of a love affair – familiar yet somehow forever changed at the same time.

'So which department are you working for?'

She asks the question without remotely being interested in the answer and wonders if the woman whom she now knows is called Iris can tell. She doesn't want to come across this way – vague and disconnected, rude even, but this is how she feels inside now: dead. She glances around the cafeteria, sees if she can spy Ros and call her over so that she can pick up the slack. Warwick's staff café is busy, filled with workers taking advantage of the subsidised breakfast and limitless coffee, about to embark upon another day's commission-led selling, and yet despite being surrounded by so many faces, many of them familiar, she's suddenly hit by a debilitating sense of loneliness, an ache in her chest reminding her how different her life is now; how different she is.

'Perfume,' Iris says, her voice cutting through her maudlin thoughts. 'It's a temp job – just in the run-up to Christmas.'

Daisey nods and smiles. She used to be so social, sometimes even the life and soul, or at least that's what had been said a few times over the years. She'd always prided herself on being able to strike up a conversation with anyone. 'You talk too much, Daisey,' she heard Luke's voice berating her again, 'you're too trusting, too friendly and accommodating. That's why people trample all over your boundaries…'

Well, now she felt the opposite of those things – now she felt prickly, wary and suspicious – and above all lonely, *so terribly lonely*.

'On the Dior section – I like your scarf, by the way,' Iris notes, pointing at it. 'Suits you.'

Daisey looks down at her coffee. She wishes she hadn't mentioned the bloody scarf. She wonders if Iris knows about her, if Ros – or anyone else – has said anything, or if she recognises her from the newspapers and is desperate to ask her about the attack, like most people are. She realises she's being a little paranoid but it's what her life has become now – everything centres round the attack. People are fixated on it, intrigued and curious about it, about her. She sees it in almost everyone she meets; it's written all over their faces, a ghoulish desire to find out more. She wishes she could just be anonymous, like she was before. Even if her life hadn't been exactly exciting – even if sometimes she had wished she'd done more, seen more and achieved greater things – she'd sacrifice it all just to go back to her mundane, uneventful and anonymous existence now.

Instinctively she touches the scarf. It feels silky between her fingers, like a gossamer layer of protection.

'You never know, you might want to make a "career" out of it?' She makes inverted commas with her fingers, shoots her a conspiratorial smile, anything to draw her away from the scarf and the scar it conceals, both physical and mental.

Iris smiles back brightly. 'Why, are the career prospects bright then?' She raises an eyebrow in recognition of the rhetoric.

'Well, if you like ridiculously long hours, standing on your feet all day, having no social life at the weekend, if you enjoy working with the general – and sometimes generally rude – public and aren't interested in getting rich quick, then you'll fit in a treat.'

Iris giggles almost childishly. 'Sounds right up my street then.' She cocks her head to one side. There's a slight pause. 'Surely it's not *all* bad? There's worse jobs out there.'

Daisey exhales deeply. Truth is, for all her grumbling, she actually enjoys her job at Warwick's – or used to, before she stopped enjoying anything at all. She knew that Luke used to secretly look down on it, dismissed it as 'menial shop work' and had appeared uncomfortable whenever any of his intellectual friends or colleagues had ever asked her the question, 'So, what do you do?' But it gave her pleasure working with all the cosmetics, learning about the different products and helping women to make themselves look and feel their best. We couldn't all be Mensa material, could we? *Who the hell was that pretentious arsehole to judge anyway?*

'Well, there is the 25 per cent staff discount, sample sales and' – she holds her cup up like a trophy – 'free coffee!' She swallows down her moribund thoughts with another sip of flat white.

'Every cloud, eh?' Iris laughs and suddenly Daisey is struck by an inexplicable sensation, like someone has walked over her grave, or whatever the saying was to describe such an unsettling feeling. 'Anyway, you sure we haven't met before? You really do look familiar.'

Daisey drops her chin slightly, stares into her coffee. She gets this a lot now, strangers thinking they somehow know her because they've seen her face splashed all over the newspapers. Often they can't quite place her, can't put their finger on why they think they recognise her.

'I'm sure I'd have remembered you if we had.' This is her favourite response. It's the politest way of ending any uncertainty. 'Where were you working before here?' She changes the subject.

'Temping,' Iris sighs. 'A slew of shitty office jobs.'

Daisey nods in understanding. At least she wasn't the only one drifting through life without much purpose, not that this was much in the way of consolation.

'You not married then? Kids?' She figures Iris is probably around a similar age – early thirties, though she could be younger. Now she looks at her though, she wonders if Iris is maybe right and that actually they may have met before. There's a familiarity to her that she herself can't quite place, but then again, her mind and memory has been shot to shit ever since her skull had been bashed in. She has trouble recognising herself, let alone anyone else. The wires in her brain haven't quite meshed back together properly yet, and it takes longer than usual for her to recall names and faces, like forgetting the words to a favourite song.

Iris shakes her head. 'Nope. Young, free and single, me… well, the last two at least.' She laughs, throws her head back and Daisey wishes she had the same kind of carefree vivacity – like she used to have. 'I live on my own… actually…' She leans in across the table towards her slightly. 'Ros told me you might be looking for a flatmate…'

'Oh! Did she?'

'Hiya, love!' As if on cue, Ros joins them at the table, carrying an espresso for herself. She addresses Daisey but smiles at them both. 'How are you?'

'Daisey and I were just talking about being single,' Iris interjects.

Ros gives a little snort, places her cup down onto the table. 'Best bloody way to be, I tell you. By the time I was your age I'd been married twice and had three kids… thank God they've all grown up and fled the nest now.'

Daisey relaxes a little now that Ros has arrived and taken over the conversation; if she smiles and nods and chips in every now again she might just pass for normal.

'I wouldn't want to be young again. There's too much pressure on women these days: pressure to get married, have kids, a glittering career, be an Instagram model, perfect mother, perfect body, perfect wife… all of it. I'm telling you now, no one can spin that many plates at the same time without dropping one.'

Iris laughs a little. 'Anyway, I need to find a room somewhere because the place I was sharing with a friend… well, the landlord, he's selling up, kicking us out – by the end of the week!'

'There you go, love!' Ros shoots Daisey an animated smile. 'Problem solved!'

Daisey had casually mentioned to Ros just the other day that she'd been thinking of renting her spare room out, although it was not so much a thought but a necessity. Luke had stopped paying his half of the mortgage just like he'd said he would – the memory of that hospital visit still crushes her whenever she thinks of it – and she's been struggling to make ends meet. He and that bitch girlfriend hadn't even given her the chance to get back on her feet properly, kicking her while she was down – at her lowest, in fact. *Sometimes she wished he had killed her.*

Iris rolls her eyes as if to illustrate the major inconvenience.

'I mean, seven days' notice! What an arsehole…'

'Well then.' Ros beams brightly at Daisey, nodding her encouragement. 'Looks like you can both help each other out, kill two birds and all of that…'

Daisey feels a sense of reluctance but isn't sure why; she needs the money – and the company, truth be known – though the idea of hurtling towards forty and sharing a flat admittedly depresses her. *This wasn't how it was supposed to be.* 'Well, I do have a spare room, but it's a bit of a trek into work every day, and the transport's a bit hit-and-miss and…'

Ros nudges her with her foot under the table.

'Why don't you go over and see the room; it's a gorgeous apartment… she could pop by tonight couldn't she, Daisey?'

'That's brilliant!' Iris knocks her coffee and takes her phone from her handbag, not waiting for Daisey's response. 'Take my number and text me the address, yeah? Is 8 p.m. OK for you?'

Daisey obliges, punching the digits into her iPhone, a little overwhelmed by the speed at which the conversation is moving. 'Um… OK.'

'Perfect, see you then!' Iris stands to leave. Daisey had been right – she is small. 'Bye, Ros, see you later; Daisey, 8 p.m.!'

'Bye, love!' Ros waves at her as she walks away and nestles in closer to Daisey at the table. She takes a sip of her espresso.

'There you go, darling.' She nudges her arm. 'Things are looking up! At least that'll be one less thing to worry about, paying your mortgage. And now you won't be on your own. I worry about you being alone, you know…'

'I suppose so,' Daisey replies uneasily. 'But I don't really know her.'

'Well,' Ros says brightly, 'what do they say? Strangers are simply friends you don't know yet or something; anyway she seems nice enough. Friendly and fun, reminds me a bit of you, like you were before—' She stops herself short. 'What did you say her name was again?'

'Iris…' Daisey says glumly, realising what Ros had been about to say. 'Hang on, I thought you knew her?'

'Me? No love.' She shakes her head, dregs her coffee cup. 'Never met her before in my life.'

CHAPTER NINE

March 1994

'Doesn't she look a proper little darling?' Mrs Merryweather from number 119 bends down and smiles at Rosie. 'Will you just look at her costume… you look just like a princess!'

'An Easter *fairy flower girl* princess,' Rosie corrects her in a high-pitched baby-type voice, even though she's almost seven. 'Mummy made it for me,' she adds proudly, looking up at Tracey as she holds her hand tightly. 'For the parade today at the street party.'

'Well now, aren't you a lucky girl?' Mrs Merryweather makes a little groan as she stands, highlighting the fact that it's a bit of an effort these days. 'Must've taken you an age to make that.' She stands back to admire the costume once more. 'Dying art these days. Women don't sew like they used to, not like when I was a girl anyhow. Your mother taught you, her mother taught her and so on… Gosh,' she gushes again, holds Rosie's chin between her thumb and forefinger, 'she really is a picture, isn't she, this one. Such a beautiful little girl – perfect.'

Tracey smiles proudly in agreement. 'Thanks, Mrs Merryweather, it took me two days solid to make it. Even if I say so myself, I'm quite proud of it – and she does look like a little angel, doesn't she? My perfect little angel…'

Rosie beams, basking in the glory her mother and the old woman are lavishing upon her.

'And how about that wee brother of yours?' The old woman gently smiles at Rosie. 'Did Mummy make him a spectacular costume for the parade today too?'

Tracey stifles a cough at the back of her throat, avoids eye contact with the old woman.

'Mummy says he's not allowed to c—'

'He's not feeling so well today, Mrs Merryweather,' Tracey interjects. 'He woke with a bit of a temperature this morning. Best for him to stay indoors.'

'Ahhh, that's a shame. I hope the little lad isn't going down with something… such a pity for him to miss the events today; the committee has gone to a big effort, lots of stuff for the kiddies to enjoy. The parade and the fun fair and the cakes and the egg hunt… such a lot of it about these days, and the kiddies are so susceptible, aren't they? Echinacea… you want to give him a few drops of that in his milk before bedtime, very good for the immune system, supposed to work miracles… my Arthur swore by it, right up until he died.'

Tracey wants to walk away but can't bring herself to be rude. 'Well, it's lovely talking to you, Mrs Merryweather…'

'Oh! Before you go, I don't suppose you've seen my Snowdrop, have you?'

Tracey swallows hard. 'Snowdrop?'

'Yes.' The old lady smiles but her eyes look a little glassy. 'My Snowy… my cat… you know, big white fluffy thing, can't miss her. She's been gone for a few days now. It's not like her, you know, to disappear. Never been missing this long before, likes her home comforts too much. I'm terribly worried. I've asked everyone down the street to check their sheds and garages, but no one's seen her. My poor Snowy, I do hope she's all right. She's all I've got left now that Arthur's gone.'

Tracey can't look the old woman in the face. 'No… no, I'm sorry, I haven't seen her. But I will look out for her, Mrs Merryweather, I promise.'

'Ahhh, you are kind. I don't suppose you've seen a big fluffy white cat around have you, my little princess?'

Rosie opens her mouth to speak but Tracey pulls at her daughter's hand firmly.

'No, she hasn't, have you, Rosie? I'm sure she would've said something… Rosie loves animals, don't you, darling?'

Rosie nods but doesn't speak. She recognises the hand tug as an instruction not to.

'Ah well, keep those beautiful blue eyes of your peeled for me then, eh, sweetheart?'

'We will do, Mrs Merryweather. Hope to see you later, at the parade.'

Tracey stares at the black sack by the kitchen door.

'What are we going to do, John?' She bites her nails and looks at her husband anxiously. 'She was asking about it earlier, the old lady up the road, Mrs Merryweather. She asked Rosie to look out for it too.'

'She didn't say anything, Rosie, did she?' He throws her a concerned glance.

'No. I made sure she didn't. Oh God, John, I feel awful… *terrible*.'

'Calm down, Trace,' he says, hovering over the sack, unable to take his own eyes from it. 'We'll just have to bury it, won't we… in the garden, down the end by the tomato plants.' He rubs his forehead with his hand. 'I'll do it this afternoon, while you take the twins to the parade.'

Tracey turns to her husband slowly. 'Oh no. I'm not taking *him* with me, with us. He can stay locked up in that room all day as punishment… I'm not letting him spoil my Rosie's moment at the parade. She's in line for first place for the costume I made her… and stop calling them "the twins", you know I don't like it.'

She takes a cigarette from her husband's packet on the kitchen table and lights it, taking an audible drag. She only smokes when she's stressed which is why he says nothing, thinks it best not to pass comment in the circumstance. John comes towards her, places his hand on her arm.

'Look, Trace, we don't know he killed her bloody cat, do we, not for sure? He said that they'd found it like that, didn't he? And Rosie backed him up, said she'd been with him and another little girl, playing in the field the whole morning and that they'd stumbled across it, and the knife.'

'I don't believe him,' Tracey says, monotone. 'I think he got Rosie to lie for him. You know they're as thick as thieves.'

'They're twins, Trace. Twins are notoriously close; everybody knows that. You say it like it's a bad thing. You can't keep the little lad locked up all day. We should talk to him; find out what really happened exactly. It might all be a misunderstanding.'

Tracey snorts. 'So, shall we tell Mrs Merryweather? Tell her that I found him standing over her precious moggie, holding a bloody knife. What do you think she'd think – what do you think *anyone* would think?'

'That there was a reasonable explanation for it?' He shrugs. 'It was probably just kids, teenagers who were bored or high or something... a misunderstanding,' he says again.

'There's nothing to misunderstand, John,' she says stoically. 'I found him, under the lilac tree in the woods, standing over the damned thing with a knife in his hand. He'd stabbed the poor thing to death, I know he had.' She visibly flinches as the moment flashes up inside her head like a scene from a horror film. 'Covered in blood it was, and he was just... just standing there staring at me, with this look on his face... this blank expression... it was horrible, macabre.' She buries her head into her hands, smoke curling upwards into her hair and starts to cry. 'There's something wrong with him, John – and I don't just mean all the physical problems – I mean there's something wrong with him inside; I've known it since the minute he was born.'

John sighs, goes to comfort her.

'Why do you always think the worst of him? Please don't start all this again, love. We've been here before. Look, I know it's been hard… what with the…' he struggles to find the right words, '… the difficulties and everything, and you had postnatal depression and—'

'NO!' Tracey objects. 'I didn't… I didn't have postnatal depression, I…' She tries to explain how she feels to her husband but she can't articulate it; she doesn't know how to explain it, doesn't understand it herself and she knows he'll only put it down to all his medical 'issues' anyway. 'We need to take him to someone; he needs help, professional, psychological help. He isn't right, John. I know it and so do you deep down.'

John turns to her, takes an audible breath. 'What that boy *needs*, Tracey, is his mother's love. Right from the moment he was born, you adored our Rosie and you rejected him – it wasn't his fault he was born the way he was, but he was – *is* – our son, *your* son. Look, no one else has raised any red flags; the school, for example… his teachers say he's a bit quiet, a bit withdrawn but otherwise, he's a perfectly normal little boy…'

Tracey's head lowers. She knows he's right – that it's true, she had struggled to love her son since his birth – but it wasn't for the reasons John had always thought. It wasn't because he had 'defects' or was a sickly and demanding child. It was something else, something she felt deep inside of her. She really had tried to love her son like she loved her daughter; she'd never mistreated him, always made sure he was well-fed, well-dressed and clean. But that inexplicable love, that unconditional love a mother feels for her child… Tracey wasn't sure what she felt for her son exactly. He was different to Rosie, completely. Not just to look at either – you'd never guess they were twins. People often mistook her son for Rosie's younger brother and seemed genuinely surprised when she would correct them and say, 'He's not just my brother, he's my *twin* brother.'

Rosie was a beautiful child, undeniably so. She'd been blessed with a pair of sparkling violet eyes and silky chestnut hair, peachy skin and long, lithe, athletic legs. She was confident and outgoing and possessed a zest for life. She was healthy and happy and... *normal.* Her son, on the other hand, was small for his age – noticeably so against his sister, and painfully thin. He was withdrawn and insular, never smiled much, and he was weak and sickly, forever unwell. Unlike Rosie who was cuddly and affectionate, she couldn't snuggle up to him on the sofa and read stories or watch Disney films together. He hardly spoke and when he did his voice was squeaky and grated on her. The contrast of her two children was marked and remarkable – they were polar opposites, like they had been born with different parents, like he wasn't theirs. When Tracey looked at him, she got the feeling she was looking at an empty shell, a little boy void of any emotion whatsoever, unable to show any love to anyone – with the exception of his sister. He adored Rosie, followed her around like a lovesick puppy – she'd only ever seen him come to life around his twin. That he had been born 'different' might have made Tracey feel more protective towards her son, and she felt ashamed that it hadn't. But these facts were not the reasons she felt as she did. There was something strange about him, something amiss; she was almost fearful of him, or *for* him – she wasn't sure which, maybe both. And now this had confirmed her worst fears.

'I know he's been troublesome, love...' John continues, his voice softer with compassion for his wife. 'All those doctors and hospital visits as a baby, him being sick all the time and the operations... I know it took its toll on you and I should've been there more, helped share the load, but I had to work, love, to keep a roof over our heads.'

'I know,' she replies, her voice low with the guilt and shame she feels.

'Look, if he has done it then he most likely did it for attention. *Your* attention, that's what he's needed. You've lavished our Rosie with it all her little life and given nothing to that boy.'

'Please, John,' she says, her eyes welling up with tears.

'I'm sorry, love,' he says. 'But I see you with him – you can barely look at him… your own son!'

Tracey sucks on her cigarette.

'He doesn't like me.' She hears how pathetic this sounds but it's how she really feels. The way he looks at her sometimes, blank and emotionless. It scares her. 'He only likes spending time with Rosie. I don't like the way he looks at her, John; I don't like the way he looks at *me* sometimes, either.'

'Looks at her? Jesus Christ, Tracey, what are you saying? He's only six years old, for Christ sakes!'

Tracey rubs her temples again. She loves her husband but she knows she can't get him to understand. He doesn't see what she does. John's job takes him away around the country, sometimes for days, even weeks on end. He's been a good father, but largely an absent one.

'Look, John, don't tell me you think this is normal… a six-year-old boy stabbing a poor defenceless cat to death. You know that's how all the serial killers start out, don't you, by killing animals?'

John sighs loudly and Tracey can tell the conversation is going nowhere and that her concerns have fallen on deaf ears. He doesn't *want* to believe her.

'Rosie said they found the poor thing like that, they'd been playing with another little girl and they all stumbled across it… it was probably teenagers; you've seen them hanging around the woods up there, right horrible-looking mob they are, roughnecks from the estates, latchkey kids… It'll be them who did it for kicks, nothing better to do,' he says resignedly, looking at the black sack by the back door.

'Yes,' she agrees with him. There's no point trying to explain how she feels anymore. She doesn't want to fight with him. Perhaps he is right: the problem is with her and not their son. Perhaps if she just tried harder. 'I'm sorry. You're right. I don't know what's wrong with me.'

John comes round the table and embraces her.

'It's OK, Trace. It'll be OK, I promise,' he says, kissing the top of her head. 'Now, do you want to start digging this hole or shall I?'

CHAPTER TEN

The sound of the doorbell startles her – it always does now, and she looks through the spyhole. The image is contorted through the fish-eye lens, but she can see it's a woman and she's holding what looks like a bottle in one hand and a bunch of flowers in the other.

'Er, helloooo… it's Iris,' the voice says tentatively, waggling the bottle out in front of her. 'I've come about the room…'

Oh Jesus. Daisey's shoulders sag as she makes the connection. The woman at work, the new one from the Perfume counter; they'd made some half-baked arrangement for her to come over to look at the room this morning over coffee. How could she have forgotten? Come to think of it, she doesn't remember even texting her the address, but she guesses she must've done otherwise she wouldn't be here. Bloody hell, she's in her pyjamas as well. She was just settling down to finish the Netflix series she's been binge-watching while slowly getting pissed on Prosecco – something she's found herself doing more frequently since the attack; well, since Luke left, if she's honest. The wine helps her to sleep, or at least it helps her to forget, even though she can't actually remember – how ironic is that? Daisey feels aggravated with herself. If anything her memory seems to be getting worse, not better like the doctors had told her it would. Sometimes she finds herself walking into a room for something only to instantly forget what it was she had come for in the first place. This was something she only occasionally did before the attack but now it was an almost daily occurrence.

'Yes… yes… *Iris*…' She releases the top bolt, pulls the chain off the latch and unlocks the door. 'Of course… come in.'

'Blimey, it's like Fort Knox in here,' Iris comments with a bright smile as Daisey finally opens the door. 'You trying to keep someone out?'

Suddenly, she feels self-conscious, standing there in her sloppy pyjamas, a little worse for wear.

'I'm not early, am I?' Iris asks, stepping inside. 'We did say 8 p.m., didn't we?'

'Yes,' Daisey says. 'We did. Sorry, in all honesty I forgot you were coming, hence the PJs.' She cocks her head in apology. She hasn't tidied up either and there are dirty dishes on the side and an overflowing ashtray on the coffee table. She scrabbles around in a bid to clear them away, plumps up a few cushions on the sofa.

At least the spare room is in order, thank God. She and Luke had turned it into a guest room when they'd bought the place; it was supposed to be used for when friends and family came to stay. Not that any of hers ever had or did – not family, anyway. She had hoped it might become a nursery in time, just like they had discussed. She had clearly envisioned it in her head; all soft white blankets, fluffy sheepskin rugs and an oak cot where their baby would sleep, clean and pristine, like something out of a high-end store catalogue. But it had remained untouched and unused since he'd left and she rarely went in it now, too much of a painful reminder of what should have been.

'Don't clear up on my account.' Iris holds out the bottle of wine. 'I brought Prosecco, I hope you like it.' She looks down at the glass on the coffee table. 'Though it looks like you already started without me.'

Iris places the bottle on the table, lays the flowers next to them – a bunch of roses, the sort you get from a supermarket, wrapped in plastic with a price sticker that never rips cleanly off. Upon the sight of them her breathing instantly becomes laboured, her heartbeat increasing rapidly as she stares at their pink heads just beginning to open, their thin spiky green stems… she wonders if this type of rose is similar to the one he left on her naked body – was it a pink rose or a red one? She hadn't thought to ask until now and no one had thought to tell her. She supposes it doesn't really matter, or does it? Roses: red, or pink, expensive or cheap?

Suddenly, it all matters. Her counsellor had warned her about this, 'triggers' she had called them, things associated with the trauma that could potentially send her into a panic. The trick, apparently, was to identify said triggers and try to eliminate or avoid them altogether, which is easier said than done. Despite her lack of recollection, her imagination is sufficient to have built a mental image of how the scene might've looked. Her naked body, blood on the sheets, her head smashed open, her throat slit and more blood, blood everywhere – *and a rose…*

She stares at the flowers on the glass table, unable to look away. She doesn't want them anywhere near her, let alone in her apartment. Luke springs back into her mind again, the bouquet of flowers he had brought when he'd visited at the hospital – lilies and gerberas and… *roses…* How could he have been so insensitive? Had it been deliberate? He'd known that her attacker had left a rose at the scene; the press had made a big deal of it. Does Iris know this too? Surely she wouldn't have brought roses if she did. Surely she wouldn't be so stupid, so… *offensive.*

Daisey smiles awkwardly. She's not sure if she's reviled or enamoured by Iris's direct approach, or her air of confidence, which is almost tipping over into arrogance. But there is something intriguing about her. She wonders if it's because Iris's personality doesn't seem to correlate with her physical appearance. She's small in stature like her, around five feet three inches, and is thin, almost painfully so. She's neither pretty nor ugly but somehow a strange combination of both. Her nose is long and pointed, and her eyes are small, sunken a little too far into their sockets and a touch too close-set. Her hair is perfect though, smooth and glossy – almost like she's wearing a wig – and she notices the thick layer of make-up on her face, a visible line on her jaw where she hasn't quite blended her foundation properly, a basic error, not least for someone working in a beauty department. She's casually dressed – jeans and a sweatshirt that hangs off her small frame and covers her hands as though it's two sizes too big for her. She hadn't really noticed any of this when they'd met that morning in the café. She hadn't really been paying attention. But now she looks at her properly she decides that Iris is a bit odd-looking – mismatched and definitely a little unusual; yes that was the word, *unusual*.

'I brought you some flowers,' she says brightly, looking around the room with approval. 'Shall I get a vase for them? Do you have one?'

What Iris lacked in sartorial finesse she certainly appeared to make up for in confidence.

'I'm allergic to them… roses in particular,' she says, rubbing her nose for effect. 'They give me chronic hay fever.'

'Oh!' she says. 'I'm sorry. I had no idea. Shall I throw them away?'

Daisey doesn't want to sound ungrateful. She assumes Iris isn't to know that these particular flowers are a painful trigger.

'No. It's fine. Leave them there. And… and thank you, it was a kind thought.'

Iris looks unperturbed. 'It's so good of you to let me look at the room. I was getting really desperate… what with the landlord kicking us out with almost no notice whatsoever… bloody bastard…'

'I didn't think they were allowed to do that. I thought tenants had protection against that sort of thing?'

Iris doesn't answer her, carries on looking around the living room.

'Wow, what a gorgeous apartment. So… trendy, so cool.'

Daisey inwardly winces. She hates the word 'cool'. It's one of Luke's favourites. He overused it a lot and she always thought it sounded contrived coming from someone over the age of thirty. '*Don't do that Daisey, it's so uncool.*'

'Yeah, really nicely done out.' She nods her approval. 'You've got great taste.'

'Thanks,' she says. *Pity it wasn't great enough to keep my fiancé from running off with one of his students.*

'How long have you lived here?'

'Just over a year now… about fourteen months.'

'And you own it?'

'Yes. Well, myself and my ex…' She thinks to add the word fiancé but decides against it. She suspects it'll be too tempting a disclosure for her not to probe further.

'Didn't work out then?' Iris casually enquires as she moves from the living room through to the open-plan kitchen area, inspecting it.

'No,' she says flatly, thinking it an obvious answer to what was clearly a question that didn't warrant being asked in the first place.

'Let's have a drink,' Iris says. 'I'll get some glasses.'

Daisey nods and for a moment she thinks that Iris is about to actually begin opening her kitchen cupboards. She wonders if people get the sense that she's a pushover, or if they somehow mistake her kindness for weakness. 'Boundary issues' – that's what Luke had called them. '*It's why people take advantage of you, Daisey – a lack of boundaries.*' Well, wasn't that the truth where *he* was concerned!

'It's fine, I'll get them,' she says, quickly moving past Iris and pulling two flutes from the kitchen cupboard. She feels nervous as she pops the cork and pours them both a glass, though she isn't sure why exactly. She lights a cigarette in a bid to calm herself.

'You smoke?'

Daisey resists firing off a sarcastic comeback, something like, 'No shit, Sherlock.'

'Yes occasionally. Socially mainly, mostly only when I drink.' She doesn't add that these days she 'mostly' drinks every day and that therefore 'occasionally' has become more like 'frequently'. Anyway, why is she even thinking about explaining herself? Why does she always feel the need to justify herself to people, even complete strangers, even strangers who need something from her? *This is your apartment, Daisey*, she reminds herself.

'I didn't have you down as a smoker,' Iris comments, 'not that I mind; cigarette smoke, I mean. Haven't got a problem with it – it's your house, your apartment, after all.'

Daisey blinks at her, wonders if she has just conveyed her exact thoughts to her through her expressions.

'What's this?' Iris asks, pointing to the red button on the kitchen wall.

'No! Don't press it!' Daisey's voice suddenly rises an octave. 'Sorry,' she apologises, lowering her tone, 'it's a panic button – if you press it, it alerts the local police station.'

Iris gives her a quizzical, surprised look, one that convinces her that she really doesn't know anything about the attack after all. She had been convinced that Ros had orchestrated Iris approaching her about becoming a potential flatmate, giving her the heads-up about Luke and about the attack and then pretending she didn't even know her – Ros worries about her living alone, it's why she often 'popped by' even though she lived the other side of town, a forty-five-minute car journey away. But looking at Iris now she isn't so sure.

'Did Ros put you up to this?' Daisey enquires, though she is careful not to sound accusatory. 'Did she tell you I was considering renting the spare room out?'

Iris takes a sip of her drink. She has her back to her and is seemingly admiring the pictures above the fireplace – old black-and-white *Vogue* prints that she'd had blown up onto canvas that Luke had deemed 'a bit clichéd and un-thought-provoking.'

Suddenly, she wonders if there was anything he had ever liked about her, or why he was ever in a relationship with her in the first place.

'Ros? Oh yeah… she mentioned it this morning, remember?'

'Really? She told me she'd never met you before.' Daisey feels confused, her mind muddled and muddied. She can't trust her own memory anymore. That crackling noise in her head is suddenly there again, the one that sounds like a radio frequency, hissing and snapping in her ears, painful like cabin pressure, and she sees herself opening the door to her apartment… '*Oh… it's you…*' She places her hands over her ears as the pressure crescendos.

'Daisey? Daisey, are you OK?'

The mental image switches off as the noise fades.

'Yes… yes, sorry… it's just…'

Iris turns round to face her.

'Ron, Ros's bloke, he fitted it for me – the panic button – after I was attacked.' There, she's said it now. If Iris didn't already know about it then she soon will. Best to get it out of the way.

'Attacked?' Iris cocks her head to one side but her expression doesn't change.

'A few weeks back… someone broke into the flat – well, I'm not sure if they actually broke in or I let them in, or if they pushed their way in or… anyway—' She's gabbling. 'They attacked me… in fact they almost killed me.' It still feels strange to say it out loud, like she's saying it on behalf of someone else. Suddenly, she wonders how she would broach telling a potential new love interest about it, not that she's thinking about finding one of those, but still – would it put them off, make them think of her as damaged goods?

'I ended up in hospital, in an induced coma…' Instinctively her hand goes up towards the raised scar on the back of her skull. It still feels tender to the touch. She's not wearing her scarf and wonders if Iris has noticed the thin red line on her neck, the one the doctors assured her would fade with time.

Iris is staring at her silently and she feels compelled to fill the empty space. 'He left me for dead. If Ros hadn't come to pick me up the following morning and found me in time, well… put it this way, you'd still be looking for a room to rent.'

Iris refills Daisey's glass, tops her own up. 'Ahh, I see, that explains it.' She nods towards the panic button.

'Yes,' Daisey says, her voice a little hoarse. It's never been quite the same, not after having a fat tube inside it helping her to breathe. It's more gravelly than it used to be.

'Well, you know what they say?' Iris smiles at her brightly. 'What doesn't kill you makes you stronger. Can I use your bathroom?'

Daisey's a little taken aback. This is not the reaction she has become used to. She was more familiar with horror – horror and disgust followed by pity and awkward silences or a barrage of ghoulish questions, wanting to know all the grizzly details. She blinks at her, unsure what to make of the strange though not altogether unpleasant woman in front of her.

'Yeah… yes, of course.'

Iris grins and places her glass onto the coffee table.

'Won't be a sec.' She rolls her eyes. 'Prosecco always makes me pee loads. Bladder the size of a walnut.'

She leaves Daisey alone in the room, holding her glass, a little perplexed. She hears her in the bathroom down the hall, the clank of the toilet seat as it's lifted and the rush of pee hitting the pan. Luke had always made her feel self-conscious of using the bathroom, had said it was a design fault by the architect, placing the toilet so close to the living room. The noise had bothered him, even though there was little she could do about it. *'I'd rather not have to hear you peeing, Daisey… why don't you put some paper down first?'*

She hears the toilet flush, the sound of a tap running briefly and waits for Iris to come back into the living room and for the inevitable questions that will no doubt ensue now that she's had a few moments to process what she's just learned. She's too busy pre-empting them to wonder how Iris knew where to find the bathroom in the first place.

'So,' Iris says brightly, returning to the living room and picking up her wine glass once more. 'When can I move in?'

CHAPTER ELEVEN

'A forensic profiler?'

'Yes. Her name is Annabelle Henderson and she's coming in to meet you today' – she checks her watch – '2 p.m. – soon.'

Gwendoline Archer – my new boss – gives me a matter-of-fact look from across her desk, which is, incidentally, much tidier and organised than Woods's ever was. She even has a small pot plant on it – one that's actually alive. I stare at its shiny leaves and at the small white buds that are just shy of opening, tentatively peeping out, checking if it's safe to reveal themselves to their new environment, which is not too dissimilar to how I feel right now. Her laptop – also shiny, looks new – is tilted open and gleaming back at me as the sunlight slides in through the blinds and bounces off the screen. I can see my own reflection in it, stare at it for a moment and try to pretend that I'm not looking more and more like my father with each passing day. Her pen – gold, looks expensive, probably a gift – sits adjacent to it, almost completely parallel to the notepad and her phone is positioned in line with it, like they have been meticulously arranged in such a precise and measured fashion. I'm no psychologist – forensic or otherwise – but I suspect she might suffer from a little OCD, or as my dad calls it, 'those anal beggars who can't stand a hair out of place'. He's so un-PC.

'She's one of the best there is. American. Worked with the FBI on some very serious cases before she came to the UK – child abduction, serial rapists, paedophiles… she knows her stuff. She helped out with Operation Winton, do you remember? The two young girls who were abducted from a care home in Suffolk? I knew the SIO on that too, James Muldowney, good copper, great actually, quite young like you, Dan and talented…' She looks me directly in the eyes, adding, 'In lots of ways.'

Now don't get me wrong, when it comes to reading women on a private, personal level at least, I'm about as effective as an ashtray on a speedboat, but I could swear she's coming on to me, or maybe not coming on to me exactly, but the remark sounds a little, I don't know, suggestive perhaps, or maybe I've just imagined it.

I carefully, surreptitiously assess my new boss. She's older than me but I couldn't tell you by how much, or at least I wouldn't want to tell *her* by how much. She takes care of herself; her smooth skin is testament to that and although her blonde hair is short, it's neatly trimmed and still quite feminine, well-maintained highlights running through it – no stray greys for Gwen. No ring – rumours round the nick say she's twice divorced, once to a fellow copper, the other a physician. She's tall and slim built, but there's a steeliness to her that immediately warns you she's no one to mess with. She has an exemplary career history, unblemished record, 'quietly yet fiercely ambitious' – that's how Woods had described her to me when he'd told me she was to be his replacement. 'She'll have no truck with some of your more, how shall we put it, *unorthodox* methods, Riley. She does things completely by the book. I might've turned a blind eye to some of your past shenanigans, but this one won't. And if you don't get the results she wants, you'll be yesterday's news, no matter how successful your track record or that handsome jawline of yours. She runs operations like a business, you're only as good as your last catch and…'

I'd been too stuck on the 'handsome jawline' part to remember what else he'd said now.

'He, Muldowney, told me that Henderson had been of significant and considerable help,' she continues, strictly professional once more.

'I've no doubt about that, ma'am, it's just that—'

'It's just that what, Dan?'

She cuts me off but her tone remains calm. I must admit, I feel slightly aggrieved by the suggestion of bringing this Henderson woman in, even though I realise this is perhaps a little churlish of me – and frankly at this stage in the investigation if someone suggested a clairvoyant I'd give it due consideration – but on a personal level it feels like a failure on my part. Archer cut short my paternity leave especially for this case. For whatever reasons, she has – or had – faith in me and I feel like I've let her down, let everyone down.

'You need help with this one, Dan, a different kind of help. We're not getting anywhere and we've got nothing, no suspects, no leads, very little forensic—'

'Well, actually,' I interject, 'we think our man has some connection with flowers.'

'Flowers?' She blinks at me.

'*Jasmin* Godden, *Fern* Lever, *Daisey* Garrett… all the victims are named after flowers.' Davis is still dining out on the fact that she realised this before I did. As a result I've got her digging around local garden centres to see if she can unearth anything – both puns intended. Anyway, that poured water on the fire of her self-congratulation. Still, if there's anything to find, Davis will be the one to find it, of that I'm certain.

'Well, a fern is technically a plant,' she corrects me.

'Yes, but I know – I *feel* – there is some connection, that it's not simply coincidence.'

'So what is it then,' she asks directly, 'this connection?'

'I don't know yet, ma'am,' I say, wishing this pathetic feeling that has suddenly gripped me would subside. 'Intuition.'

She smiles, or perhaps it's more of a small smirk.

'Ah yes, this infamous intuition of yours. I've heard all about it. Woods mentioned it to me. Interesting,' she muses. 'You may be in touch with your feminine side, Dan, with this intuition of yours, but I need facts. Cold hard evidence that's backed up and supported by facts. Hunches are great – if they lead you to those things; until then, I don't need to know about them.'

I feel like she's chopped my manhood off with her tongue. Feminine side? Is she trying to emasculate me?

'Anyway, we'll soon know if your intuition is correct, won't we, by the name of his next victim – because there is going to be a next, Dan – we both know this – and so does the bloody press. They're whipping people up into a frenzy of fear, and they know we're struggling, and so does our killer most probably – which is why we need a different approach, someone who can maybe steer us in some kind of direction. Henderson will give us logistical guesses based on crime scene evidence, witness reports – what little there is of them – and victim testimony. She'll be able to give us an analytical description of our man, behaviour patterns, victimology, personality traits, maybe even physical appearance…'

'I thought you said she was a forensic psychologist, ma'am, not a psychic.'

Archer smiles thinly but doesn't bite. 'I've suggested an informal meeting in the local, The Swan. You can grab a bit of lunch and get to know each other – she's something of a maverick. I think you two will get along. Just make sure it stays professional, yes?'

I glance up at her; shocked she would even suggest such a thing, and on what grounds? The fact that I'm a man and Henderson is a woman? I'm pretty sure no one has ever used the words 'womaniser' and 'Dan Riley' in the same sentence together, not even in my heady prime as a young – younger – man, not even when I once went on holiday with a group of friends to Magaluf back in the 90s and had definable abs and hair like

David Hasselhoff, although come to think of it, that's probably why no one ever has called me a womaniser.

'I'm happily…' I stumble, unsure of exactly what it is I want to say. 'I'm already involved with someone.'

She looks at me from across the desk. 'Ah yes, the journalist, that's right, isn't it? Your baby's mother?'

I feel the lightest film of perspiration forming on my top lip. This conversation is making me feel increasingly uncomfortable. *Baby's mother*? Did she really just say that?

'Yes.'

'Shame.' She says it so quietly I'm not even sure it's what she's actually said at all or if I'm imagining it again. 'Well, I hope you're not giving anything away that you shouldn't, pillow talk and all of that. Loose lips sink ships, Dan.'

'Of course not, ma'am, I wouldn't dream of jeopardising this case, or any case for that matter. Besides,' I add, 'by the time I get to bed I'm usually too exhausted to say anything at all.'

She looks up at me, raises her eyebrow ever so slightly.

'So' – her voice returns to an audible level – 'Henderson. Two p.m. The Swan. And remember, she'll be working alongside you, Dan, not for you, OK?'

'Great,' I say biting my tongue so hard I think I may have drawn blood.

Jesus, I could do with a drink.

CHAPTER TWELVE

'So, what do you fancy tonight, spaghetti meatballs or pesto pasta with Parmesan?' Iris throws the shopping bags enthusiastically onto the kitchen counter and exhales. 'I got us a bottle of that wine you like and some of your favourite bread from the bakery down the high street – that rosemary stuff. The girl who works there, she saved me a loaf – was so thoughtful of her...' She pulls off her coat, discards it over the back of the kitchen stool and wraps her oversized baggy cardigan around her small frame. 'I thought we could have a glass while watching the rest of that Netflix series tonight.'

Daisey, fresh from the shower with a towel wrapped round her head, bites her bottom lip.

'Oh God, Iris, I'm sorry.' She takes a cigarette from her packet on the side, lights it with damp fingers. 'But I'm, well...' She thinks about how to say what she wants to say without causing offence. 'It's just that I... I've invited someone over tonight... for dinner...'

'Oh!' Iris blinks at her. 'Great! No worries. There's more than enough to go round. Although we may need another bottle of...'

Daisey inwardly cringes. 'The thing is, Iris' – Daisey shuffles a little awkwardly – 'I was... well, I was kind of hoping... if you don't mind that is, if you could... if you could make—'

'Make myself scarce?' She finishes the sentence for her.

'I don't want you to feel like I'm forcing you out or anything, I'm really not, it's just that, well...'

Iris raises her hand. 'Really. It's fine. Honestly. It's perfectly OK. I understand.'

'You do?'

Daisey feels her shoulders sag. The last thing she wants to do is hurt Iris's feelings; she's been so kind to her already. She really has appreciated having Iris around the place; she likes hearing the sound of someone else's key turning in the lock and another set of footsteps on the floorboards. It gives her comfort knowing there is someone else to witness her day-to-day life, reminding her that she does in fact still exist – and she has felt safer, particularly at night when the static seems to be at its worst and the nightmares come.

Another stab of guilt twists in Daisey's guts. 'I'm really grateful for everything you've done, everything you do, Iris. Perhaps we can catch up on that series tomorrow night; maybe I'll cook dinner for us this time? And it's only for a couple of hours tonight.'

Iris nods although Daisey can tell by her body language that she feels a little rejected.

'Of course; no worries, I'm sorry… I should've mentioned it to you at work today. I should've checked to see if you had plans already. I guess not everyone is like me; some people actually have a life!' She gives a little self-deprecating laugh.

Now Daisey feels like a complete shit. Iris hasn't mentioned many friends since she's known her – any, in fact – which strikes her as kind of odd given Iris's vivacious personality. She had expected her to be something of a social butterfly. Come to think of it, she hasn't mentioned any family either and suddenly Daisey realises that selfishly she's been so wrapped up in her own life that she hasn't really asked Iris much about her own at all.

'How about we open that bottle of wine while I'm getting ready?' Daisey suggests by way of compensation. 'You can come and help me choose what to wear tonight.'

Iris's demeanour brightens slightly as she follows Daisey into her bedroom, grabbing the wine and two glasses.

'So, who's the lucky man then?' she enquires as Daisey turns away from her, discards her towel and wraps a kimono around her nakedness. As she does, she briefly catches Iris's eye in the mirror. She swiftly looks away.

Daisey begins to apply her make-up in the mirror.

'How do you know it's a man?' she replies with a raised eyebrow.

'Just a wild guess…'

'It's my ex actually, Luke.'

'The one you own this place with?'

'Uh-huh; my cheating, lying ex-fiancé. He ran off with one of his former students last year – he's a university lecturer – we were due to be married this summer. We'd been together seven years.'

'Jesus, Daisey, I'm sorry, what a total shit.' Iris throws herself down onto the bed. 'If someone did that to me, I'd *kill* them.'

Daisey laughs sardonically. 'Yes, well, trust me, the thought has crossed my mind a few times!'

Iris rolls over onto her front, props her chin up with her elbows and swings her legs up behind her in a childlike way.

'Tell me to mind my own business, but if he's such a lying, cheating bastard, why are you inviting him over for dinner?'

Daisey exhales loudly, takes a large glug of wine. It's a valid question. One she isn't sure how to answer.

'He invited himself.'

'Ah, so you still love him,' Iris deduces. 'Even after he betrayed you, you still love him?' It sounds more like a statement than a question. 'I understand.' Iris sighs softly. 'I know what it's like to keep running towards the source of your pain.'

'Do you?' Daisey stops what she's doing and looks at her in the mirror.

'He's a bad tenant,' Iris says.

'A bad tenant?'

'Yep,' Iris says, stretching out on the bed. 'He took up residence inside your heart, and now you can't evict him, even though he hasn't paid rent for a long time, metaphorically speaking – a bad tenant.'

'Great analogy,' Daisey says.

'Yet still you miss him?'

Daisey swallows the remains of her glass, pauses.

'Yes,' she admits reluctantly, briefly stopping getting ready. 'I do.'

'What do you miss most about him?'

Daisey shrugs. 'Oh, I don't know… the little things, I suppose – you know, like his penis.' She starts to laugh at her own joke but Iris's face doesn't even crack a smile and she stops abruptly.

'A penis isn't everything, you know,' Iris says, her voice low and serious.

'Well, no, of course not…' Daisey laughs a touch nervously. The conversation is getting a little weird. 'It was just… just a joke.' The real issue really had nothing to do with the size of Luke's manhood, more what he liked to do with it, i.e. put it in other people behind her back. There's an awkward pause between them.

'So, aside from his small penis,' Iris continues, 'what do you really miss most about him?'

It's difficult to tell if Iris is joking or being serious – she can't gauge it.

She tries to think of examples, of any example, but now she's been put on the spot her mind has gone blank.

'Just… I don't know… like, coming home to someone… watching a film together, cooking dinner… planning stuff… the comfort, I suppose.'

Iris watches her thoughtfully. 'Ah, so it's not really *him* you miss, not Luke the person, more what he represented to you…'

Daisey blinks at her in the mirror, a little surprised. She really hadn't had her flatmate down as being the deep and meaningful type, but then again, she hadn't had Luke down as being a philandering, duplicitous two-timing cheat either.

'Anyway, it's your own fault,' Iris says, her tone almost accusatory. 'People project their needs and desires onto others; onto people they know don't really possess the qualities they're looking for deep down. They merely convince themselves that the other person is who they want them to be, rather than who they really are, and then they get all disappointed and hurt when they turn out to be an arsehole – or a cheat or a loser or whatever – when really they were those things all along and the other person just chose not to see it. They tricked themselves with their own hope and self-denial. "Hope is the worst of all the evils because it prolongs the torments of man."'

Daisey blinks at her, a little stunned.

'Anyway,' Iris continues, 'this Luke character sounds like a total arsehole who doesn't deserve you.' Her eyes meet Daisey's in the mirror again. 'Because I think you're beautiful, inside and out.'

Daisey laughs uncomfortably. It's not the compliment per se that has unsettled her – although she's never really known how to take one well – it's more the strange intensity of the whole conversation and the way the compliment was given, a bit like something a lover might say.

Iris tops up her wine and they briefly chink glasses.

'So, how about you?' Daisey asks, desperate to take the spotlight away from herself.

'How about me what?'

'You said you were single when we first met. Anyone at Warwick's taken your fancy yet? Not that there's much in the way of talent. I mean, you'd think, wouldn't you, given the size of the place and how many men work there, there would be at least a few half-decent contenders?'

Tommy White's face flashes up in her mind, begrudgingly handsome with a look about him that suggests he's always on the verge of saying something a little… what was the word? Lewd? No, that was too strong… Cheeky? Yes, that was more accurate. Tommy had sent flowers to her in the hospital, huge pink blooms encased by lush green foliage – at least he'd been sensitive enough not to send her roses – and she remembered they had looked expensive and hand chosen, as if he had given it considerable thought. The handwritten note accompanying the bouquet had been sweet too, expressing how sorry he was, how bad he'd felt about what had happened to her and how he hoped that she'd make a full recovery. He'd finished off by leaving a row of kisses, ten at least. Luke had only ever left her a standard lone 'X' in correspondence he'd sent her.

She realised it was a bit pathetic, a woman in her thirties judging someone's affection by the amount of 'X's they put in a card or text. She knew it was childish and shouldn't matter but the truth was that it *did*. It did matter what people said as well as what they did, didn't it? Sometimes words were like missiles – once fired they could not be reversed and once they had hit their target, the destruction was often inevitable and irreversible.

Suddenly it returns, the static and that high-pitched ringing in her ears and she drops her mascara. *She's standing in the kitchen of her apartment, the light from the fridge door casting a glow through the darkness. She's looking for something, wine… yes, she's checking the fridge for wine. She hears Tommy's voice from down the hall but the words aren't clear – she just knows it's his voice, recognises it – and then she feels his presence, behind her in the kitchen, the coldness of the floor tiles on her bare feet and…* The noises in her head stop and her breathing begins to regulate once more. The recollection has lasted no more than a second, but it was there. *She'd remembered Tommy being in her apartment that night.*

Daisey places a hand on her chest to steady her heartbeat, regains composure and looks at Iris in the mirror. She can't remember if Iris has answered her question – the flashback has completely thrown her – so she tries another.

'And your family? I've never heard you mention them much.'

Iris is standing with her back to her now, rifling through Daisey's wardrobe with one hand, glass of wine in the other.

'My parents are dead,' she replies causally, pulling various garments from the rail and discarding them onto the bed.

Daisey puts her make-up brush down. 'God, Iris, I'm sorry. I had no idea…'

'Don't be,' she says, matter-of-fact. 'I wasn't particularly close to either of them, my mother especially.'

Daisey gives a little snort of recognition. 'My mother lives in Australia with her "other" family, her husband and their kids, my half-siblings, I've only ever met them twice in over a decade. They're fourteen-year-old twins.'

Iris still has her back to her but stops what she's doing. 'Twins?'

'Yeah, her perfect little matching pair of angels,' Daisey says, unable to disguise her resentment. 'I was the teenage mistake – she had me at eighteen. Some older bloke she had a fling with – left her holding the baby – literally.' Daisey doesn't like discussing her mother for this very reason; it makes her feel melancholy.

'I was always seeking her attention as a child,' she continues, unable to hold back now that she's opened the floodgates, 'I think it's why my choice in men – my last one in particular – has always been so spectacularly shit.' She glances back at Iris in the mirror, smiles at her. 'If it doesn't hurt then it doesn't work, you know? Arseholes, bullies, controllers and cheaters; I know where I am with them at least.'

Iris is staring at her intensely in the mirror.

'What?' Daisey asks, catching her.

'Nothing,' she says. 'It's just that you could be describing my life too.'

Daisey sighs. 'Birds of a feather flock together, eh?'

Iris tops up both their glasses again.

'There must've been some happy moments with your mum, surely? Good memories of the two of you together?'

Daisey places her flute onto the dressing table, the glass dinging musically as it connects.

'Yes; plenty. I do remember we got drunk together on my eighteenth birthday. We drank champagne and listened to ABBA, danced together...' She stares out the window, gripped by the vivid memory before shaking herself out of it. 'Anyway, she met her husband soon after that and moved to the other side of the world. She did ask me to emigrate with them but my life was here, you know, so I stayed and she went. I don't get to see her much now; she has epilepsy and can't fly because of it. We FaceTime and talk on the phone, but it's not the same...'

'Happiness is always interrupted, why is that?' Iris sighs. 'I suppose if it wasn't then no one would ever truly understand what it is to be happy in the first place, would they?'

'No. I... I suppose not,' Daisey agrees. 'And the rest of your family?'

'I have a brother,' Iris says. 'We're very close, were extremely close as children. He visits me from time to time, and I have a sister too, though I wish I didn't; I hate her.'

Daisey's increasingly unsure of how to take the whole conversation.

'I was bullied quite badly as a kid but my brother always stood up for me. My mother had no time for me when she was alive. I was a big disappointment.' She suddenly sits up, crosses her legs on the bed. 'I understand what it feels like to be inadequate – look I'll show you.' The blueness of Iris's eyes suddenly appears to reflect the colour of her sadness and she raises her left arm and pulls up her baggy sleeve.

Subconsciously, Daisey places a hand over her mouth to stifle a horrified gasp, then, realising how this must look, quickly removes it and attempts to regain composure. Two of Iris's fingers are missing, giving her hand a strange claw-like appearance, almost like a pincer. She wonders how on earth she hasn't noticed this before and figures that like her, Iris has become adept at hiding her flaws. The baggy jumpers make sense now.

Iris gives a little knowing laugh. 'I know, gross huh?'

'What happened? I mean… were you… were you born like that?'

'An accident as a child,' Iris casually explains, 'a hit-and-run when I was eleven; crushed under the wheel. They had to amputate two of my fingers. I spent the rest of my childhood and teens being the butt of everyone's jokes, picked on and bullied… because of this.' She wiggles her two good fingers and thumb. 'I was the weirdo with the claw who everyone avoided. Except for my brother. He took care of me, watched out for me…'

Daisey sighs. 'Human beings can be so cruel sometimes… where is he now, your brother?'

Iris suddenly jumps up from the bed, the sleeve of her top sliding back down to cover her hand once more.

'I think you should wear the red top tonight, the tie-up thing,' she says, holding it up on the hanger. 'Red always suits blondes.'

'Do you think?' Daisey doesn't push. She knows how painful it is to open up old wounds. 'You don't think it's a bit barmaid-y, a bit tarty?'

Iris shrugs. 'Depends on how you want the evening to progress with Luke, I suppose.'

Daisey laughs but it sounds hollow, just like she feels inside. Suddenly, it all seems so pointless. Iris was right; why had she ever agreed to let Luke come over? Why hadn't she just told him to piss off, or not accepted his call in the first place? He'd caught her off guard when he'd called that morning.

'We need to talk, Daisey,' he'd said sagely, which she knew translated as *he* needed to talk. 'Can I come over, tonight? Maybe we can have dinner together? I'll bring some wine…'

She'd been blindsided by his friendly approach, and a little intrigued, if she was honest.

'Please, Daisey,' he'd said after a few seconds' silence. 'I really do want to see you.' That's what did it: the word *want*. And so she'd agreed, told him to come round at 8.30 p.m.

She doesn't want Luke to know about Iris. She doesn't want him knowing that because of him she's been forced to find a tenant, someone to help pay the mortgage because he can't anymore or won't. She wants him to believe she is coping with everything, wants him to see how strong and capable she is.

Daisey suddenly thinks about *him* then, the man who had attacked her; she wonders who he is and why he had chosen her. Why anyone had. Was Luke right? Was it because she is an easy target and people saw her coming, like the proverbial sitting duck? He is still out there, maybe stalking his next victim, maybe even thinking of coming back for her despite Detective Riley's assurances. She knows this fear is why she never leaves the apartment alone anymore, not for any length of time anyway.

Now, she is going to throw herself to the wolf once again, go back for more punishment from a man she knows does not love her and probably never did. But he *wants* to see her. And more than anything she wants him to want to see her, her shattered self-esteem crying out to claw back some of the power that Luke and her almost-killer had stolen from her. And yet even as she thinks this, she already knows how the evening will play out, how it was always going to play out.

Iris is on the bed staring at her in a strange way, almost adoringly.

She turns to her.

'Then I guess the red it is,' she says.

CHAPTER THIRTEEN

'A forensic psychologist – they're bringing in a shrink?' Davis repeats the words back to me. 'So, I'm guessing that the conversation with Cupid didn't go well?' She raises an eyebrow, hands me a lukewarm cup of coffee across the desk. I accept it, sip it and pull a face. 'Rumour has it that she's packing more in the downstairs department than most of the blokes here at the nick. Although if you ask me, the boys are just pissed off that they'll be answering to a woman.' She snorts. 'Still, at least it's good to know that rampant sexism is alive and well. I mean, she couldn't possibly have got the job on merit *and* be a woman; no, she's got to be secretly packing a set of male genitals or she's slept her way into the job.'

I'm mildly amused by Davis's little rant. Not because she's isn't right – she is, absolutely – but because I rarely get to see her so het up.

'Cupid?' I shoot her a baffled look. 'You called her Cupid?'

'Archer,' she explains, making a bow-and-arrow shape with her hands. 'Archer… Cupid… bow and arrow, get it?'

'Jesus.' I roll my eyes. 'Couldn't they have come up with something a bit more original?' I swivel round on my chair to face Mitchell.

'Any joy yet, Mitchell?' I'm in receipt of the answer before I've even asked the question, yet hope still compels me to ask it. If there's anything to find in that pile of hundreds of thousands of names, then Mitchell is the one to find it. She'd seemed genuinely pleased when I had tasked her with such a laborious job – making her the right person for it.

'Nothing yet, gov,' she replies, miraculously upbeat. 'No one of any real interest so far, just a couple of people with a few minors on their record, a couple of thefts and a fraud – all of which have checked out so far. Warwick's are pretty stringent on employee checks.'

Davis audibly sighs.

'Keep going,' I say trying to mirror her enthusiasm back to her.

DS Baylis approaches my desk. He's a good solid member of the team, trustworthy and diligent. He works particularly well with DC Harding – we call them 'the set of soaps' for obvious reasons – it's a joke that never gets old.

'Nothing on the flowers yet, boss,' he tells me. 'We've contacted every florist, every petrol station within a ten-mile radius of Daisey Garrett's apartment…'

'He must've got them from somewhere,' I say. 'They don't bloody well grow on trees.'

Davis goes to make a clever remark but thinks better of it.

I turn to the board up on the wall; stare at the gruesome images of the victims and the map, at the pins and arrows identifying each of their locations, all of them within a ten-mile radius of each other. *Where will you strike next, you slippery bastard?* It's impossible to say exactly but my instincts are telling me he's going to stay local, that he knows the area well and doesn't want to step out of his comfort zone, at least not for now.

'So,' Davis says. 'We've got no suspects, no weapon, no DNA match, no CCTV, no motive, and no witnesses…'

The silence from within the incident room speaks volumes. I'm losing this one, can feel him slipping beneath the shadows, always one step ahead of us. He's made a name for himself now – notoriety is every serial killer's dream, and he knows we have zero on him – at least not yet. His confidence will be growing, his ego unchecked. He's going to strike again soon; I can feel it, like a knot inside my guts, tightening with each passing day. And as dreadful as it is for me to even contemplate it, in some small way I almost hope that he does. Not because I want another body on my hands or another family's lives destroyed forever, but because I know through bitter experience that he will slip up eventually, because they always do. *Always.*

'You're wrong about one thing, Davis,' I say. 'We *do* have a witness. Get your coat. We're going to pay Daisey Garrett another visit.'

CHAPTER FOURTEEN

'Hi, can I help you?'

I don't recognise the woman who opens the door of Daisey Garrett's apartment. She's small, of similar build to Daisey with bobbed mousey blonde hair. If I didn't know better I might think they were related.

'Is Daisey in?' I enquire. 'It's Detective Riley and DS Davis.' I flash my badge and Davis follows suit.

'Oh, yes! Detective Riley.' Her eyes flicker in recognition. 'Hang on, I'll go and get her.' She smiles, disappears behind the door, leaves it open a crack. 'Daisey! Daaaisey. There's a policeman here to see you. That detective you told me about…'

There's a pause as I hear the sound of footsteps approaching and the door swings open.

'Detective Riley!' She looks pleased to see me, which is not always the case in my line of work – and therefore appreciated. 'You didn't say you were coming over… come in, come in,' she greets us brightly.

'You look lovely,' Davis observes, beating me to it. She's wearing a red wraparound top with a low V-cut at the front, tight jeans and heels. Her hair is styled in glamorous waves, her face fully made up, and I get a waft of strong perfume, something sweet and fruity. I suspect she's going on a date with someone.

'Come through to the kitchen.' She ushers us through the door. 'I've got time to make you a cup of tea if you like.'

'No… no trouble,' I say, waving my hand at her. 'We were just passing; thought we'd pop by.'

'It's nice to see you,' she says, looking at me.

'You too, Daisey,' I reply. 'You look great, by the way. Going anywhere nice?' I'm pleased that she's putting her life back together; she deserves it after all she's been through, but I can't help feel concerned. I think of Juno and how I will have all this worry to come; boys, parties, staying out late, serial killers, rapists and paedophiles… you know, the general kind of thing every father who works on homicide fears. I know Daisey Garrett is a grown woman in her thirties – she's not a teenager – I'm only a few years older myself, yet there is something childlike and vulnerable about her, perhaps because she's small, or perhaps it's something else, plus I can't forget that the man who tried to kill her is still out there, and we can't rule out the possibility that she's still in danger.

'Thanks, Dan,' she says, blushing slightly. 'I'm… I'm meeting up with an old friend for dinner… actually, they're coming over.'

'They?'

She doesn't follow up with any more information and I'm reluctant to pry.

'Don't worry,' she says as though second-guessing my thoughts, 'it's someone I know and trust… well, trust won't attempt to kill me anyway.'

She smiles again, almost too brightly, and I wonder if her cheerfulness is simply a smokescreen.

'Well, that's good,' I say, slightly relieved that she'll be staying in the safety of her own home. 'What's on the menu?'

'The only thing I'm good at.' She gives a light-hearted laugh. 'Pasta bolognese.'

'Well, if it makes you feel any better I'd even make a hash of that,' I say. And I'm not joking. I think of Rachel then. 'I lived with a chef once,' I tell her. 'She tried to teach me to cook but had to admit defeat in the end. It's a talent; some of us have it and some of us don't. And I'm afraid I definitely fall within the latter camp.'

'Well, we've got something in common then,' she replies. 'Are you sure I can't make you both any tea?'

Davis waves her hand and I shake my head.

'Just a quick visit. We won't keep you from your plans, just wanted to check in on you… see how you are.' I notice the woman who answered the door standing in the entrance to the kitchen, leaning against the side of the doorframe listening to the conversation. I turn to look at her.

'Oh God, sorry!' Daisey apologises, lightly smacks her forehead. 'This is Iris. Iris, this is Detective Dan Riley and…'

'Lucy,' Davis says. 'DS Lucy Davis.'

'They're working on my case,' she explains. 'Iris is my new flatmate.'

'Hi.' Iris shuffles forward into the kitchen. 'It's nice to meet you.'

I go to extend my hand but she begins rearranging a bunch of flowers in a vase on the table. Though innocuous, it somehow strikes me as a slightly odd thing to do.

'You too.' I smile back. 'So, when did you move in?'

'Just recently,' she says, as she begins to deadhead some of the blooms. 'We both work at Warwick's.'

'That's great.' I turn back to Daisey. 'Good to have some company.'

'Yes,' Daisey says, smiling at Iris. 'It is.'

Iris hovers around tentatively for a moment. 'Well, it was nice to meet you both.'

I nod. 'Likewise, Iris.'

She hesitates by the door, turns round to face me.

'You will find him, Detective, the man who tried to hurt Daisey and killed those other women… it's pretty terrifying to think there's someone like that still at large. In the meantime, don't worry, I'll take care of her.'

'Thank you.' I give her a reassuring nod; watch her as she walks from the kitchen. 'And rest assured we will find him, *we absolutely will.*'

'She seems… nice.' I turn to Daisey once she's gone. 'I'm glad you're not here on your own.'

'Yes, well, I can't say I haven't felt safer since Iris has been here.' She begins pulling things from the fridge, placing them onto the counter. 'Are you here to tell me something, Detective, something about my case?'

Davis and I exchange a brief glance.

'We're following up a few lines of enquiry, Daisey,' I say vaguely. She nods as if she understands that I have nothing new to tell her so I follow the statement up with, 'I made you a promise, didn't I? And I will keep it, Daisey.'

'You're here to ask me if my memory's come back… I know that's why you're really here, isn't it?' There's no anger in her tone as she says it, just the slightest hint of resignation. 'You know I would tell you if I'd remembered anything.'

'Anything at all.' I say it as a statement when in truth it's more of a question really because there's something in her body language – her demeanour and the lack of eye contact – that suggests she's holding back from me. She's rearranging the produce from the fridge on the counter with a lack of purpose. 'I mean, if there was the slightest thing, Daisey…'

'We have every reason to believe he is going to kill again,' Davis cuts in – and to the chase, 'and soon. You are the only person to have seen this man, Daisey. So if there's anything you…'

I watch her eyes stay firmly focused on the tins and pasta on the counter.

'Static,' she says quietly. 'It's like static in my head…'

I feel my adrenalin kick in like a shot of amphetamine in the arm.

'What is?'

'The noises,' she says quietly with her back to me. 'Images… all broken up, fragments, nothing that makes sense, nothing in any sequence… just flashes, like a slideshow on fast forward, all speeded up.'

'You think it's trying to come back, your memory? It's trying to return?'

She nods, and Davis looks over at me, her eyes wide and shiny in the artificial light of the kitchen.

'Did you remember something, Daisey? These flashes, what were they? What did you see?'

She shakes her head. 'It's like a glitch… like trying to tune in a TV without an aerial.'

'And…?'

'And nothing really…' She sucks in breath. 'I was in the kitchen, right here where you're standing, that night, the night it happened. I opened the fridge… I was looking for wine I think, and I heard Tommy down the hall. He was speaking but I don't know what he said; I just know it was Tommy: his voice. He used the bathroom and then he was behind me and…'

I'm holding my breath, too excited to breathe.

'Go on.' Davis nods encouragingly.

'And nothing… that's it.'

I exhale.

'And this is the only time it's happened?' I ask. It may not be much but this is the best news I've heard in weeks.

'Well, there was another time… a few split seconds where I was standing outside, at the party, the night of the party… I was smoking a cigarette and this man…'

Iris suddenly reappears in the doorway. 'Your phone's ringing,' she tells Daisey. 'I just heard it from my room.' She looks at Davis and I respectively. 'Sorry to interrupt.'

'Thanks, Iris,' Daisey says. 'I'll be there in a minute.'

She nods and smiles, disappears again.

Daisey straightens up.

'You said something about a man… you were smoking a cigarette and a man.'

She shakes her head, like the moment has passed.

'I can't remember what he looks like; I just remember talking to a man.'

I try not to appear as crestfallen as I feel.

'I'm so sorry. Look, I don't know if I'm imagining things that didn't happen, or if I'm making it up in my mind, trying to piece things together. It's like when you try to relay a dream to someone. I can't quite explain it as it happened, you know. It's like a block, like a mental block in my mind…' She begins to rub her temples with her forefingers and I can see she's becoming distressed and I don't want to upset her, especially since it seems she's doing so well, yet at the same time I want to shake her until her memory slips back into place like the missing last piece of a jigsaw.

'Daisey!' Iris calls out from down the hall. 'Your phone again!'

It's time to retreat and I signal to Davis.

'We'll leave you to get on with your evening, Daisey,' I say. 'We can see you're busy.'

She nods, appears relieved.

'I'm sorry, Detective,' she says quietly as Davis and I make our way through the kitchen. 'I know it would be such a help if I could remember more but…'

'You're doing great,' I say. 'I've every faith in you. I sense from what you say it won't be too far off now.'

She nods in agreement, though it belies the fear I see in her eyes. She's terrified of what's coming – she doesn't want to remember, and as much as I need that day to come soon, my heart still goes out to her.

'We'll be in touch soon, OK?' I place my hand on her arm; give it a reassuring little squeeze. 'You won't have to go through any of this alone, remember that.' She smiles thinly, nods. 'You know you can always call the station, day or night, anytime. If you get scared, if you notice anything or anyone strange, if there's anything, anything at all… I want you to call, OK? You've got the number – use it if ever you need to.'

'OK,' she says, less flustered now. 'I'm OK, now I've got Iris here, it's not so bad…'

We walk through the hallway towards the front door. I notice the spare bedroom door is open a crack and I sense someone is behind it.

'Good to meet you, Iris,' I call out. But no response comes.

CHAPTER FIFTEEN

July 1996

'What did you do to him? Tell me! TELL ME!' Tracey Eggerton has her hands on her son's shoulders and is shaking him violently. 'I know what you've done! You did something to him, didn't you? God help me… if you've… Oh God! You're evil… do you know that – EVIL!' She bangs her lips with her hands manically.

'Tracey, stop! STOP IT!' John pulls his wife away, locks her arms in an embrace to prevent her from attacking their son.

'Look!' she screeches, spittle flying from her mouth as she attempts to lurch towards him. 'The little bastard isn't even denying it… look at him, John! You're evil, an evil bloody freak! That's what you are! Right from the moment you were born I knew it, I *sensed* it! You… you should never have been born!'

'THAT IS ENOUGH!' John bellows so loudly that it causes everyone in the room to stand statue still. 'Enough!' he says again, his tone markedly lower this time. 'The boy can't even answer you with all this screaming and shouting going on… how is he supposed to explain if you won't let him speak?'

Tracey is hyperventilating, her chest heaving. She puts a hand up to her heart in a bid to steady her rapid pulse. She feels like she might have a heart attack, or pass out. Rosie glances at her mother, wide-eyed with fear; Tracey meets her daughter's eyes, closing her own momentarily and nodding as if to reassure her it's OK, that she's OK and not to look so worried.

'Right.' John lights two cigarettes and passes one to his wife. 'Let's try and stay calm, shall we, talk about this rationally, find out exactly what happened, yes?'

'I know exactly what happened, I—'

'Ah!' John raises his finger at his wife to stop her from saying any more. 'Let's hear what the boy has to say first… and Rosie too. Then we will decide what's what and what to do about it, OK?'

Rosie looks like a rabbit caught in headlights as she stares between her mother and father and finally at her brother.

'Go on…' John nods at his son, and he looks sideways at his sister for approval. She dips her head slightly, a silent exchange of communication between them, one only they understand.

'We was playing down by the river… me and Rosie. We was throwing sticks and rocks into it, watching them travel downstream, running after them along the bank… that's when we see him.'

'Saw him,' Tracey mutters underneath her breath. 'That's when you *saw* him.'

'He was on his own… we thought… we thought his mum must be nearby because… well, he was only small… we… I asked him if he was OK and he nodded. We asked him if he wanted to play with us…'

'OK,' John says sagely, 'and then what?'

'And he said OK and so we gave him some sticks and rocks and he started throwing them in the river, like we was doing.'

'Were,' Tracey whispers to herself. She's not sure if anyone else has heard her.

'And then we was playing together for a bit and Rosie asked him where his mum was and he pointed behind him and she said he should go back to his mum soon and then we said we was going to go now and we said goodbye and left him there.'

'By the river?' John clarifies.

'Yeah.'

'On his own – there was no one else there? You saw no one else?'

He looks sideways at his sister nervously. 'Well, there was this girl.'

'What girl?'

He shrugs. 'Just some girl we sometimes play with.'

'Who? Who is she?'

Tracey puffs anxiously on her cigarette, letting her husband do all the talking. She knows she won't be able to control what comes out of her mouth if she opens it.

'She's…'

'We don't know her name,' Rosie interjects. 'She's just some girl we've seen around a few times… she's nice… fun to play with.'

He shuffles from foot to foot and watches his sister as she speaks.

'And when you left, she – this girl – stayed behind with the little boy?'

'No. Yes… Well, I dunno,' he stammers, glancing sideways at his sister again. 'Me and Rosie left and went back to find Mum.'

'And you never saw him again after that? That was the last time you saw him?'

'Yes.'

'OK.' John nods at his son. 'Right. Is that how it happened, Rosie?' He turns to his daughter for clarification.

'Yes, Daddy, we were playing under the lilac tree, the three of us.'

'Three?'

'Yes.'

'You, your brother and this girl?'

'Yes. Then us three started playing pooh sticks on the river and then we saw the little boy and he joined in for a bit and then we said goodbye and went to find Mummy.'

John sighs deeply. 'OK. Well then…' He turns to his wife. 'There you go, that's what happened… this is what you'll need to tell the police when they arrive, tell the truth as it happened and everything will be fine, OK?'

They both nod silently.

'Go upstairs now, the pair of you, and I'll call you down once the police get here. I need to talk to your mum.'

They quickly do as they're told, leaving Tracey and John alone in the kitchen together. Tracey sighs heavily, breaking the palpable silence, and lights another cigarette. She feels exhausted, like she's run a marathon.

'I need a drink,' John says, opening a cabinet and taking out a bottle of Jack Daniel's. He doesn't ask his wife if she wants one; he automatically pours her a large measure. They sit in silence for a moment, sipping their drinks and trying to digest the situation.

'Oh God, John, it was horrible… so *awful.*' Her head drops into the palm of her hand. 'His poor mother, she was just hysterical, running around the park like a maniac, screaming his name, calling out for him, asking people if they'd seen her little boy… saying that she'd turned her back for a minute and he'd wandered off…' She stifles a cry that's threatening to escape from the back of her throat. 'I mean, you read about this sort of thing in the papers, don't you? One minute they're there and the next, *pouf* – gone, snatched by some sicko, bundled into the back of a van somewhere – every parent's bloody nightmare!' She drops her face into her hands again, covers her eyes.

'I could see the terror on that woman's face, John; I can only imagine what was going through her mind. People started to get up and help look for him, trying to calm her down and comfort her. She was so distressed, I've never seen anyone so… so… ter-rified…' She drags on her cigarette, gulps back her glass.

'Someone must've called the police at some stage but by the time they arrived it was too late – one of the dads who was helping with the search found him face down in the stream.' She buries her head into her hands again. 'I ran down there, everyone did… but I didn't want to look, I couldn't bear it. Apparently, he had hit his head, or something – *someone* – had hit him on the head and he'd fallen face down into the river and drowned. He was only four years old, for Christ's sake!'

John blinks at his wife, refreshes her glass with another measure of Jack Daniel's. God knows they needed it. She wraps her shaking fingers around the glass and John gently squeezes her shoulder. They're both silent for a moment.

'I think she's covering up for him, John,' she says, looking up at him across the table. 'I think… I think he killed that little boy, bashed him over the head with a rock and then drowned him in the river and Rosie's covering up for him.' There. She's said it.

John shakes his head, audibly exhales.

'Jesus Christ, Tracey, that's absurd! Can you hear yourself? *Killed him?* You honestly believe that our son actually murdered that little boy, that child? He's not capable! I mean, even if he was, you've seen him; he's only the same bloody size as a four-year-old! And Rosie would've stopped him! This other girl would've… she'd have seen it and told someone, her mum, the police, anyone…'

'They haven't found her yet… the other little girl… no one knows who she is! He could've made it up, made her up to divert the attention elsewhere…'

John takes a swig of his drink. She senses he's beginning to get angry, can feel it coming off him in waves.

'For Christ's sake, Tracey… it was nothing but a terrible, tragic accident. His mother wasn't watching him, let him wander off, he went down to the river and fell in and hit his head – that's what happened. You should be pouring scorn on the mother's negligence, not accusing your own bloody son of murder! Saying all those terrible things to him like that. Wishing he'd never been born, killed at birth… and you call him evil!'

Tracey swallows a mouthful of her drink, and a measure of guilt with it.

'He killed that little boy, John.' She says the words with quiet resolve as she stares into her glass. 'I'd stake my own life on it. Just like he killed that poor old woman's cat too.'

'For goodness' sake, don't start with all that again,' he says deadpan. 'And I suppose Rosie is lying too, is she, making it all up?'

Tracey shrugs, nods. 'Lying because she's scared of him, yes.'

John stands, exhales loudly and smashes his cigarette into the ashtray to extinguish it. She's never seen him this hostile in all their years together.

'Bullshit! You're talking absolute bullshit! What is wrong with you?'

She doesn't answer him; instead sits silently at the table, her head dipped.

'You'll say none of this to the police. Do you understand me, Tracey, none of it? They've already said it was a tragic accident, and it is; they just want to take the kids' statements as a matter of procedure.'

Tracey starts to cry then, short sharp sobs escaping from her throat. John watches her, sighs as he goes over to her, crouches down next to her at the table and places a hand on her arm.

'Listen to me, love. I really do feel for the little lad and his family, but you're not going to destroy ours with your wild accusations. I won't let you do that, love, do you understand?'

She nods, against everything she knew was true in her heart, she did.

'She didn't mean it; you know that really. She's just angry. People say bad things when they're angry, things they don't mean. She doesn't mean it,' she says again, stroking his hair.

'But she does,' he sniffs, 'she does mean it. She hates me; she wishes I'd died at birth. She's always hated me.'

'Shhh,' she says, attempting to soothe him.

'She never wanted me.' He wipes the mucus from his nose with the edge of the bedcover. 'Do you think it's because you was born all perfect and I was different… do you think that's why she hates me so much?'

She pulls him closer to her and they cuddle up on the bed together, interlocked.

'She doesn't hate you, silly,' she says. 'And even if she does, so what? Daddy loves you; *I* love you. You're perfect to me.'

She wipes the tears from his face with the hem of her sundress.

'Am I?'

She props herself up, rests her head on her hand and looks at him.

'Yes. You're my baby brother, my baby twin brother.' She smiles at him. He smiles back a little. 'And I love you very much and you're loyal and kind and sweet.'

'I am, really?' He looks up at her adoringly.

'We are a circle,' she says, 'a seamless circle where neither of us knows where I end and you begin. We cuddled up inside Mummy's tummy just like we're doing now. I am you and you are me,' she says brightly. 'Our love for each other is all we need.' She says it with such resolve that immediately he feels better.

He nestles into her warm body, into the comfort of it. She can always make him feel better.

'What about *her*?' he asks quietly after a few moments. 'The police will want to know about her, won't they?'

Rosie sighs gently.

'Don't worry about *her*,' she says confidently, stroking his hair once again. 'They'll never find her.'

CHAPTER SIXTEEN

'I brought the files along for you,' I say, sliding them across the sticky pub table towards her.

Dr Annabelle Henderson smiles widely, bearing neat white teeth – very American – but her accent is soft, only a slightly detectable lilt, like she's done her best to try and shed it.

'You guys have got your hands full with this one, huh?' she says, putting on her glasses. She begins to flick through the pages.

'You could say that,' I reply. 'We're lacking in the way of evidence, suspects and witness statements. We're having to reply on painstaking police work, grass roots stuff, back to basics, you know.'

'But you do have a witness, I'm right, right?'

'Well, yes, we do…'

'Only she's got temporary amnesia, right?'

'Traumatic amnesia,' I correct her. 'Daisey Garrett, the last victim. I'm pretty sure he meant to kill her, but by the hand of God she miraculously survived somehow.'

'So, he's getting sloppy, huh…' Her eyes are cast down, scan-reading the pages, glasses perched on the tip of her small nose. I can't help but wonder, given her looks and finesse, what made her choose the profession she has, working with society's degenerates and murderers, rapists and child molesters, violent, sadistic people devoid of conscience, of humanity and compassion for their fellow man – and woman. Then again, maybe she's thinking the same about me.

'Maybe,' I say. 'But I think it was more down to sheer luck and timing. You've familiar with his MO, I assume?'

'Yes,' she says without looking up. 'He hits them over the head, incapacitates them, presumably rendering them unconscious, though those injuries alone wouldn't have been enough to have killed any of them outright. Then he strangles them until they stop breathing and slashes their throats just to make sure, lets them bleed out.'

She sips her drink thoughtfully as she reads, unperturbed by the brutality of what she's just said; all seemingly in a day's work for Dr H. 'But he didn't want to kill this one,' she adds, finally looking up. 'The pathologist's report states that the slash to her neck wasn't as deep as the others, not too much more than superficial. He gave her a chance.'

'Why would he do that? Why her, why Daisey and not the others?'

Henderson shrugs gently. 'It was possibly subconscious; like he didn't mean not to kill her exactly. But he felt more empathy towards her for some reason, more of an affinity.'

'Something she said to him, perhaps?'

'Possibly. Maybe she reminded him of someone. So, tell me, Dan. You've been on the force a long time, right?' She likes to use the word 'right' a lot.

'Right.'

'Must've witnessed a few horror stories, a fair amount of suffering, the worst of human nature?'

I nod. 'My fair share, I suppose, much like yourself.' I pause for a moment before continuing. 'I think he knows them… I think he targets his victims, stalks them, gets close to them somehow, maybe even befriends them enough for them to recognise him anyway, not feel too threatened by him. There's no sign of any break-in at any of the crime scenes.'

'You married, Dan?'

The question stops me in my tracks, blindsides me.

'No,' I reply. 'I'm not married.'

'But you have a daughter, right?'

'Right.' I wonder how she knows this. Archer must've told her, though why I don't know; I can't see how my marital or parental status bears any relevance to the case.

'Have you ever been married?'

'No.'

'Because of the job?' Her green eyes are looking directly into mine like a spotlight, forcing me to engage.

'No.'

'Why then?'

'Why then what?' I'm not especially comfortable with her line of enquiry.

'Not found the right one yet?'

'That's a pretty personal question,' I reply.

She gives the faintest smile. 'Funny,' she remarks.

'What is?'

'You.'

'Oh?'

'You ask people the most intimate and personal questions all the time in your professional life; you dig around into their private lives, rake up their pasts, their history, families, friends, lovers… you uncover other people's dirty secrets, things they would rather keep hidden, and yet you cannot answer such basic of questions yourself.'

I don't know whether to be offended or to laugh but either way I suppose she has a point.

'The key word there is *professional*,' I gently remind her. 'And this isn't about me,' I add.

She raises her finely arched brows. 'You're wrong, Detective. This is very much about you. To understand our killer here, you need to first understand yourself.'

I refrain from rolling my eyes. 'I'm not the patient here, Dr Henderson. I'm here to catch a maniac, a serial killer, a predator, a dangerous individual who brutally kills women – and I thought that was why you were here too, to help me, to help us, do that.'

She takes a measured sip of her drink, places it back down onto the table carefully.

'I am,' she says. 'That's exactly why I'm here.'

There's a pregnant pause. Silence.

'I nearly got married, a few years ago,' I say, realising I've filled it, which I assume is exactly what she wanted. She's using my own tricks against me. 'I had a fiancée, Rachel. We lived together.'

'But you didn't marry her?' She asks the question causally. 'Why? Fear of commitment, greener grass syndrome, or was it that you were already married to the job?'

'No,' I say, 'it was none of those things. I loved her very much, *very much*, and I was looking forward to sharing my life with her, becoming a father and—'

'She had your child?'

I sigh audibly. I don't want to have this conversation but something tells me Dr Henderson isn't going to play ball unless I do.

'No.'

'No?'

'We didn't get that far.' I take a gulp of my beer. I wish I'd gone for something stronger now. 'She was killed in a motorbike accident – she was hit by a drunk driver. She was a few weeks pregnant at the time, although I wasn't aware of it; I'm not even sure if she was herself.'

I finish my drink; place the glass back onto the table. It makes a louder impact than I consciously intend. 'I'd appreciate it if we could go back to the matter at hand, if it's all the same to you.'

She doesn't take her eyes off me for a second.

'What makes you say our man is a lunatic, Detective?'

I raise my hands a little off the table. 'Well, I think it's pretty much a given to say that it's not entirely normal behaviour is it, Doctor, stalking, killing and maiming women?'

'Doesn't make him mad, Detective, bad maybe, but not necessarily mad. There's a marked difference.'

'OK, so he's perfectly sane then, *right?*'

She smiles, one that suggests she knows she's getting to me.

'Anyway, he's young.'

'The killer, you mean?'

She nods affirmative. 'No older than mid to late thirties, I'd say, and his motive isn't sexual. This is not a sexual crime.'

'You're sure? They were all discovered naked and you know they found traces of semen on Daisey Garrett's body, although it doesn't match the other DNA found at the other two crime scenes – and there was no semen present in them either.'

'He doesn't strip them for sexual gratification,' she ponders. 'Purity, their nakedness is something to do with purity and inno-cence… his own or theirs maybe. And it's not the killer's DNA – the DNA on Daisey Garrett; it's not his semen. He didn't sexually assault her, or any of them. His motive is more… more psychological, per-sonal. It fulfils something in him, something lacking, something he needs. These killings are not for gratification, they're for affirmation of some kind, almost ritualistic – I'm not even convinced he even actually enjoys killing them, or the act of it. I suspect he knocks them out first because he doesn't want them to suffer too much pain in death, doesn't want to hear them begging for their lives…'

'Are you saying he has a conscience?'

'Yes, possibly, I think so; he's not excessively violent.'

'You don't call smashing someone's skull in with a hammer violent? Or strangling someone and cutting their throat?'

'What I mean is, the attacks aren't frenzied; he does the job cleanly, methodically, no theatrics.'

'So if he's not getting a kick out of it, then what the hell is he getting?'

She finishes her drink and I point at her empty glass. 'Another?'

'Not for me, but you go ahead. This is something very personal for him,' she continues. 'There was no forced entry in any of the crime scenes, which leads me to believe they all knew him, or recognised him and yet I suspect none of them felt particularly threatened by him' – she pauses – 'which would suggest he is not an imposing character, not physically anyhow. They represent something to him, the victims – hence the calling card, the rose. He leaves it for them as a gift, an act of kindness, of love even.'

'Love?'

'Yes. He cares for these victims. He positions them in an almost religious way, with the arms folded across their chests; he neatly arranges the bodies, folds their clothes next to them and leaves them flowers. To him it's an act of kindness.'

'I can think of better ways to show you care, Doctor.'

She smiles.

'And the connection, with the victims' names… floral names…'

'Ah yes! I was getting to that. I wouldn't be surprised if his mother or someone influential in his life had or has a Christian name that represents a flower of some kind. An ex-lover perhaps; anyhow, someone of meaning, of importance to him.'

'So is he out for revenge? Spurned in love? Getting back at women who remind him of his cheating lover perhaps?'

'It's possible, yes. I definitely don't think it's a coincidence.'

I think of Davis then – she'll be pleased.

'It would be highly probable that his next victim will also have the name of some kind of flower.'

'I'm hoping there isn't going to be a next,' I say, though there's uncertainty in my voice and I suspect she detects it.

'I think you're right in that he watches them, Detective. They're chosen, selected – these are not random attacks. This means, I'm sure you've already established, that he walks among us in daily life, unnoticed, unremarkable probably. He may well be an upstanding pillar of the community, or an average Joe you wouldn't look twice at in the street.'

'Great,' I say, 'that narrows it down then.'

She smiles again. 'A watched kettle never boils, Detective. Sometimes we cannot see what is right before us when we're looking too closely.'

'That's what I'm paid to do, Doctor, look closely.' I feel like screaming.

'He's a chameleon. He isn't what he seems. He befriends his victims easily because he can.'

'Why doesn't he bother cleaning up the crime scene? We've got his DNA… they'll be no escaping justice once we've got him in custody. DNA doesn't lie.'

She runs her finger round the rim of her glass; we both watch.

'He hasn't offended before. He's not known to the authorities and doesn't expect to be. He doesn't care about DNA because he's confident his identity will remain unknown.'

'That's pretty confident!' I say with a little snort. 'Why so much confidence?'

'Because he's not who or what you think he is,' she says, matter-of-fact.

'So if he isn't who we think he is then who is he?'

'Oh, I'm afraid I cannot tell you that, Dan, I can only give you a profile of who I think he *could* be, given the information I have and my experience with such crimes and the people who commit them – and why. I can only make suggestions based on my professional knowledge.'

'And you say he's no fruit loop?' I don't care about political correctness right in this moment.

'The term "fruit loop" could cover a very broad spectrum,' she says, unmoved by my choice of words. 'In my opinion, he has probably suffered some kind of psychological damage at some stage, most likely during childhood, some kind of traumatic experience that has affected his mental health. He may well have been institutionalised at some point; it's certainly possible.'

'Paranoid schizophrenic perhaps?'

'I couldn't completely rule it out, although his crimes appear to be quite organised and methodical, which is not usually indicative of those managing such a condition. It's possible he has some kind of borderline personality disorder – he shows some sociopathic tendencies, but there isn't a complete lack of empathy in his methods which one would expect to see from a fully fledged psychopath… there's something else.'

We sit silently for a moment as I digest the conversation or attempt to. I'm undecided if she's been extremely helpful or the complete opposite, my mind swinging back and forth between the two like a pendulum.

'Your current situation,' she says eventually. 'You live with your partner and child, she's… how old is she?'

'My partner?'

She smiles, indulging me.

'Your baby.'

'Coming on for a year now, eleven months,' I say, my face automatically breaking into a grin. 'Juno. I call her Pip. She's an angel. Though she's teething at the moment, so not so much an angel as a little devil and—' I realise I'm going off track. 'Anyway, she's the best thing that's ever happened to me.'

'I'm sure.'

'And we're not… her mother and I… well, we're not partners exactly.' I don't know why I have offered this information but it's too late to retract it. 'I don't know what we are exactly.'

She nods as though she fully understands.

'Things become clear when we start looking at them clearly, Detective,' she says. 'When we stop overthinking them.'

'Well, thanks for the relationship advice, Dr Henderson, but I have a serial killer to catch.'

'Yes,' she says, 'what do you think would help you right now?'

I want to say, 'A large whiskey with ice and a cold shower,' but stop myself short.

'Well, if Daisey Garrett could give us something… anything, we'd have a profile at least, something to work with… a start, but she can't remember anything, at least not yet.'

'Hmm.' She swishes her hair from her face, giving me a waft of something that reminds me of beaches and coconut sun cream. 'I'm pretty sure she has simply mentally blocked it all out through trauma. The brain is pretty adept at protecting itself. But it's there, her memory of that night is there, it just needs to be unlocked.'

'That's as may be, Doctor, but unfortunately, I don't seem to have the key.'

She gives me a Mona Lisa kind of smile.

'Maybe I do,' she offers. 'Hypnotherapy can be an extremely effective way of removing blocks in a patient, helping them to retrieve memories or thoughts they've buried through trauma. It's been very successful on some of my patients in the past. Unlocking and releasing those memories can be very cathartic for the individual – as well as, in this particular instance, beneficial to others.'

'And it's not dangerous?'

'I wouldn't be practising it if it was, Detective.' She bristles slightly and although I really don't want to admit it to myself, I feel a tiny hint of malicious glee. Not because I want to offend her, but because I feel she has somehow had me on the back foot throughout the conversation.

'No.' I smile. 'Of course not. But Daisey is, I suspect, more fragile than she's letting on. I think she's hoping that her memory of that night won't come back to her so that she doesn't have to relive the ordeal – and I can't say I blame her but…'

'Well, no one wants to relive painful memories, do they, Dan?' She stares at me intensely with piercing green eyes. I want to look away but somehow can't, and for a moment I feel like I may have been hypnotised myself.

'We'll reconvene again soon,' she says, matter-of-fact, snapping the file shut. 'Maybe next week?'

'OK, sure.' *Sure?* Now I'm convinced she's hypnotised me.

'Great.' She smiles, places the files inside her leather tote and stands. I duly follow and she shakes my hand again. 'It was good to meet you, Dan.'

'You too,' I reply quickly, too quickly perhaps.

'And if you think it will help, I could always speak to Daisey Garrett myself. Explain the benefits of her undergoing a hypnotherapy session with me, how it would help her in the long term, help her to regain her life and come to terms with what happened.' She flicks her hair from her shoulders again, slings her bag over her arm into the crook of her elbow and stares at me. The thought pops into my head before I can prevent it. *She really is very beautiful.* 'You never know, I may have more luck persuading her.'

'Of this I have no doubt,' I find myself saying. *No doubt at all.*

CHAPTER SEVENTEEN

May 1997

'*Underneath the lilac tree, just you and me, just us three, happy as can be…* Sing it with me, *Underneath the lilac tree…*' Rosie skips around the tree trunk barefoot, holding her floral skirt above her knees.

'Come on!' she coaxes them. 'Join in, you two, don't be spoilsports…'

His friend looks sideways at him for affirmation, unsure of whether he should follow suit, take his shoes off and chase her around the tree. He can see he wants to though and this makes him feel a little cross. Michael had come to see him today – the very first time he'd ever had a friend over to play, a friend that wasn't hers, one he'd made all by himself, one that actually seemed to like him.

*

'Of course he can come over. Invite him for tea!' Tracey Eggerton had seemed as pleased as she had been shocked when her son had asked if his friend could come to their house that afternoon. He'd never asked before; he'd never had cause to. He didn't have any friends, none that she knew of anyway, until now.

'See, Trace.' John had wrapped his arms around her waist as she'd stood over the oven, stirring pasta. 'He's making progress, he's got himself a little playmate, that's a good thing isn't it, eh, babe?'

Tracey leans into her husband's embrace as she continues to stir the pasta and smiles.

'Well, it's definitely a step in the right direction,' she agrees with him. 'Michael seems like a nice little boy – from that new family round the corner, they've not long moved here. I spoke to his mum earlier, Sandra; she seems nice too… normal, not up herself at all.'

He nuzzles her neck affectionately.

'All that worry for nothing… that business with the cat and the little…' He decides not to finish the sentence, doesn't want to set her off again. 'He just needs a chance, love, a chance to fit in, be like the rest of the kids. He is just like the rest of them really.'

Tracey nods. She wants to believe him. 'Like I say, it's a step in the right direction.'

'Well, it makes a nice change him having a little mate over. It's always Rosie's friends who come here… always Rosie who gets all the playdates and invitations. If it goes well I'm sure they'll invite him back to theirs another time. We should encourage it more; encourage him to play with other boys his own age instead of having to tag along with his sister all the time; it's not good for him.'

She nods but says nothing. She doesn't want to talk about all those birthday lists he's been left off from at school, all those party invitations never received. It stung, of course, but deep down she understood. Deep down she knows she would feel the same way if the boot were on the other foot. In the early days, a few of the friendlier mums had made the effort. After all, it was difficult to invite Rosie to a party without her brother, her *twin* brother. But on the few occasions he had attended any such events in the past he had acted strangely, refusing to join in and hanging on to his sister's dress, unable to interact with anyone but her. It had made Tracey feel awkward and embarrassed and in the end she had simply stopped bringing him and the mums had stopped inviting him. It had been easier that way.

'Maybe you should go up to the field, check they're OK,' Tracey suggests. 'Tell them tea will be ready in about half an hour.'

'Stop panicking, love,' John says. 'They're just having fun. Nothing bad is going to happen. Relax.'

Tracey smiles nervously, unable to stop the jitters dancing like butterflies inside her stomach. Try as she has, she cannot shake the sense of unease she has felt ever since Michael came over to play, a feeling of impending dread – like a bruise, tender and sore inside her solar plexus, shortening her breath. But she can't relay her fears to her husband. He'll just start up about her paranoia again; tell her to take one of her pills.

'They're just kids, Trace,' he says, as though reading her. 'Just normal kids.'

'Yes,' she says, opening the cupboard and reaching for the small bottle of JD she's stashed there. 'Just kids.'

*

'I'll be the Queen and you two can be my foot soldiers!' Rosie is cartwheeling across the grass, her skirt flying up over her head as she flips herself over and over in succession, briefly exposing her floral underwear. 'Start marching!' she commands.

Michael looks at him and he nods. They both begin to march; one-step, two-step, *attention*!

'That's it,' she says. 'Good soldiers! Now,' she says, stopping and turning to face them, 'one of you will become my King!'

'Which one?' Michael asks keenly, hanging off her every word. 'Can I be King?'

She taps her lip with a finger, goes over to him and begins to circle him, inspecting him. 'Hmmm,' she says. 'We shall have to see what you're made of first, young man!'

Michael giggles.

He watches his friend and sister interact, can see that Michael has lost interest in him and that now all his focus is upon her, just like it always is, just like it is with everyone. This was supposed to be *his* playdate.

'I'm going to give you some tasks, a competition and there can only be one winner,' she announces, clearly enjoying her role as Queen. 'There's going to be a race… from here to the lilac tree… whoever wins will be one step closer to becoming my King!'

He feels instantly deflated. He cannot run fast, she knows this and is doing it deliberately. Michael is bigger, stronger and taller than him. He will beat him easily. He doesn't want to take part. He doesn't want to feel the inevitable humiliation and failure that will be his, sensations he is all too familiar with. He just wants to play with Michael on the zip slide and the makeshift swing that hangs from the lilac tree. He'd told Michael all about it at school that week and he'd seemed excited to see it. Now all his attention is focussed upon her instead.

'Ready… set… GO!'

Michael sprints off in the direction of the lilac tree and he reluctantly follows, already knowing the outcome. Michael reaches the tree a good fifteen seconds before he comes panting up the rear behind him.

'I won! I won!' Michael punches the air, triumphant. 'Does this mean I'm your King now?' He looks at her with wide hopeful eyes. He's under her spell already.

'Not yet!' she says provocatively. 'Now let's see who can climb the tree the highest! The one who makes it to the top first wins!'

Michael has a foothold on it already before he can even digest the challenge.

'Hang on, that's not fair,' he objects, 'I wasn't ready!'

'Come on,' she says to her brother, 'are you going to beat him or are you just going to stand there like a clown, whining?'

He feels the anger rise within him, an uncomfortable paradoxical mix of resentment and the need to please her. He knows the tree better than Michael does, has climbed it a million times before. He can get up it faster, quicker, he feels sure.

Spurred on by this knowledge he begins to climb. He looks up above him and sees the soles of Michael's shoes. It's a big tree, maybe twenty-five feet, and Michael seems to be struggling a little already. Ha! He'd misjudged it, hadn't realised how tall it was.

'I'm coming after you!' he calls out to his friend, suddenly enjoying the game now that he has gained a little confidence. Michael is bigger though, his legs are longer, more powerful than his and of course there's his other disadvantage, the one he was born with... but still he knows the tree better than him. He begins to make a bit of pace, navigating the branches, gripping them with all the strength he has, using his knowledge of the tree to find the quickest and safest route. He's catching him up.

'Shall we introduce him to our other friend?' Rosie's voice carries upwards through the branches where they're both frantically climbing. 'She can decide who gets to be my King!'

'What friend?' Michael is almost at the top now, but he's tired and panting and looks a little scared.

'You don't want to meet her,' he says, a few feet below, beginning to accept defeat. 'I don't want you to meet her. I'll let you win. You can be her King,' he says.

'Why don't I want to meet her?' he asks. 'Who is she?'

He doesn't answer. He needs to concentrate on holding on. If he fell at this height he would surely break his neck.

Michael makes a final push, the sound of the branches snapping and cracking with the strain of his weight as he reaches the pinnacle.

'I won again!' he calls out, not daring to look down. 'I'm the King! I get to be Rosie's King!'

He can hear his sister clapping below at the base of the tree.

'We should go back now,' he says. 'Tea will be ready soon. If Mum comes up here and sees us in the tree she'll be cross.'

Michael nods, begins to make his descent. 'Yeah, all right.'

'As you're the winner, Michael – and my King for the day – you get a special surprise,' Rosie calls up at him in the tree. 'You get to meet our special friend! Not many people get to meet her so consider yourself lucky. She's going to crown you my King!'

'Let's go, quick,' he says to Michael, beckoning him down. 'You really don't want to meet her. Look, you won, you're King, OK. Let's just get back home. Mum says we can have ice cream with chocolate sauce for afters if we eat all our tea.'

'But I want to meet her,' Michael says, intrigued. 'If she's anything like your sister then she'll be fun.'

'No, Michael, we have to go,' he says, panic rising up through his small diaphragm. He likes Michael, he really does.

'Come on! She's waiting down here!' Rosie's voice rings out across the field. 'Come and see her, Michael; she has something for you, something for my special King!'

'A crown!' Michael says, eyes wide in anticipation. He tries not to look down, the sunlight slipping through the branches like laser beams blinding him. 'Every King needs a crown.'

He feels his entire body deflate with hopelessness. Michael wants to meet her now, wants to know who she is. He can't dissuade him. He couldn't dissuade any of them. He wishes she would just go away, leave them be; he wishes he had never introduced her to Rosie in the first place.

Michael looks down again, tries to spot Rosie and her special friend but can't see anyone. Suddenly, he realises how high he is and feels a rush of fear.

'So… so where is she then, your special friend?' he calls out. 'I can't see anyone.'

He knows what's about to happen but can't stop it – he's never been able to stop her.

'She's right behind you!' The loud voice, close in Michael's ear, that comes from behind him, causes him to jump in alarm and lose his grip on the branch. He shrieks as he slips, kicking out with his feet as his balance goes and he begins to fall.

He can only watch as he hears the sound of branches snapping and crackling like gunfire, the rustling of leaves, and the crunching of bone that causes him to inwardly wince. He waits for the sickening thud as Michael's body hits the ground. And when it comes, he closes his eyes.

CHAPTER EIGHTEEN

'You look great, Daisey,' Luke remarks, following her through to the kitchen and throwing his keys and wallet onto the worktop, a force of habit that causes her to feel a twinge of sadness.

'Thanks,' she says, opening her mouth to automatically return the compliment but stops herself short. Truth is, he doesn't look great, not really; he looks tired and a little drawn. His beard isn't as neatly clipped as usual and she notices the faintest of dark circles under his eyes.

'I brought a bottle of Chablis; you like Chablis.' He places it down onto the kitchen table.

'You remembered, thank you.' She smiles, though the real truth is that she couldn't tell a Chablis from a Chardonnay if her life depended on it; she'd always just pretended to. Luke referred to people who knew nothing about wine as 'Philistines'.

'Well, the place still looks great,' he remarks, scanning the apartment with approval. 'You've kept it nice, clean and tidy.'

'What did you expect it to look like? A squat?' She hears the confrontation in her tone so adds a quick laugh at the end to take the edge off. Iris's cardigan is slung over the back of the sofa and, spotting it, she quickly picks it up and surreptitiously stuffs it behind one of the cushions.

'Do you remember when we viewed this place?' he says, his voice tinged with nostalgia. 'You fell in love with it on sight, started jumping up and down like a little girl, all excited. That estate agent was mentally spending his commission before we'd even left.' He laughs.

'Yes.' She smiles with her back to him but supposes he can tell. 'Of course I remember. I'd practically given up finding somewhere after all the shitholes we'd viewed, like that place round the corner, the one where there were tea bags in the sink and a pair of dirty pants on the bathroom floor – do you remember?'

He laughs again in recollection and for a moment she feels a bittersweet ripple of comfort as they reminisce.

'We definitely made the right choice,' he says. 'Once you'd set your heart on this place you were like a woman on a mission, never seen you so determined about anything before.' He pauses. 'Do you remember what we called it?'

She does. She remembers exactly. It was their 'Forever until we have lots of babies' home, but she doesn't want to say this – it's too painful. She wonders how much small talk they'll endure before he gets to the real reason why he's here. It can't simply be for a trip down memory lane. She pours them both a glass of wine, a Chardonnay she picked up from Sainsbury's. It had been on special but the label looked quite posh. She hopes he'll approve.

'How's work?' he enquires, throwing himself down onto the sofa like he owned the place – even though he still did, technically.

'It's good to be back. Actually, I've enrolled on a college course in Make-Up and Special Effects for TV and Film at the art college, starts early next year.' This is only a white lie – she has every intention of enrolling on such a course but just hasn't got round to it yet. 'I'd like to work in prosthetics, maybe help people, you know, people who've suffered burns, or… been scarred in some way.' This is the first time she's thought this, but now that she has it seems like a good idea.

'That's cool, very altruistic. I'm happy for you.'

Cool. God, she hates it when he uses that word; it sounds so… contrived.

'I'm glad you're moving forward, Daisey, really I am, especially after… well, after everything you've been through.' *You've put me through, you mean.*

He clears his throat. 'Here's to new beginnings.' He chinks her glass and she feels like throwing the contents over him, overcome by a confusing mix of love and hate; that age-old fine line blurring.

'Does Charlotte know you're here?'

He shoots her a sideways look that suggests she already knows the answer.

'So you're lying to her? That's twice already that I know of, Luke.' She makes a tut-tut noise. 'It's not boding well, is it?'

He cocks his head to one side. 'I just wanted… I just needed to see you, to speak to you… You know, sometimes in life, Daisey, it's not always the best thing to do, to tell the truth.'

She snorts a little. 'Well, you'd certainly know, wouldn't you?'

He drops his chin, sighs. 'I teed that one up for you, didn't I? I guess it's no more than I deserve.' He looks a little pitiful and she tries not to feel any empathy for him.

'Dinner will be ready soon,' she says, lightening the tone. 'Spaghetti bolognese, I'm afraid. You know I'm not much of a cook.' She wonders if she's much of anything and that's why he left her. She glugs back more wine, notices his glass is empty and pours him another. He's outpacing her – a first for him. Something must've happened.

'So,' he says, crossing his legs and taking another sip, licking his lips. He looks so at home that for a split second she thinks that nothing has happened, that there was no affair and no attack and that it had all been just one big horrific, dreadful nightmare. 'Why don't we cut the bullshit, eh?' He leans forward in his seat. 'How are you really, I mean *really*, Daisey?'

She flicks her hair, shuffles a little in the armchair, wonders if he can smell her perfume from where he's sitting, the perfume he'd once remarked had smelled of 'sex and regret'.

'I'm fine, Luke, really. I'm… I'm just wondering why you're here, that's all.' She can't hold back any longer; she wants to know the purpose of his visit – the real purpose. 'I haven't heard from you since… since the time you visited me in the… in the hospital.'

He dips his head again, exhales slightly. 'Yes, about that.'

He rests an elbow on his knee, holds his glass with the other. She tries not to feel any emotion as she recognises the familiarity of his body movements, tries to push back the flutters of desire that have begun to stir in the pit of her stomach. She should never have agreed to him coming here tonight.

A noise breaks the surface of her thoughts; it sounds like it's come from one the bedrooms, a small clattering sound as though something has been knocked over, a lamp perhaps.

'What was that?'

'What was what?' He stops talking, looks behind him through to the hallway.

'I heard a noise.'

He shrugs. 'I didn't hear anything.'

She thinks to go and investigate but doesn't want to come across as jumpy and paranoid – even though she is.

'Do you want me to go and see?' He stands, places his wine on the table.

'No, it's OK!' She doesn't want him poking around in the bedrooms. He'll see Iris's stuff, start asking questions and she'll have to come clean. 'It was nothing, next door probably. You always said the walls were a little thin.'

He cocks his head to one side. 'You see,' he says, almost with a touch of self-satisfaction. 'I knew you weren't all right, not really.' He leans forward again, places his hand on her knee. 'It's only to be expected. Jesus, I'm surprised you're not a nervous wreck. Most people would be. I mean knowing that… that that man, that lunatic who attacked you, is still out there… Has the doctor prescribed you anything? Valium, Citaloplan?' Concern is etched upon his face – a face she can't help but find handsome still – and wonders if it's genuine. He'd been so cold and unfeeling, so dispassionate when he'd come to visit her in hospital. Why the sudden turnaround?

Nerves jangling, she moves into the kitchen area to check on the food.

'I wanted to apologise,' he says, calling back to her.

'Really? Well, in that case it'll be a long night.' She's being facetious again but can't seem to stop herself.

He laughs gently. 'I know,' he says. 'I've been a complete arsehole, a complete and utter arsehole.'

'A cheating, lying, insensitive, cold, cruel arsehole,' she adds, but she's smiling as she says it in a bid to take the sting out.

'Yes,' he agrees softly, 'a lying, cheating, insensitive arsehole.'

Daisey can't quite believe what she's hearing. He really does sound and look genuinely regretful.

'I wish…' He gets up, follows her into the kitchen space, standing with his back against the worktop next to her, watching as she stirs the pasta. 'I wish, sometimes, that I could go back. That we could go back… to how it was, how we were before…'

'Before what, before you starting sleeping with someone else?'

'In truth,' he says, throwing back more wine and pouring himself another, tipping the rest of the bottle into her glass. 'I was scared.'

She raises an eyebrow but doesn't say anything. She wants to hear this; with a bit of luck she might even get the closure she's been searching for.

'Scared of what?'

'Oh, I don't know, growing up, I suppose. Scared of my youth slipping away, of becoming old and boring. The idea of marriage terrified me, Daisey. Even saying the word aloud made me feel trapped, stifled, caged… the thought of spending my whole life with just one person, of my... autonomy being taken from me.'

'Bit dramatic.' She pulls a face. 'Anyway, it was your bloody idea to get married – you asked me!' she says, animated, the wine giving her the confidence to say what she really feels. 'I thought the whole concept of marriage is that you *want* to spend the rest of your life with one person, that you can't wait to share your life together... or was it more like you were scared by the idea of never having sex with anyone else ever again? Was it that you felt you needed someone different, someone more, I don't know, like you...'

'Like me?'

'Yeah, you know, highly educated, intellectual, someone you could talk to endlessly about politics and philosophy and literature and the rest of it. Someone you wouldn't bore the pants off. Someone like Cho.'

He laughs then and suddenly she sees him as she remembers him at the start of their relationship. He'd been much more easy-going, easier company, less pompous and judgemental, less up himself. He'd even been quite self-deprecating at times, fun and silly. There hadn't been any of this overly politically correct seriousness and vegan diet rubbish. He even used to eat Pot Noodles for lunch, for Christ's sake.

'Sometimes I miss the easiness of us, Daisey.'

'Easiness?' She's not sure what he means by the remark.

'Yeah. There wasn't any pressure to be... you didn't make me feel like... Oh, I don't know. I could be more...'

She watches him closely as he struggles with his words, tries not to experience a modicum of glee from his discomfort.

'More myself, I suppose. You were quite low maintenance really, never asked anything of me, never demanded or made me feel like I wasn't up to scratch.'

Aha! So that's why he's really here. Things aren't going great with Cho and he needs an ego boost.

'What I mean, Daisey, is I miss you... miss this... you were always so, I don't know, refreshing sometimes, funny, even when you didn't mean to be.'

Daisey can't grasp what she's hearing.

'You thought I was thick and stupid,' she says, 'you still do. That's why you ended up with her. Cho and her unfeasibly large b— brains!'

He continues to laugh but it peters out.

'I made a mistake,' he says, suddenly serious. 'I'm a fraud, Daisey.' He drops his head into his hands. 'You never pretended to be someone you weren't, not like me... you're stronger than me. I'm weak, weak and pathetic. I mean, look at you. Most people would've fallen apart after what's happened to you, but here you are, looking better than ever, rebuilding your life, moving on. You're the most courageous woman I've ever met – do you know that?' He's facing her again now, inches away, and looking deeply into her eyes.

'Your scar,' he says, lightly touching her neck with his finger; she can smell his skin, the scent of him on his fingertips. 'It's healing well.' He's so close now that she can feel his breath on her cheek. 'Then again... physical ones usually do; it's the emotional scars that take the longest.'

She gathers the strength to pull away from him, busies herself with the pan on the cooker, or pretends to.

'Have there been any updates in your case, from the police? Has that detective, whatshisface – the suave-looking one who came to visit me – come up with anything? Is he any closer to finding him...?' He doesn't finish the sentence, doesn't need to. 'Jesus, I still can't believe something like that happened to you, something so... so horrible. I mean, you see it on TV, read about it in the newspapers, but you never think... you never think it could happen to someone close to you. And to think he's still out there... prowling... searching for his next victim and... I worry about you, here, alone... I mean, how do you sleep at night?'

'I could ask you the same question,' she says dryly. 'And the suave-looking detective, Dan Riley, the one you lied to, the one you made *me* lie to about when you last saw me – he makes sure I'm OK. You know, I really should've told him the truth. The DNA they found on me – in me – it was yours, from the morning before... we could both get in a lot of trouble for withholding that information. I feel really guilty about it; terrible, in fact. It could've hindered the investigation.'

He looks a little sheepish, bites his bottom lip subconsciously. 'Yeah, well... I refused to give a DNA sample as well so he probably thinks I'm the killer.'

'Jesus, Luke, lucky for you, you had an alibi,' she remarks, 'otherwise I might be inclined to agree with him.'

'Don't be bloody ridiculous, Daisey. You'd never have let me through the door if you'd ever truly believed that even for a second. Speaking of which, it's good to see that you've upped the security in the place; I noticed the new locks.'

'Yes, and I've got a panic alarm too, so don't get any ideas.' She's smiling as she says it. 'Anyway, there's CCTV everywhere now. If he... if he tried to come back for me then he'd have to be pretty stupid.'

Her hands are shaking as she says it though and she hopes he can't tell. 'They think there may be some connection with me and his second victim, Fern Godden, maybe a connection with Warwick's; she used to work there too – and flowers, roses... but, oh, I don't know...'

'So it wasn't random then? He targeted you...?'

She shrugs; she doesn't want to think about it, tries her best not to. 'Perhaps.'

'Christ, Daisey, what's to say he won't come looking for you again? I mean, it was a miracle you survived; he obviously meant to kill you and… what if he's still watching you, waiting for the right time to…'

'Can we talk about something else please?' she says. 'Like, why you're really here.'

He ignores the question, continues. 'Surely you must remember something about that night, the night it happened? Hasn't anything come back to you, nothing at all?'

She doesn't want to tell him about the noises in her head, the split-second flashes of her memory that have been threatening to return. She doesn't want to tell him about her paranoia or her nightmares. Then she hears another noise; it sounds like floorboards creaking, like someone moving around. It sounded like it was coming from the bedroom. Or maybe it was just the noises in her head.

Daisey rubs her temples, feels like she's going mad. She shuts her eyes, tries to regulate her breathing, calm herself—

A high-pitched sound suddenly pierces her head like a skewer, causing her to wince and grab her temples. The crackle is louder this time, shrill and more painful than ever before. She hears the hammer as it impacts with her skull, a sickening crack, the thud as she falls to the floor, the metallic smell of blood, her own blood. Shockwaves… almost painful as they pass through her body…

*

… she's pulling herself up… Oh God… Oh God! No! Fear erupts inside her chest like an explosion. She cannot move, can only feel. He's pulling her… dragging her… she's semi-conscious, moaning, she wants to cry out but can't, her head hurts, the pain sharp and unforgiving, is pulsing through her and is all she can focus on.

'Stop…' She hears her own voice but it's a muted whisper inside her mind. She's in the bedroom and he's holding her, placing her on top of the bed. Her limbs feel heavy, dead, like lumps of raw meat. Her vision is blurred, as though she's looking through a smeared windowpane, the image of him is fuzzy, like a watercolour left out in the rain.

He's leaning over her now, straddling her. She feels the weight of him on her chest, his knees, sharp, digging into her sides, squeezing her torso, the smell of him, a strange sweet scent, almost like perfume, *like flowers*.

'*Underneath the lilac tree, just you and me, just us three…*' He's singing! Humming a rhyme of some sort.

'No… no…' She's coming round a little, her vision sharpening, her voice has more clarity. His hands are around her neck… He's speaking but she can't quite hear him, his voice is soft and low, almost gentle.

'I'm sorry, Rosie…' Yes! That's what he'd said, those were the words, he'd called her by the wrong name: Rosie. She can feel her arms; loose and floppy as though they're boneless as she tries to move them, tries to lash out at him. She wills herself to grip his forearms, to stop the squeezing and the pressure on her neck, but fear has rendered her powerless. There's blood in her eyes but she can sense the darkness coming, like dusk about to fall, her peripheral vision gradually closing in, an ever-decreasing circle, getting smaller and smaller. Her mind is struggling to fight; it's telling her to stay awake, battling against the grip he has around her neck, but she's slipping, slipping downwards, as though she's falling through the bed, sinking into the floral bedspread through the duvet and layers of mattress and… the glint of the blade! The smallest flash as the moonlight from the window bounces off it and she opens her eyes wide in horror and looks up…

*

'Jesus Christ, Daisey, are you OK? Talk to me, talk to me, Daisey!' Luke is shaking her gently, bringing her round. 'Are you OK? Daisey! Are you all right?'

Her breathing is laboured, heavy as she regains focus.

'Yes… yes… I'm fine.' She shakes her head, rubs her aching temples. 'I'm… I don't know what just happened.' Her thoughts begin to settle, fluttering gradually back to a normal frequency. 'I just had a moment, that's all,' she says. 'I'm fine.'

He's kneeling down in front of her, his hands on her forearms, looking at her, concern etched on his brow.

'You fucking scared me,' he says, pulling her into his arms. 'What the hell was that?' She doesn't resist, instead sinks into them, closes her eyes and breathes in his familiar smell, soap and cologne with the faintest undertone of banana. He pulls back for a moment, looks at her. He's so close that his nose is practically touching hers.

'God, you're beautiful,' he says as his lips begin to touch hers.

CHAPTER NINETEEN

Exhaustion hits me like a heatwave as I put the key in the door to my apartment and tiptoe through it so as not to wake Pip. It's gone 3 a.m. so I'm surprised to see Fiona still up and dressed in the kitchen. She's always been a night owl like me, but what with her job and Juno, these days she's usually flaked out before 9 p.m. – or so she tells me, because I'm rarely home before midnight.

'Dan.' She looks up, smiles, glances at the clock. The rims of her eyes are red and I wonder if she's been crying or if, like me, she's just tired. 'You look shattered. Tough day at the office?'

I exhale my response; throw my keys onto the table and collapse into a chair. I take my jacket off, the movement giving me a sour waft of my own body odour. I haven't showered since yesterday morning, but in my defence I haven't been home since then either.

'You too by the looks of it?' I say, nodding at the bottle of Remy Martin on the table, an empty glass next to it. I reach for it, pour myself a measure and hold the bottle up towards her but she shakes her head. 'How's Pip? Are her teeth still giving her gyp?'

'Marie says she's been good today; the tooth has finally broken through so she's been a little more settled. Only a few more to go now…'

She smiles again and I laugh a little, roll my eyes. Marie is our part-time nanny, a Vietnamese lady with the patience of Mother Teresa and the wisdom of the Dalai Lama rolled into one.

'Great.' I take a long sip of brandy and it slides down my throat, warming my empty insides. I can't remember the last time I ate anything.

'So,' she says tentatively, taking a seat opposite me. 'Anything?'

She asks the question though I suspect it's rhetorical. Fi knows I'd be buzzing with energy if I'd had any real breakthrough on the case. I run my fingers through my hair; it smells of the station, of the sweat and toil of a hundred men and women. 'Jesus, Fi... this one... I don't know... we're no closer... I mean, we've got all the DNA we could shake a stick at but no identity, no suspects, no leads...'

She looks down at the table. 'I'm sorry,' she says. 'You'll get a break soon, I know you will – you always do, Dan.'

I shake my head. 'We need one, Fi. I sense he's close to doing another... this sick feeling of impending dread inside me...' I thump my chest with a fist in a bid to dislodge it.

She sighs. 'How about Daisey? Her memory?'

I shake my head again. 'The poor woman's petrified, doesn't *want* to remember, I think that's where the problem lies.' Annabelle Henderson jumps into my consciousness then and I get a waft of her beaches and sun-cream scent.

'I met a forensic psychologist today, an American woman; she's been assigned to help on the case. She thinks she might be able to hypnotise her, unlock the memory of that night.'

Fiona blows air through her lips. 'It might be worth a shot.'

'If I can convince her,' I say, unhopeful.

'Well, I guess I wouldn't want to remember having my head bashed in and my throat slit open either – you can't really blame her.'

'I don't,' I say miserably. 'But right now she's our only hope. This one's clever, Fi, elusive... he'll strike again, and soon. I'm worried I'll...'

'You'll what?' Her head is cocked to one side and her eyes are looking into my own. Juno has the same eyes as her mother, dark and almond-shaped – eyes I could look at forever. 'Don't tell me the great Dan Riley is doubting himself because I won't believe it.'

She reaches for my hand across the table, slides her own on top of it briefly. This small act of solidarity brings a lump to my throat and I have to take another sip of brandy in a bid to soften it.

'You'll get the break you need,' she says softly, raising an eyebrow. 'And then you'll give me the scoop before anyone else.'

I laugh. She never takes a day off. Perhaps that's why I love— why we get on so well.

'If I tell you something will you keep it to yourself, just for now?'

She's smiling and nodding but I can tell something's not quite right; she doesn't seem herself – the brandy, the red-rimmed eyes... 'Flowers,' I say, 'the victims all have floral names. There's a connection.'

Fiona's eyes light up in that way all journalists' eyes do when you give them a morsel of information – only hers are more genuine than most.

'I'll need to get in touch with Warwick's. Get them to give me a list of staff named after flowers. I think one of them could be his next victim, couldn't she?'

Suddenly, I think of Iris, Daisey's flatmate. She works at Warwick's.

'I've been so close to this case, Fi, closer than anything else I've ever worked on and...' Dr Henderson's voice is in my ears again. '*A watched kettle never boils, Detective. Sometimes we cannot see what is right before us when we're looking too closely.*'

'And that's why you're the right man for the job. Listen, Dan...'

She continues to speak but my mind had spun off in a new direction, the connection between Fern Godden and Daisey Garrett and Warwick's. Now I'm more convinced than ever that our man worked there, maybe still does.

I stand, reach into my pocket for my phone to call Davis. That's when I spot the suitcase on the floor, next to the table. It's open and some of Fiona's clothes are folded neatly inside. A spike of adrenalin rises through me, the heat reaching my earlobes.

'You leaving me?' I say, only half joking, nodding at the suitcase.

She looks down at the floor. 'Sit down for a minute, will you?' she asks gently. 'We need to talk.'

I can feel my heartbeat increasing, the thud of it against my ribs. 'Has... has something happened?'

She nods. 'It's my mum, Dan, in Korea. She's sick, really sick. In fact, she's dying, Dan. My brother just called me, just before you got home, to tell me she's not got long left.'

I fall back into the chair again. Pour another brandy and one for her. She accepts it this time.

'Jesus, Fi, I'm sorry,' I say, because it's all I know to say, even with all the regrettable experience I've had of imparting bad news to others. 'How... how long is not long?'

She shakes her head, shrugs. 'A couple of weeks, a few maybe... she only got the diagnosis last week and then... well, the decline has been so rapid, everyone's shocked and upset and... and she wants me to go there, to see her, be with her at the end.'

'Yes... yes of course. I... I...'

'I booked us the tickets immediately, me, Leo and... and Juno... the cab's coming in' – she looks at the clock again – 'twenty-five minutes. We're getting the first flight out of Gatwick.'

'You're taking Juno?' My voice sounds louder than I intend it to.

'Yes, Dan, it will be the first and last time she will ever see her.' She pauses, watching my reaction. 'Look, I know it's a long way, I know it's not ideal, but it is what it is, Dan. I have to go.'

I nod but can't speak; too many emotions have flooded my brain for me to be able to grab hold of a single one and articulate it. I swallow back another mouthful of brandy.

'I could come too,' I find myself saying, though we both know that this is not possible. She smiles thinly, doesn't need to follow it up with anything.

'How long will you be gone for?' I ask after a few moments' silence.

'I can't say, Dan, two weeks, three, four… however long it takes for…' She doesn't finish the sentence, doesn't need to. 'I've been given compassionate leave at *The Post*, but I'll still be dipping in and out while I'm away.'

Like I say, she never takes a day off. I rub my temples; try not to think about how I feel and think of her instead, but all that's going through my mind is, *she's taking Pip away from me*, like a hideous mantra, over and over.

We sit in silence for a moment.

'Maybe it will be good, Dan, the space, for both of us,' she says gently. 'Maybe while I'm gone – while we're gone – you'll have the chance to think about things… about what it is you really want.'

'What I really want?'

Her eyes flicker a little. 'You know what I'm talking about.'

I do. And she knows I do.

'We can't stay like this forever, Dan.'

'Like what?'

She frowns, but there's no real crossness behind it. 'We can't avoid it forever.'

'Avoid what forever?' I can hear myself, how I sound, and wish I had a gun handy so I could shoot myself in the face.

'Avoid this!' She laughs a little. 'Avoid you avoiding having this conversation with me, about us, about what we are, what our future is, if we even have one together. We can't stay as we are, in this limbo of "are we, aren't we?". Juno needs stability, whatever form that comes in, whether we are a couple or not. You're a great dad, Dan,' she says, her eyes glassy now. I say a silent prayer to myself, hoping that she doesn't start to cry because I fear I will follow suit. 'You really are, and whatever happens you will always be that girl's father, always be part of her life, a big part,' she adds as though to reassure me. 'But we both have lives to lead; we both deserve a future, even if it's not together.'

I feel as though I've been hit with a brick. 'So you *are* leaving me?' She sips her brandy.

'What I want is already here, Dan. It's been here all along.' She smiles, takes a deep breath. 'The cab will be here soon.'

'But I can take you to the airport… I'll drive you!'

She shakes her head. 'No, Dan, airport goodbyes aren't really our style, are they? Besides, you look like you haven't slept in a week. You're needed here on this case. You need to get some rest, catch this killer – only you can do it, Dan, everyone knows that. I have every faith in you.'

'But I'm needed… I mean *I* need…' I try to say that I need her, that I need Juno and Leo, I need them all, but the words don't come.

'I'll call you once we land, let you know we've arrived safe.' She stands, pulls the suitcase onto the table and zips it up. 'I'll go and get Juno.' A few moments later she brings her downstairs in a car seat. Remarkably she's still asleep, her eyes tightly shut like two ticks on a page. She places her onto the kitchen table and goes back upstairs to get Leo organised.

I watch my sleeping daughter huddled up in a fluffy blanket. Her little legs twitch slightly and I wonder if she's dreaming, and what she might be dreaming about. Do babies dream? I guess it's something we'll never really know, but I'm sure they must do. Perhaps she's dreaming about milk, or the pureed pear she loves for breakfast, or maybe she's dreaming about Bingo, her fuzzy panda bear, one she's had since birth and that lately she's been chewing, so much so that one of his ears has fallen off.

I kiss the top of her head, my lips lightly touching her soft skin, and I breathe her in, inhale that scent of hers, the one that smells of purity and joy.

'You be good for your mummy, yes?' I say gently. 'Look after her. You're going on a big adventure, to see your nanny and your family and…' Something splashes onto her cheek and I realise that it's me; that I'm crying, and I quickly wipe it away with the edge of her blanket, use the corner to wipe my own eyes. 'Daddy wishes he could come too, but Daddy has to stay here and catch a very bad man who does very bad things…' She stirs a little, makes a snuffling sound and I stop talking until she settles. 'Daddy's going to miss you so much, Pip… Daddy loves you more than anything else in the whole world, do you know that? Daddy loves you to the moon and back and then back again and…'

I turn and see Fiona standing in the doorway, watching me. I think she might be crying too.

CHAPTER TWENTY

She watches him, naked, as he gets up from the bed and removes the condom with a snap, discarding it into the waste-paper bin by her dressing table.

'What time is it?' he asks through a yawn.

She presses her phone, watches as the screen illuminates. 'Just gone 9.15,' she replies. 'Will Cho will be wondering where you are?' She props herself up on the bed with an elbow as he scrabbles around for his clothes and begins to dress.

He casts her a withered look that she just about catches in the low light of the bedroom.

'Don't be like that, Daisey,' he says. But already she can feel a change in him, a shift from his earlier repentant mood, more detached. The knot in her stomach tightens. Suddenly, she realises something – the condom, he'd brought one with him! Oh my God! Had he planned all of this, to come here tonight with the sole intention of seducing her? The 'poor misunderstood me' routine, the apology and self-regret, had it all been contrived and disingenuous, just so that he could get her into bed?

Daisey feels the familiar sense of dread creeping in like fog around her; like something bad has just taken place and that, worse, she's been complicit in it.

'The condom,' she says. 'You brought a condom with you… why?' He's pulling his jeans on, zipping them up. 'Bit presumptuous, wasn't it?'

She can't keep the anger from her voice, though in truth it's more like fear; fear that she's been duped, that he's managed to manipulate her again – and that she's let him. The knot in her belly squeezes even tighter.

'Oh, come on, Daisey, don't come the innocent – we both knew what was going to happen tonight, what always happens when we get together... it's not like you had to fight me off, was it?' He walks from the bedroom, down the hallway into the living room.

Indignant, she wraps the bed sheet around her and follows him, slamming the bedroom door shut behind her.

'I didn't... I wasn't planning to... I... I... just thought you were coming over for dinner to *talk*, you said you needed to see me, said you wanted to!' She wills back the rage she feels, the panic and anger and hurt and confusion all mixed together, coming to the surface in some sort of diabolical hybrid.

'I did,' he replies quickly, still struggling with his shirt buttons as he sits down on the sofa. 'I did want to see you.'

She blinks at him, waits for him to elaborate but he doesn't.

'Oh wait... hang on...' The realisation crashes down upon her like a landslide. 'You wanted to see me... you needed to see me *because you needed an ego boost*? She recognises the question as a rhetorical one, is pretty sure he does too.

He sighs heavily, rolls his eyes.

'So all that stuff you said... the regret and the "I wish we could start again, Daisey... do things differently, Daisey..." that was your idea of foreplay, was it? Bullshit just so that you could fuck me?'

He has the nerve to throw her a contemptuous look of disgust.

'Jesus, Daisey, do you have to make it sound so... so tawdry?'

He's dressed now save for his socks and she stares at his bare feet – she'd always liked his feet; they were soft and delicate for a man's, almost feminine.

'Look.' His tone drops an octave, softens slightly. Adrenalin causes her to shake beneath the bed sheet and she wraps her arms around herself tightly. 'I wanted to tell you earlier, I had planned to, but well, being back here, seeing you again, the wine, all of it…' He throws his hands up towards the ceiling. 'I think it went to my head.'

Daisey's throat feels bone dry as she attempts to swallow. Instinctively she knows she doesn't want to hear what he is about to say.

'Tell me *what*, Luke?'

He looks down at the floor, doesn't meet her eyes.

'It's Cho,' he says. His voice is definitely softer now, more in keeping with his earlier repentant tone. 'She's pregnant. She's pregnant and… and we're getting married.'

Daisey closes her eyes momentarily. The knot that she thought couldn't get any tighter squeezes harder, almost garrotting her intestines and causing her to double over. She blinks at him as he finally looks up.

'She's only a few weeks gone, eight or nine, I think… it's… it's early days.' There's a weary resignation to his voice not exactly reminiscent of a proud father-to-be. 'And the wedding, well, when she found out about the baby… when *we* found out… I thought I had to do the decent thing, Daisey, you know… she wants to do it before the baby is born, doesn't want it to be born out of wedlock – well, her family don't anyway,' he adds, unable to hide his resentment.

She stares at him, paralysed mute by the revelation and by what's just taken place between them.

'We'll have to go to court,' he says flatly. 'I don't want it to come to that but she's set her heart on this place so if you don't agree then we'll have no option.'

'Set her heart on it? How could she have set her heart on it, she's never even seen it and…' She pauses, her hand subconsciously covering her mouth as it dawns on her. 'Oh God…'

She looks at him, eyes aflame. 'She's been *here*, hasn't she? You brought her here, didn't you, while you were having the affair; you brought her *here*, to our home, to our bed!'

Suddenly, it all makes terrible sense and she picks up one of the scatter cushions, throws it at him in rage but it narrowly misses and bounces onto the floor instead.

'I'll tell her,' she sneers, defiantly. 'I'll tell her what we just did… what we did that day on the kitchen table too, when you last came over to "talk". I'll tell Detective Riley as well, tell him you lied about being here the day before I was attacked, I'll say that it came back to me, that I've just remembered.'

He looks up at her miserably, a pathetic hunched-over figure on the edge of the sofa. She despises him.

'You wouldn't, Daisey,' he says, his arrogance incongruous with his demeanour.

'Why not?' She shrugs, the bed sheet threatening to slip from underneath her armpits. She pulls it tighter around her torso. 'I'll tell her everything. She'll find out who you really are, a lying, cheating, self-serving…'

'Yeah, yeah,' he says, 'change the record, eh? It's getting really boring now, Daisey. You won't say anything to Charlotte because you still love me. You know it, and so do I. Despite everything that's happened you still love me, which is why you're standing here naked underneath that sheet, and why it hurts so much to know I'm getting married and having a baby with someone else.'

She exhales sharply in utter disbelief. For a split second she thinks about running to the kitchen and grabbing a knife from the butcher's block, plunging it into him repeatedly until there's no life left in his wretched body. She'd be doing herself – and Charlotte – a favour.

'You're a scumbag, Luke Bradley, a low life, do you know that?' She hears the snarl in her own voice, is almost startled by the malice in it, like it's come from someone else. 'Look at you! You think you're so clever, so intelligent, so *interesting* when really, like you said yourself, it's all just an act to disguise the weak, spineless, pathetic, selfish excuse of a man you really are underneath.'

He laughs a little, but she can tell her words have impacted, *like missiles on target.*

'Like I said' – he looks up at her – 'you still love me. And do you know what, Daisey? I realise now that I still love you too.'

She puts her fingers to her lips, tries to stop the tears that are stinging the backs of her eyes from coming to fruition. She doesn't want to give him the satisfaction of seeing her break down.

'Love you?' She laughs then, a hollow sound. 'Love you? *I loathe you…* everything you are and stand for… that expensive education of yours, what a waste of money that was, not a shred of decency or integrity in your body. Leave. Now. Get out,' she says, her voice flat and cold. She hopes he can hear the resolve in it, that she means it this time. 'I never want to see you ever again, Luke. Never.' She turns away from him, barely able to swallow back the rock of emotion lodged inside her oesophagus, one she seems to carry around with her wherever she goes now.

He stands, opens his mouth to speak.

'Don't say it!' She gets there before him. 'Don't you dare say you're sorry.'

He looks away, closes his mouth.

'I never wanted it to be like this, Daisey, please, if you can't believe anything else then believe that at least.'

She pulls open the door, waits next to it silently, looking past him. He pauses, hovers for a few seconds.

'If you say anything – to Cho, I mean – I'll be forced to deny it. I'll say you're making it up out of spite, revenge for the affair, or that your memory isn't right, that you haven't been right since the attack because – let's face it, Daisey – you haven't been, have you? It's like you're two different people.'

'Goodbye, Luke,' she says coldly. 'I'll see you in court.'

CHAPTER TWENTY-ONE

Daisey wipes her eyes, takes the leftover bottle of Chablis from the kitchen table and pours herself another large glass. 'Don't mix it, it's the superior stuff.' She snorts derisively as she hears his pompous voice resonate inside her head, like he's still in the room with her. The kitchen looks like a representation of her life – a complete mess. The pasta on the hob has boiled dry, burnt and stuck to the bottom of the blackened pan, which is beyond salvageable. An acrid smell fills the room and she opens a window in a bid to air it out.

Catching a glimpse of herself in the reflection of the window she is horrified by what she sees – her mascara is smudged, black tear tracks staining her cheeks. The red lipstick she'd taken time to perfect earlier is smeared over her mouth and chin, giving her an almost ghoulish appearance reminiscent of The Joker. She only wishes it were a joke though, all of it. She wipes her mouth with the back of her kimono sleeve in a bid to erase the evidence, the residue of him on her lips that she's sure she can still taste. She glugs back more wine; pulls a face. It tastes like she feels, bitter and acidic. She wishes he'd not bothered with that fancy stuff and just brought a cheap bottle of Prosecco instead; she'd have much preferred that. *Pretentious arsehole.* Now she thinks of it, she's sure she has an emergency bottle of it somewhere, hidden away for an occasion such as this – a commiseration bottle. She begins to search for it, opening cupboards randomly, pots and pans clattering noisily as they spill out onto the kitchen floor. 'Shit!'

She paces the kitchen, chewing her thumbnail and thinks about calling Ros. Ros would know what to do, what to say to make her feel better because right in this moment she isn't sure she could feel any worse. She glances out of the window, down at the street below. It's dark and miserable out, indicative of how she feels.

She spots a car parked across the street, directly opposite her apartment. She leans in closer to the window, her nose almost pressing against the glass. There's a man sitting in the driver's seat; she thinks it's a man, anyway – it's difficult to tell exactly in the dark. For the briefest second she thinks he glances up at her; sees her standing in the window, and she jumps back, flattens herself against the wall, her heart pounding in her chest. Is it him? The Rose Petal Ripper, the man she wishes now had simply killed her and put her out of this misery? Is he watching her, waiting for her? Does he know she is alone?

Fear sweeps through her like fire and she tells herself to calm down: it's probably just an Uber driver, waiting to pick someone up, or perhaps Detective Riley has sent someone to keep an eye on her, yes, maybe that's it… but she's hyperventilating now, her fear mixing with the anguish and self-loathing, a diabolical stew swirling inside her guts and making her feel nauseous. She starts to cry again, sipping wine between sobs.

Next, she hears that shuffling sound again, like someone's inside the apartment moving around and… hot fear spikes through her body like a virus and she holds her breath. Quickly she slips into the kitchen, grabs a knife from the block, grips it as she holds her breath, too terrified to move or breathe.

The door to the front room opens slowly, tentatively.

'Hello?'

'Oh Jesus Christ,' Daisey exhales loudly, relief gushing through her like a burst water pipe. 'Iris, you scared the shit out of me.'

'What you doing in the dark?' Iris switches the light on. 'Are you OK?'

Daisey blinks at her, unable to answer. Iris's hair is wet; it must be raining out. She places something down onto the kitchen table, a paper bag of some sort.

'I… I didn't hear you come in.' She shakes her head. 'I didn't hear the door go… I thought… I thought you were him…'

'Him?' Her eyes move down to the knife Daisey's holding in her hand, by her side. 'Oh, *him*… the killer, you mean? Is that why you're holding a knife?'

Daisey exhales again; she can't seem to regulate her breath; she thinks she might pass out.

'I thought I heard something… I'm sorry. I'm just a bit on edge.'

Iris takes her coat off, folds it up neatly, carefully placing it next to the paper bag on the kitchen counter.

'Jesus, are you sure you're OK? Has something happened? Where's Luke? I thought he was coming here tonight?'

'He was… he did… he's left already.'

Iris moves into the kitchen, switches the kettle on.

'I'm sensing it didn't go so well then.' She throws a couple of tea bags into two cups. Daisey joins her in the kitchen, places the knife down onto the work surface, the blade making a musical sound as it connects with the granite.

'You could say that.' She swallows back the emotion that's swelling at the base of her throat again, threatening to erupt like projectile vomit. 'He's marrying his girlfriend' – the words push themselves past it, up through her windpipe and from her lips – 'the one who he cheated on me with – and they're expecting a baby.' Her voice sounds strange, detached and monotone. It hasn't sounded the same, not since that night. 'They want the apartment, they're going to force me to sell it, take me to court.'

Iris stops then, turns to look at her.

'And the kimono,' she says, looking her up and down. 'You weren't wearing that when I left…'

No flies on Iris, Daisey thinks as her eyes drop to the floor.

'He only told me after we'd…' She can't finish the sentence; she's too awash with self-loathing, chocked by her own shame. 'He told me how sorry he was, expressed regret for everything, how he wished he could start again, that we could start all over again and…'

'And you believed him?' Iris says, though there's no real judgement in her tone. She pours the tea she's just made down the sink. 'Something stronger, I think,' she says, opening one of the bottom cupboards and pulling out a bottle of Jack Daniel's. 'I think this calls for it.'

Daisey doesn't argue but is surprised; she didn't know Iris has a secret stash – she's full of surprises, such a paradox.

'My mother always kept a bottle handy,' she explains. 'In case of emergencies.'

Two large tumblers in, and Daisey's self-loathing has dissipated into something nearing rage.

'He planned it, that sly, calculating bastard! He came here tonight with an agenda to get me into bed one last time before he ties the knot and becomes a dad. He used me, Iris, *again*! How could I have let him do that to me? Why did he let me keep believing? Tonight he said I'd changed, said it was like I was two different people. But it was him all along; he was the one who was two different people – it was all an act, the pretend Luke and the real Luke. Jekyll and fucking Hyde!'

Iris is next to her on the sofa, her feet tucked beneath her, her hair beginning to curl up at the ends as it dries. She's listening intensely, her expression grave and full of concern.

'Maybe Luke *is* two different people, Daisey,' she says. 'Maybe we all are really. Perhaps he was battling with himself internally, the good Luke versus the bad Luke – and bad Luke won in the end; he was just the stronger of the two.'

Daisey wipes her nose with the sleeve of her kimono, her face a mucus-y mess. She swallows back more JD. She wants to erase tonight, or at least rewind it to the beginning and do everything differently.

'You mustn't blame yourself,' Iris says as though reading her exact thoughts. 'He knows that you still have feelings for him – after all, most normal people can't simply switch them on and off like that, like he can – and because of this he knows how to manipulate you, how to win you over. He knows the right words to say almost instinctively, like he's programmed to; he also knows that right now you're vulnerable. He knows he represents familiarity and comfort, that he is a reminder of happier times, good times even – a time before the attack happened, a time when you felt safe.'

Daisey has stopped crying now and feels a little dunk; she is mesmerised by Iris's words.

'People like Luke,' she continues, 'they're chameleons. They'll change themselves to achieve whatever they desire in that moment. They capitalise on the emotions of others, exploit their weaknesses, use the love you have for them as a weapon against you – it's incredibly cruel – *he's* incredibly cruel.'

Daisey lets out a little gasp.

'God, Iris, it's like… well, I've never heard anyone explain it like that before and it's so… so accurate. You've summed him up better than I could ever put into words.' She looks at her with admiration. 'How come you're so knowledgeable about these things, so wise and… understanding?'

Iris gives a wan smile. 'Let's just say I've known a few people like Luke in my lifetime. My sister being one of them.'

'Your sister, ah yes, you mentioned her. But at least you got on with your brother, the kind one…'

Iris shakes her head. 'I don't have a brother, just a sister… well, she's dead now; you must've got it wrong.'

Daisey is confused. She's sure Iris mentioned a brother when they'd been talking earlier that evening while she'd helped her get ready; a brother she was close to, yes, that's what she'd said, one who had stuck up for her when they were younger, against the bullies.

'But I could've sworn…' Daisey shakes her head as though it may help rearrange her brain into working order. It's her memory; it's playing tricks on her again. She feels a little embarrassed.

'I'm sorry; I must've got it wrong. I didn't realise your sister was dead. Oh God, Iris – your mum, dad and sister, all dead…'

Iris laughs, looks at her strangely. 'No, no,' she says, 'Mum and Dad are very much alive; it's just my sister who's dead. She was eleven years old, accidentally hung herself from a tree – a terrible, tragic accident.'

Daisey's confusion has chartered new territory; she can't think straight. But Iris had told her that both her parents were dead, hadn't she? Yes, she feels sure that's what she'd said, convinced of it; they'd chatted about it, about her mother being distant and disinterested in her. Jesus, her memory must be even worse than she thought – now she's imagining conversations that never took place. She's lost the bloody plot.

'I'm sorry,' Daisey says. 'I got confused, I thought… well, anyway… that's awful, about your sister…'

A faint smile passes across Iris's lips. 'It was a long time ago now… anyway, Luke,' she says, bringing the conversation full circle. 'What are you going to do?'

Daisey's sadness quickly switches back to anger at the mention of his name. 'I'm going to grass that bastard up to Dan Riley – that detective, remember, the one who came here earlier tonight, the one who's working on my case? I'm going to tell him everything.'

'Everything? What do you mean, everything?'

'He lied to the police, Luke I mean, about the last time he saw me. He was here, you see, the day before the attack. We had sex on the kitchen table.' She spits the words out like poison. 'The police found DNA; it was his. It was his semen they found.'

Iris's eyes widen; she actually looks pleased, Daisey thinks.

'God really, but how can you be sure it was his and not the killer's?'

'Because the killer's MO isn't sexual, apparently, or so Dan Riley says. He didn't rape his other victims and there was no evidence to suggest assault, plus the DNA sample didn't match the other samples found at the crime scenes.'

'Why didn't you tell the police about this initially? This is vital information, Daisey.'

She looks away, a little shamefaced. 'I know I know…' She buries her head in her hands. It was all such a mess. 'Luke asked me not to say anything about the encounter to the police so that bloody Cho didn't find out and dump his rotten cheating arse. And like the fool I am, I agreed.'

'Jesus, he really does have a hold on you, doesn't he?' She refreshes their glasses – they've almost finished the bottle. 'Well, if you want my opinion, for what it's worth, I think you should get on the phone to that detective right now and tell him what you've told me. Say that you only just remembered, it's feasible after all, what with your amnesia.' Iris pauses tentatively. 'You still have amnesia, don't you?'

Daisey nods. 'Yes… but it's coming back, Iris, my memory of that night, slowly, bit by bit… I keep having these strange flashbacks, all broken up and fragmented…'

'And what do you remember?' She's sitting forward in her seat now, engrossed.

Daisey shakes her head, lights a cigarette and blows the smoke noisily from her lips.

'Not much, not in the way of detail anyway… I was standing in the kitchen with Tommy, the doorbell rings and… well, I remember being hit on the head, the pain and the sound, a sickening crack… oh God, it's horrible…' Instinctively her hand goes to her head and she rubs it. 'He was on top of me, on the bed, the blade, the glint of the blade…'

'Can you see his face? Do you remember anything else about him?' Iris is transfixed upon her every word, her eyes wide and glistening in the low light of the room.

'No. It's like a mask, a smooth mask with no features.' She shudders. 'I can't visualise him in my mind, though something tells me—'

'Tells you what?'

'Something tells me that I know him. That whoever he is I know him somehow, that I've seen him before, met him before. That night of the party, there was this guy standing outside. I was smoking a cigarette, he gave me a light and there was something…' She screws her eyes tightly shut, strains to recall. 'I don't know what it was exactly, just something odd about him physically but it's buried… it's buried inside my head and I can't seem to reach it… but I think it was *him*… I think he was the man who tried to kill me.'

Iris takes hold of her hand between the sleeves of her oversized hoodie.

'It will come to you,' she reassures her. 'And when it does I will be right here.'

Daisey smiles at her gratefully as Iris shuffles closer on the sofa, cuddles up next to her. Her head feels woozy thanks to the combination of wine and Jack Daniel's and she drops her head onto Iris's shoulder.

'Thank you,' she says, wiping away the residue of her tears from the outer corners of her eyes. Iris begins to stroke Daisey's hair.

'Everything is such a mess,' she says, breaking down, giving in and allowing more tears to come. 'I'm terrified he'll come back for me, Iris…'

'Who, Luke?'

'No… the killer… I'm frightened. I think that maybe he's watching me… stalking me… and I've lied to the police, maybe hindered the whole investigation because of that bastard Luke. And now maybe the killer will get away because of me and…'

'Shhh… stop that… stop punishing yourself; none of this is your fault. You did what you did for the best reason there is.' Iris's voice is soft and soothing and coupled with her stroking her hair, Daisey begins to feel a little sleepy.

'And what's that?'

'Love,' Iris says. 'You did it for love.'

Daisey looks up at her. 'Thank you for being here; I don't know what I'd do without you right now.'

Iris looks genuinely touched as she stares closely into Daisey's watery eyes, their faces only inches apart.

'It's OK,' she says, 'we have each other… we'll always have each other.' Iris kisses the top of her forehead and then pauses, draws back and brings her lips down onto Daisey's.

Confused, Daisey pulls away from her and abruptly sits up.

'Sorry… I… I…' she stammers, unsure of what's just happened. Did Iris just try to kiss her? 'I think I'm a little drunk.'

Iris smiles.

'It's late,' she says. 'You should go to bed, get some sleep. Things won't seem so bad in the morning.'

'You're right,' Daisey replies, rapidly sobering up. 'Goodnight,' she says, shuffling out of the living room, feeling utterly wretched.

'Goodnight, Daisey, and don't worry about Luke,' she calls out to her. 'He'll get what's coming to him, mark my words.'

CHAPTER TWENTY-TWO

On first sight, Miriam Jones strikes me as the type of lady who was born to work in Human Resources. She's short and stocky with steely grey eyes and looks like she could withstand a nuclear holocaust. Formidable is the word that springs to mind. I'm surprised, then, by how soft her speaking voice is, gentle and musical, almost like a lullaby. I'm reminded of Pip then, of the lullabies I sing to her in a – futile of late, anyway – attempt to get her off to the land of nod, but to be fair to her I've not got much of a singing voice. 'Don't give up the day job, Danny boy!' That's what my father says to me any time he hears me break into song.

Fiona messaged me as soon as the three of them had touched down in Korea, letting me know they were safe and well and that Juno had practically slept through the entire journey. As well as relief, I'd felt proud somehow, as though my little Pip had instinctively known what an important journey she was making and not to play up. I'm trying not to think about the days and nights I will be without her – without them all – and of all the tuneless lullabies I'll miss singing to her.

'I've compiled the list of employees and former employees, Detective Riley, just as your colleague requested,' Miriam Jones announces efficiently, pushing her glasses further up her nose and handing me a file. 'I've sent you a virtual copy too, to your email. It was surprisingly longer than I'd anticipated, but then again, I have gone back some years. They're all in there though, every Poppy, Rosie, Marigold, Ivy, Bryony, Clover, Fleur, Heather, Holly, Hyacinth, Saffron, Lily, Olive… the list is endless, oh, and of course,' she adds solemnly, 'Jasmine, Fern and Daisey. There were a few surprises in there too, for example I had no idea that the name Margaret derives from an exotic flower and that—'

'Thank you, Miriam,' I interject, 'this will be very helpful.'

'Well,' she says, smoothing her dress down – incidentally floral – with short stubby fingers. 'I do hope so; it took quite a while to compile, you know. I've marked all the current serving employees with a red dot. I went as far back as 2016, like you said, and I included as many as I could, even derivatives of particular names, just to be thorough. Took me an absolute age it did and—'

'You've done a great job.' I smile at her. 'Thank you again.' I begin to flick through the file.

She nods, seemingly satisfied that I've shown enough gratitude.

'So,' she says, her grey eyes twinkling slightly, 'do you think he's got his sights set on someone on that list? Can you believe, a few of the younger ones in the office even have a sweepstake on it, on what his next victim will be called, unless you catch him first, of course, which I'm sure you will.' She laughs a little nervously, realising what she's just said and who she's said it to. 'Obviously I find such a thing highly distasteful,' she quickly backtracks. 'But you know what the youth of today are like – no integrity, any of them. Good job there's not a war on, else we'd all be—'

'A sweepstake, really?' I interject, unable to keep the shock from my tone. 'So, who's the front-runner then?'

Miriam looks deeply embarrassed. 'I… I shouldn't have said anything…'

'No, really, I want to see it, this sweepstake.' I'm careful to keep the anger I feel at bay. It's not Miriam's fault that people can be so insensitive.

She hands me a sheet of paper sheepishly.

'I can assure you I had no part in this, found it terribly disrespectful to those poor women he killed. I mean, these things shouldn't be taken lightly and…'

I read it. The name Lily is at 3-1 with Poppy a close second at 5-1.

'Well, well,' I say, 'now there's a first. I've never heard of a serial killer sweepstake before.'

Jesus, the public has clearly lost all faith in the police, so convinced of him striking again that they're actually putting money on it.

'Such a chilling thought,' she continues, 'that the next victim could be on that list. I mean, my own middle name is Iris.' A look of concern suddenly flashes across her face. 'God, you don't think he'll go as far as including middle names, do you?'

Iris! That reminds me, I need to speak to Daisey's flatmate, make her aware of the name connection, although no doubt the press has already done that for me. It was splashed all over the headlines this morning with alacrity: *The Rose Petal Ripper and His Fetish For Flowers; RPR and His Bouquet of Bodies*. I don't want to terrify the poor woman but given that Iris could indeed be a potential candidate for our killer, forewarned may be forearmed. Besides, I'm still not entirely convinced that he won't try to come back for Daisey. They say lightning doesn't strike twice but I know that's not true. The church near the house I grew up in was hit three times when I was a child and eventually burned to the ground.

'What? Erm, no, no I don't think so, Miriam,' I reassure her. 'We can't even be sure that it will be anyone on this list at all – it's simply precautionary; there's no need to be alarmed.'

She glances at me, not entirely convinced.

'Well, we've sent an email out to all staff, warning them to be on their guard and to try and travel to and from work in pairs, just in case. It's awful, just dreadful to think that the killer might be targeting our girls. I mean, it can't be coincidence, can it, that two of his victims worked here?'

I shrug gently, not wanting to commit to a definitive answer. 'I can't say for sure at this stage, Miriam.'

'There's rumours going around that he works here, or did at one point, and that he stalks them, follows them home from work and then...' She visibly shudders. 'Everyone's paranoid, looking at their colleagues suspiciously, thinking, could it be *him*, is *he* the Rose Petal Ripper? I mean, that poor man who works in Sportswear,' she continues, unable to stop herself, 'the one who was with Daisey the night of the attack... Tom something or other... White, that's right, Tommy White, he's suffered greatly ever since, people gossiping and pointing the finger, you know how it is. Mud sticks, doesn't it, Detective? No smoke without fire and all of that... don't supposed it helped him having a bit of reputation with the ladies either and—'

'Well,' I assure her once again, 'Mr White was been exonerated completely, so rest assured he is not the man we're looking for. He has a watertight alibi and his DNA sample ruled him out as a suspect early on.'

'Well, that's a relief, for him anyway; well, for all of us I suppose because—'

'Tell me, Miriam,' I cut in, 'you recently took on a new employee; someone called Iris. I think she works in the Beauty department.'

'Well, we take on a lot of new staff every day, Detective, especially at this time of year in the run-up to Christmas and—'

I clear my throat. 'If you wouldn't mind taking a look for me.'

'Yes, yes, of course. Any surname?' She clicks on her PC.

''Fraid not.'

'Age?'

'Couldn't say exactly, early thirties, at a guess. She's Daisey Garrett's new flatmate.'

'Doesn't ring any bells.' Miriam is tapping something into her computer. 'How long ago did she start working at Warwick's?'

'Again, I couldn't tell you,' I say apologetically. 'A few weeks… I can't be specific.'

She taps some more on her computer, pushes her face closer to the screen.

'Ah yes,' she says after a short time. 'Iris Egan, in the Perfume department.'

'Any address?'

'Hmm, let me look… I thought you said she shares a place with Daisey Garrett?'

'She does,' I reply, without elaborating on why I'm asking; truth is, I'm not sure why I am asking.

'Well, it says here she's listed her address as a Cliveden Road… East Sussex, probably where she was living before she came to London.'

'No doubt – can you email the address to me?'

'Yes, of course, Detective, I'd be very happy to.'

'Right, well, thanks and thanks again for compiling this.' I wave the file at her.

'Glad to be of assistance, you know.' She adds thoughtfully, 'Perhaps you should speak to Des.'

'Des?'

'Yes, the store maintenance man; he's retired now, just recently in fact. Poor thing has the onset of dementia, but I think he might be a good person to speak to. Des has worked here almost since the beginning – what he doesn't know about the comings and goings here isn't worth knowing; he's seen more people through those doors than you and I could shake a stick at, although personally I've never really understood what that saying quite means exactly, anyway.' She's waffling a little, something I'm fairly confident is one of Miriam's baseline traits. 'He's your man for who's who and what's what around here – or he was anyway, up until a few weeks ago before he left. Lovely send-off it was,' she reminisces wistfully. 'There were a lot of tears, I tell you, shed a few myself to be honest and… anyway, like I said, he's your man for gossip, not that I'm one for that, obviously.' She looks away, blushes slightly.

'Obviously,' I indulge her. 'And how would I get hold of Des? Do you have a contact number, an address?'

Miriam shuffles around her desk. 'Yes, let me get it for you, hang on…'

My phone rings – it's Davis – and I hold my hand up by way of an apology.

'Excuse me, Miriam – Davis,' I say, answering.

I've come to know Davis extremely well these past few years; perhaps better than anyone else I've ever worked closely with in all my time on the force. It's much the same as a romance, but without the, well, romantic side. As such I have become familiar with all her little nuances; her body language and gestures that communicate silent exchanges between us, that give clues as to what she's thinking. And so the way she draws the tiniest breath before speaking instantly tells me that what she's about to say is not going to be good.

'There's been another one, hasn't there?' I say rhetorically, before she can say anything, my sphincter muscle loosening as my stomach drops.

Miriam is edging a little closer to me, no doubt having noted the look on my face.

Davis sighs.

'Where?' I ask.

'Shortland's Parade, gov, above Yanis's Newsagent's. Sounds like our man. Uniform are down there now. SOCO are on their way.' Her voice sounds heavy, weary.

'Shortland's Parade, that's only round the corner from Daisey Garrett's apartment, isn't it?'

'Less than a mile, boss.'

'Any ID on the victim yet?' Instinctively I hold my breath, and rightly or wrongly I play a mental guessing game as to which flower our newest victim is named after, Poppy, Lily, Fleur…

'Leilani,' Davis says, 'her name's Leilani Stewart.'

'I'm on my way, Davis,' I say. 'I'll meet you there.'

Miriam steps back a little as I end the call, pretends she's not been listening and busies herself at her desk.

'Everything OK, Detective Riley?' she casually enquires.

I nod, manage a half-smile that I know belies my demeanour. She watches me intensely as I look down at the names on the sweepstake. Leilani is on there, a rogue outsider at 20–1.

CHAPTER TWENTY-THREE

The traffic is thick through the West End, forcing me to put the siren on and curse a lot as I will people to pull over and give me a clear path.

I'm hyperventilating by the time I pull up sharply outside Shortland's Parade some thirty minutes later. I'm also dismayed by the amount of press that has already congregated outside, like a swarm of locusts spilling out onto the pavement and scuttling around, directionless, searching for scraps. I've always had a love/hate relationship with the press – Fiona excluded, of course – on occasion they can be an extremely useful tool in your arsenal; a vital source of information, helping to raise public awareness, giving victims and their families a much-needed platform, a way to reach people quickly and effectively. On the other they can be a hindrance, a nuisance and sometimes even downright obstructive.

'Get this lot out of here,' I bark at a random uniform. 'Tell them to get back. *Everybody* get back. Seal the whole place off. This is a crime scene not a bloody circus.' I hear the sounds of cameras snapping and popping like fireworks around me as they scramble to get access.

'Has he struck again, Detective? Is this the work of the Rose Petal Ripper?' a voice cuts through the commotion.

'Why haven't you caught him yet, Detective?' says another. 'Do you think he's working alone or does he have an accomplice?'

'What have you got to say to the public, Detective? Women are terrified to leave their homes…'

I ignore them as I try to navigate my way towards the door and am relieved to see Davis's familiar form jostling through the clock of bodies towards me. She nods at me and I pat her shoulder in solidarity as uniform push back the hacks. Davis leads me up the narrow stairs of the apartment block, muffling the din as she closes the door behind us. While we both suspected this moment was coming, it still does nothing to dampen the sense of shock, of horror. Neither of us speaks as we dress in PPE – our silence does all the talking.

I'm hit by the – sadly familiar – scent of death as we get closer to the front door of Leilani Stewart's flat, a scent that is somehow different every time I've encountered it, yet also instantly identifiable. A scent that lingers longer in your psyche than some love affairs do, a unique smell you never forget. Both Davis and I look at each other in a silent exchange and brace ourselves for what we know is behind that door. I'm guessing, by the pungency of the smell, that Leilani has been dead for more than a few hours.

A warm, putrid wave smacks me like an uppercut as we enter the bedroom and both Davis and I instinctively recoil. Thankfully I haven't eaten breakfast this morning otherwise I suspect it might make an abrupt reappearance. I can't speak for Davis. I can't speak at all.

'Who found her?' I eventually ask the uniform standing guard in the doorway, my voice muffled by my protective mask.

'The owners of the shop below, sir, Mr Yanis and his wife,' he says through pursed lips. I suspect he's trying not to breathe. 'They noticed the… smell, sir. Some of their customers did too. So they tried knocking…'

'I see. And what can you tell me about her?'

He checks his notes. 'She worked at the bakery round the corner. Aled's Artisan Bakery.' I can see his eyes are watering and he wipes them quickly. 'No one reported her missing but her employer did try and contact her, sir, when she didn't turn up for work – says she was always very reliable.'

I get a horrible sense of déjà vu as my eyes drink in the scene. There's no sign of a break-in and the apartment looks untouched. It's a small space – not much bigger than a studio, but is neat and tidy, nothing immediately out of place. She's naked on the bed, a futon, sofa-bed-type thing that sits low to the ground; Japanese, I think – they were quite trendy in the 90s, if I remember. Her body has been positioned just like the others, naked and vertical, her arms folded across her chest. I note the neat pile of clothes next to her on the floor, her trainers positioned alongside them. The bed is so heavily blood-stained that it's almost black. There's noticeably more blood than there was with Daisey, but I guess that's only to be expected because this time there's no ambiguity as to whether or not she's alive. Aside from the putrid smell, the poor woman's head has almost been severed entirely from her body, the deep cut across her neck exposing congealing tissue and bone and ugly yellow bubbles of subcutaneous fat.

'Jesus Christ,' I say aloud.

I see Davis bury her head in her hands momentarily as she absorbs the gruesome scene alongside me. The rose on the victim's chest has been placed between her fingers. I suspect it was once pink but soaked in blood it has now taken on a strange purple hue. I look down at her face. Even in the condition she's in – her skin is mottled and waxy-looking, bluish green in parts and her lips are a pale white – I can see she's young, possibly even younger than the others. Her eyes have sunk back into her skull but thankfully they're closed. I wonder if she closed them herself during the attack, or if he had shut them for her after he'd finished. Either way I cannot imagine the horror they must've witnessed in those final moments.

Suddenly, I'm gripped by a macabre urge to gently pull back her eyelids and look into them. I've read somewhere that a dying person's eyes record their last moments much like a camera does, capturing the images of those final few seconds. There's absolutely no physical evidence to support this but something compels me to want to do it in the very slim chance that there may be something in it.

I clench my fists in desperation and dread, overcome by a mix of anger and frustration, of sadness and disgust. But my overriding feeling is one of guilt – guilt that I didn't save Leilani Stewart, and that I allowed her to become this monster's next victim – and right under my nose as well. On my patch, less than a mile from his last attempt. My guilt soon manifests itself into white-hot rage and I take a few deep breaths from behind my sleeve, trying not to take in the foul and fetid air. Somehow, it feels like I'm breathing part of her in.

'Vic Leyton's arrived,' Davis tells me gently, as if she knows I'm on the brink. It's a relief just to hear her name.

'Detective Riley,' Vic greets me with a friendly smile as she walks through the door, though it's not a happy one – and I note the subtle difference. 'We meet again,' she says, 'and regrettably so soon.'

'Don't you start, Vic,' I say, 'the press is baying for my blood as it is.'

'Understandably,' she replies in that matter-of-fact way of hers, adding, 'though also unfairly.' She looks over at the body on the bed and I see a fleeting flicker of sadness in her eyes, which is not something I usually detect from the staunchly professional and emotionally detached Ms Leyton – I guess this case has got to everyone.

'Well, it's certainly looking like our man's handiwork at first glance,' she surmises. 'Though he seems to have made more of a mess of this one.'

I know the feeling, I think miserably to myself.

'Her name's Leilani Stewart, twenty-six, works in the local bakery round the corner.' I turn to Davis: 'Get uniform down there ASAP. Interview the owners, co-workers, neighbours, members of the public… find out as much as you can about her, how long she worked there, if anyone has been harassing her, stalking her, if she was concerned about anything, anyone, and get hold of any CCTV there is from both the bakery and downstairs – anything on the parade. With a bit of luck this time he'll be caught on camera – his luck has to run out sometime, doesn't it?' I say this aloud, though it's predominantly to myself. 'He's not the invisible fucking man!'

Vic looks up at me sharply, presumably surprised by my use of bad language, though I can tell by her expression that she's more concerned than she is offended. I don't usually swear in the company of women – I'm old-fashioned like that, I suppose – but I'm really struggling to hold it together.

We both move closer to the body as Vic begins her initial assessment, the sound of the forensic cameras popping in the background.

'He's left the weapon this time,' I state, nodding towards the kitchen knife that has been placed – seemingly deliberately – on the small bedside table next to the body. 'Hasn't bothered trying to hide it.'

'Yes… I can see he's becoming progressively brazen… and,' Vic notes as she inspects the body, 'more violent. The wound looks considerably deeper than any of his previous. The head is practically severed from the torso.'

I watch as Forensic bag up the blood-stained weapon and silently pray to a god I don't believe in that his dabs will be on them. Maybe he's become as sloppy as he has brazen – the two often go hand in hand. One can only hope.

'There's blunt trauma wound to the back of the skull as I expected,' Vic says as she gently manipulates the body with gloved fingers. I'm almost touched by her lightness of hand. I think it's as much out of respect as it is to preserve evidence.

'He hit her first, just like the others, possibly with a hammer, something blunt. But judging by the size of the wound, and the lack of bleeding, I wouldn't necessarily say it would've been enough to render her unconscious, incapacitated perhaps, stunned, but not unconscious.'

'So she was compos mentis when he killed her?' The thought turns my blood icy.

Vic sighs. 'Difficult to say until I get her on the slab, but possibly, and regrettably yes. I can't quite tell due to the depth of the wound on her neck if she was strangled beforehand like the others were; I don't detect any obvious contusions at this point.'

'Well, if he went straight in, cutting her throat, surely she would've screamed out, someone would've heard a commotion?'

'Looks like there's a few superficial wounds to the hands and forearms though – defence wounds.' She turns to look at me slowly. 'I think she may have put up a bit of a fight.'

I shake my head, my stomach lurching violently. Despite the gruesome nature of his previous crimes, there was at least some small solace gleaned from the fact that he's – thus far anyway – spared his victims any unnecessary suffering by knocking them unconscious before he gets to work on their throat. Now, if Vic's observations are correct, which I've no doubt they are, then it appears he's not been quite as 'considerate' with Leilani which means he's upping the ante, escalating the violence and the savagery – *he's becoming more dangerous.*

'What about time of death? How long has she been like this?'

'Hmm,' Vic prevaricates. 'I'll need to do a temperature reading to be more specific, Detective – as you well know by now, or at least should do.' She glances sideways at me and for a moment I think she might be about to go into one of her well-meaning lectures in a bid to educate me, but she refrains. As well as being adept at reading dead bodies, I suspect she's well-versed at reading living ones too.

'She's still got a touch of autolysis though is beginning to soften, which would indicate she's about to go into the next stage, the bloating phase to put it simply for you, Detective.'

I nod at her gratefully. 'She's emptied her bladder and bowels and judging by the consistency – it's started to dry – I would surmise that she's been here for over twenty-four hours. The central heating will have helped speed up the decomposition process though, which is why the smell was detected.'

Instinctively I reach for the radiator behind me. It's hot to touch.

'Someone turn it off,' I say, trying not to think about poor Leilani emptying the contents of her bowels all over herself, not that she'd have known, of course, but it's just the thought of the whole indignity of it. My mouth begins to water as the nausea rises up through my own intestines. 'So, where would you put TOD, roughly, I mean?'

I'm well aware that my favourite pathologist prides herself on precision and doesn't like to guess at something as vital as this, but I need something I can work with, and fast.

'Well, without a proper autopsy, as you know I can't be exact, but my professional guess is that she died somewhere between the hours of 8 p.m. and midnight on Tuesday evening – roughly a day and a half ago.'

'Thanks, Vic,' I say and she nods at me, smiles.

'Always a pleasure, Detective Riley.'

I only wish it was. 'How's that wee girl of yours coming on? Juno isn't it?'

'She's wonderful, thanks for asking. Although…' I think to explain to her that she's all the way in Korea with her mother visiting her dying granny and that she's teething madly and that I miss her terribly and… but I can't indulge myself; I have to focus on the matter at hand.

'Well, fatherhood seems to suit you anyway,' she observes. 'Has softened your features a bit.'

'Really?'

'Yes,' she says, looking at me thoughtfully. 'Oh, and by the way,' she adds, as though she's just had an afterthought, 'I think, though again, I can't be certain until I get her on the table, that she might have been sexually assaulted.'

'What? Why? What makes you think that?'

'Semen,' she says. 'There's traces of what looks like semen on her inner thighs. It's dried, of course, but I'll know more once we've got her down to the lab for the autopsy. I should have something more conclusive for you by the morning.'

It's odd to say it, to even think it, but this is good news. Semen is DNA and DNA makes identifying a suspect much easier. Semen is a good thing.

Davis re-enters the room, nods at Vic by way of acknowledgement. She has an energy that suggests she has something to tell me.

'Do you want the good news or the good news?' she asks me, her eyebrows raised.

'There's good news?' I reply, heavy with sarcasm. 'Hit me with it, Davis,' I say, 'God knows it's about time.'

'Well, there's CCTV footage from both the bakery and from the newsagent's downstairs. The camera is positioned above the door to the side and covers the entrance to Leilani's flat so there's every chance our man will have been caught on camera.'

'Great,' I reply, 'get the team onto it right away. And the other good news?'

'Daisey Garrett called the station, gov. She's been trying to reach you apparently.'

'Is she OK?' I feel a sudden sense of fear rush through me like a cold wind.

'She says she has something to tell you – something important.'

CHAPTER TWENTY-FOUR

'They arrived this morning, around 8.30.' She glances at the bouquet of roses on the kitchen table, then looks away again quickly. 'I was getting ready for work when the doorbell went.'

'And the man who delivered them?'

'A courier, I think. Had a motorcycle helmet with him. Just handed them to me and asked me to sign for them.'

I nod. 'You didn't recognise him?'

She shakes her head. 'No, never seen him before.'

'Any note with them, a card?'

She hands it to me with shaking fingers. She looks terrible; her face is pale and drawn, her hair scraped up into a messy bun on top of her head, a total contrast to when I last saw her.

'*Silence is Golden*,' I read it aloud.

'It's a message, isn't it? A threat,' she says, her voice gravelly and unsteady. 'He's stalking me, he's going to come for me, I know it… why else would he send these? He's telling me to keep quiet, in case I remember something.' She audibly swallows, wraps her kimono around her almost in protection. I can feel the terror coming off her in waves.

'Riviera Florist's… on the high street…' I hand Davis the card. 'Call them, see if there's a trace on the credit card used…'

'Boss,' Davis says enthusiastically. I can tell she's excited – this might be the break we've been looking for, only my intuition stops me from sharing her exuberance entirely. Surely our killer wouldn't make such a basic, potentially traceable mistake as this? Davis leaves the room.

'I saw a man,' Daisey says once she's gone, 'the night you came to visit me. He was parked outside the apartment, across the street, just over there,' she points. 'I looked out of the window and he saw me, looked up at me. It could've been him, couldn't it? Watching me... waiting for me...'

'What time was this?'

She shakes her head. 'Sometime around 11.30... Iris will know exactly, she'd only just got home and found me hiding in the dark holding a knife. I was terrified.'

'And this man, did you get a description of him, of the car? Make, model, number plate?'

She shakes her head again, wraps her arms tightly around herself.

'Where is Iris, by the way?'

'She's gone to the supermarket for a few bits. She took the day off to be with me. I didn't want to be alone.'

'Of course.' I touch her forearm. 'You're not alone, Daisey. You're safe, OK; I'll make sure you're safe.'

She manages a thin smile but it does nothing to ameliorate the fear in her eyes.

'I heard something... someone... that same night... it sounded like someone was here, in the apartment. I thought I was imagining it, just being paranoid, you know, but now this...'

'And did you check? Did you check the apartment when you heard these... noises?'

'Yes, well, I didn't, Luke did...' She lowers her eyes. 'He was here that night. He was my dinner guest...' Her voice trails off momentarily. 'I thought I was just being paranoid because no one can get into the apartment; it's not possible without a key. But I swore I heard someone creeping around.'

'And it was just you and Luke that were here – alone?'

She nods tearfully. 'Iris was out. I'd asked her to… you know, make herself scarce for a few hours. Luke wanted to come over, *to talk*…' She hisses the last part, pauses again, rubs her temples with her fingers. 'I think I'm losing my mind, Detective Riley. Hearing things, seeing things… I'm confused all the time, I keep misplacing everything, thinking I've had conversations that I haven't… I'm… I'm…' She turns away from me, visibly upset and reaches for the cigarette packet on the table.

'What things, Daisey? What things have you heard and seen?'

She stares out of the window, eyes glazed as though she's slipped into some kind of a trance. '*Underneath the lilac tree, just you and me, just us three*…'

She's singing something and I move in closer in a bid to hear her. 'What's that, a song?'

'I don't know,' she says, 'yes, like… like a nursery rhyme maybe… he sang it to me.'

My senses sharpen up a notch. 'Your attacker?'

She nods. 'He was singing it to me… and… and he called me by another name… Rosie… yes, I think he called me Rosie instead of Daisey.'

I can feel my heartbeat galloping inside my chest cavity. *Rosie?*

'And that's all you can remember… there's nothing else? His face, what he looked like… anything at all?'

She shakes her head again, more vehemently.

'The night of the attack… at the party… a man… I was standing outside and he gave me a light for my cigarette. I think he may have worked at Warwick's.'

'Did you notice what he was wearing; a watch, a tattoo, any small detail?'

'That's just it, Detective Riley… There *was* something strange about him… something I noticed, but I can't remember what it was… I keep trying but…' She shakes her head, drops it back onto her shoulders in frustration. 'It's weird but I feel like I knew him, or know him somehow… I think he may have been my attacker.'

I squeeze her arm. 'That's brilliant, Daisey, you're doing so well,' I say. 'Listen, how would you feel about undertaking some hypnotherapy?'

'Hypnotherapy?'

'Yes… there's this forensic psychologist, her name's Annabelle Henderson, she's extremely well qualified, highly professional – the best in her field. She thinks she might be able to help you, help release some of the memory blocks from that night.'

She looks fearful. Almost takes a step back from me.

'Put me to sleep, you mean?'

'No… no… just…' I don't quite know how the procedure even works myself. 'Look, I know you're scared, Daisey, but please, just think about it, yes? Dr Henderson thinks it could really help you with the healing process, says it has helped many people in a similar position to you and… of course,' I add, not wanting to sound disingenuous, 'it could possibly help us too.'

Her eyes drop into her lap.

'There's something I need to tell you,' she interrupts me, lighting a cigarette with unsteady hands.

'OK.' Her tone of voice concerns me. 'Shall we sit down?' I have a horrible feeling I may need to.

She nods, scrapes back a chair and I let her take a moment or two to gather herself.

'The DNA you found on me after the attack… the traces of… semen.' I nod. 'Well, it belongs to Luke.'

I inwardly sigh. I can't say it's come as a shock.

'I see. You're sure?'

She nods, her leg furiously tapping against the floor.

'The morning before the attack, he was here and we… we ended up in bed together.'

'And you just remembered this?'

She doesn't look up at me, doesn't commit to an answer.

'He didn't want his girlfriend to find out which is why he lied about when he'd last seen me.'

'And that's why he refused to give us a DNA sample?' It all makes sense now. 'Thank you for telling me, Daisey.' I lightly touch her forearm again. I know that none of this can be easy for her. 'We'll need to request another sample from Luke, match it to the one we found on you, just to be sure, just to eliminate him.'

She nods again, blows smoke forcibly from her lips.

'And when he came here the other night...' Her eyes drop back down to her lap. 'Well, again we ended up... we ended up...' She doesn't finish the sentence, doesn't need to. I get the picture.

'It's OK,' I say gently. 'It's OK.'

She starts to cry then. Rubs her temples with a thumb and forefinger.

'He's having a baby... his girlfriend is pregnant and they're getting married.' She looks up at me with a tear-stained faced. 'Maybe you could, when you go to see him, I mean, I don't know, be discreet?' She pauses again, adding, 'I didn't know, you know. I didn't know she was pregnant until the other night; he didn't tell me until after we'd...' She closes her eyes, shakes her head as though she's trying to shake off the memory. 'That's what he'd come over to tell me, why he was here.'

She looks so vulnerable and fragile that I have to resist the compunction to take her in my arms and hug her.

'I'm sorry, Daisey' is the best I can manage. The fact that she doesn't want me thinking badly of her, judging her – and I don't, quite the reverse in fact – confirms what sort of a person she is. That she has even asked me to be discreet tells me that even after all the betrayal and heartbreak and horror she's suffered, she doesn't wish harm on anyone else. We're silent for a moment.

'Has it hindered the case…' she asks, 'withholding about Luke's DNA, I mean?' She chews her bottom lip, looks at me through watery eyes.

The doorbell rings before I can answer and it startles us both, shattering the moment.

'I'll get it.'

It's Ros, Daisey's friend, the one she works with; the lady who found her that fateful morning.

'I came to check you were OK,' Ros says, hurrying over to her, acknowledging me with a brief smile. 'They said you'd called in sick and I've been trying to reach you all morning.' She gives her the hug I had wanted to moments earlier and I'm glad I refrained now as it undoes Daisey completely and she starts to sob. 'What's happened, my darling? Oh God.' She casts me a look of concern over Daisey's shoulder as she comforts her.

'Someone sent me these this morning,' she says, pointing to the bouquet on the table, 'roses… with a note warning me to keep quiet.'

Ros turns to look at me, eyes wide.

'God, they're not from… you don't think they're from *him* do you, Detective?'

'We're looking into it,' I say, glad that Ros has arrived. Daisey's going to need all the support she can get once I've told her what I'm about to. 'Look, I'm sure it's being reported as we speak – but I'd rather you hear it from me than on the news.' I draw breath. 'I'm afraid there's been another murder.'

I see a curtain of horror fall across their faces simultaneously.

'Oh God, no…' Daisey's head drops into her hands. 'And it's him, you think it's him?'

I nod. 'Yes,' I say, 'regrettably I do.'

Ros gasps. 'Oh Jesus, no! Not another one.'

'It wasn't far from this place, Daisey,' I say gravely, 'Shortland's Parade. Do you know someone by the name of Leilani Stewart?'

She thinks for a moment. 'No... no I don't think so. Who is she... who was she?'

She shakes her head, tears streaming down her cheeks. She doesn't bother wiping them away this time.

'She worked at the bakery on the high street, Aled's Artisan Bakery, do you know it?'

She takes a sharp intake of breath. 'Oh God... yes, yes, I do... hang on... not the girl behind the counter... the young girl! Oh no, don't say it's her! We buy bread from her. Iris gets it every day practically... look, we have some on the kitchen counter, still in the paper bag! Oh Jesus Christ, no!'

'Yes,' I say, 'she was twenty-six.' I think about Leilani's parents then. Harding and Baylis have been tasked with telling them the unthinkable news that their daughter is dead, brutally murdered in the most unspeakable way, her head almost severed from her body. I can almost hear their anguished screams in real time, high-pitched and piercing; I can feel the horror, tangible as it cuts through them like an axe, the disbelief, the raw pain and grief. I know these feelings, I understand them; I have experienced them myself when Rachel died, but however hard I try I simply cannot imagine if it was my own daughter, my own child – my Pip. I clench my fists tightly, try to banish their howls of anguish that are amplified inside my head. *You should have stopped him, Dan. You could have stopped him.*

I swallow back my own emotions; take a moment before I speak.

'I think, given the proximity of the latest victim and now with the flowers, that you shouldn't stay here, Daisey, in your apartment, just to be on the safe side. I think both you and Iris should stay somewhere else.'

As if on cue, Iris breezes into the living room, Davis following close behind her.

'What's happened?' she asks, clocking the expressions in the room. 'Why are the police here?'

'He's struck again,' Daisey says. 'He's bloody well killed the girl from the bakery. You know, the nice one we get the bread from… he's killed her!'

Iris places the shopping bags onto the kitchen table with an audible clatter as a tin escapes and rolls across the wooden surface.

'What? No… Nooooo! But… I only saw her the day before yesterday!' She grabs onto the back of a chair, seemingly in shock. 'Oh my God, that's *awful*. And it's definitely him? The same man who tried to kill Daisey?' Our eyes meet.

'It would seem so, yes.' My interest had piqued. 'You said you saw her just the other day, when was that, Iris?'

'I went in for a loaf of the bread we like. Day before yesterday I think… yes… Tuesday.'

'What time was that?'

She shrugs. 'I couldn't say exactly, maybe around 7.30 p.m., not long after I left here. I went to the cinema afterwards.'

'Alone?'

'Yes.' Iris looks over at Daisey. 'Daisey… Daisey had a guest over…'

'And what time did you get home?'

She shrugs again. 'I guess it was around 11.30, midnight, something like that.'

I nod; smile. 'What did you see?'

Iris begins to unpack the shopping, removing items from the carrier bags on the table.

'Me? Um… nothing,' she says, 'I didn't see anything. I just went into the bakery, bought a loaf of bread like usual. We exchanged pleasantries and then…'

'No, I meant at the cinema,' I explain. 'What film did you see?'

'Oh! Ha!' She laughs, rolls her eyes. 'Sorry, I thought you meant… yeah, I watched that new one, the one starring whatshisface out of that Disney film… *The Maverick*. It wasn't all that really,' she goes on to explain. 'I fell asleep at one point.'

I nod in understanding. They've only got to dim the lights in a movie theatre and I'm out like a light. It used to drive Rachel mad. Suddenly, I realise that Fiona and I have never been to the cinema together. In fact, I'm not even sure we've ever sat and watched a film, just the two of us, which is terrible really when I think about it – I don't even know what type of films she even likes. I make a mental note to ask her when we next speak.

'I was just explaining to Daisey that it may well be prudent if the two of you were to stay elsewhere for a while – be on the safe side in case he is stalking you or casing the apartment.'

Iris exhales, runs her fingers through her hair and I notice her hand – she has two fingers missing on her right hand, something I've not noticed until now.

'The killer, you think he's stalking us? Watching the apartment? Surely he wouldn't be dumb enough to hang around here?' Iris scoffs a little.

'It's just a precaution,' I say.

'They can stay with me,' Ros announces. 'I'm not having you here alone with that maniac prowling around. You can come to my place, both of you; Ron won't mind.'

'I think that's a good idea, Ros.' I nod at her.

'Well, I can go and stay with my aunt,' Iris says. 'I was planning to go and see her this weekend anyway.'

'Were you?' Daisey says. 'You didn't say…'

'Yeah.' Iris nods. 'I told you the other day that I was visiting an aunt, near Brighton, don't you remember?'

Daisey shakes her head. 'I probably forgot,' she says apologetically, rubbing her temples. 'I'm pretty good at forgetting at the moment.'

Ros strokes her arm.

'Well, anyway, my aunt, she has a spare room, and I don't want to put you out, Ros.'

'It's no bother, love,' Ros says, 'really.'

'No honestly, it's fine,' Iris insists. 'Like I say, I was going there anyway.'

'Well, as long as you'll be safe, love.'

'That's sorted then,' I say, reassured. I see Davis in my peripheral vision waving her hands, trying to catch my attention.

'Gov… gov…' she whispers as she beckons me out of the kitchen into the hallway.

'What is it, Davis?'

'Good news!' she announces breathlessly. 'The florists… Mitchell contacted them and it turns out, well… you won't believe this…'

'Try me,' I say dryly.

'Well, it turns out the credit card used to pay for them is registered to none other than Luke Bradley, Daisey's ex!'

'Is it indeed? Well, well, well, wouldn't you know…'

'The order was placed over the telephone last night, around 10 p.m.'

'Interesting,' I say, my head spinning into overdrive. 'But it doesn't prove anything other than the fact Bradley's a nasty piece of work.'

'Gov?'

'They had a fight on the night Leilani Stewart was killed, an argument, Daisey and Luke. He was her dinner guest that night and she's just told me that the DNA we found on her – the semen, well, she thinks it's his.'

'Really!' Davis says.

'I knew he was holding something back that time we paid him a visit, slippery bastard. He clearly didn't want to give us a DNA sample because he didn't want his girlfriend – his pregnant girlfriend, no less – finding out he'd cheated on her with his ex.'

'Well, we can't exactly nick him for sending an anonymous bunch of flowers, can we?' Davis sounds a little disappointed.

'No we can't, Davis,' I agree with her absolutely. 'But let's bring the bastard in anyway.'

CHAPTER TWENTY-FIVE

'What part of "I did not send those flowers" do you not understand?' Luke Bradley, it's fair to say, is not a happy bunny as he sits opposite Davis and I in the interview room, legs crossed, his face even crosser. 'What possible reason could I have to send her roses with a card warning her to keep quiet?' Agitated, his leg begins swinging manically over the other.

'Daisey told us about the argument the other night,' Davis says. 'She threatened to tell your partner, Charlotte, that you had slept together, didn't she?'

'Yes,' he says, 'but I knew she wouldn't do that. Daisey isn't... well, she isn't the malicious type – or wasn't anyway.' He snorts. 'Not so sure these days; she's been quite different since the attack. Anyway, I didn't take it seriously. It was said in the heat of the moment. Besides, I would've simply just denied it anyway even if she had – no need for a bunch of roses and a menacing note... it's really not my style. It's all a bit *Godfather* for me,' he says, his arrogance reverberating off the walls.

'Where did you go after you left Daisey's apartment that night – the night of the argument when she threw you out?'

I study Luke Bradley carefully as Davis conducts the interview. His body language is closed and guarded, but then that's to be expected. He's clearly appalled at being brought into the station under caution for questioning. His cowardice however is in opposing correlation to his arrogance – I thought he was about to burst into tears when we picked him up.

'Firstly,' he says, 'Daisey's apartment happens to be *my* apartment as well,' he corrects her. 'Secondly, she didn't *throw* me out, I left of my own accord, and thirdly, I went straight home.'

'Can anyone corroborate this?' Davis asks politely, though I can tell she's enjoying Bradley's discomfort almost as much as I am.

He sighs heavily, puts his head into his hands briefly.

'Yes,' he says with resignation, 'my fiancée, Charlotte. She was in bed when I got home.'

'Asleep?'

'Yes. Until I got into bed and woke her briefly.'

'And what time was that, Mr Bradley?'

'Oh, I don't know, around 10.30. I'm not sure exactly. Why?'

Davis gives him her professional smile, a smile that's slightly different to her personal one, though I suppose only those who know her well can tell the difference.

'Look, what is all this? Are you going to tell Charlotte where I was that night because I'd rather you didn't.'

'We will need her to corroborate your story, Mr Bradley.' Davis nods, non-committal. 'We're not here to judge you, just to find out the facts.'

'Yes, but do you have to tell her where I was? You do know she's pregnant? All this will obviously be extremely upsetting for her… she could lose the baby or something and…'

I stop myself from asking him whose fault would that be and instead let Davis do all the talking. I simply stare at him, waiting for the right moment to interject.

'So.' Davis sits up straight. 'You arrived at Daisey's, sorry, your apartment around 8.30 p.m. and left around 10 p.m., correct?'

'Correct,' he says, exasperated.

'You were supposed to be having dinner, weren't you? Didn't stay long…'

'Well, it's like she told you herself,' he sighs deeply. 'We had an argument and I left.'

'What route did you take on your journey home?'

'What route?' He shrugs. 'The usual route… look, why are you asking me this? I thought I was here because of some bunch of flowers I'm supposed to have sent even though I never sent them and this is all just a ridiculous waste of time and resources.'

His agitation is morphing into anger now; his leg swinging so furiously that I'm concerned his trendy trainer may come flying off his foot and smack Davis in the face at any moment.

'Look, someone must've cloned my bank card, got hold of my details somehow and bought them with it. You should be looking into that instead of interrogating me! Someone has committed a fraud against me. I'm the bloody victim here!'

'It's OK, Mr Bradley, Luke… I can call you Luke, can't I?' I ask with my best friendly face. 'Try to stay calm. We're simply making a few enquiries. Another murder took place that night, the night you were at Daisey's apartment – your apartment – together.'

His eyes move from Davis onto mine. I watch them as they widen, his bearded chin disappearing into his neck.

'What! And you think…' He sits forward in the chair. 'Surely you don't think I had anything to do with it? Jesus Christ! So I've gone from being a phantom flower giver to a vicious murderer – a bloody serial killer – now, have I?' His outrage has now morphed into something else – fear. I can almost smell it on him. 'Should I call my solicitor?' he says, tsking under his breath and trying to mask it. 'Bloody ridiculous…'

'No need – at this point anyway,' I add affably. 'But if you would answer DS Davis's question…'

He folds his arms tightly across his chest. 'Which was again?'

'The route you took home,' I prompt him.

He shakes his head, closes his eyes for a second as though this whole encounter is a terrible drag that is beneath him.

'I went down St James's Avenue, up through Marlborough Park, down into Sherwood Road and then onto Days Lane, which is where I live. Takes about twenty-five minutes at pace, a little over half an hour at leisure. Do you want me to draw you a map?' His tone is facetious.

'Yes!' I reply, mimicking it. 'That would be extremely helpful.'

I nod at Davis which is a silent way of telling her we'll need to see if he's been picked up somewhere on CCTV. 'So, you didn't go anywhere near Shortland's Parade on your way home?'

'No,' he states firmly. 'It's in the opposite direction to where I live. Why would I?'

'Do you know Leilani Stewart?'

'Leilani who? No… no I don't. I don't know anyone called Leilani, never heard of her.' His eyes dart between Davis's and mine respectively.

'Have you ever been to Aled's Artisan Bakery on Shortland's Parade?'

He looks bewildered and confused; beads of sweat beginning to form an oily sheen on his forehead.

'I didn't even know there was a bloody bakery on Shortland's Parade in all honesty,' he says defensively.

'Why did you send Daisey a bunch of roses with a card saying, *Silence is Golden*, Luke?' Davis asks. 'You knew that her attacker had left a rose on her body. You also knew that she was scared, didn't you? Scared of her attacker coming back to hurt her again, finish the job. Did you capitalise on that fear? Do it to frighten her into submission, try and stop her from making good on her threat to tell your fiancée that you'd slept together?'

He stands up now, his chair making a sharp scraping sound with the sudden momentum.

'Please, Mr Bradley – Luke – sit down,' I say calmly.

'I DIDN'T BLOODY WELL SEND THOSE FLOWERS!' he bellows, his face red with rage, angry purple veins protruding from his neck. Even his beard looks vexed.

'So how do you explain that they were paid for with your personal credit card, Luke?'

I nod at him to sit down and he complies reluctantly, petulantly scraping the chair back.

'This is police harassment,' he says. 'I have rights, you know! I have already told you, over and over again, that I did not send those flowers. Jesus, I don't ever send *anyone* flowers, not even my own mother! They're a waste of bloody money. Forty-five pounds you said they cost – well, I can tell you this for nothing, I'd never spend that sort of money on a bunch of dead stems, not for anyone and certainly not for—'

He stops himself from using her name.

'Could anyone have had access to your card? Your girlfriend, perhaps?'

His eyes widen. 'Now look, don't you bloody bastards bring her into this! She's nothing to do with it. Jesus Christ, *I'm* nothing to do with it! I honestly don't know how someone could've used my card… I really don't know… I swear…' Luke Bradley looks like he's about to burst into flames. 'This whole thing is a nightmare!'

'Seems odd though, doesn't it, Mr Bradley,' Davis says, 'that soon after cheating on your pregnant girlfriend and following an argument with Daisey that she receives an anonymous bouquet of roses with a card suggesting she keep quiet? Bit of a coincidence, wouldn't you agree? Especially as you say your card hasn't even been stolen and that no one else had access to it.'

'Yes!' he shrieks. 'I absolutely would agree. It *is* a coincidence. That's exactly what it is! I mean, she was paranoid as hell that night, thought there was someone in the apartment, someone hiding in wait for her. She says she keeps seeing things, hearing

things. I mean, clearly she's worried that the killer's still at large…
but I tell you now, I'm not him and I'm not lying.' He bangs his
fist onto the table, though more for effect than anything else as
it doesn't make a particularly loud thud. 'Why on earth would I
be stupid enough to use my own card with my name on it and
not even report it stolen? Not exactly the work of a criminal
mastermind, is it?'

Reluctantly I have to admit that he's right, about that anyway.

'Check my phone if you want,' he says defiant. 'The number
would be there, wouldn't it, the florist's number, if I'd rang them
to order flowers then it will be in my call list?'

'Yes, Luke, we will check that.' Davis nods efficiently. 'But
you have lied to us before, haven't you?'

He blinks at her and then looks at me, confused. 'Lied about
what?'

'About when you'd last seen Daisey.' Davis flicks through the
notes in front of her, runs her finger down the page. 'When we
interviewed you on the… seventeenth, the day after Daisey's
attack, you claimed that you hadn't seen her for a little over a
month – 12 June, to be exact. That wasn't true though, was it?'

'Can I have some water please?' he asks, his voice a little
scratchy. 'It's rather hot in here.'

'Of course.' Davis stands to leave, excuses herself to the
recording.

We are alone and silent for a moment.

'I know why you lied, Luke,' I say, breaking it. 'Daisey told me.'

'Oh did she?' he says, coolly, his eyes resting on mine. 'Jealous are
you, Detective Riley?' I think I detect a small smirk cross his lips.

'It's an offence to give false or misleading information in a
murder inquiry, Luke. I'm sure an educated man such as yourself
is aware of that.'

His smirk disappears almost instantly.

'It wouldn't shock me if she's bloody well done this herself,' he says, 'stolen my card details and ordered them herself in a bid to stitch me up, get back at me for…'

'For what…?' I say. 'But I thought you said she wasn't the malicious type, Luke…'

'She isn't, or wasn't, generally speaking, but she's not been the same since the attack, head's all over the place – no pun intended,' he adds inappropriately. 'And she wasn't best pleased when I told her about me and Charlotte and the baby.'

'I don't suppose she was, Luke,' I humour him. 'Especially given your… timing.' I raise my eyebrows at him and he looks away sheepishly. 'Anyway, the florist claims it was a man who called up to order the flowers, that it sounded like a man's voice.'

'Doesn't prove anything conclusively,' he shoots back.

'The DNA we found on Daisey, one set presumably is yours, from the encounter between you, the morning before she was attacked?'

He sighs heavily. 'Go into detail, did she? Get you off did it, Detective?'

I'm struggling to hide my disdain for Mr Bradley with each passing second.

'We're going to ask you to give us a voluntary DNA sample,' I say. 'So we can compare it to the sample we have on file from the crime scene. I presume you're happy to give a sample this time?'

He makes to object but I cut in. 'We wouldn't want to have to use reasonable force or anything, which we'd be perfectly entitled to do.'

'Oh, be my guest,' he snaps angrily as I take the large cotton bud from the DNA kit and swab the inside of his mouth. 'And yes, for the record, Daisey and I did have sexual intercourse the morning before she was attacked and yes, I'm sure my DNA sample will no doubt match one of the sets you found on her – but it's not a crime to have sex with your ex, is it, or have I missed something here?'

I shake my head. 'Not a crime at all, Luke,' I say, 'although your pregnant fiancée might not see it that way.' I smile at him affably, can't help myself.

'Bloody bastard,' he mutters underneath his breath.

Davis re-enters the room. 'A word, gov,' she says.

I excuse myself on record, step outside the interview room and look at Davis, shake my head. 'He's too slippery, too sly to have bought those flowers with his own card – and too tight by the sounds of things. Which leaves me wondering—'

'Boss,' Davis interjects, 'you might want to reserve your judgement for a bit because… well, you are not going to believe this!'

'What – what is it, Davis?'

'Forensic has just come back and' – she shakes her head in a mix of disbelief and excitement – 'and there's been a match.'

I can feel my heartbeat quicken. Bingo! At last! A break!

'And…?'

'And the semen sample found on Daisey… well it matches the DNA found on Leilani Stewart.'

I can't be sure but I think my jaw may have involuntarily fallen open.

'Jesus Christ, you're sure…?'

Davis nods.

'They faxed it over just now – you can take a look for yourself, gov.'

I shake my own head in disbelief. 'But that means… that means, Davis, that if Daisey's right about who that semen sample belongs to then…'

We both turn and look at door of the interview room and then at the plastic bag I'm holding containing Luke Bradley's DNA sample.

'… then we've got him,' she says, finishing my sentence.

CHAPTER TWENTY-SIX

'Ah! Riley! Dan!' Gwendoline Archer pokes her head round the door of her office. 'A word, please.'

'Ma'am.' I raise an eyebrow at Davis, tell her to go on ahead to the incident room and close the door behind me. She greets me with a professional smile and I notice that her hair looks professionally styled and that she's wearing lipstick, some of which is on her front teeth. I think to politely tell her but decide against it.

'Brilliant news on Bradley, well done to you, and the team, of course!' she says, gesturing for me to sit down. She places the pen she's holding neatly down next to her laptop, rearranges it a few times until it's perfectly symmetrical. 'Now that Forensic have confirmed that Bradley's DNA matches the DNA found on Daisey Abbott…'

'Garrett,' I correct her, 'Daisey Garrett.'

'Yes, Garrett, that's what I said. And now that it's a definite match with the DNA also found at the Stewart crime scene' – she pauses momentarily, as though checking she'd used the correct name – 'I'm going to call a press conference, let them know we have a man in custody, someone helping us with our enquiries. And I think you should be with me when I address them. After all it's down to you that we have our man – and they'll want to ask questions.'

I'm guessing my subconscious has relayed my reaction directly to my face because she quickly adds, 'The public wants some reassurance, Dan – needs some – and we have something positive to give them at last. The bloody press hasn't spared us over this case: I've had pressure from all sides; them, the Commissioner, the parents…'

I glance up at her.

'Though that's obviously understandable,' she swiftly adds. 'Anyway, I think your presence will be very reassuring – and you have a good face for the camera.' She begins to observe me, as though looking at a painting in an art gallery. 'The public tend to be more forgiving of a pretty face, more trusting.'

I open my mouth to speak but nothing comes out. *Pretty face?*

'The conference is at 3 p.m. today. I've spoken to the parents of the dead victims; they're fully briefed and up to spec. I thought you might like to brief Daisey yourself though, seeing as though you're close.'

'Close?' What does she mean by that? Is she alluding to something?

'She trusts you, Riley; you have a rapport with her.'

I swallow dryly. It's airless in the room, or perhaps it's simply my disbelief sucking up all the oxygen. I feel as though this conversation has got off to a shaky start and I'm pretty sure what I'm about to say isn't going to do much to remedy that.

'You think a press conference at this stage is a good idea, ma'am?' I ask tentatively. Personally, I think it's a terrible one, but at least it explains the freshly styled hair and lipstick. While I understand Archer's exuberance – this is the first time that we've had any real break in the case – I feel it's premature to hang out the bunting just yet. Matching Bradley's DNA to the semen found on Leilani Stewart may well be cause for celebration – but something isn't right. My intuition tells me that he is not our guy. Besides, the fingerprints found on the knife – three of them, a thumb, index and middle finger – they aren't his; they don't belong to Bradley.

'Don't you think you might be…'

'Might be what, Riley?' She raises an eyebrow ever so slightly.
'Jumping the gun a bit?'

She tucks her chin in to her chest slightly. 'No, Riley,' she
says sharply. 'I don't. We need some good headlines, something
positive to work with. We've been vilified throughout this case as
little more than a clueless bunch of halfwits chasing our tails and
getting nowhere. People are scared, Riley – women. We need to do
this to give them some reassurance, win back a bit of confidence
from the press – and the public.' The way she says it convinces
me she's slightly more concerned with the former.

'I would agree with you about needing some good headlines,
ma'am,' I say, 'if I believed Luke Bradley was actually our man.
Only he's not.'

'Oh?' she says. 'And you're absolutely sure of that are you,
Dan? We have a DNA match on him, on two of the victims,
at least. Even if Daisey Garrett says she did have sex with him
consensually, it doesn't explain how his semen managed to find
its way onto Leilani Stewart's body, does it?'

'Admittedly not.' I'm careful to agree with her again. 'But
Bradley has a watertight alibi the night Daisey was attacked. And
somewhat macabrely, she herself is his alibi for the night Leilani
Stewart was murdered. Besides that, the fingerprints found on
the knife, they're not his.'

'But,' she interjects coolly, 'it's possible that Bradley, after
Daisey Garrett threw him out of her apartment, made his way
to Stewart's flat, isn't it?' It's more a statement than a question.
'Perhaps he was angry, wound up about the argument with Daisey,
maybe he followed her home… he could've had an accomplice.
Bradley may well only be responsible for two of the attacks; both
could've been copycat killings; all the information was out there
for anyone so inclined… you've only got to look at the amount of

false confessions we've already had, all manner of cranks phoning in saying they're the Rose Petal Ripper... or knows who is... Bloody time wasters.'

I shake my head.

'It's possible,' she states again. Though it sounds like she's trying to convince herself more than anyone.

'Look, ma'am, I understand why you want to believe he's our man. If he was then it would make my job a hell of a lot easier and—'

'Are you patronising me, Riley?' she says coolly.

'He doesn't fit the profile for one thing,' I say. 'The one Dr Henderson compiled – your good friend, Dr Henderson,' I add for weight. 'Bradley may be an arrogant arseh—' I stop myself short. 'He has no previous, no history of violence, no history of mental health issues, and no motive to kill any of the victims, arguably with the exception of Daisey Garrett – who ironically is the only one still alive. It doesn't make sense, ma'am,' I say.

'And what about the flowers, Riley, with a note warning her to keep quiet?'

'He vehemently denies sending them, ma'am,' I say. 'And even if he did, it doesn't make him a murderer.'

'And you believe him?'

'Yes, ma'am, I do.'

She sighs heavily, readjusts her pen on the desk.

'So who in the hell did send them? And how in God's name did his DNA end up at Stewart's flat?'

'I don't know yet, ma'am. Perhaps someone planted it, someone trying to frame him?'

'And who would want to do that, Riley? Abbott?'

'Garrett,' I correct her for the second time. 'It's possible, but unlikely. Again, I don't know.'

'You don't know much, do you, Riley?' she sighs. 'And stop calling me ma'am!' she says shrilly. 'It's irritating.'

'I'm sorry, m—' I cough into my fist. 'We can only hold him for another twenty-four hours and with what we've got, well, I can't see the CPS giving us the green light to charge him, can you?'

'I'll deal with the CPS, Riley,' she says stonily. 'You just concentrate on Bradley at this stage. Search his apartment, collate any CCTV evidence, speak to the girlfriend, gather as much intelligence and forensic as you can.'

She gives me a look that reminds me of the ones Woods used to give me – like I've just thrown a bucket of water over her.

'His DNA matches and he has no explanation of how it got there,' she reiterates sternly. 'It's tight but feasible that he had enough time to have committed the murder the night he was with Daisey.'

I shake my head again, unconvinced.

'We're waiting on the autopsy report for a more concise TOD. He was at Daisey's apartment from 8.30 till around 10 p.m. If TOD falls anywhere in between then he can't be our man. Besides, he's alibied for the other two murders – both of which checked out.'

'Well, like I say,' she replies authoritatively, 'he may be responsible for the attacks on Daisey and Leilani and used the previous killer's MO in a bid to throw us off track. You know it's feasible.'

'Perhaps, but I don't believe so, ma'am. I think we're looking for just one offender. Besides, I'm pretty sure Daisey would've known if Bradley had been her assailant,' I say. 'They were together for seven years and—'

'Yes, but she can't remember a bloody thing about it!' she snaps. 'Mind's a total blank, so she says. Look, do what you have to, Dan,' she says irritably, 'but I want you to try to make this stick, OK? For now at least, make us look like we've actually got something.'

Make it stick? I'm dumbfounded. Luke Bradley is not our killer and I'm pretty sure she knows it as well.

'Ma'am,' I say, careful to keep my tone measured and respect-ful. 'If we go after Bradley and try to "make it stick", as you say, and it transpires that we've got the wrong man – which I'm pretty sure we have – then the press will hang us out to dry and the killer will remain at large. Think about it; it would reflect extremely badly on us if we were to be seen wasting time with Bradley while the real killer is at large and could potentially strike again, wouldn't it? They'd feed us to the wolves.'

I watch her as she thinks about this potential scenario, her demeanour changing with every passing blink of her made-up eyes. She knows I'm right, only I suspect she's too wrapped up in the idea of all the reflective glory if the public were to believe we had caught our man. Woods had warned me that Gwendoline Archer is a results-driven woman, but even so, the idea of 'making it stick' on the wrong guy leaves a very bad taste in my mouth indeed.

She's silent for a moment, thoughtful.

'Right, well, as you wish. I'll do the press conference alone,' she says, staring at me with her piercing grey eyes. 'Leave you to what you do best.'

'And what's that, ma'am?' I ask.

'What you're told, Riley.' She smiles at me affably. 'What you're told.'

CHAPTER TWENTY-SEVEN

'Luke? *Luke?*' A sliver of icy fear hits Daisey's stomach and explodes like a mushroom cloud. 'No…' She shakes her head repeatedly. 'No, no, no… it's not him… it can't be Luke… not possible!' She turns to look at Ros, sitting opposite her ashen-faced on the sofa of her front room. She can't believe what they're saying to her, what they're telling her. 'I'd absolutely know if he'd been the one who attacked me,' she says resolute, looking at the faces around the room. 'I'd… I'd remember, wouldn't I?' She asks the question aloud, looks to Ros again for affirmation.

'We found Luke's DNA on Leilani's body, Daisey,' Detective Riley explains gently. 'It matches the sample we found on you, after you were attacked.'

She shakes her head again, his words hanging heavy in the air around her; she's unable to absorb them.

'But… I've explained that,' she says, panic-stricken. 'We'd had sex the morning before the attack, in the kitchen, in the apartment, over the table.' She doesn't know why she has shared this particular candid detail; where they had sex is not relevant, but somehow she thinks it might add weight to what she's saying. 'He didn't even know her, did he?' she protests. 'He didn't know that girl from the bakery, or any of them, except for me… why would he… how can it be possible…? I… I… don't understand.' She wants to cry but the shock has paralysed her tear ducts and her face feels numb.

'I'll make some tea,' Ros says. 'Or maybe something a little stronger. A brandy?'

'Yes,' she agrees quickly. 'Brandy.'

Ros nods, glances at the two detectives as she stands. 'Never trusted that bastard anyway,' she mutters as she leaves the room.

An army of questions hit Daisey's brain and explode in a kaleidoscopic flurry. *Luke.* She's known him for almost a decade, lived with him, *loved* him… she would've known if he was some kind of homicidal maniac, a serial offender who attacked women, wouldn't she? Yes, of course she would. But then again, she hadn't known that he'd been having an affair, had she? Leading a double life for almost two years without so much as a fleeting suspicion? She grapples with the internal struggle inside her mind and suddenly she recalls the conversation she'd had with Iris the other night after Luke had been here, the one about him being two different people, Jekyll and Hyde… '*Perhaps we're all two different people at the end of the day, Daisey…*' Fear sweeps through her like fire. Luke was many things: a cheat and a liar, yes; he was weak and spineless, for sure. He was pretentious and affected, sneaky and devious, but a violent serial killer? No. No she couldn't buy that one, DNA or otherwise.

'The flowers, Daisey,' the female detective's voice cuts through her thoughts, shattering them like glass. She still can't remember the woman's name even though she's met her countless times. It just hasn't sunk in; none of this has. 'The card, the Visa card used to order them, it was registered to Luke.'

'What?'

Ros returns with the brandy and hands it to her. She swallows a large mouthful, relishes the burn at the back of her throat. She's not sure how much more she can take and holds her glass out for another. 'The roses, you mean? Luke sent them?'

'His card was used to purchase them,' the female detective explains, 'although he categorically denies it had anything to do with him.'

She shakes her head again. It feels like she's slipped into some strange twilight zone, a parallel universe where nothing is as it seems or bears any resemblance to her life whatsoever.

'Luke doesn't really do flowers,' she says, remembering the pathetic bunch he'd brought along to the hospital with him that time he'd visited her, cheap with the price label still on them – markedly different to the expensive-looking bouquet she'd just received with the note. 'It's not really his style.'

'I think he may have sent them to try and scare you, make sure you didn't say anything to… Charlotte, is it?' The female detective checks her notepad. 'About the two of you… Could anyone have had access to his credit card that night, aside from yourself and Luke? Did you see it; did you see it in his wallet?'

Daisey casts her mind back, replays the events. *Luke entering the apartment, throwing his wallet down onto the kitchen surface… the noises… like someone creeping around, a clattering sound, like a lamp being knocked over… 'God, you're beautiful'… his kiss and the quick sex that had followed…*

'Yes, I did see it. He put his wallet on the kitchen work surface,' she tells the detective, 'like he always used to when he came home from work. I don't recall seeing it after that.'

'And you're absolutely sure no one else could've had access to it?' Detective Riley is looking at her with those kind eyes of his – eyes she likes and trusts and only wishes she'd met in much different circumstances. '*He wants to fuck you!*' Luke's voice reverberates in her head. He'd been jealous when she'd mentioned Detective Riley that evening and it had made her feel good.

'Yes, I'm sure.' But now he asks the question she wonders if she had in fact seen it all. Her mind is so confused, so overloaded with questions and thoughts and emotions that it's malfunctioning and cannot be relied upon to reflect the truth. Perhaps, she thinks, that no one ever really 'sees' anything anyway and that it's all just the eye's interpretation or power of suggestion at the end of the day. After all, what one person 'sees' can be distinctly different to another – even if they're both looking at the same thing.

'Have you arrested him?' Ros says. 'Luke, is he in custody?'

'Yes.' Detective Riley looks at Daisey. She can tell he's trying to gauge her reaction. 'We have and he is, but if we're going to charge him – we need more, a lot more.'

Daisey gets up and stands by the window of Ros's front room, staring out onto the street below. Ordinary people are milling about, doing ordinary things and she only wishes she were one of them, like she used to be. Dan and Ros are talking but she's tuned them out to background noise as her mind struggles to comprehend the thought that Luke could be responsible for the brutal murder of three women – and of attempting to murder her. She tries to allow herself to imagine this but the idea is so inconceivable, so preposterous, that she thinks she might suddenly burst out laughing instead. Luke Vincent Bradley, the politically correct intellectual university lecturer and self-proclaimed vegan humanitarian, her former fiancé, a sadistic serial killer? He didn't even like the sight of blood, said it made his hands and feet 'go tingly' whenever he saw it. He was even squeamish when she had her period, for goodness' sake.

But as her thoughts reach the pinnacle of doubt they tip over into something else. Because it *could* and *did* happen, didn't it? She's read about it, seen it on TV, people who'd been married to murderers and rapists and paedophiles for decades without knowing; ordinary people who had families and jobs and friends and led perfectly normal, unremarkable lives. The very idea that this could've happened to her makes her feel sick right through to the calcium in her bones. How had her life become this… this charade, this nightmare? Has she been so blind, so trusting and blinkered that she hadn't known her fiancé was a vicious maniac who slaughtered women? Has Iris been right and she's only seen what she's wanted to see? Does Luke have two faces, one for the public and one for his own depraved and dark deviancies? Surely, in hindsight, there would've been clues, red flags, something, *anything* that might've aroused some kind of suspicion in her. The cognitive dissonance was too wide a chasm for her to mentally navigate. How is it possible that his DNA, his semen, had been found on that girl from the bakery? He'd been with her that night, they'd been together in their apartment – they'd had sex on the bed they'd once shared and…

Just then, she remembers the condom; he'd taken it off afterwards and thrown it in the waste-paper bin! In her upset she'd clean forgotten about it. She hadn't emptied the bin so it will still be there, won't it? A strange, cold sensation settles upon her like fresh snow. What if…?

'I need to go back to my apartment,' she says suddenly. 'There's something I forgot, something I need.'

'I'll get it for you, love,' Ros offers. 'Just tell me what it is you want and I'll pick it up for you on my way from work later; it's no bother.'

She doesn't answer, can't think straight. She swallows some more brandy.

'There must be some other explanation for this, Detective Riley,' she says, looking over at him, pleading with him. As much as she hates Luke's betrayal, his deceit and treachery and his abysmal treatment of her, she doesn't want this to be true. 'I just can't believe…'

'You said yourself that you think you knew your attacker didn't you, love?' Ros reminds her softly. Everyone speaks to her softly now, like she's a child, a sickly child who needs careful handling. 'Perhaps that's why you've blanked it out; maybe it was him and you just blanked it out because it's too painful to think that Luke…'

She refreshes her glass for the third time and notices Ros and Detective Riley exchanging glances.

'No… no… I would've known if it had been Luke, I'm sure of it… I… I…'

Static. That high-pitched whining, so loud and painful, like her eardrums are about to explode. 'You want one of these…' His voice sounds oddly familiar as he takes the lighter out of his pocket and…

'Daisey! Are you OK? Daisey…'

She's hunched over the sofa, her hands pressed against her ears, rocking back and forth. Ros puts an arm around her shoulder.

'Love… Are you OK?'

She closes her eyes, rubs them with her fingers until she sees spots.

'The flashbacks,' she says, looking at their concerned faces in turn. 'They're getting worse… I know there's something… something about him… I can see it but I can't quite reach it, just can't seem to grasp it, get it into some kind of focus. I'm trying but…'

'Have you thought any more about what I said, Daisey?'

Dan Riley is sitting next to her now, his hand resting gently on her arm. He smells nice, clean and soapy, not too dissimilar to how Luke used to smell and she wants to fall into him, into his arms and stay there until all of this has gone away.

'About the hypnotherapy I suggested? I really do think it could help. Look, I know it's scary, God knows I'd be scared too but you'd be in good hands – the best hands – and perhaps, once you've confronted this fear of remembering, these images might stop plaguing you, and well, if, like you say, it wasn't Luke who attacked you then it might help to exonerate him too; if you remember something, it might help him.'

Daisey shuts her eyes. Her head feels woozy and she's not sure if it's the booze, the news of Luke's arrest or the static that's causing it, perhaps all three.

'OK,' she says. 'When?'

CHAPTER TWENTY-EIGHT

September 1997

'I've made the appointment for next Wednesday, at 3.15. It's only an initial assessment, so the doctor says, and then, once that's done, he'll be able to suggest the next step, how we move forward. His name's Dr Barber, supposed to be one of the best in his field. He comes highly recommended; we were lucky to get him. John… John, are you listening to me?'

Tracey Eggerton turns to her husband. He's sitting at the kitchen table, reading a newspaper and sipping a Scotch. He doesn't look up. 'John?' she says, trying to keep the irritation from her voice. 'Did you hear what I just said?'

She sips her own glass of Scotch, lights a cigarette and pulls up a chair, sits opposite him. He looks up slowly, folds the newspaper shut.

'Yes, I heard you.'

'And?'

'And what, Tracey?' He sighs. 'What do you want me to say?'

'Well… And what do you think? Will you come with us, to the appointment?'

Her husband stares at her, gives her a look that makes her heart drop like a stone in her chest.

'What do I think?' His voice is weary as opposed to angry, although she suspects he's doing his best to mask it. 'Well, I think that my wife is putting our son – and herself – through unnecessary trauma, that's what I think. And no... I won't be coming along. There's nothing wrong with him, Trace.' He flicks open the newspaper again, resumes reading, his piece said.

Tracey gulps back another mouthful of Scotch, sighs internally. She has never in all this time been able to get her husband to understand – despite all the 'coincidences' and the 'accidents'; 'hapless mishaps', 'just bad luck', that's how he'd explained them away – Mrs Merryweather's cat, the little boy down at the lake and then Michael...

Tracey thinks about the boy who'd 'fallen' from the tree while playing with her son. He'd suffered such dreadful life-changing injuries as a result – a fractured skull and vertebrae, a punctured lung and brain damage, leaving the poor boy with severe learning difficulties, barely able to walk or talk. A 'misdemeanour' is what John had called it, the police 'a tragic accident', not that this had been any consolation to poor Michael and his parents who had subsequently been forced to move away and would now have to provide round-the-clock care for their disabled son for the rest of his natural life. Tracey could barely stomach the guilt she felt; it was corrosive, gnawing at her insides every single day and she wondered how many more 'accidents' there might be, how many more lives would be ruined or taken or damaged before her husband would listen to her.

'I'm frightened, John,' Tracey addresses him. 'I know you don't want to hear it; I know you think I'm the one with the problem but—'

'*That's* the problem,' he says without looking up, tapping the half-empty bottle of Scotch on the table. 'It's not even midday yet, Trace. Why don't you slow down a bit? It's not doing you any good, this obsession with our son, it's so... unhealthy.'

She knows he's right – she does drink too much, but it's a symptom of the problem, not the cause. His words simply make her want to pour another, try to blot out this terrible feeling inside of her, a feeling that she has tried so hard to quash over the years but instead seems to be growing stronger and stronger to the point where she can no longer ignore it, pretend it's not there.

Having her son seen by a child psychiatrist is, for Tracey at least, the first logical step; a professional will be able to diagnose him, tell if her instincts are correct and there is something wrong with him; something seriously, dreadfully wrong. She'd explain everything to Dr Barber, had rehearsed it all in her head, the feelings she's experienced since he was born – even while he was being born – a horrid sixth sense that there is something inherently wrong with him, something malevolent, something *evil*. She'd tell him that this feeling had nothing to do with his issues at birth; something John was convinced had caused her to reject their boy and that had sparked these thoughts and feelings inside of her, but then again perhaps it did have something to do with it? Perhaps it was all somehow related. She only hoped she could articulate it all well enough for the doctor to believe her – *if someone would just believe her.*

She will tell him about the 'accidents', about the terrible things that seem to happen when he is around, accidents that she can't just put down to coincidence like John and everyone else seemed capable of doing. She'll make the doctor see what she sees and she hopes, more than anything, that he won't think she is a paranoid obsessed alcoholic with mental health issues of her own – just like she knew John thought, deep down anyway. Perhaps they'd deem her son a danger, to himself and more importantly to others, and maybe they will take him away, lock him up so that he'll be safe, that they'll *all* be safe. Guiltily, this is Tracey's greatest hope of all.

'John,' Tracey pleads with her husband, 'please, I know you think… well, I know what you think of me – that I'm the one with the problem – but I really think we need to do this, for his

own sake as much as ours. I'm scared, John, really scared. I have
this dreadful feeling…'

John Eggerton sighs heavily, closes his paper again and looks
up at his wife.

'Trace, love, you've *always* got a dreadful feeling. You've had
this dreadful feeling for the past ten years…'

'Yes!' she shrieks. 'You're right! I have, I don't deny it. And it's
not going away, John; in fact, it's getting worse, getting stronger…
I feel like something very bad is about to happen, something
imminent, something to do with *him*.'

She knows he's exasperated with her, frustrated and angry, but
she can't give up; she loves her husband and she wants him to
listen; if only he were on her side she would feel so much stronger,
so much more capable of dealing with everything.

'I think, when you take him to see this doctor, that you should
see one yourself too, love.' John addresses her kindly but stoically.
'I'm worried about you, Tracey. You're right, it's got worse, this…
this feeling of yours, and the drinking too… I'm not a doctor but
I think you may have depression. I really do think *you* need to see
someone. Let me help you, love,' he says, reaching for her hand.

'I'll come with you, stand by you, but all this' – he holds his
hands up – 'it has to stop. It's not good for you, or for the kids. I
mean, look at them today, they're as happy as Larry, off playing
down in the woods together, no dramas, nothing *bad*, just doing
what other normal ten-year-olds do in the summer holidays. It's
like every day you're waiting for something terrible to happen,
something dreadful…'

'But bad things *have* happened, John…' she implores. 'The
cat and the kid, and Michael…'

'No, Tracey… those things, they were tragic accidents that
could've happened to anyone. Jesus wept, woman, how many
times have we been through all of this? How many more times
do you want to? Michael slipped! He was twenty-five feet up a

bloody great tree, for goodness' sake! No one pushed him. Rosie *told* you what happened; she told you time and time again. The kid at the lake, accidental drowning – even the bloody police said it. And the cat… that was four years ago! God, please don't make me go there again, Trace. I can't, I just can't.'

He shakes his head and she hears the exhaustion in his voice, feels bad that she's the source of it. She feels like screaming. Perhaps she will see a doctor, if only to have someone else listen to her; maybe a doctor would believe her, wouldn't make her feel as if she's losing her mind, as if she's the one who needs locking up.

'I'm sorry, John,' she says quietly. 'I know you think I'm mad but…'

He sighs yet again, folds the paper up and finishes his Scotch, smacks the glass down onto the table.

'Look, it's a beautiful day out, why don't we go for a walk, eh? Get a bit of fresh air, make you feel better, clear your head. We'll walk up to the field, go and find the twins, watch them play for a bit, all of us together. What do you think? It'll do you good.'

She nods her agreement, wishes she could somehow dislodge this feeling, like a boulder crushing her chest cavity, hard and heavy and unyielding, *a sense of impending doom.*

There's a light wind outside but the sun is strong and high as they stroll across the field behind their home. John takes his wife's hand and kisses it as they walk in the direction of the woods – towards the lilac tree, where their children like to play. He seems less angry now that they're outside in the sunshine.

'A holiday,' he says after a few moments of them walking silently together, 'that's what you need. We haven't had one in a while… I was thinking somewhere hot, somewhere on the Costa del Sol… all sandy beaches and Sangria, sunbeds and a swimming pool for the twins… what do you think? I'm sure

Bob wouldn't mind if I took a week off work; we're not too busy at the moment.'

She hates it when he calls them 'the twins', always has even though she knows that's what they are.

'Can we afford to?'

He snorts gently. 'Can we *not* afford to?'

She drops her head for a moment.

'Well, it does sound lovely,' she agrees, trying to imagine the soft sand between her toes and the carefree feeling that has been absent from her life for so long – or at least, since *he'd* been born. The talk of a holiday suddenly makes her think of their honeymoon in the Canary Islands and she casts her mind back some thirteen years to when they had been newlyweds, high on each other, on love and lust and happiness – their future together stretched out in front of them like a glorious precious gift. It feels like a lifetime ago now; she'd been a different person back then, so vivacious and confident, so hopeful about life, a stark contrast to how she feels today. So much has changed since she'd had the children – she's changed, and the memory only serves to highlight to her just by how much.

'Great.' He squeezes her hand in his. 'We could grab some brochures from the travel agent on the high street on the way back if you like, take the long route, get an ice cream…'

She musters up a smile for him as they continue to walk through the field, the lilac tree becoming visible on the horizon – its heavily blossomed top bobbing into view as they take the incline towards where the twins are playing. She tries to remind herself how lucky she is, something she attempts to do most days in a bid to stop the darkness from creeping in. Positive affirmations, they were called; she'd read about them in some book about Buddhism and finding inner peace and happiness. 'I'm grateful for my beautiful home, for my wonderful husband… for my health and for my friends and for my *children*…'

But as they near the lilac tree she cannot ignore the sensation in her body – an insidious ache creeping through her guts, almost painful, like she's been disembowelled and is dragging her entrails behind her as she walks. She squints through the bright sunshine, brings her hand up over her eyes like a visor. John is still talking, something about traveller's cheques, but she's not really listening; something about the scene coming into her view feels wrong. She sees a dot on the horizon, but still she knows it's him, his strange small form identifying as her son. He's standing to the left of the tree, a small distance from it, looking up. Her eyes search for her daughter but she can't see her, she can't see Rosie and suddenly an egregious panic grips her tightly, crushing her ribcage and restricting her breath.

'Where's Rosie?' she says aloud. 'Can you see her, John? I can't see her!'

John looks towards the tree that's coming closer into their vision.

'I can see *him*,' he says, waving at his son and smiling.

'Yes, but where is *she*?' Tracey says, her voice gravelly with fear. 'I don't see her, John… I don't see our girl…'

'Don't panic, Trace, for goodness' sake,' he says, a touch snappy but something in his voice makes her think that he feels it too, senses something, and she's right because suddenly he picks up pace, breaks into a jog, pulling her along with him and then suddenly they're running, sprinting towards the lilac tree, her terror increasing with the gathering momentum, her summer dress whipping up against her calves in the breeze. She's a little way behind him by the time they approach the tree and…

'OH JESUS CHRIST! NO! NO! OH GOD, NOOOOOO!'

Her husband's cries send shockwaves through her as she runs up behind him, breathless and sweating in the sticky heat. She sees her son. He's standing at the bottom of the tree, looking up; there's something on him, on his clothes – his T-shirt and his hands, what is it? Red… blood… *Oh my God! It's blood!*

John is screaming, making a sound she has never heard him make before and confused she tries to make sense of the scene before her, her eyes darting furiously in an attempt to gain some clarity, panic rendering her almost blind, taking nothing in, like reading the same line in a book over and over again without digesting the words. John is on the ground, on his knees and he's wailing – why is he wailing?

'Where's Rosie?' She's barely able to push the words up through her throat it's so constricted by terror and panic. 'Where's your sister?'

He says nothing as he stands there, covered in what she thinks is blood, his eyes hollow and dead, almost black, like they've disappeared into his skull. He looks up, points slowly and silently.

Tracey follows his eyes and looks up into the tree and sees the body of her daughter hanging from the rope, her head dangling to the left side of her neck, distorted, forming an unnatural, ugly shape that her eyes can't seem to discern or accept. Tracey tries to scream as her knees give way beneath her, but nothing comes out and she drops to the floor.

'It was an accident, Mummy,' he says. 'Just an accident.'

CHAPTER TWENTY-NINE

The buzz in the incident room back at the nick is palpable as Davis and I walk through the door, only I can't quite fully bring myself to share in the team's exuberance – not yet.

'Let's not get too excited, folks,' I address them cautiously. I don't want to be a total buzz-killer but I also don't want to get their hopes up – or my own. 'We've got a lot more work to do yet.'

'Did you see her, boss?' Harding sniggers a little. 'Cupid on TV, the press conference?'

I shake my head. Truth is, I couldn't bring myself to watch it, thought it was a mistake to go public so soon, and I told her as much. 'She had brown lipstick on her teeth.' The gang start to titter among themselves. 'Made them look all yellow under the lights, like she's on sixty a day – she'll be mortified when she watches it back.'

'All right, all right,' I say, allowing them their five minutes of fun at Archer's expense. 'That's enough.'

I resist the small pang of guilt I feel in my guts. I probably should've told her about the lipstick, in hindsight. But maybe Woods had been right; I suspect that Archer is seriously ambitious and something of a glory hunter. Cracking this case will invariably put her face on the map, lipstick on her teeth or not.

'Right then, jokes aside,' I address the team, their noise settling down to a hush. 'We've got a twelve-hour extension on Bradley before we can charge him or release him, which buys us only a little more time to do a lot more work, so I hope none of you have any plans for the foreseeable because if you have then cancel them.'

A few groans emanate but this is mandatory and to be expected; I suspect they're just as eager as I am to get on with the job in hand.

'So, what have we got?'

'His DNA, gov,' Harding shoots back, causing the team to titter again.

'Yes, yes very good, Harding,' I reply dryly. 'We've established that. But how did it get there? How did it get in Leilani's apartment, on her body?'

I watch as the team exchange glances, puzzled by my obvious question – or is it really as obvious as it sounds?

'It places him at Leilani Stewart's apartment, boss.' A voice I don't recognise causes me to look up.

'And you are?'

'Parker, sir.' He stands up. 'DC Josh Parker. I was sent over from Leyton, gov. They thought you could use the help.'

'Oh, did they?' I say. He coughs a little, pushes his glasses up his nose. He's young, early twenties, but I get a sense of him already: intelligent, eager to please and learn, ambitious – just the sort I need on side right now. 'Only it doesn't make much sense,' Parker adds.

'Go on,' I encourage him.

'Well, Forensic found semen on the victim's body but no sign of sexual assault. No sign of sexual assault on any of the other victims either.'

'Maybe he just masturbated over her, after he'd killed her,' Baylis suggests. 'Didn't touch her but got a sexual thrill from killing her.'

Parker's face flushes slightly. 'Why not the others then? Why didn't he mast— why was Leilani the only one they found semen on?'

'And Daisey Garrett,' Harding interjects. 'His semen was found on her too.'

'Yes, but Garrett was, is, Bradley's ex-fiancé and by her own admission, they'd had consensual sex the morning before her attack. There was no semen found on her body at the crime scene, nothing fresh.'

I smile to myself. I think I like Parker. He reminds me of someone.

'Doesn't mean just because he and Daisey had consensual sex that he didn't try and kill her, or kill Leilani Stewart – that he isn't linked to her death, or the attack on Daisey,' Davis pipes up, I suspect playing Devil's advocate, testing Parker.

'No,' Parker agrees, 'but it's like this: he had sex with Daisey the morning before her attack, right?'

'Right,' I say, intrigued by Parker's thought process.

'Assuming Bradley is the killer, by the time he gets to Daisey he's killed twice already – Fern Lever and Jasmin Godden. We've got DNA from both scenes, neither of which match Bradley's, and no signs of sexual assault. Skip to Leilani Stewart and suddenly he's left semen on her body? Just seems… I don't know… a little strange.'

'Serial killers tend to be,' Baylis snorts.

'Yeah, but couple that with the bunch of roses that were sent to Daisey… why use a card registered in your own name and address, something so easily traceable? It's asking to draw attention to yourself.'

'These are extremely good questions, Parker,' I say, giving credit where it's due.

'Thank you, sir,' he says, flushing pink again and suddenly I know who it is he reminds me of: myself, at least back when, like him, I'd just started out.

'So? Possible explanations…'

'Someone set him up,' Parker says. 'Planted his DNA at the crime scene and stole his card to buy the flowers to give it weight, put the focus on him.'

'Listen and learn, people!' I say, slapping Parker on the back.

'So who set him up, gov?' Baylis asks. 'And why?'

'Could've been Daisey Garrett?' Harding suggests. 'She had access to his credit card that night – she could've written down the details and ordered them herself, had them sent to her address. Maybe she wanted to get back at him, get him in trouble. She said they'd argued about his girlfriend and selling the apartment.'

'Hmm, it's possible, Harding.' I nod. 'Only the florists say they thought a man had placed the order, which reminds me, we need to check Bradley's call log on his phone – anyone done that yet?'

'I'll get on it, boss.'

'Even if someone did try and stitch him up on the flowers, gov,' Davis says, 'it doesn't explain how his semen found its way onto Stewart's body, does it?'

I tap my lip with my finger – that thing I hate that people do when they're thinking hard about something and… well, maybe it does actually work because I've just remembered something Daisey Garrett said, something that has made me think…

'Who else, aside from Daisey, has access to her apartment?'

'Umm, Ros, I think – she has a key – and her flatmate, Iris.'

'Check both their alibis for the night of Stewart's murder, OK. I think Iris said she went to the pictures – double-check it.'

'What you thinking, gov?' Davis's eyes have lit up in such a way that it makes me involuntarily smile.

'I don't know yet, Lucy,' I say, 'but you'll be the first to know when I do. Anyway,' I bring my thoughts back to the room, 'Parker's right. We know Bradley has alibis for the dates and times that Fern Lever and Jasmin Godden were murdered, one from his girlfriend and another from friends he was out with.

I want these triple-checked and tight as a nut. Now that the fiancée – she's pregnant, by the way – has found out he's been a naughty boy with his *ex*-fiancée, if she's been covering up for him then she might retract, so, Davis, I want you to go and see her, use that gentle touch of yours, see what you can get out of her. And while you're at it send a couple of uniforms down to the university Bradley works at – dig around, find out if he was popular with his colleagues and students, any enemies, grievances… you know the drill.'

'Gov.' She nods.

'Anything from the newsagent's CCTV yet?'

'Bad news, boss,' Harding says. 'The camera outside Stewart's flat wasn't working.'

I close my eyes, curse under my breath. 'Jesus bloody Christ.'

'Although the one inside the shop was…'

'And…?'

She shakes her head. 'Sorry, boss, nothing.'

'Brilliant, bloody brilliant. And what about anything from the route Bradley says he took home – any cameras pick him up?'

'Waiting on that now, gov… and on the full autopsy report, then we'll have a more accurate TOD, which might let him off the hook anyway.'

'Right,' I sigh, 'well, let's get on with it, eh?'

I turn to look at the whiteboard in front of me, watch as a Post-it note flutters to floor. Jesus, I can't even make *that* stick.

'Gov.' Mitchell comes up behind me, approaches me tentatively, clearly sensing my mood.

'What is it, Mitchell?'

'I don't know, boss,' she says, 'probably nothing.'

I refrain from asking her why she's bothering me in that case; I'm aware I'm on a short fuse. A lack of sleep, sustenance and evidence will do that to a person.

'I've been going through the back catalogue of former employees again… Warwick's… checking and re-checking names,' she adds. 'It's sent me boss-eyed, boss, and…'

I clear my throat, an indication for her to get on with it; we're up against it as it is.

'And well, like I say, it could be nothing, a coincidence maybe.'

Coincidence. I like the sound of coincidence.

I sit down and she comes round towards my desk with a pile of papers. 'I've been cross-referencing every male who worked at Warwick's around the same time as Fern Lever and Daisey Garrett. Checking them on the database, seeing if they've got any previous, anything flagged up, and well… something struck me as a bit odd.'

Odd. I like the sound of odd even more than I do coincidence. I nod at her to continue.

'There were a couple of POIs – namely a small-time criminal's son and someone who was married into a family known to have criminal connections, but then I came across this guy… Garth Eggelston.'

'Garth Eggelston?' The name doesn't ring any bells. 'Who is he?'

'He worked at Warwick's for less than three months at the same time Lever worked there – and when Daisey first joined too, incidentally – as the maintenance man's assistant, an odd job man sort of thing. Apparently, he just didn't turn up for work one day and no one ever saw him again – a few days after Fern Lever was murdered.'

My interest piques. 'Really…?'

'Uh-huh.' Mitchell looks pleased with my reaction. 'So, I thought I'd do a bit of digging,' she says. 'And nothing came back…'

My interest dips again. 'Nothing on a Garth Eggelston anyway… but I dug a bit deeper and something interesting came up on someone called *Gareth Eggerton*... it could be nothing, they could be completely unrelated but well, he's a whole different story altogether.'

She throws a file down onto my desk. 'I think you might want to read this, gov,' she says and I nod, my interest piquing once more.

CHAPTER THIRTY

Gareth Eggerton. The more I say the name over and over in my head, the more I think it sounds the least likely name for a serial killer and more befitting to some softly spoken bookish English-teacher type. But then if you look back at infamous serial killers many of them have ordinary, unremarkable names and often present as affable, educated, even attractive human beings. Fiction – and perhaps even our own primeval fears – have fed us the idea that killers should somehow look as monstrous as the crimes they commit, therefore making them more identifiable, only it doesn't work that way; that is why many killers go undetected, unnoticed and under the radar. People like, I suspect, Gareth Eggerton might've done.

I take Mitchell's file home with me, a little light bedtime reading before I catch my now statutory three hours' shut-eye. I make myself a ham sandwich from a solitary piece left in the fridge and the last two slices of almost stale bread. It has gone curly and hard at the edges but with enough mustard doesn't taste too offensive and I settle down to read. The apartment feels empty and still, reminding me I am alone and that my Pip isn't here, bringing noise and life and vibrancy to the place and I realise how much I have become used to constant noise, how it has brought something of a reassurance to me.

The sound of my phone ringing bursts my thoughts and I groan. It is gone 2 a.m., but then I see Fiona's face flash up and my heart lurches inside my chest because somehow I instinctively know it's going to be *the* call. She's FaceTimed me.

'Fi.'

The line crackles a little as her image comes into view. She looks pale, like she's been crying and my heart drops further still.

'I didn't wake you, did I?' Her voice sounds faint and I'm not sure whether it is the connection or not. 'I keep forgetting we're eight hours ahead.'

'No… hey, don't be silly. Anyway, I don't sleep, remember; I'm a homicide detective. Which is also why I look like the walking dead.' I try to inject a little humour into the conversation because I know what is coming. And then I realise I've used the word 'dead' and wanted to punch myself in the face.

She laughs gently. 'You look fine to me,' she says generously.

'How's Pip? Where is she?' I ask instinctively, suddenly struck by an urgent ache to see my daughter, to feel her and hold her, bury my head into her sweet chubby neck where that scent of hers seems to be at its most potent. 'God, I miss her, Fi. This place feels like a mausoleum without her… without you all.'

Now I've used the word 'mausoleum' as well. And I wonder, in that moment, how I can be so mindful and sensitive and considerate of what I say to others in my professional life every day and yet make such an epic hash of it in my personal one – it reminds me of something Davis said to me, something about everyone having *two different personas. Doubling,* that's what the psychologists call it.

'We miss you too, Dan,' she says. 'Look.' She moves the phone until Juno had comes into view. She is lying on her back with just a nappy on, her chubby legs in the air, reaching for her toes and smiling.

'Hey, Pip! It's Daddy! How's my girl? Hey, sweetheart… it's Daddy, yes… Daddy misses you… hello!' I wave and coo at her image like a maniac and she coos and gurgles back at me, which admittedly makes me fight back tears. She probably has no idea who I am, this goon grinning back at her from a small screen, but I like to think she might recognise me.

'She looks different,' I say, swallowing back the lump in my throat, 'bigger, like she's grown.'

'We'll be home soon,' Fiona says, her face returning to the screen. 'Mum passed away early this morning, just gone 6 a.m.'

And there it is.

'I'm so sorry, Fi,' I say, my tone low with respect. I want to wrap my arms around her, tell her it will be OK and that I love her, because I do. I think I really do.

'It was expected, peaceful,' she says, wiping her face and composing herself. 'We were all with her, my brothers and I… and she got to meet Juno; it made her very happy to have seen her.'

I nod; frightened to speak in case I put my foot in it again.

'That's good, Fi, I'm glad.'

'Yeah…' she says, her voice almost a whisper. 'There are a few loose ends to tie up here, Dan. So it may be another week or so before we can fly back. Got to organise the funeral and sort out all her things and…'

She starts to cry and I try to think of something I can say that will be of some consolation to her in her moment of grief. But instead I say, 'Well, you'll be pleased to know I remembered which day to put the bins out.' And she laughs, which I suppose is something.

After the phone call I don't much feel like reading; my head feels sore and overcrowded, but I am too intrigued to sleep, the name Gareth Eggerton stuck on loop inside my mind. The files consist mostly of newspaper cuttings that Mitchell had found. I switch the nightlight on.

'*Twin Terrors,*' the headline screams, '*tragedy as twin sister hangs while playing with brother.*'

'*Boy, 10, distraught in game gone wrong death of twin sister,*' said another.

I look at the photographs, two small, adjacent pictures, of a little girl and boy. The girl is pretty, with long chestnut hair and a wide smile. The boy looks younger than his twin, smaller, thinner, with short brown scruffy-looking hair. He isn't smiling like his sister – he isn't smiling at all.

'*A girl from Newhaven in East Sussex was found hanging from a tree on Wednesday…*' I look at the date, 17 September 1997. '*Rosie Eggerton, aged ten, was playing with her twin brother, Gareth Eggerton, in local woodland when the tragic accident happened. The twins – who were said to be inseparable – had been climbing a tree and swinging from a makeshift rope swing when it became caught around Rosie's neck. Her distraught brother had attempted to try and help his sister by cutting the rope using a penknife but it was too late. Paramedics were called but the girl was pronounced dead at the scene. Police are currently treating the incident as a death by misadventure.*'

Rosie. Roses… Daisey had said he had called her by that name – that her attacker had called her Rosie. She thought it had been a mistake; that he'd made a mistake – but maybe it wasn't a mistake at all? And Newhaven, that's near Brighton, isn't it? Someone recently mentioned it… Iris… yes! I'm sure that's where she said she was going to stay, with an aunt; maybe that was it.

I flick through the rest of the cuttings, my heartbeat amplified in the still silence of the room. '*Twin questioned over death of his sister.*' The cutting is dated over six months later.

'*A distraught mother whose ten-year-old daughter was hanged in a game gone wrong six months ago has spoken out about how she feels her daughter's death was "no accident". Tracey Eggerton, thirty-five, from Clivedon Road in East Sussex claims that while Rosie Eggerton's death was officially recorded as misadventure, the grieving mother suspects foul play and believes that her own ten-year-old son, Gareth Eggerton – Rosie's twin brother – was responsible for his sister's death.*

'*Tracey Eggerton says: "The police may have recorded Rosie's terrible death an accident, but I am convinced there was more to*

it than that." Asked whether she believed her son may have played
any deliberate or malicious part in his sister's untimely death – the
ten-year-old was found hanging from a tree in local woodland – Mrs
Eggerton replied, "Yes, yes I do."'

'Good God,' I say aloud.

Suddenly, my phone rings again, startling me once more.

It's Mitchell.

'Sorry to call so late, boss,' she apologises. 'I know it's gone 3
a.m.; hope I didn't wake you.'

'You didn't,' I reply. 'I was just reading the file.'

'Well?' Mitchell asks.

'Well, it's definitely a possibility that Garth Eggleston and
Gareth Eggerton are the same person – and if they are, it seems
he may have begun his killing career from quite a young age.'

'More than a possibility,' Mitchell says, sounding pleased
with herself. 'Garth Eggleston doesn't exist. I ran him through
the system – the database, public records, checked them against
the details he provided for Warwick's – and there's no match, no
one by the name Garth Eggleston born in 1987 in the UK. There
is, however, a Gareth Eggerton with the exact date of birth that
Garth Eggleston gave when he joined Warwick's. I think they're
one and the same person, gov.'

A rush of adrenalin causes me to sit bolt upright and throw
my bedcovers back.

'The family fell apart after the death of the daughter, Rosie,'
Mitchell continues. 'Seems the mother was convinced the son
had murdered her, that he was responsible for his twin's death
and she was quite vocal about it too.' Mitchell draws breath. 'She
tried to convince people that her own son had killed his sister,
that he was, and I quote "evil"… anyway, it put a strain on the
marriage and the father eventually left.'

'The father?'

'John Eggerton.'

'And where is he now?'

'Dead, gov. Died of a heart attack less than a year after the death of his daughter.'

'And the mum, Tracey, is she still alive?' My breathing is laboured now; there's a tightening in my chest.

''Fraid not, gov, after the death of her husband it seems she really lost the plot and had the boy put into care, when he was twelve years old…' Mitchell pauses; I suspect she's reading something. 'A place called Allerton Manor, a care home predominantly for children with special needs, problem kids… he was under the care of someone called Dr Barber – a child psychologist. Tracey died five years ago, alcohol related; liver disease, I think.'

'Any recent photos of Eggerton?'

'Nothing I've found, boss, just the pictures in the cuttings, when he was a kid.'

'Get CGI onto it; see if they can come up with an e-fit of what he might look like now. And an address – we need an address of the place in Newhaven, where the Eggertons lived and the care home – we need to find out as much as possible about Gareth Eggerton. Oh, and the tree.'

'The tree, boss?'

'Rosie Eggerton was found hanging from a tree in local woodland – find out what type of tree it was, the name of it…'

Underneath the lilac tree, just you and me, just us three, underneath the lilac tree. It's the rhyme Daisey had remembered her attacker singing to her.

'On it, boss.'

'I'll be there in half an hour, Mitchell,' I say, my earlier fatigue replaced by a driving force more potent than drugs. 'Call Davis – tell her to meet me at the station.'

'Boss.'

'Oh – and Mitchell,' I say, 'well done.'

I can almost hear her grinning down the phone as I reach for the crumpled shirt I'd discarded next to the bed and put one arm through it hastily. I look down at the picture of the little boy on my bed, his small thin expressionless face staring back up at me.

'Gotcha!' I say as I grab my keys.

CHAPTER THIRTY-ONE

She knows she isn't supposed to go back to the apartment; that Detective Riley has told her it isn't safe, but she has to go. Something isn't right and it's nagging at her. The condom Luke had used when they'd had sex the night he supposedly murdered Leilani Stewart, he'd discarded it in the waste-paper bin in her bedroom and she needs to find it, make sure it is still there. But what if someone took it, planted his DNA at the crime scene? It was unlikely – she's clutching at straws – but it was possible wasn't it, and it would certainly explain a lot. Besides, she wants a break from Ros's place – it's doing her head in, making her feel claustrophobic. Ros has been fussing over her, checking in on her every few minutes and bringing her endless cups of tea. Tea. Why did the English think tea was the answer to everything? Someone dies; let's have a cup of tea. Lost your job? Drink some tea. Just found out your ex-fiancé is a serial killer? Cup of tea should do it!

Well, she doesn't want bloody tea. She wants answers – and wine, preferably in that order, because none of this makes any sense. The shock that maybe Luke could be responsible for her attack, and Leilani Stewart's murder, maybe even the others, felt somehow worse than when she'd first woken up in hospital attached to a load of machines. She had tried hard to absorb the thought that maybe she had been living with a murdering psychopath all this time, been a few months shy of marrying him even, but it wouldn't take hold. The more she ran it through her mind, the less convinced of it she was.

'You had a lucky escape,' Ros had said as they'd watched the police press conference on TV, the prim-looking female police superintendent explaining how they had someone in custody, a 'person of interest, helping with enquiries'. She'd noticed that the woman had lipstick on her teeth – a basic beauty faux pas – and she'd wondered why no one had thought to tell her before the cameras had started rolling.

Anyway, Ros is probably right, she has had a lucky escape, but not for the reasons she thought. Daisey realises now with some clarity that while Luke may have come across as the more superior of the two of them in their relationship, she has in fact been the stronger one all along, and yet it has taken all of this to have happened for her to recognise it.

She catches a glimpse of her reflection in a glass shopfront as she makes her way to her apartment. She looks just the same as she always has, everyone tells her this as though it should make her feel better, but she isn't the same. Nothing is. She feels like there is no ground beneath her anymore, nothing secure to get a foothold on.

She checks her watch – if she's quick she can be in and out and get back before Ros returns home from her shift and realises she's borrowed her car.

She turns the key in the lock and walks through the hallway down towards the kitchen. As she gets closer she thinks she hears voices, a man and a woman talking. Her first instinct is to think that she must've left the TV on, though she was pretty sure that wasn't likely. Fear suddenly grips her aorta, fizzes through her bloodstream and prickles her skin. Tiptoeing into the kitchen she grabs a knife from the block and stands still, the thud of her heartbeat reverberating in her ears. The voices sound like they're coming from Iris's room – she recognises one of them as Iris's voice.

'Iris!' Daisey places the knife back onto the kitchen table and tentatively walks towards her flatmate's bedroom door, taps it gently. 'Iris, are you OK? Is everything OK in there?'

The voices suddenly stop dead. She taps on the door again, slightly louder this time. 'Iris! Are you OK? It's me, Daisey; open up.'

A few moments pass before the door creeps opens.

'What the hell are you doing here?' she hisses. Her face looks somehow different, though Daisey isn't sure how, perhaps because she's never seen her so angry. 'I thought you were staying at Ros's?'

'I was… I am…' she stammers, taken aback by her abruptness. 'I needed to come back and get something.' Something is wrong and she senses it. 'Why are you still here, Iris? I thought you were going to visit your auntie in Brighton. Detective Riley said it wasn't safe.'

Iris laughs then, a strange reaction that does nothing to abate the trickle of fear she feels.

'Riley! That clown? Ha!' she snorts derisively. 'He couldn't find his arse with two hands and a flashlight! He's an idiot.'

Daisey doesn't understand. Iris's whole manner and demeanour have changed somehow.

'I heard you talking to someone… is someone else here?' She peers into the room behind her and Iris pulls the door in closer to her.

'There's no one else here, Daisey,' she says a little defensively.

'But it sounded… you were talking to a man; I heard a man's voice.' She swallows dryly. 'What's going on?' Suddenly, Daisey realises what's different about Iris's appearance. Her hair. It's slicked back off her face and is shorter, much shorter. 'You've had your hair cut,' she says before she's thought about it. 'When did you do that?'

Iris blinks at her, audibly draws breath.

'It's not a crime to get your hair cut, Daisey,' she says coolly. 'Don't you like it?'

'Yes… yes… it suits you.' Her instincts are telling her not to say anything to upset her. There's a slight pause.

'I was on the phone to my brother,' Iris explains. 'He was on loudspeaker; that's why you heard a man's voice.'

'Oh right, I see.' Daisey smiles at her weakly and then remembers. 'But I thought you didn't have a brother? A sister you said, a sister who died.'

Oh but hang on, she had mentioned a brother once before, hadn't she? One who had stood up for her against the bullies who'd teased her about her hand when she was a kid. Daisey's so confused that she instinctively massages her temples.

'I do,' Iris replies. 'She did. But I have a brother too; I told you that, Daisey.' Iris rolls her eyes. 'Anyway, why are you so interested in my family all of a sudden? I don't pry into yours, do I? I don't keep asking you about that bitch mother of yours…'

Daisey's eyes widen in shock. 'I'm sorry… I wasn't… I didn't mean to pry; I was just… it's just that…'

Iris is standing with one leg bent, her hip against the door; she raises her eyes expectantly.

'Why are *you* here?' Iris asks, her tone almost accusatory.

She wants to say it's because she lives here and that Iris has no right to even ask such a question, but she doesn't want to inflame her any more than she already appears to be.

'I need to get something,' she says. 'Did you hear about Luke?'

'Luke?'

'Yes,' Daisey says. 'He's been arrested.'

Iris's eyes light up. 'Oh, so it's *him* they're talking about on the news! Well, well, well.' She laughs a little. 'I heard on the radio that they've got someone in custody; a person of interest, they said…'

'Yeah, well, it seems that Luke is that person of interest,' Daisey says, adding, 'though I don't believe it for a second. I mean, Luke, the Rose Petal Ripper… the man who tried to kill me, has killed three others…' She shakes her head.

'Why is that so unbelievable?' Iris asks. She hasn't moved from the door. 'You said yourself he was a deceitful liar. He had an affair behind your back for two years without you even suspecting, so why is it such a stretch of the imagination to think he could be a killer?'

Daisey blinks at her. 'Because cheating on your girlfriend is one thing, and brutally murdering someone – three, almost four people – well, that's another thing altogether, don't you think?'

'No,' Iris replies flatly. 'I don't. If you really think about it, both things require a considerable ability to conceal and to lie and deceive. It's not so far a chasm to leap to believe it. What have they got on him anyway? Did the police tell you?'

Daisey's mouth is opening and closing like a fish. She isn't sure how to react, what to say, how to respond; Iris's attitude is unsettling.

'They found his DNA, semen, on that bakery girl's body – on Leilani Stewart.'

'Did they now. Well, what do you know… revenge is sweet, eh, Daisey? Bet that stuck-up cunt of a girlfriend of his isn't so smug now, is she? If I was her I would be straight down the abortion clinic.'

What was Iris saying? Why was she being so vile, so horrible? She doesn't recognise her.

'I'm going to go and look… I've got a few things I need to pick up before I go back to Ros's.' She points in the direction of her bedroom self-consciously. 'Will you be going to your aunt's house today? I really don't think it's safe to stay here, Iris, and—'

'Well, they've got their man now, haven't they.' She shrugs. 'Panic over, but if it makes you feel better…'

'I think it would.' Daisey smiles. Suddenly, she doesn't feel safe in the same room as her. 'Leave your auntie's address in Brighton, just in case,' she says. 'The police might ask for it, might want to know where you are.'

'Why would they want to know where I am, Daisey?' Iris's head is cocked to one side, her expression blank.

'I… I don't know, to know that you're safe, I suppose, or if anything happens to me.'

'And what's going to happen to you?' Iris is almost smirking.

'I don't know, nothing… it's just well, I'm going to see this psychologist, someone Dan wants me to see, an American doctor; she's going to put me under…'

'Put you under what?'

'Under hypnosis… to try and unblock my memory, see if I can remember anything of the attack, of my attacker…'

'Why would you want to do that?' Iris looks genuinely puzzled.

Daisey brushes her hair from her face nervously. Her hands are shaking slightly and she hopes Iris hasn't noticed.

'Because I want to help – there's no guarantee it will work but at least if I do remember something it might help to exonerate Luke at least.'

'Ha!' Iris throws her head back. 'And why would you want to exonerate him? I thought you'd be pleased that the snivelling little rat was behind bars… Jesus, some people.' She rolls her eyes. 'They just don't know when to look a gift horse in the mouth. I thought you'd be grateful.'

'Grateful, for what, to who? I think he's innocent… I wouldn't want to see him behind bars for something he didn't do. I just don't think he's capable of committing such horrific, awful crimes…'

Iris is shaking her head, sighing. 'You really are just so… *nice*, aren't you, Daisey? Doormat Daisey coming to the rescue of the man who lied to her, cheated on her repeatedly and humiliated her, brought his mistress into her home and fucked her in her own bed, cheated her out of her perfect life, of being the perfect wife and mother she's always dreamed of being, even trying to take her home from her… yet still she wants to help him! Incredible really.' She shakes her head again. 'Luke might be innocent of committing these – what did you call them – "horrific", "awful" crimes, but he is hardly innocent is he?'

'Yes, but that doesn't mean…' Daisey thinks to try and defend herself, to defend Luke but her instincts are screaming at her to leave, to get away from Iris and her sudden strange and unpleasant shift in character. 'Look, I've not got a lot of time,' she explains. 'Ros will be back soon and I don't want her to know I've borrowed her car, so I'll just go get my things. I'll see you soon. I'll be back once the police say it's safe… have a nice time at your aunt's.'

She walks swiftly to her bedroom, closing the door and standing behind it. She stands still for a moment, waiting for her breath to regulate before walking over to the waste-paper bin. It's as she left it; a few tampon cartons, an empty moisturiser bottle, some cotton wool, a Durex wrapper… but the condom isn't there. She sifts through it, pulling the items out one by one, checking and double-checking. But it's gone.

Instinctively her hand goes up to her chest as a horrible slew of thoughts scatter through her brain like confetti. Placing everything back into the bin she grabs a few items of clothing from the drawer to make it look as though she has come for them instead and throws them into her tote bag.

'I'm leaving now!' she calls out to Iris. Iris is outside her bedroom door as she opens it, causing Daisey to gasp and take a step back.

'Did you get everything you need?' Her demeanour seems to have switched back to normal, her stance softer along with her tone. 'I did some washing for you.' She holds out a pile of clothes to her. 'All ironed and folded – nice and fresh.'

'Thanks, thank you,' she stammers, tentatively taking them.

'Can I get you anything before you go?' Iris asks. 'Something to eat maybe? We could grab a quick coffee, if you like.'

'No!' Daisey says, a little too quickly, adding. 'I'm sorry, Iris, I'm pushed for time, got to get back…'

Iris nods. 'Of course. I'll see you soon then.'

'Yes.' Daisey swallows. 'See you soon.'

'Take care of yourself, and keep safe.'

'I will, thanks, you too.'

'Oh and try not to worry about Luke,' she adds in a manner that is in stark contrast to the one she'd had moments ago. 'I'm sure if he's innocent then the police will find out and let him go.'

'Yes.' Daisey nods. 'I'm sure they will!' Her eyes move to the shelf in the hallway, next to where she's standing. Iris's phone is on it. How could it be that she'd been talking to her brother on loudspeaker if her phone was right here?

She turns to open the door but the movement somehow triggers a memory burst. *He's standing there, at the front door as she answers it. His hand raised, the hammer he's holding in his fingers and… Oh God!* Daisey gasps aloud. *His fingers!*

Suddenly, Iris is behind her and sensing it she scrabbles to open the door.

'You know, if you want a job doing properly round here,' Iris says, striking Daisey over the head with the hammer she's holding, 'you've got to do it yourself.'

CHAPTER THIRTY-TWO

'Garth Eggelston,' I say the name again, 'he worked with you at Warwick's for a short time back in 2017, as your assistant; do you remember him, Des?'

Desmond Taylor, a rotund, balding man who looks to be in his early seventies, sips on his second cup of tea since I've been here and blinks at me thoughtfully. I check the clock on the wall surreptitiously, mindful of the time. Daisey has agreed to meet with Annabelle Henderson today and I'm hopeful that the fragrant doctor will manage to persuade her to go through with her hypnotherapy session. According to Henderson, the worst-case scenario is that Daisey won't recall anything of 'significant value' to the investigation and we'll be no better off, and the best-case scenario is that she will be able to give us a full description of her attacker, maybe even identify him outright, which understandably is the preferred outcome.

'Either way,' Annabelle informed me, 'Daisey will benefit on a psychological level from releasing the blocks in her mind, even if it doesn't seem so at first.' I only hope she's right because time is of the essence. We need to identify and locate Garth Eggleston – and fast.

'He was around thirty at the time,' I say, attempting to jog his memory and hide my impatience at the same time. I remind myself that he has the onset of dementia and not to expect too much from him.

'Worked there all me life, I did,' he says proudly, 'man and boy... Reggie Arkwright, he was the fella what employed me, he was me governor, taught me all the tricks of the trade he did, bit of this... bit of that... lovely old boy he was, from the West Country, had a set of false teeth that were too big for his mouth, always losing them... I found them in a bucket once that he'd been using to wash some windows... been looking for them all day he had.' He chuckles at the recollection.

I've read somewhere that this is common among those poor souls suffering with dementia – they can recall a long-term memory from way back with remarkable detail yet don't recognise one of their offspring who they saw just yesterday.

'Anyway, you was just a twinkle in your father's eye back then...' He points at me, gulps back more tea. 'Me whole life spent at that place, like a second home to me it was. When my Lillian was alive she used to say I had two wives, she was one of 'em and Warwick's was the other, God rest her soul. Haven't known what to do with meself since I left the place... rattling around here on me own. I even got up and went into work the other day, totally forgot I'd retired, force of habit you see, over fifty years of habit! They had to send me home again...' His voice trails off wistfully and I feel a stab of empathy for him. 'I miss the place,' he sighs. 'Sorry, who was it you said you was looking for again?'

I take a deep breath. 'You may have known him as Garth Eggleston,' I say for the third time. 'He worked with you, Des, for around two months or so back in 2017, helping you out with odd jobs and maintenance work.'

He shakes his head. 'They come, they go... some of these lads I've had under me wing over the years... well, they didn't last five minutes, did they, didn't have what it takes, you know? People think: "maintenance", how hard can it be? Changing a few lightbulbs here and there, but it was much more than that, Detective – what did you say your name was again?'

'Riley,' I say, 'Detective Riley.'

'Yeah, well, Riley, like I say, they come and they go. For me, it was a labour of love, a purpose, something to take pride in, but for others, well, they were just passing through, weren't they? Didn't have the minerals, the mettle you needed to—'

'Was Garth just passing through?' I cut in. 'Was Garth one of the people who couldn't hack it? He left abruptly, didn't he? Just didn't show up for work one morning – that's right, isn't it?'

'Who's Garth?' he says and I stuff my clenched fist into my pocket.

'He worked with you for a while, Des,' I say again, 'an apprentice of yours, back in 2017, he only lasted a few weeks, around thirty? You remember him?'

'That's my daughter, my Miranda,' he says, nodding at a photograph of a young girl and boy on the mantelpiece beside me. 'Proper little belter, ain't she?'

'Yes.' I smile, though if I'm honest it's more of a prelude to a scream. 'She's lovely,' I say, glancing at it briefly. Terrible cruel thing, dementia, I think to myself as he picks up the photo and looks at it. Our memories are the fabric of who we are, what all of our lives are made up of. They're the back catalogue of our very existence, a visual soundtrack of where we have been, what we've seen and how we felt about it all. It must be like slowly losing a piece of yourself every day.

''Course she's not so little anymore.' He looks at the photo adoringly. 'All grown up now… haven't seen her in a while.' He frowns at the picture. 'Not sure who the fella next to her is though…'

'Anyway,' I say, gently taking it from him and placing it back down onto the mantelpiece, noticing the handwriting on the back of the frame. It reads: *Miranda and Jason, Bournemouth 1982.* Brother and sister, I assume. 'Garth Eggleston.'

'Garth… Garth Eggleston… hmm.' He pauses for a few moments and I inwardly hold my breath. 'Ah yes, Eggleston, I do remember him, now you say the name!'

I fist-pump the air in my head.

'Young lad, strange boy…'

'Strange?' I say. 'In what way, Des?'

His eyes glaze over. 'Small but surprisingly strong, not a lot of meat on him… quiet, kept himself to himself.'

'Anything else you remember about him; hair colour, eyes… you wouldn't happen to have a photograph of him, would you, Des?' It's a long shot, I realise, but you never know.

'Can't say I do,' he says. 'Can't really remember the lad well. Like I say, small, on the thin side, bit of a strange way about him… shy, like he wouldn't say boo to a goose. There was something different about him though, something…' He strains to recall, a visible frown etched on his brow.

'Different how, physically you mean?' I press gently.

He pauses for a moment. 'Nope, it's gone, sorry.' He pours himself another cup of tea from the pot, gestures to an empty cup next to it.

'You sure I can't get you one, Mr…?'

'Riley,' I remind him. 'And no thank you, Des. Did he ever talk to you about anything, where he was from, family, girlfriends, that kind of thing?'

'Who?'

'Garth Eggleston,' I say.

He looks at me puzzled. 'Young fella?'

It's time to retreat.

'Thanks, Des,' I say, standing to leave. 'You've been very helpful.'

'He worked with me for a bit. Small chap, wasn't there for long. Don't think he was up to the job. Why do you ask?'

'We're investigating a series of murders, Des,' I explain. 'Two of the victims both worked at Warwick's at some point; we think there may be a possible connection, that the killer might've worked there himself.' I can see I'm getting nowhere; it's not his fault, but I'm wasting valuable time.

'It's been good to talk to you, Des.' I shake his hand. 'I wish you all the best in your retirement.'

I scan his apartment; it's small but neat, not a lot to show for over fifty years of hard work and suddenly I'm hit by a wave of sadness as I imagine Des's slow and lonely decline into dementia. 'And if there's anything else you remember, please do call me; it could be extremely helpful.'

'A sister,' he says suddenly. 'He talked about a sister... and well, I'm sure there was something unusual about him, something about how he looked but... I just can't remember what it was; me memory isn't what it used to be, Detective Rogers.'

'A sister?'

'Yes, though why I've remembered that I've no idea.' He chuckles, almost pleased with himself.

'Did he ever mention her name, this sister's name?'

He shakes his head. 'Well, if he did I'm afraid I can't remember it.'

I nod.

'She was dead though,' he says, 'I do remember that.'

My blood runs to ice.

'How do you know she was dead, Des?'

'Because he told me he'd killed her,' he says, adding, 'You sure I can't get you a cup of tea, Detective Richards?'

CHAPTER THIRTY-THREE

In direct contrast to poor Des, Dr Barber is remarkably fit looking for a man in his seventies. Tall, with a lithe physique, he's not long returned from a five-mile run when Davis and I show up at his impressive residence on the outskirts of North London.

'I was expecting you earlier,' he says, convivial as he shakes our hands respectively.

'Traffic,' I say. 'Hazard of the job.'

'Among many others, I'm sure,' he says, smiling. 'Let's go through to my study, shall we? I'll ask Mary to bring us in some refreshments.'

His study is just how I would expect a psychiatrist's study to look – decorated with bookshelves, an antique desk with a leather top and a large comfy-looking armchair scattered with cushions. There's a box of tissues on a small side table next to it.

'As you know, I'm retired now,' he says, 'five years ago. I do occasionally see private clients here at home, but it is mostly to keep me occupied, keep a toe in the water so to speak. Do take a seat.' He gestures to Davis and I to sit down and we duly comply. 'Ah, Mary.' An older-looking, well-dressed lady comes in with a tray of refreshments. I presume she's his housekeeper.

'There's coffee, tea and some iced water,' she announces efficiently, placing it down onto the desk. 'Help yourself to whatever you prefer. Oh, and there's some banana cake left. I made it just yesterday so it should still be moist.'

'Mary's banana cake.' Dr Barber winks at me. 'It really is delicious.' He pats his slim stomach. 'And also the reason I try and run a few miles every day.'

I smile, watch him as he pours us all some tea.

'I believe you know a Gareth Eggerton, that he was a subject of yours, a patient, back in 1997, at Allerton Manor, a care home for troubled juveniles. You were the resident consultant child psychiatrist at the time, is that right?'

He takes a sip of his tea, holding the china cup almost daintily between his fingers.

'Yes, that's correct. My job was largely in an advisory capacity for other members of the medical teams working there. I would oversee patient diagnoses, recommend medication where appropriate and other treatment strategies, plus offering support on managing behavioural health conditions.'

I nod. 'But you knew him – Eggerton?'

Dr Barber nods. 'Yes, of course. I'd forgotten about Gareth when you called to enquire about him,' he says, stroking his neatly clipped beard. 'Haven't heard that name in an awfully long time.' His voice trails off. 'Of course, when I say "forgotten", I mean I hadn't thought of him in many years, no reason to. Hearing his name jogged my memory though, reminded me of what an interesting case he was.'

'How so, Doctor?'

He sips his tea, draws breath.

'Well, he came to Allerton in 1999, as you rightly say, when he was twelve years old. His father had died some months earlier – a sudden heart attack, I think – and his mother, Tracey, had undergone quite a severe a nervous breakdown which as a result rendered her incapable of looking after him. He was placed into the care of the local authority where he was assessed and diagnosed to have some considerable psychiatric issues, hence ending up at Allerton.'

I nod at him to continue.

'Gareth was a twin. He had a sister, Rosie, to whom he was exceptionally close. From what I gathered, she was the dominant of the two, not uncommon among twins. What was uncommon however was that his mother had alleged that her son had killed her – the twin, I mean. Her mother and father found her, hanging from a tree where she had been playing with Gareth. Although the death was officially recorded as an accident, a misadventure, Tracey was convinced that Gareth was somehow responsible for his sister's death and that it was a deliberate act of murder. Once the father had died she became quite vociferous about this accusation, insisting that she believed he had in fact killed and attempted to kill others as well as his own sister.'

'Others?' Davis says, writing in her notebook. 'Do you know who?'

'I'm afraid I cannot recall any names.' He smiles apologetically. 'Anyway,' he continues, 'according to Tracey Eggerton's account, Gareth had killed an animal some years previously. She alleged that she had found him in the woods standing over the carcass with a knife, although both Gareth and his sister claimed to have stumbled across it while out playing.'

I raise my eyebrows.

'There's more, Detective. Some years later, a child, a toddler, was found drowned in a stream in a local park near to where the Eggertons lived. The official verdict was "accidental death" but Tracey insisted that Gareth was responsible and that he and his sister had been playing with the little boy moments before he had met his unfortunate demise. Some years following, there had been another incident where they had been playing in a tree – incidentally, the same tree where Rosie was found hanging – with a friend of Gareth's from school. Both Gareth and the boy had climbed the tree and at some point the boy fell. His injuries were life-changing; broken skull, neck and back, resulting in paralysis, plus some injuries to the brain, leaving him with quite severe learning difficulties as a result.'

'And Tracey believed that Gareth had pushed him?'

'Yes,' he says. 'Yes, she did. Even though again, it was officially recorded as a misadventure.'

I look over at Davis; wonder if she's thinking the same thing I'm thinking.

'Tracey believed that the sister, Rosie, was covering up for her brother, that she was scared of him, despite him being physically much smaller than she was. Which leads me on to explain about his birth abnormalities.'

'Abnormalities?'

'Yes. Tracey was told she was expecting twin girls – the ultrasound identifying both infants in the womb as female. It was something of a shock, then, when she gave birth to what she thought was a boy.'

'What she *thought* was a boy?'

'I'll explain.' He nods in recognition of my confusion. 'It seems that Gareth was born with ambiguous genitalia; he was an intersex baby.'

I glance sideways at Davis. 'You mean a hermaphrodite?'

'No,' Dr Barber, says, 'not exactly – there's a difference, and this is a simple way of explaining a complicated condition, a rare condition where an infant's external genitals don't appear to be clearly defined as either male or female at birth.' Clearly he has read both Davis's and my expressions as he gives a gentle laugh.

'Gareth Eggerton was born with both ovarian and testicular tissues; in his particular case, his penis was abnormally small with the urethral opening positioned closer to the scrotum. There can be many variations of these malformations – these ambiguities: an infant born with female genitalia and internal male organs, hormones and tissues, and vice versa.'

'So.' I clear my throat; try to get my thoughts around what he's saying. 'You're saying he was born both a boy *and* a girl?'

'It's more complex than this, Detective.' He smiles gently. 'Like I say, intersex. It's a genetic condition. Reading the medical notes taken at his birth, he possessed both male and female chromosomes. Perhaps you may remember from biology lessons at school that after conception the XX chromosome results in a female infant, and the XY chromosome a male. In Gareth's case, he was born with XXY. Although it is not a common condition it is not perhaps as rare as people would think. In most cases – back then anyway as I believe things are different today – the doctors would assign the baby with a dominant gender and surgery would be performed to remove any... ambiguity. This is what happened with Gareth. As he presented outwardly as male – albeit with some abnormalities – he was assigned male gender and underwent various surgeries as an infant to remove any female tissues and organs – in his case, ovaries, I think – and a partially formed womb.'

I try not to look as horrified as I feel. 'I see. Did Gareth know about this? Was he told? If so do you think this resulted in him having some identity issues.'

Dr Barber looks almost pleased. 'Yes, Detective, I do. It seems his parents never spoke about it to him, and rarely to each other even. I believed he found out from his sister. She'd overheard her parents discussing it and told her brother.' He momentarily pauses, allows us to digest his words. 'I spoke with Gareth at length when he arrived at Allerton and continued to work with him on and off until he left. He was suffering from dissociative identity disorder – often, and wrongly in my opinion, described as split personality or personalities plural, as there can be many.'

'Gareth had a split personality?'

He snorts gently. 'Again, it was more complicated than that, Detective.'

'Did he admit to killing his sister?'

He shakes his head. 'No, never to me anyway. Gareth loved his twin. She was his closest ally, his "other half", if you will; he doted on her – and she on him, I believe.'

'But do you think he killed her?' Davis asks, scribbling furiously. 'In your professional opinion, I mean.'

Dr Barber sighs deeply. 'Physically, perhaps, but psychologically, I'm not so sure.'

'I don't follow.'

He smiles in a way people do when they're discussing things most people have little understanding of.

'Gareth told me they'd been playing on a rope swing, him and his sister – one that he'd made and attached to the tree – when apparently it had somehow got caught around the little girl's neck. He claimed that Rosie had made the loop herself and had dared him to put his neck in it, swing from the tree and see how long it was before he passed out. Then she would cut the rope, cut him free so that he wouldn't die, wouldn't hang.'

'That sounds like a pretty dark and dangerous game for two ten-year-olds to play,' I remark.

'Indeed it does, Detective, and it is interesting if in fact, as Gareth had claimed, that it was Rosie's idea. He told me he'd been reluctant at first but she had insisted – the dominant twin – and so eventually he acquiesced, he put his neck in the loop and had passed out. He remembered waking up on the grass beneath, dazed and dizzy. As they had agreed, Rosie had cut the rope. But when it came to her turn something went wrong, Gareth couldn't manage to cut the rope in time, or so he said, and she died.' He sits back in the chair, folds one leg over the other.

'And you believed him?'

He looks at me, taps his lips with his finger, that pet hate of mine that seems to serve no purpose at all.

'I believed him when he told me that *he* didn't kill her, and by *he* I mean Gareth, because actually they were not alone at the time his sister died.'

'There was someone else present?' I ask.

'The little girl they mentioned?' Davis interjects. 'The one they always played with but no one knew who she was, that someone else?'

He nods slowly. 'Yes; only the little girl who no one knew was, I believe, actually Gareth himself. She was part of his dissociative disorder – a separate identity. They may have shared the same body, but it seems this is where the similarity ended.'

'So,' I say, leaning forward slightly, which is also another thing I've noticed people tend to do when they're trying to concentrate, 'let me get this right – you're saying that this other identity, this female identity that Gareth had inside him, took over and killed the sister?'

The doctor nods again. 'In my opinion it's possible, yes. I'm not saying that this is what took place, but I suspected that it was definitely possible.' He pauses, draws breath. 'Gareth appeared to deteriorate after his twin's death. When he came here as a child – and that is what he was, Detective Riley, just a child – he was a painfully shy little boy, very softly spoken, a touch effeminate I suppose due perhaps to his birth condition, a hormonal imbalance. But he was likeable, pleasant and polite, at least while he presented as Gareth. After Rosie died, after his father died and his mother technically abandoned him, this other part of his identity began to become, I suspect, much more prominent.'

'How do you mean?'

'The splitting became more frequent, more prevalent. To put simply, it began to take over. Less of Gareth and more of the other... she had a name, now, what was it...' He taps his lip again. 'You'll forgive me; it was some time ago now.'

'This other identity inside of him had her own name?'

'Yes, yes she did. And her character was the antithesis to Gareth's own. She was brasher, more vocal, confident, she could be rude and abrupt, disruptive, cruel even.'

'You met her?'

'Oh yes,' he says, as though this is a stupid question, 'many times over the years. At different stages the female identity was the more dominant. She tended to show up when Gareth felt under duress… goodness me, what was her name again? I should know it…' He strains to recall, shakes his head. 'Anyway, it will come back to me.'

'Violent?' Davis asks the question for me. 'Was she ever violent?'

'Not that I ever recall but she was certainly less amenable and less likeable. She presented very differently to Gareth. It would be a struggle to the unexperienced eye to have known they were one and the same person.'

He pauses again, sips his tea. 'Dissociative identity disorder is commonly triggered by severe trauma at a young age. Essentially the mind splits so as to lessen the trauma one experiences. It creates another "self" as a means of survival, it happens a lot in severely abused children for example; they create another identity, one that they go to in a bid to escape what is happening to them. It is a very real disorder that not many people – professional or otherwise – have a great understanding of. There are even some who suggest that it doesn't exist at all and that those allegedly affected with such a disorder are simply "faking" it, perhaps to use as a means of defence. But I can assure you that it does exist and I have treated quite a number of sufferers during my time as a psychiatrist. These are not simply "voices in the head"; they are real people with a whole set of different characteristics, mannerisms, even a different gait to the original body they are hosting in. They can have a completely separate history, memory and thought process. They can be a different age, race and gender, they can even speak another language, and there can be many co-existing in one body – I had a patient who had five different selves once. It was often very crowded during a therapy session with him.' He smiles.

'So, did Gareth know, I mean, was he aware of his "other self"?' I ask him, enthralled.

'Some people are aware of the other or others existing alongside themselves, whereas others are not. I think, if I recall, Gareth was aware, and became more aware still, even frightened, as she became more prevalent.'

'So was it trauma or his birth condition that caused him to split?'

'It is very difficult to know that exactly, Detective. There is absolutely no evidence whatsoever anecdotal or otherwise to suggest that intersex babies are more prone to such a disorder, none at all. Many infants who're born intersex have no idea they were born this way – it was a taboo subject, more so back then. Now it is treated differently; physicians are more likely to wait until the infant is older and naturally identifies with a particular gender before they undergo surgery, and some remain gender fluid. I do however think the trauma of losing his sister – or perhaps indeed even being responsible for her death – exacerbated the splitting he subsequently experienced.'

'How was he treated? Was he on medication?'

'There is no magic pill for dissociative identity disorder, although I suspect he was prescribed anti-depressants, maybe anti-anxiety drugs alongside therapy and counselling. It's a troubling condition for those affected.'

'When did he leave Allerton, Dr Barber?'

'When he became old enough to be deemed able to make decisions on his own, when he was legally classed as an adult, which back then was sixteen years old. We were not able to prevent him from leaving. He was not deemed a danger to himself, or others, and he had no convictions. I have no idea of where he went or what happened to him after that – and I never saw him again. Though I would be lying if I said I hadn't wondered over the years about what had happened to him, if his condition had worsened, how or if he managed to maintain any sense of a satisfactory existence.'

He places his teacup down onto the desk, looks at me sagely. 'You think that maybe Gareth is somehow responsible for the murders of these three women, and the attack of another?'

'Yes, it's possible,' I reply, using his turn of phrase. 'And knowing what we now know from you, it's also possible that he may well be living as two different people.'

'And that one of them is murdering the women, yes, I see.' He nods.

'Would you say, having known Gareth, that he is capable of murder, Dr Barber?'

He raises his eyes. 'You above all people should know the answer to that question, Detective Riley. We are all, are we not, given the right circumstances, capable of such an act?' He smiles kindly.

'You have been exceptionally helpful,' I say, standing. Davis follows suit, finishing the dregs of her tea and stealing a slice of banana cake while the doctor isn't looking. 'Exceptionally.'

'But of course.' He nods graciously. 'Like I said, if I can be of any further assistance… there are files somewhere, perhaps still at Allerton, or maybe they've been archived somewhere. I will make an attempt to locate them for you – all the detail will be in there, all his notes, medical information, photographs too. Actually!' He stands abruptly. 'Now I think of it, I may well have something of interest for you.' He begins routing around on one of the bookshelves. 'An album.'

'Photo album?' I say.

'Yes, like a yearbook, I suppose. The staff compiled them for the students, the patients. They did one each year, a photograph of a student with an accolade underneath, documenting their achievements during their time with us; it was mostly an exercise in positive reinforcements, bringing a sense of normality to their existence. Now, where is it? Aha!' He begins flicking through the dusty book, turning the pages slowly. 'Here he is.' He taps at the page satisfactorily, turns it around for me to look at.

I stare down at the book, at the photograph on the page. He looks younger than sixteen, more like the age he was when he'd first arrived at Allerton. He's sitting on a school chair, hands folded neatly in his lap. He's smiling in the picture but it isn't reaching his eyes and I sense it's not a smile of happiness but one he'd been asked to give for the camera. There is something about his face that suddenly strikes me as faintly familiar, though the connection isn't forthcoming. I stare at it a little longer, my eyes burning into the page. *Gareth Eggerton – gentleman, champion table tennis player and chief ironer!*

'Chief ironer?' I look up at Dr Barber.

He shrugs. 'He was particular, very neat, always kept his bedroom and himself – his clothes – freshly washed and ironed.'

'All the victims have had floral names, Doctor,' Davis says, hiding the slice of cake behind her back. 'And a rose left on their naked bodies.'

'He treats them with respect after he kills them,' I add, 'places their clothes neatly beside them, meticulous, almost as though he is caring for them.'

'Ah, well, I see…' Dr Barber gives me a resolute look that needs no explanation.

'Gareth's sister was called Rosie – which would seem an obvious connection – and perhaps explain the reason why he leaves one on their bodies. Could he be killing them as some kind of sacrifice, re-enacting the death of his sister? Or perhaps the "other identity" is responsible for their deaths and he isn't even aware he is killing them?'

The doctor looks at me, shakes my hand.

'Yes, Detective Riley, it's possible, it's all possible.'

'Thank you again.' I nod as we leave.

'My pleasure, oh! And enjoy the cake, DS Davis.' He smiles at her. 'I really can recommend it.'

CHAPTER THIRTY-FOUR

'I'm issuing an APB on Gareth Eggerton AKA Garth Eggleston,' I address the team back at the nick. 'Check if CGI has come up with that e-fit yet and get this photo of him over to them ASAP.' I hand Baylis a copy of the image taken from the Allerton yearbook. 'He's thirty-three, originally from Newhaven in Brighton – so get onto Brighton and tell them to keep their eyes wide open because there's every chance he could've gone back there, to his home town, where his sister was killed.'

'I went to canvass the neighbours, boss,' Parker says.

'And?'

'And most of them have moved away since the Eggertons lived there, apart from a…' – he refers to his notebook – 'Mrs Runacus, Edith Runacus, eighty-four, who lived a few doors down from them. She remembered the Eggertons, said they were a lovely family, ordinary, but that the boy, Gareth, was a little "off colour", was how she put it. She said the mother favoured the girl, was rarely ever seen out with the boy. After Rosie died the family fell apart apparently. She used to hear the mum and dad arguing, Tracey crying, and then she didn't see the dad anymore, thinks he must've left the family home.

'After he died of a heart attack, Mrs Runacus went to see Tracey Eggerton to offer her condolences. She told me that all Tracey could talk about was her son, how he was evil and wicked and that he'd killed his sister and the dad, effectively. She remembers smelling strong alcohol on her breath and had called in social services because she'd been worried about the boy. After Gareth was taken away, Edith Runacus said Tracey Eggerton became an alcoholic recluse who rarely left the house. She lived at the address up until she died a few years later.'

'Good work, Parker, anything else?'

'Yes, boss, the tree where Rosie Eggerton was found hanged. It's still there and I had a surgeon check it out. Apparently, it's a Japanese lilac tree, the biggest of its variety, grows to around twenty-five feet in height, famous for its beautiful white blossom.'

That and dead children hanging from it, I think to myself as I close my eyes momentarily.

Underneath the lilac tree, just you and me, just us three…

Three. It's been bugging me, the rhyme that Daisey's attacker sang to her, as to who this third person might've been, but having spoken to Dr Barber I now think it was referring to Gareth's other self, the girl…

'Where are with speaking to old colleagues from Warwick's? We need to get a recent ID of Eggerton, his appearance could've, and probably has, drastically changed since he was sixteen.'

'I've been tracing them, gov,' Mitchell says. 'I've spoken to a few people who worked there around the same time but no one really remembers him.'

'Ros!' I say aloud. 'She'll have been working at Warwick's around that time. Get her on the phone, and Daisey too obviously – now we have a name, it might jog something. Shit!' I look at my watch. 'Henderson.' I turn to Davis. 'Daisey's appointment with Henderson, it's in ten minutes. Let's go.'

I grab my jacket and keys.

'Boss!' Parker stops me as I'm walking out of the door.

'Be quick, Parker, I have somewhere to be.'

'Yes, boss, the night of Leilani Stewart's murder… I checked out Ros and Iris's alibis like you asked me to… seems Ros's checks out; she was at home with her partner Ron; a neighbour popped by too, corroborated the time. But Iris...'

'Go on...' I chivvy him along impatiently.

'She claims she went to the cinema, right? Well, CCTV does pick her up buying a ticket at approximately 7.45 for the 9.30 later showing that evening.'

'What, and she never showed up?'

'Yes, boss, she did show up; cameras pick her up again around 9.45 entering the Odeon, carrying something, a paper bag – I can't be sure but it may be a loaf of bread, or some kind of groceries. The cameras pick her up again leaving after the film finished around 11.30 p.m. So there's no accounting for her whereabouts between approximately 7.45 and 9.45 p.m.'

I stop, pause for a moment.

'Find out where she is, Parker. She said she was going to stay with an aunt, find out where, if she left an address, call her, tell her we need to speak to her. Oh and run a check on her, Parker.'

'Gov.' He nods. 'You have a surname on her?'

I stop, think and look at Davis for help.

She shrugs and flicks back through her notes.

'Iris... Iris... *Egan*,' she says, looking up at me slowly. 'Iris Egan.'

Egan. Eggleston. Eggerton...

A loaf of bread, Iris said she'd been into the bakery that day, the day of Leilani's murder, and I remember seeing it still on the kitchen worktop at Daisey's apartment when we went to inform her about Luke. A thought spins through my mind like a top before Parker breaks it.

'Oh, and someone called Des called for you, sir; said it may be nothing but can you call him back?'

'Will do.'

Davis and I are halfway out of door before Archer spies me from her office and pokes her head around the door.

'Dan, a quick word please,' she says curtly.

'I'm sorry, ma'am.' I carry on walking past. 'I have something urgent to do.'

'And what is that, Riley?' she asks, a little indignant.

'What I do best, ma'am,' I call out behind me, 'what I do best.'

CHAPTER THIRTY-FIVE

'Dan!' Annabelle Henderson opens the highly decorative stained-glass front door to her smart London town house, a residence that is befitting of her, and greets me like one might an old friend who they hadn't seen in a while. 'I've been expecting you. Come in.' She smiles widely, warmly at me and swishes her long, high-lighted, honey-blonde hair back from her face, giving me a waft of that unique scent of hers, coconut and beaches and sun cream, something I cannot help suspect that she's done deliberately.

'It's great to see you again,' she remarks as she sashays down the tiled vast hallway, barefoot, the tie-dye kaftan she's wearing billowing out behind her. It looks expensive, like everything else about her, and her impressive home, which is elaborately decorated in an artistic manner. It reminds me that I should give my own apartment a lick of paint before Fiona and Juno return, freshen the place up a bit, maybe even add a feature wall or whatever they're called. Fiona has mentioned them before – feature walls – though she may as well be speaking to me in her mother tongue because DIY in my case pretty much abbreviates as Decorating Isn't Your thing.

'You too, Doctor,' I reply. Davis slips round the front door behind me a few moments later.

'Oh.' She smiles thinly. 'You brought a colleague with you. Pleased to make your acquaintance...'

'Davis,' she says, shaking her manicured hand. 'DS Lucy Davis.'

She nudges me in the back as we both – I think – note the slightest hint of disappointment in her voice.

'I'm sorry we're a bit late.' I cough into my fist. 'It's been an eventful morning.'

'Really? How so, Detective? And you're not late, not technically anyway. Daisey hasn't arrived yet.'

'No?' I check my watch. It's 3.45 p.m. Her appointment was at 3.30.

'She must be held up; can I get you both something to drink? Juice, tea, coffee, iced tea, iced latte, a Scotch on the rocks, perhaps?'

'The latter is tempting,' I say, 'but we're on duty.'

She nods. 'Right. Well, everything's ready for Daisey when she gets here. Actually, I think it might be useful if you are present during the session, Dan.' She rests her hand on my arm and gives me a meaningful book. 'She trusts you; she might feel safer if you're in the room with us, right?'

'Right. Well, if you think so, Doctor.'

'Oh come on,' she says, her accent slightly more detectable now, 'it's Annabelle, remember… call me Annabelle please!'

Davis visibly turns away and I suspect she might actually be laughing.

Dr Henderson does have a somewhat unorthodox manner about her, which is why, I'll admit, I think I'm slightly attracted to her. She comes across as a bit bohemian; a free spirit, and considering the nature of her profession, I find this quite refreshing. She disappears for a moment, leaving Davis and I in what appears to be a sort of therapy area; there's minimal furniture in the room, just giant, plump white scatter cushions and an array of rugs and throws, a low Perspex coffee table with a selection of scented candles and a huge palm pot in the corner – a trendy LA doctor's waiting room, I suppose.

'Stylish,' Davis observes. 'Very Haute Hippie.'

'I have no idea what that even means, Davis,' I remark.

'Well, at least I can now see why Archer warned you about "keeping things professional".' She sticks her tongue into the side of her cheek. 'Did you see her face when she saw me tagging along?'

'Don't be ridiculous, Davis,' I reply, feeling slightly warm through the cheeks. 'She's just American, from California; they do things a little differently than us uptight Brits.'

Davis glances sideways at me and smirks. 'Riiiight. Very differently,' she says, mimicking Henderson's accent.

I turn away from her so she doesn't catch me smiling.

'Daisey is late,' I say, looking at my watch again. 'I'm worried she's changed her mind.'

'She'll be here,' Davis says with more confidence than I have, 'if only in an attempt to help get that cheating ex of hers off the hook. I think she still loves him, you know, even after everything…' Davis picks up a candle, sniffs it. 'Sad really,' she adds. 'I'd bloody well have John's bollocks as earrings if he even thought about doing half of what Bradley did to that poor woman. My pride wouldn't allow me to continue to love someone who had treated me so badly.'

'Pride is the mask of one's own faults, Lucy,' I say, not wishing to deliberately remind her of her own brief and regrettable infidelity with Delaney, an ex-colleague who I'd taken an instant dislike to some years back.

I drop down onto one of the huge beanbag cushions and sink into it, attempt to get comfortable but don't know what to do with my limbs; they feel awkward and unnatural. I think I prefer the structure of a good old-fashioned chair; you know where you are with one of those. I fish around in my pocket for the page I'd torn from Allerton's yearbook that Dr Barber had given me, unfold it and stare at Gareth Eggerton's young face. I try to look for something – I'm not sure what – some kind of clue, some kind of marker that could ever suggest he was capable of committing the crimes – dreadful, heinous acts of violence. Yet the more I stare at the image, the more he looks to me like a sad little boy, an unwanted child alone in the world. It's an uncomfortable juxtaposition.

'You definitely think it's him, boss?' Davis says, nodding at the picture. 'After everything Dr Barber told us about his identity issues, his sister's death, her name being Rosie… and that Des bloke saying something about him having said he'd killed her… it makes sense, he fits the profile, anyway. We just need to link him to the murders. And find him.'

Des! Davis has reminded me. Parker had said that he'd called me, said he'd remembered something else.

'Call Parker and ask him to get Des Taylor on the phone, Davis,' I say, staring at the photo. 'And call Daisey too, find out where she is. I'm getting concerned.'

Something about the photograph… I don't know what but there's something. I look at it some more, study Gareth's face, his small slightly sunken eyes and small hollow cheeks, the thin Mona Lisa almost-smile and… I look down at his hands, clasped together in his lap, small and childlike and… I cock my head to one side, bring the page in closer.

'Parker for you, boss.' Davis hands me the phone. 'Des Taylor's on the line.'

My heart is banging against my ribs and adrenalin causes me to stand.

'Detective Inspector Riley.'

'Mr Riley, it's Desmond Taylor from Warwick's, well, formerly of Warwick's, fifty years in fact!'

'Yes, Des, you called me earlier, said you had something to tell me… something you remembered after I came to see you the other day – something about Garth Eggleston?'

'Who?' he replies and I swallow dryly, close my eyes for strength.

'You called me, Des, to speak to me… did you have something to tell me?'

There's a pause on the line.

'Oh yes! Detective Riley, you came to see me the other day.'

'That's right,' I say, 'the other day, to talk to you about Garth Eggleston, a man who worked with you – for you – back in the summer of 2017. You said he was on the small side, a bit sickly looking, do you remember?'

'Of course I remember!' he says, a touch affronted. 'I'm not completely senile, at least not yet.' He chuckles a little and that pang of empathy is there again. 'Small lad, pale and a bit odd-looking but stronger than he appeared, could lift a ladder and bucket easily enough, even with his funny hand.'

'His funny hand?'

'Yeah. Poor little bugger only had three fingers – well, two fingers and a thumb, actually. That's what I was calling to tell you, about his hand.'

I look down at the photo I'm holding in my other hand, at Gareth's hands folded neatly in his lap, bring it closer to my face. They're clasped together, interlocked, and I count them, one, two, three, four and a thumb on his right hand and one, two… The room starts to spin then, starts to blur, the colours melding together, greens and whites and browns. Momentarily, I feel dizzy, almost faint even, and the sensation is strong enough for me to place a hand against the wall to steady myself, dropping the photograph in the process.

'Detective Ronson… Detective Ronson, are you still there?'

I try to regulate my breathing as it all comes at me at once; like forgotten memories unlocked after living in a dusty vault for hundreds of years, whirling, fast and furious flashes, almost blinding me. *Picking the petals off the flowers inside Daisey's apartment, 'You will find him, Detective, the man who tried to hurt Daisey and killed those other women.' The presence I'd sensed behind the door of her bedroom as we left; the condom, she must've somehow stolen it, taken it to Leilani Stewart's flat and planted Bradley's DNA on the body…*

'Yes, Des,' I say, hoarsely. 'I'm still here.' Just about.

CHAPTER THIRTY-SIX

For the briefest moment, as her eyes flicker open and she starts to regain consciousness, Daisey thinks she's in her own bed at home, safe. But as she makes to roll over and feels a searing pain, a sharp and spiteful rush of it as it shoots through her skull, it tells her that she's not either of those things. Instinctively she tries to bring her hands to her head, to relieve some of the pressure she feels but quickly realises that she can't. Her hands are tied. She looks down her body at them; her wrists are bound with red cord, stretchy red cord with plastic hooks on the ends, the kind you might use to secure a suitcase with. The same red cord has been used to tie her ankles too. She tries to move them, wiggle her feet, test for any slack – but there isn't any; they're bound tight.

She groans, a low gravelly sound. Her voice doesn't sound like it belongs to her, like it did when she first came round from the attack – the attack, she'd remembered she'd been attacked, and the thought horrifies her all over again. There's wetness on her lips and instinctively she licks them; they taste tinny, like iron, like *blood*. She's bleeding, can feel it trickling down the side of her face and into the corner of her mouth. As her vision comes into focus she realises she's in the back seat of a car, hears the rushing sound of cars whooshing past at speed. But whose car is she in? And who's driving it? Fear hits her then, smashes through her chest like a wrecking ball, exploding into every fibre, every crevice and cell in her body, activating her adrenal glands, sending urgent fight or flight messages to her brain. She's not sure which is worse, the pain or the fear; she only knows that combined they're a potent and toxic mix. She tries to sit up, shifting herself on the seat.

'Don't try to scream,' the voice says measuredly. It's female and she recognises it. 'If you scream, I'll simply kill you here, now, like this, OK? So just stay calm and you won't get hurt, OK, you got that, Daisey?'

'Iris?' The voice sounds like Iris's, her flatmate's voice, but that can't be possible, can it? She smiles, relief causing her bladder to involuntarily relax, a warm rush against her skin. 'Oh thank God, Iris,' she whispers, barely able to move her lips, but then she realises what Iris has just said and her relief is replaced by confusion and fear again.

Images begin playing through her mind, cloudy at first but gradually gaining more clarity, like morning mist evaporating above an ocean. She's at home, in her apartment, with Iris. She's hitting her over the head with a hammer, knocking her to the floor… she's incapacitated, groggy, slipping in and out of consciousness but is aware of being tied up. The cords belong to her, yes; they're from the kitchen drawer. She'd used them to secure the luggage when she went on holiday to Croatia a couple of years ago with Luke.

Luke! Her ex, her lying cheating ex… he's been arrested, hasn't he? What for? They think he's been killing women… that he tried to kill *her*… Sharp pain pierces through her skull and she winces, sucks in air through her teeth. It feels like someone has taken an axe to her head and that her brains are hanging out, grey and bloody and exposed. She really wants to touch her head, examine the damage and put pressure on it to help ease the pain, anything to stop the pain.

'Iris… what's… what's going on? I'm bleeding, Iris…'

'It won't be long now, not too much further,' she says, much as a mother does to a child on a long journey who asks, 'Are we nearly there yet?' 'Then I will explain everything.'

The words 'explain everything' give her a modicum of comfort as she grasps on to any reassurance that she's going to be OK, that she's going to survive this, just as she did before.

'Where are we going? Why are you doing this? Why did you hit me?' The questions force themselves from her bloodied lips, pushing themselves up through her larynx. She doesn't understand, cannot reconcile her conflicting thoughts and feelings.

'A-ahh.' Iris wags her finger in the rear-view mirror at her and tuts. 'No questions. All will be revealed in good time. Just lie back and enjoy the ride for now. And don't try and sit up; you'll only make the bleeding worse.'

Daisey watches her hand in the mirror, her claw-like hand with the missing fingers as she wags it at her.

'*Do you need one of these?*' Suddenly, she's outside the club again, the night of the party, of Warwick's party, that fateful evening that changed her life. He's standing opposite her, holding out a lighter to light her cigarette for her. She puts her fingers over his to protect the flame; it's a warm night but there's still a little breeze. She notices something, his hand… he has two fingers missing and… a wave of nausea suddenly rises up through Daisey's intestines as a horrible thought begins to creep slowy into her mind, wrapping itself around her mind like posion ivy. No. No. It was impossible, unthinkable. *It couldn't be… could it?*

CHAPTER THIRTY-SEVEN

'We need back-up… call for back-up, Davis, and put another APB out as soon as possible. Send uniform round to her apartment, right now… do it, Davis…' I'm shouting as I call Daisey's phone for the third time in succession. It rings out again.

'Jesus fucking Christ,' I swear as panic sends a sharp rush of adrenalin to my joints. 'Let's get round there quick as we can, Davis. Put the lights on.'

I'm driving full speed, thoughts flashing through my head like strobe lights as I press my foot down hard on the accelerator. She's been here, all along, right in front of me, right under my nose. She's looked me in the eyes, conversed with me; she even asked if I would catch the killer… *'You will find him, Detective, the man who tried to hurt Daisey and killed those other women?'* She's been goading me, taunting me, laughing at me… A mix of anger and fear and humiliation burn, corrosive, inside my solar plexus. How had I not seen it? Or had I? *'Sometimes we cannot see what is right before us when we're looking too closely.'* Annabelle Henderson's dulcet voice pings through my conscious. She'd been right all along.

I think back to the time I'd first met her, Iris, in Daisey's kitchen. I remember that she'd not offered to shake my hand as we'd been introduced, not entirely unusual, but not entirely common either. I wonder now if it was because she hadn't wanted me to see that she had fingers missing on her hand, although I had noticed this eventually, on another occasion. All this time, *all this time* we've been looking for a man. Forensic confirmed that the DNA found at the crime scenes belonged to a man – and Iris was a woman, wasn't she? She sure as hell looked like a woman, acted like one too, her mannerisms, posture, gestures, all of them feminine… there was nothing about her that had stopped and made me think otherwise, made me think to question her gender in any way, nothing at all.

'We couldn't have known, gov,' Davis says and I suspect her thoughts are mirroring my own. 'There was nothing about her, nothing to suggest… nothing that struck me as odd, or different, or…' Her head drops slightly. 'And remember what Dr Barber said, about her presenting completely differently to Gareth in both appearance and personality… different mannerisms, voice, even a different gait, maybe it's why no one recognised her at Warwick's, why no one put two and two together.'

My mind races to try to piece everything together, tries to make sense of the nonsensical. 'The prints… the dabs we found on the knife. There were only three of them… two fingers and a thumbprint. Eggerton only has two fingers on his left hand, two fingers and a thumb.' I pause. 'We didn't make the connection, Davis… we should've made the connection…'

She shakes her head. 'We were looking for a man, boss.'

'She *is* a man, Davis. She was born with male genitals, male DNA.'

'Yes but her condition at birth, being intersex, made it easier to pass herself, himself off as female. I mean, he is small, almost delicate-looking for one thing and…'

That reminds me of something Des, Warwick's old mainte-nance man, had said to me, '*small but surprisingly strong.*'

I shake my head.

'He was stalking her, Davis, after he failed to kill Daisey the first time, he began to stalk her. He needed to get close to her again, find out how much she knew… he got a job at Warwick's just to befriend her, so that he could finish the job without anyone suspecting him… least of all Daisey herself. Jesus Christ, Davis.' I bang my hand against the steering wheel hard and in quick succession. 'We've been desperate for Daisey to remember that night of the attack, hoping for her amnesia to lift so she could give us something, and yet the irony is, it may well have been what has saved her, bought her more time.'

'Why do you think he didn't just kill her straight away?' Davis asks. 'She's… he's been living with her, as her flatmate for a while already. Why wait?'

'I don't know, Davis,' I say. A dark and horrible thought enters my mind. 'Oh Jesus, what if she's told him, told Iris, she was coming to Henderson's today, for a hypnotherapy session to try to unlock her memory? He couldn't risk that happening, could he? Oh Jesus Christ, *Daisey*… where are uniform?' I scream. 'Are they at the apartment yet… *Jesus H fucking Christ*… he could've already killed her; she might already be dead, Davis and it's my fault… it's my fault!'

Davis opens her mouth to speak, her eyes wide with panic. I don't think she's ever seen me so rattled.

My phone rings suddenly. I put it on speaker.

'Riley!' I say urgently.

'Ah, Detective Riley.' There's a pause. 'It's Dr Barber, you came to see me, day before yesterday… enquiring about Gar—'

'Yes, yes, I remember,' I cut him off. 'What is it, Dr Barber?' I sound short. I don't have time for niceties right now.

'Well,' he says in his convivial tone, clearly unaware of the situation, 'I've been thinking about Gareth's case ever since we met, trying to remember anything else that could be of use to you and—'

'I'm sorry, Doctor, but we have a bit of an emergency on our hands right now.'

'I see, well I'll get to the point then,' he says. 'Gareth's other self, the female that was, maybe still is, part of his dissociative identity. I told you she had a name, I couldn't recall it at the time but I knew it would come back to me in the end – and it did, it has.'

'Iris,' I say. 'Was her name Iris?'

He pauses for a moment and for some reason I imagine him taking his glasses off.

'Yes! Good God, yes it was.' He sounds surprised. 'How did you know?'

I turn to look at Davis and our eyes meet.

'Just a lucky guess, Doctor,' I reply. 'A lucky guess.'

CHAPTER THIRTY-EIGHT

The car comes to a standstill and she hears the engine switch off.

'We're here,' Iris says.

'Where?' Daisey tries to sit up, to get some semblance of her location, but it hurts to move and she's paralysed by fear. The night of the attack, she's remembered it finally and she wonders if the blow to her head earlier had been what had unlocked it all at last, a horrible irony that has not escaped her. The man she'd been talking to outside the party, the one who had given her a light, he'd had two fingers missing. She recalls that he'd been aware that she'd noticed this and had self-consciously stuffed them back in his pocket.

Naively, Daisey had clung to the hope that the fact Iris also has two fingers missing on the same hand is nothing but a bizarre and strange coincidence, her survival instincts desperate to offer her another rational explanation in a bid to keep her from tipping over into unbridled hysteria. But she couldn't quite lie to herself; the only conclusion she could reach was that Iris and the man who had attacked her – and the other women – had to be one and the same person. Only this seemed too absurd, too disturbing a truth for her mind to accept.

But her newfound clarity is forcing her to see things clearer now, to add things up. Iris's obsession with washing and ironing, laying her clothes in a neat pile for her on the bed – her attacker had done the exact same thing, hadn't he? Then something else strikes her; the things that keep going missing around the house, has Iris been deliberately moving them around to gaslight her, to keep her in a state of confusion? Make her think she's losing her mind?

Fear is a strange mistress. It comes at her in stages, in peaks and troughs, an out-of-control rollercoaster ride. But as her mind clears, a strange sense of calm usurps her terror, almost like acceptance, the mind's way of coping with the unrelenting horror that was unfolding within it.

Iris turns to face her in the back seat.

'In a moment,' she says, 'I'm going to untie you. If you scream or try to run, try to escape, then I will kill you. I have a knife,' she says, her voice calm and matter-of-fact. 'And I don't want to have to do that, Daisey.'

Daisey nods silently as Iris begins to untie the cords around her ankles. Her fingers are nimble, despite her physical disadvantage.

'I suppose you've realised by now that it was me who set Luke up.' She sounds almost proud as she navigates the knotted cords.

Survival instinct instructs Daisey to engage with her. It's Iris after all, her flatmate, *her friend* – that's what she must keep thinking of her as, *her friend*.

'The night he came over, that night you wanted the apartment to yourself. Well, I never actually left, not when you thought I had anyway. I was there practically the whole time you were with Luke, in my room, listening to it all unfold.'

Daisey swallows, though it hurts to. She needs water, something to wash away the iodine taste of her own blood. It's making her feel nauseous.

'So it was you I heard moving around in the bedroom… the noises… I wasn't imagining it?'

'No,' she says. 'You weren't. I knocked something over… clumsy of me… I really thought you would come looking then, come to investigate the noise, or that Luke might've checked the apartment over, but' – she laughs a little, incredulous – 'he was too much of a coward…'

She wants to correct her, tell her that it was because she'd told him not to because she hadn't wanted him to discover that she had taken a flatmate, that her pride had prevented her and she realises now, more than ever, that it's true what people say about pride, that it really does come before a fall.

'I heard you having sex, in the next room, through the wall,' Iris continues. 'I heard *everything*.'

Daisey tries to hide the horror she feels but suspects she hasn't done such a great job because Iris follows up with, 'Oh don't worry, I didn't… I didn't get off on it, if that's what you're thinking. In fact, I was pretty disgusted by it, actually, disgusted that you could think so little of yourself as to open your legs to him after all he did to you…' She throws her a look of contempt. 'Afterwards, when you both went into the living room and started arguing, I snuck into your bedroom and found the condom in the bin. I took it with me, to Leilani's flat. Left the contents there for the police to find. Quite inspired, I thought. I wanted to do you a favour; I did it for you.'

Daisey is shaking; she can feel her body going into shock and wraps her arms tightly around herself. She tries to breathe; in, out, in, out, deep breaths, like her therapist had told her to do every time she experienced a trigger. 'I sent the flowers as well. Took a snapshot of his credit card from his wallet in the kitchen while you were fucking him in the bedroom. I thought that was a nice touch, even if I say so myself.'

'Why, Iris?' Daisey croaks. Her throat is scratchy; it feels like it's been cut.

Instinctively her hand rises up towards her neck. He'd cut her throat once before; was he going to do it again? Suddenly, she recalls the first time she ever met Iris, that moment in the canteen at work when she'd commented on her scarf, the one she wore to disguise the scar, a scar he'd given her. An icy chill runs down her vertebrae. It had all been planned, from the very beginning. He already knew her… he had come back for her, to befriend her so that he could finish her off, finish what he'd started. Only she wasn't able to remember him, to remember anything. She thinks about the intimate moments she's shared with this monster sitting opposite her. The candid conversations they'd had, the private thoughts she'd shared about her mother and Luke, about her hopes and desires and her bitter disappointments. She thinks of all the times she has walked around her apartment semi-clothed, of the moments they had snuggled on the sofa together, drinking wine and watching Netflix, Iris preparing and cooking them both a meal. The night of Leilani's murder, after the fight with Luke, Iris had comforted her, they'd drunk Jack Daniel's together and she'd held her, touched the scar on her neck, had tried to… to kiss her…

Daisey really thinks she's going to be sick. She can feel her guts swirling, going into spasm, her mouth watering, the contents threatening to rise and spew all over the back seat.

'I did it for you, Daisey. To get back at him, for everything he did to you, betrayal after betrayal… hurting you, lying to you, humiliating you and using you. Someone had to stop him; I mean, you weren't going to, were you? You covered up for him, actually lied to the police to try to protect him and the woman he fucked in your own bed for years behind your back! So… I got him back for you… as your friend I did for you what you couldn't do for yourself.'

'I need some water, Iris,' Daisey says. 'I can't breathe.'

Iris takes a bottle from her bag and hands it to her silently, watching her closely as she gulps back the contents, spilling it over her lips and down onto her T-shirt.

'Why did you do it? Why did you try to kill me?' Daisey asks the question instinctively, without thinking, and immediately wishes she hasn't. She must think before she speaks; she must consider every word that comes out of her mouth. She cannot afford to upset her, antagonise her. She must hold on to the fact that Iris is her friend, her kind and considerate flatmate who could never seem to do enough for her. If she continues to treat her this way then she might stand a chance, mightn't she?

Iris looks at her and their eyes meet. She looks different, something so subtle in her demeanour that it cannot be articulated, only sensed. She doesn't answer for a while and the two of them sit facing each other in silence, Daisey's laboured breathing the only audible sound.

'I didn't want to kill you, Daisey,' she says, only her voice sounds completely changed, lower, a different inflection, more masculine. 'Out of all of them, I wanted to kill you the least; perhaps that's why you survived – my heart wasn't completely in it. You reminded me of her, of Rosie, of myself, of all the things I saw in myself, I saw them in you too. But *she* wouldn't let me get away with it, even after I did another one to please her, she wanted you… she wanted you because she knew, she knew I liked you, that I do like you, Daisey… in fact I love you.'

The idea that Iris loves her sickens her but it also gives her something to work with. Maybe if she says she loves her too then she won't kill her. It's worth a shot, isn't it?

'I like you too, Iris,' she says. 'I feel love for you too.' She has no idea who Iris is talking about, the 'she' she is referring to, this person who is jealous and angry with her for not killing her. But then she remembers something Iris had said to her that night, the night of the argument with Luke, the night of Leilani's murder. *'Maybe we all are really. Perhaps he was battling with himself internally, the good Luke versus the bad Luke – and bad Luke won in the end; he was just the stronger of the two.'*

'Where are we, Iris?' Daisey asks. 'What are we doing here?' She looks out of the window, sees that they are in a small clearing surrounded by woodland – she can see only trees, a dense forest stretching out as far as her vision allows. The autumnal light outside is dimming; darkness will be drawing in soon; an hour or two, she guesses. The thought of it scares her, her hope diminishing along with the light.

Suddenly, she recognises the car; it's Ros's car. Ros. Ros will be wondering where she was by now, surely? She'll have realised that her car is missing and will have alerted the authorities, won't she? A sliver of hope renews itself inside her. Ros had rescued her once before; maybe she will come to her rescue again. She clings on to this thought, strangles it like a limpet.

'She made me kill that girl from the bakery by way of compensation. She knew I didn't – that I *couldn't* kill you – especially when I realised that you had lost your memory, you couldn't remember me, or anything that had happened that night. And the more I got to know you, the more I wanted to be your friend, the more I enjoyed being close to you, being part of your life, like we were sisters… even lovers, maybe. I wanted to confess, to tell you the truth, but I didn't think you'd understand, that anyone could ever possibly understand. Only she understands me, that's what she says.'

'Who are you talking about, Iris?' Daisey's voice is a hoarse fearful whisper, yet still she feels compelled to ask. 'Who is this *she* you're talking about?'

'Let's go for a walk,' Iris says, opening the car door. 'There's something I want to show you.'

CHAPTER THIRTY-NINE

The apartment is empty. I sensed it was going to be even before the team arrived with the enforcer and battered the door in.

'We're too late,' I say to Davis as she tears through the rooms, calling Daisey's name frantically. 'She's gone.' My knees feel unsteady and I place my hand on the arm of the sofa in a bid to support myself, help me to gain a hold on my thoughts.

'Search everything thoroughly,' I instruct uniform. 'Look for an address, for anything that might give us a clue to where she's been taken, and do door-to-door; maybe the neighbours saw them leave, saw *something*.'

We'd been on our way over to Ros's house to locate Daisey when the call had come in from Ros herself.

'She's taken my car,' she explained, her voice breathy and low. 'Daisey's taken my car and I don't know where she is… I can't get her on the phone and I…'

I hear the panic in her voice, hope that my own doesn't mimic it in return. It's my job to keep Ros calm even though I feel anything but myself.

'I think she… I think maybe she is with Iris,' I said. 'That maybe they have gone somewhere together.'

'Iris? But I thought Iris was staying with her aunt, somewhere in East Sussex? That's where she said she was going.'

'You don't happen to have an address for her do you, this aunt? Did Iris happen to leave any address?'

'No,' Ros says, and I can hear her concern level shift up a gear. 'She didn't; well, not that I'm aware of anyway. Why would she have taken my car? I'm not angry,' she clarifies, 'just worried. It's not like Daisey to take off without saying where she was going. Maybe she went back to the apartment, yes! She said she'd needed to pick something up now that I think of it. That'll be it. Oh thank God, I was starting to panic there for a moment.'

'Do you know what she needed to collect, Ros? Did she say?'

'No. No she didn't. What makes you think she's with Iris?'

'How well do you know Iris?' I asked her.

'Not very well at all. Met her at work, at Warwick's when she started working on the Perfume counter as a temp. Iris mentioned to Daisey and I one morning over coffee that she was looking for a room, and Daisey needed a flatmate to help out with the mortgage so I thought... well, I thought she was a good candidate, similar age, working together, and she seemed nice, a fun sort of girl, quite confident... and I know she's good around the house because Daisey's told me that she can't do enough for her. It makes me feel better knowing she has someone there with her, safer, you know, after the attack. I didn't like the idea of her living alone. Why do you ask, Detective?'

'Did Iris ever talk about her family to you? A sister perhaps?'

'A sister, no. No I don't think she ever has... You're scaring me, Detective Riley,' she said, shakily. 'Has something happened with Iris and Daisey?'

I pause.

'What's the registration number of your car, Ros?'

She gave it to me and I wrote it down while Davis watched me, relaying it into her radio while I was still on the phone.

'It's a Vauxhall Corsa, silver,' she'd said. 'She's all right though, isn't she? Daisey, I mean?' The concern is back again, audible in her inflection. 'You're not worried something has happened are you?'

'Keep trying her phone, Ros, I said. 'Just keep trying.'

Now, my eyes dart around the living room, scouring it for any clue as to where Daisey might've gone, where Iris has taken her, because instinctively I think this is what has happened, that Iris has kidnapped her.

I walk into her bedroom where Davis is searching through a chest of drawers.

'There doesn't seem to be anything missing,' she says. 'No clothes taken by the looks of things.'

I see the waste-paper bin by the side of the dressing table. It looks like it's been moved, the indentaion ring on the carpet visible underneath it.

'Ros said she came back here for something; what do you think that was, Davis?'

She blows air from her cheeks. 'Impossible to say, could've been anything, I suppose. Some essential item, make-up, a handbag… piece of jewellery?'

I begin fishing through the bin, rifling through the contents, some applicators, make-up, tissues, plastic bottles, a condom wrapper… *a condom wrapper…*

'Jesus,' I say the word aloud and Davis swings round to look at me.

'She took the condom from the bin, a used condom, and she planted it; she took it with her, *he* took it with *him*, to Leilani's flat and planted Luke's DNA on her body.'

Davis blinks at me.

'Do you think Daisey knew? Do you think that's what she came back for – to look for the condom? Realised that someone could've taken it and used it to frame him?'

Davis's radio crackles and she speaks into it as I stare at the waste-paper bin.

Where has she taken her? I try and think like Iris, like Gareth Eggerton, try and think what he would do, where he would go. I wonder if Daisey may have confronted him, maybe she realised the condom was gone and put two and two together. Maybe she'd told her that she was going to see Dr Henderson too and that Iris, Gareth, knew the game was up. I look around the room again; there's no evidence of a struggle, not in here.

'Gov!' Davis calls out to me, wrenching me from my thousand-yard stare. I go out into the hallway. 'There's blood, boss,' she says, her voice heavy with resignation. 'By the door.'

I stoop down and see spots of it on the wood, a small splash on the wall. It looks fresh, maybe a couple of hours old. Panic, fear, anger and desperation flood through me at the same time. I stand quickly. The sound of a phone ringing sends my alert button into panic mode and my eyes dart around in tune with my ears in a bid to locate the source. I don't need to look far because it's practically next to me, on a shelf in the hallway, I imagine where she'd left it, or been forced to. Ros's name flashes up on the screen until it rings out. There are twenty-three missed calls. It's Daisey's phone.

'Get SOCO up here now – and get everyone out. Let's seal everything off. Let's move now, Davis, NOW!'

A voice on her radio comes through again but I don't hear what it's saying. My eyes flick from the phone to the blood and back again. It's Daisey's blood, I feel sure of it, though no one alive in that moment could know just how much I am hoping I'm wrong, how much I want to be wrong.

'The vehicle – Ros's car – was picked up on the A23 about forty-five minutes ago, boss, heading towards Brighton. There was another sighting a few minutes later. Female driving, no one else visible in the vehicle.'

My heart sinks like the *Titanic* as I try to banish the image of Daisey's battered body in the boot of a Vauxhall Corsa.

'I think he's going back to the place where he grew up, back to the place where he killed his sister. I think he's going home, gov,' Davis says.

'I think you're right, Lucy,' I say. 'And I want us to be there to welcome him when he does.'

CHAPTER FORTY

'It's not too much further now,' Iris says as they push deeper into the thick woodland. She has hold of her tightly by the wrist. There's a knife in her other hand, even though she has assured her she won't use it.

'I don't want to kill you Daisey,' she explains. 'I just need to show you something, OK; there's no need to be frightened; don't be scared.'

Daisey complies silently, surprised by the sheer strength of Iris's vice-like grip around her wrist. Her reassurance has done nothing to quell the ever-increasing dread inside of her, the sense that with every unsteady step she makes, she is edging closer towards her own death. Hopelessness and despair sweep through her like fire and her head is pounding relentlessly, as she stumbles through the brambles and bush. This place is vast and unrelenting, and seems to go on for miles.

She thinks about running, yanking her arm from Iris's firm hold and making a break for it, sprinting as fast as she can in the opposite direction, but she can only just about keep herself upright and is struggling with her balance, her head woozy and throbbing loudly in her ears. Instinctively she touches the wound, can feel the swelling and trauma; she looks down at her fingers, sees the fresh blood on them. She needs medical attention; she can feel herself weakening, like she's slipping into a surreal dream-like state. She mustn't allow that to happen.

'Slow down,' she says but her voice sounds faint, like it's coming from someone behind her, twenty yards away. 'I can't keep up. My head… my head hurts, Iris.'

If she's heard her it has made no difference because she's really pulling her now; her wrist feels like it's about to come out of its socket. Maybe if she just complies – just listens to her and hears what she has to say – maybe if, like she's requested, she just tries to understand then Iris will let her go, and that it will be enough and she'll set her free. But then she remembers that Iris isn't actually Iris at all and that she's the man who attempted to kill her and her hope is shattered once more.

'What's your name?' she asks, making another attempt to engage. She's read somewhere that victims sometimes do this in a bid to appear more human to their attacker. 'Your real name, I mean.'

Iris doesn't answer and they carry on walking, up a slight incline now, thick brambles and tall grass scratching against her arms and face and legs, catching at her skin. She feels like they've been walking for hours when in reality it probably hasn't even been fifteen minutes; she's exhausted and just wants to sit down, for the throbbing inside her skull to subside; the pressure is excruciating.

Iris is panting heavily by the time they stop, yet her eyes are wide and bright, almost sparkling in the rapidly disappearing light amid the denseness of the trees surrounding them. They come to another small clearing and, breathless, Daisey looks around her in a bid to get some kind of bearing on where she is, not that it matters. She's deep in woodland, injured and without any means of communication. There is no point in screaming; no one will hear her; it would simply be a waste of vital energy.

'It's beautiful, isn't it?' Iris says, breathing in a deep lungful of air. She looks up at the tree in front of them; the blossom has all but disappeared now, only the last few faded petals remaining.

'It's past it's best now,' she says with a hint of sadness. 'Can you still smell it though, the blossom?'

Daisey sniffs the air audibly but can only smell the scent of her own fear – and blood.

'Yes,' she lies. 'I can.'

'I've always wished I could bottle it, the smell.'

Daisey tries to appease her with a smile but her face feels paralysed.

'You can see my house from here,' Iris says, 'on a clear day, anyway, if you stand on the hill.' She looks out over the brow. 'This is where we played as children.'

Daisey wants to sit down, thinks she might fall if she doesn't.

'As children, you and your sister… and your brother…?'

She remembers the song then; the rhyme he'd sung to her during the attack. *Underneath the lilac tree, just you and me, just us three, happy as can be…*

'That song,' she says, falling to her knees; she can't physically stand anymore, can't support her own weight; the exhaustion and agony and fear is too much, too overwhelming. 'The song about the lilac tree, you sang it to me that night… the night you… is this the tree, the lilac tree?'

'You remembered the song!' Iris actually looks pleased, maybe even impressed. 'Yes, it's the tree, the lilac tree. The tree where my sister died, where she hung herself, where I hanged her.'

Daisey thinks she might be slipping unconscious.

'You killed your sister?' She doesn't think it's possible to feel any more fear than she does in this moment: it's off the chart.

Iris sits down next to her, pulls her up against the tree trunk so that she can rest her body against it.

'When I was born I was neither one thing or another.' Iris pulls her knees up to her chin. 'I was not a boy nor a girl but something, somewhere in between, I suppose.' She pauses. 'I was a twin. My sister, Rosie, she was born a few minutes before me, though there was no mistaking that *she* was a girl, a perfectly formed little baby girl. Ten fingers and ten toes.'

Daisey swallows. *Rosie… Hello, Rosie…* It hadn't been – like she'd hoped – a case of mistaken identity at all. Her mouth feels bone dry; she needs more water but doesn't dare interrupt her as she speaks.

'The doctors,' Iris continues, 'they decided I was more of a boy than a girl; I had a penis, you see, of sorts anyway… and so they cut away the female parts of me, things that hadn't formed properly… and they made me a boy.'

Daisey begins to whine a little; she wants to cover her ears; she doesn't want to hear this but knows she has no choice.

'Anyway, it was a dreadful disappointment, for my mother especially. She'd been told that she was expecting twin girls, and instead she got only one, the other a hybrid freak of both, born with things it shouldn't have and with other parts missing…' She waggles her two fingers and laughs.

'Rosie was the one who told me… my parents never did; they kept it from me, never once spoke about it, but I wish they had, because it would've explained so much. Maybe then I would've understood why *she* was there all the time…'

'Why who was there?' Daisey asks, continuing to try to engage. If she shows empathy, if she listens and sympathises then perhaps she will come out of this alive.

'Her,' she says, 'Iris.'

'But you are Iris,' Daisey replies. 'Aren't you?'

'Partly,' she says, 'only I'm Gareth too. I was born Gareth John Eggerton. And I had a sister called Rosie, a twin sister who I loved very much…'

'What happened to her, Iris?' Daisey says, careful to keep her tone soft. 'What happened to Rosie?'

'Rosie was the only one who ever saw her,' she says, 'the only person I ever allowed to meet her, to know her. I was scared of her, you see…'

'Of Rosie?'

'No, of Iris,' she corrects her. 'She was dormant for many years, always just below the surface, but gradually she became stronger. I felt her presence growing within me day by day. It was Rosie who encouraged her to come out, encouraged me to embrace her. She'd always wanted a sister you see…' Her voice trails off. 'Iris is much more fun than me… much more mischievous, and Rosie liked to play with her and so sometimes I would let Iris play with us… but then Rosie wanted to see her all the time, began to prefer her, to love her more than she loved me, and Iris… well, Iris sometimes did bad things to people… things I could never do, horrible, dreadful, wicked things…'

Daisey is slumped against the base of the tree, listening to Iris's words with a sickening sense of horror as she realises once again that she is alone, in the deep of the woods with someone who is clearly mentally disturbed and extremely dangerous.

'What horrible things?' She doesn't want to know the answer to the question but yet is still instinctively compelled to ask it.

'She killed people, hurt them,' Iris explains. 'She liked to see pain and suffering in others – she enjoyed it. She was bad. She *is* bad.'

Daisey wonders who is talking now, Iris or Gareth. She assumes the latter and it strikes her that if she can reach out to Gareth – who seems to be the kinder of the two – if she can appeal to him, keep him talking then perhaps Iris will disappear and she'll be safe; right now she just wants to be safe more than anything else in the world.

'Why don't you just tell her to go away,' Daisey says, 'tell Iris that you don't want her here anymore and to leave you alone?'

She starts to laugh then, a sound that only exacerbates Daisey's sick feeling.

'If only it were that easy, Daisey! Don't you think I've tried that already? It's the reason Rosie is dead,' she says.

Daisey looks at her, and suddenly she sees *him*, the boy, the man that he is, his features appear masculine and nothing like Iris's at all, but those of a complete stranger – a male stranger who she doesn't recognise.

'In the end I realised that Iris was taking over; she was gradually killing Gareth off. I was scared of her, of what she was going to do, who she was going to hurt next. Rosie wouldn't let me get rid of her though; she did nothing but encourage her; she enjoyed having a bad sister... she covered up for her...'

'Please, Gareth,' Daisey says gently, 'why don't we go back to the car? It's getting late and dark and I really need to go to the hospital. Look, maybe I can help you. I can talk to Detective Riley. We can help each other, Gareth. You could help me and I could help you...'

He looks at her strangely, his head cocked to one side.

'That's exactly what you're doing, Daisey,' he says. 'Helping me is exactly what you're about to do.'

CHAPTER FORTY-ONE

'We've got a hostage situation, ma'am,' I explain to Archer on the phone as Davis and I race down the M23. 'Gareth Eggerton is in fact Iris, Daisey's flatmate and colleague, the woman she's been sharing her apartment with.'

'What?' Archer's surprise is evident by the rise of an octave. 'Gareth Eggerton *is a woman?*'

'Look, ma'am, I haven't got time to explain everything right now. We're going to need a helicopter and an armed unit. I think he's taken her into woodland close to where he grew up, specifically to the tree where his twin sister was found hanged twenty-three years ago. We need the whole area sealed off, roads blocked, no one in or out.'

'Jesus Christ, Riley,' she says, 'the press is going to have a field day… a hostage situation?' I can hear her breathing accelerate down the line. 'Whatever you do, Dan, make sure you go through all the correct channels. Do not go in there all guns blazing. This needs careful handling, proper risk assessment, all of it… I want everything done by the book, do you hear me?'

'They will have a field day if we don't get to her on time and he kills her, ma'am – and I think she may already be hurt. We found traces of blood in her apartment; it's with Forensic but I'm pretty sure it's Daisey's blood.'

'Jesus Christ,' she repeats herself. 'Do we know if Eggerton is armed?'

'No, ma'am, though I suspect he may be; he's not the biggest man in stature, no bigger than Daisey herself. I think he may have her in the boot of a car, tied up.'

Archer pauses. 'Do you think she's still alive?'

'I can't allow myself to think otherwise, ma'am,' I reply.

'Yes, but I mean do you *feel* it, Riley? This infamous intuition of yours, what's it saying to you?'

I can't help but give the tiniest smile to myself. *I need facts. Cold hard evidence that's backed up and supported by facts. Hunches are great – if they lead you to those things; until then, I don't need to know about them.*

'It's saying we've got to get to her fast, that time's running out, ma'am.'

'Don't do anything rash, Dan, OK?' Her tone is stern, authoritative. 'Wait for back-up; do not go in there after them alone – that's an order, Riley. Woods warned me about you… about your penchant for going off script. We don't want any more dead bodies on our hands – and that includes yours.'

I hang up and Davis glances sideways at me as she drives, waiting for me to speak but my phone goes again; it's Annabelle Henderson.

'What's going on, Dan?' she asks, her voice laced with concern. 'Daisey never showed up for her appointment. Have you heard from her? Is everything OK?'

I take a deep breath and explain everything to her, everything I've just learned, everything I think I know about Gareth Eggerton and who he is, his background and his past.

'What do you think he's trying to do?' I ask for her insight.

There's a pause on the line. I can almost hear the sound of her mind ticking over as she attempts to digest everything I've just told her.

'He's tormented by this other self, by the splitting that Dr Barber told you about. I suspect he's battling with himself, with the two people he feels are inside of him, one who I suspect became even more prevalent after his sister's death.'

'So you think he's going to kill her? That he's taken her there specially to kill her?'

'It could be that he thinks that by killing Daisey – by killing her there, under that same tree in that same spot – that it will somehow finally kill that part of him off, like he's trying to emancipate himself from her, from Iris, once and for all – and Daisey's the ultimate sacrifice, someone he cares about, someone he loves. If he offers her up, then maybe Iris will be satisfied finally and he'll be set free at long last.'

I close my eyes and exhale loudly.

'I only hope you're wrong, Doctor,' I say. Only I have a feeling she isn't, that she's absolutely on the money. 'But you were right about one thing.'

'What's that?' she asks.

'About being so close to the truth that you can't see what's right in front of you.'

'Ah, that,' she says, and I think she might be smiling a little.

I thank her and go to hang up.

'Eggerton,' she says, gravely, 'he's dangerous, Dan. I know we've only just met but… well, somehow I think this world is a better place with you in it. Stay safe, won't you?'

'Thank you, Annabelle,' I say, 'I'll do my best.'

As I hang up I suddenly think of Pip, of my little Pip and of Fiona too; I see their faces as though they're right here in front of me. And suddenly, I know exactly what she means.

CHAPTER FORTY-TWO

'It's getting dark,' I remark aloud as Davis and I pull up outside Newhaven woods and I switch the ignition off. 'Stay here, Davis. As soon as the team arrive, brief them. Seal off every entrance and exit to the woodland and surrounding areas and roads – shut him in so he can't move; let's block him in. The chopper will almost certainly alert him of our presence so we have to be prepared for that. It'll be dark soon so we'll need infra-red, see if we can pick them up that way once the light goes.'

'Yes, gov.'

'Have you dug up that Google Map yet? I need an aerial view of these woods. We need to find that tree.'

'But it could be anywhere, boss; this place is across three and a half hectares… where do we even start?'

'His house.' I take the iPad from her and look at the map. 'Eggerton's old house is here…' I point to it. 'Clivedon Road. He used to walk into the woods from there with his sister as kids. My guess is that it's in a southerly direction, up over the brow of the hill – ten, fifteen minutes if you know where you're going.'

'Yes, boss, but that's just it, we don't; we don't know where we're going.'

I smile at her. Oh ye of little faith!

'Gareth and Rosie Eggerton were ten years old when she was found hanging from that tree. By all accounts the Eggertons were good people, right?' I pose the question.

'I s'spose so, yes, from what we know.'

'Well, it's unlikely, given if they were decent parents, that they would've ever allowed their kids to wander off too far from the house on their own, not at that age, so my reckoning is that the tree is round about…' I press my finger down onto the screen. 'Here.'

'OK, boss, so that's where we'll brief the team to start the search.'

'Correction, Davis,' I say, 'it's where *you'll* brief the team to start the search. I'm going in now.'

Her eyes widen.

'Gov? No, gov, you can't go in there on your own! Are you mad?' She stares at me, eyes widening even further. 'You heard what Archer said. She'll have your balls as earrings, and more importantly' – she looks at me, meets my eye line – 'it's not safe.'

I smile at her, touched by her concern.

'You couldn't find me, Lucy,' I reply. 'When they ask you where I am, you say you don't know.'

'But, boss… oh Jesus, gov.' She rubs her forehead with her hand, but she knows me well enough to know that there's no talking me out of it.

'It's going to be dark soon, Davis. And you know as well as I do that this lessens our chances of finding her – alive anyway. Time is running out.' I turn to face her, look her directly in the eyes again.

'Well, in that case I'm coming with you, boss, I can't… I'm not letting you go in there unarmed and alone! I *can't* do that. Don't ask me to do that, Dan.' She's used my Christian name – she's serious.

'I'm not asking you, Lucy, I'm telling you,' I reply, pulling rank. 'I made a promise to Daisey. I promised her that I would get the man who tried to kill her and that I'd keep her safe. I made promises to Fern Lever's family, Jasmin Godden's and Leilani Stewart's too. And I intend to keep them.'

Davis buries her head in her hands.

'What do I tell Archer, boss? She wants to be kept informed at every step via radio… what do I say?' She looks at me, imploringly.

'Tell her I had to go and follow something up.'

I get out of the car.

'Follow what up, boss?'

'My intuition, Davis,' I say as I slam it shut behind me.

The light seems to fade with every step I take deeper into the woods, dropping like a blanket over a body. I can't help but feel my hope of finding Daisey Garrett alive is fading along with it. I know she's in here somewhere – that they both are – hidden among the trees, shrouded by their imposing branches, *underneath the lilac tree.* I just need to find it. A sense of purpose overcomes all other emotions that are threatening to break the surface of my thoughts. Fear is secondary, though it's there, like a butterfly trapped in glass, dancing inside my guts. I make friends with it, use it to my advantage, allow it to help me forge ahead and into the abyss in front of me.

I know that Davis is right, Archer's going to have my guts for garters after this, or 'balls as earrings' as she'd put it – not the most pleasant of images, I have to say. But the truth is, none of that worries me, not right now. All that matters is that I keep the promises I made – and that I find Daisey alive.

CHAPTER FORTY-THREE

'It was a beautiful day,' he says, 'the day Rosie died. We'd been playing here, right where we are now, in this very spot.'

'Tell me what happened, Gareth,' she asks gently. 'Tell me about that day.'

He smiles and places a hand on the rucksack sitting next to him on the ground; she hasn't noticed it before. She stares at it, both wanting and not wanting to know what it might contain simultaneously.

He brings his knees up, rests his elbows on them. He's Gareth now, she thinks to herself; she can tell by his body language, the subtle nuances and inflections in his voice and demeanour. She needs him to stay that way; instinctively she thinks she stands a better chance with Gareth than she does with Iris.

'I'd made a swing,' he explains. 'Out of old rope and a branch, tied it to the tree, spent hours playing on it, back and forth... back and forth...' He laughs gently as he reminisces. 'Simple pleasures, eh, not like it is for kids nowadays with all their gadgets and electronics... back then we had to make our own fun.' He smiles at the ground. 'I loved this tree as a boy, it was my favourite one in these entire woods – something about it, something magical, something, I don't know, hopeful.'

He glances at her briefly and she wonders how she looks to him, her face all bloodied, her eyes swollen from crying and filled with fear. She wonders if he can really see her at all.

'We came up here almost every day, Rosie and I, and sometimes Iris came too…'

'That day…' she interrupts him, not wanting him to think about Iris, to mention her name. 'Tell me about that day.'

'It had been the first time we'd been up here since Michael's accident – well, I say accident…'

'Who's Michael?' She's doing well. Asking questions, engaging him.

'Michael was my friend. I didn't have many of those growing up, just Rosie really and… well, Michael was in my class at school and I'd invited him over for tea. Mummy was happy that I had a playdate, think it might even have been officially my first ever. Anyway, I was pleased that she was pleased – and I liked him; he was nice.'

'Did something happen to him, Gareth?' Daisey asks, unable to take her eyes from the rucksack.

He nods solemnly. The light is dropping rapidly. Soon they will be in complete darkness. She wonders if the police have been called by now, if they're already out looking for her. She can't be sure how long she's been gone; she has no sense of how much time has passed. Perhaps she'll make front-page news again, like she did when he attacked her before. She remembers how she'd felt, seeing herself on TV on the evening news. Such a strange, surreal sensation to see her own image staring back at her from a TV screen, to see herself how others must view her. She'd looked different somehow, not quite how she saw herself in the mirror anyway, and it had made her cringe, like when you hear a recording of your own voice…

She remembers that Gareth is talking to her and tries to listen, but her mind is wandering off in different directions, like it's trying to find its way out of a maze, perhaps in an attempt to protect her, to take her off somewhere else, someplace else, anywhere but here, where she is now.

'... Rosie made her come out to play that day,' he continues. 'I was content with it being just the three of us. I didn't want Iris there spoiling things; she always spoiled everything. But Rosie insisted, and I could never say no to Rosie; no one ever could, or ever did I think.' He snorts a little but it sounds more melancholy than derisive.

'And Michael,' she asks, 'what happened to him?'

'I tried to tell him,' he says, 'I really did; you've got to believe me, Daisey,' he says, almost pleading with her. 'I told him he didn't want to meet her, that it wouldn't be good and that we needed to get back home.'

His head drops to his chin and she thinks how much he is like a child in that moment, a small, sad and lonely child, and although she tries not to feel sorry for him, to feel any empathy for him, she finds she cannot help it.

'We were in the tree.' He points above them and they both look upwards. 'She pushed him,' he says. 'And he fell, smack, smack, smack... until...' He looks down at the floor.

'Was he dead?' She tries to look at him, doesn't want to, but she tries. She must try. 'Did she kill him, Gareth?'

'Anyway, it was the final straw,' he doesn't answer her. 'First, she killed the cat, and then the little boy who drowned in the river and now Michael...'

Daisey stifles a cry, has to cover her mouth with her hand to prevent it from escaping through her lips.

'Mummy was furious, wouldn't let me out for a long time afterwards, tried to have me seen by a shrink... and for a while I thought she'd gone, left finally, and I was happy, you know, happy to be free of her and all the trouble she brought. But that day... while we were playing here, with the swing, Rosie wanted to see her again, said she missed her, missed playing with her and that I was mean to keep her away. On and on she went. I begged her and begged her to stop, told her that I hated Iris and never wanted to see her again, that I was scared of her and what she was capable of. I was frightened that Mummy was going to have me sent away forever if she ever came back… but Rosie wouldn't take no for an answer…'

He shakes his head, closes his eyes as though the memory is too painful for him to recall. 'I knew…' he says, 'in that moment something inside me knew that I would never be free of her, all the time Rosie was alive, she would want to see her, to play with her, to be her sister… and something in me just snapped, but it was an accident, Daisey, I'm telling you the truth; you do believe me when I say it was an accident, don't you?'

'Yes! Yes, Gareth, I do, I really do,' she agrees with him quickly, zealously. 'It's OK,' she says, trying to reassure him. 'I believe you.'

'No you don't,' he says. The tone of his voice has switched again and a fresh wave of fear silences her. It's almost dark now, the last of the daylight evaporating. He stands suddenly, picks up the rucksack and she watches, her heart pounding painfully in her chest as he opens it and takes out a rope and the knife.

'How are you at climbing trees?' he asks, smiling.

CHAPTER FORTY-FOUR

'I'm scared of heights,' she says. It's the first thing that comes into her throbbing head. 'And it's dark, Gareth.' She uses his name deliberately. 'Please…'

'Don't be a spoilsport, it's not too dark – and I'll hold on to you – where's your sense of fun, your sense of adventure?'

He's standing over her now, swinging the rope from side to side, a gesture that appears that much more sinister in the impending blackness.

Daisey screams silently inside her head. She doesn't want to die like this, not like this, in the dark, alone in some strange woods at the hands of a mentally disturbed killer. She doesn't want them to find her lifeless body swinging from a tree, her neck snapped and her head all bashed in. It isn't supposed to happen this way, not to her, *not to anybody*. Her mind races as she desperately tries to think of something she can do or say that will stop this horror, but she's exhausted everything; she's exhausted full stop.

Suddenly, she feels cheated, angry and cheated that he didn't kill her the first time around and that he's been able to put her through all of this again only to die at the end of it.

'Please,' she says, 'don't make me climb the tree. I'll fall, hurt myself, I'm already hurt…' She's pleading now, her earlier strategy of attempting to establish a connection all but abandoned.

'Will you just stop whining for a second!' Daisey is convinced that Gareth had disappeared and that Iris is talking now. 'The view is much better from up there.'

'But it's getting dark; it's dark now and…'

But Iris is pulling her up off the floor, telling her to climb, forcing her to put a foothold on the tree.

'See, there you go,' she says, 'it's not so difficult, is it, a lot of fuss about nothing. That's your problem, Daisey, always complaining, always the victim…'

Her arms feel like they're on fire as Daisey clings to the branches and embarks upon climbing. She's weak from blood loss and her legs feel boneless, like they're made of rubber, making it difficult for her to get any purchase on anything. Iris is above her now and she can feel her tugging at her hair, pulling her upwards. She slips a little, loses her grip momentarily and screams out as she yanks her by her scalp, grabbing at her arms until she's regained her footing. It feels like her chest is about to explode by the time they reach the top.

'We made it,' Iris says, panting, positioning herself on the branch. She begins to swing her legs back and forth in a childlike manner. 'Look down, Daisey, look how high we are!'

Daisey can't breathe and horrible rasping noises escape her dry throat when she tries to. She doesn't want to look down; she's terrified of heights, but she's more terrified of Iris pushing her if she doesn't do as she's told. One shove and she'll surely meet the same fate as poor Michael.

'What are we doing up here?'

'I'll show you,' she says, beginning to tie the rope around the thick branch, looping it round and making a knot to secure it. Daisey watches eyes wide with horror in the dark as she ties another loop at the other end of the rope. She's making a noose, a noose that she's sure she's about to put around her neck, just like she did around Rosie's, around her own twin sister's throat.

'W... what... what's that for?'

She wants to scream, to shout out, but thinks this may antagonise her, maybe make her do something rash, only what could be more rash than forcing someone to climb a tree and putting a rope around their neck?

'No... no...' She edges away from her, upwards of the branch towards the trunk, but she knows there's no escape, there's nowhere else to go except down. She forces herself to peer forward at the darkness beneath her, like a black hole of despair. How has she arrived at such a place as this? A place where she finds herself mentally weighing up whether to throw herself from a tree or have a noose placed around her neck. She is forced to contemplate which might be the better option of the two, which death would be quicker, less painful. She stares at the rope in Iris's hands, can't take her eyes from it. At least this way it would be certain death. Falling from the tree might not be enough to kill her outright; there was potential for more suffering. A fall could leave her a paraplegic, in a wheelchair for life, a vegetable who needs feeding through a tube, alive but no longer living. She's always hated the thought of being a burden to anyone and...

What was that? Daisey thinks she sees something in her peripheral vision, or maybe hears something, a rustling noise perhaps, the crunching sound of leaves. It's caught Iris's attention too because she's telling her to 'shhh,' to 'shut up and be quiet'.

Daisey looks at the knife she's holding in her fingers, in her pincer-like claw, and for a split second she thinks to snatch it out of her hand and plunge it into her, only one wrong foot and she'll fall, do the job for her. The sound is getting closer.

'Hello,' she calls out instinctively, 'is somebody there?'

CHAPTER FORTY-FIVE

I see their shadows as I draw closer. I was right, the lilac tree. He's brought her here just as I'd predicted. It's dark, but not yet pitch black and my eyes struggle to focus, to gain some clarity on what's in front of them. I peer from behind a tree, careful to conceal myself, and I look up. My heart bursts and drops simultaneously as I see them both in the lilac tree, Daisey clinging to a branch. It's a horrible paradox of relief and horror, an unsettling combination that I have no desire ever to experience again.

'Suspect and victim located…' I whisper into my radio. 'Due south, about 400 metres in… Suspect may be armed.'

As the fading light falls on the branches, I think I see Iris a little clearer. She's holding something… I can't quite make out what it is through, no… it's a rope.

'Suspect has a rope,' I speak quickly into the radio before discarding it onto the ground. I make my move from behind the tree, walking slowly, stealthily towards them, into the small clearing.

Daisey spots me first and the second she does she starts crying, screaming my name and making a noise.

'It's OK, Daisey. Stay calm!' I call out to her. 'I want you to stay calm now! Stay. Calm.' I keep my voice low but authoritative as I take slow, measured steps towards the tree, my hand outstretched in front of me, palm facing her. 'This is Detective Inspector Dan Riley,' I announce myself. 'I'm unarmed. I'm not here to hurt anybody, OK? I just need everyone safe… calm and safe… Is anybody hurt?'

'Dan!' Daisey screams again. 'Oh God, Dan, please help me. She's got a knife…'

I hear rustling from the tree and hold my breath as I stand still.

'Iris? Iris, is that you?' I call out to her. 'I want you to drop the weapon, Iris. Drop the weapon; throw it down to me. And I want you to let Daisey go, OK?' The rustling stops and silence ensues. 'Talk to me, Iris, let me know you're OK.' Branches start to shake with movement and I hear another scream.

'She's got a rope!' Daisey's voice rings out across the open space, the acoustics sharp. 'She's got – no… Noooooo!'

Jesus Christ.

'Daisey… Daisey… I want you to grab hold of something… hold on…'

I hold my breath, expecting to see fall her at any moment. *He's going to push her; he's going to hang her, just like he did his own sister.*

'Iris…' I call her name. 'Iris, I need to talk to you. Can you hear me, Iris? I need you to let Daisey go. She's hurt, Iris… she's scared. You're a long way up… it's not safe… let her climb down… it's not safe for either of you.'

Silence. I pause; hold my breath again until my lungs force me to open them. 'We can sort this out, Iris… it doesn't have to be like this – let Daisey go. She doesn't deserve this, Iris…'

I've had to coax down a couple of suicides during my time on the force. One was a woman who'd just lost a child and was going to throw herself under a moving train, which was particularly harrowing. They train you for such encounters, but nothing really prepares you for it when it actually happens and you're faced with it in reality, the crushing sense of responsibility and terror of witnessing such a fine line between life and death. One wrong move, one wrong word and it's the difference between a sense of euphoria and relief, the achievement of helping a fellow human being in their darkest moment, or a lifetime of sleepless nights and 'what ifs'.

'Well, well, if it isn't the village idiot himself – Dan Riley, the man who makes Inspector Clouseau look competent.' Iris's voice rings out across the clearing. 'How good of you to join the party. But I'm afraid you're a little late – and no balloons?' She tuts... 'What a pity...'

I stop still; don't go any further. *Back-up will be here soon*, I tell myself. *You've just got to keep her calm, Dan. Stay calm.*

'I want to talk to Gareth,' I say after a moment. 'Let me speak to Gareth.'

'What do you want to talk to that fool for? That waste of space... Mummy was right, you know, that pathetic spineless little freak should've been killed off at birth. I was the stronger one... It's all because of him... it's all his fault that she has to die.'

'No one has to die,' I say gently, trying to appeal to the softer side of him, the part of him who is Gareth. 'No one; you can choose. You can do the right thing. You can let Daisey go and we can talk. We can help you. I know you've suffered, Gareth. There are people who can help you...'

I can hear Daisey whimpering and want more than anything to be able to just grab her, hold her in my arms, make sure she's safe. I can feel her terror from where I'm standing, can almost taste it and touch it like it's tangible in the air around me.

'I didn't mean to kill her, you know.' His voice has changed. It's lower now, softer round the edges.

'I know you didn't, Gareth. I know that you loved her, that you loved her very much.'

'I just wanted her to go away... to stop hurting people, but she wouldn't go... she wouldn't leave... and Rosie didn't want her to, Rosie wanted her to be bad and... and... I thought if I stopped Rosie, then maybe she would stop... I didn't mean to kill her... we were playing, right here, together... and she put the rope around my neck, made me jump. It was a game… I didn't want to play it… you believe me, don't you?'

'I believe you, Gareth,' I say as a deep sadness washes through me. He sounds like a child now, a terrified child that bears no resemblance to the cold-blooded killer he is, who Iris is. 'Why don't you come down, come down and talk to me, where I can see you? I promise I will help you, Gareth; you have my word on that.'

'When it was her turn to jump I watched her… I was supposed to cut her free, like she did me, but instead I just stood there and watched.' His voice sounds anguished; he's crying. 'It was like I was in a trance. When I came out of it, I panicked, realised what I'd done and I tried to cut her down, but I was too late, the rope was too tight around her neck. I cut her throat trying, trying to sever the rope… *Rosie! Rosie! No! Mummy! Daddy! It was an accident…*'

I can hear his distress tipping over into hysteria as he recalls the nightmare scene of his sister's death.

'I thought, afterwards, that she wouldn't come back… she left me alone for a while… but she came back,' he says, his voice low and laced with what sounds like hatred. 'She came back bigger, better, stronger even than before…'

I can hear the sound of back-up in the distance, of sirens, a commotion not too far off. No sirens, I think to myself, turn the damn things off! I edge a little closer now.

'What's that noise?' he asks, his voice sounds shaky with fear. 'Are they coming for me?'

I swallow.

'It's OK, Gareth.' I'm careful to keep my voice gentle, soothing even. 'It's all going to be OK.'

'I never meant to hurt her or Daisey… any of them… you understand that? She… she just wouldn't stop… my head… always in my head…'

I look up and see him beating the side of his temples with his small fist and then in a swift movement I see him place the noose over Daisey's neck, hoop it over her head like he's hooking a duck.

'Oh God, oh God, Dan! Daaaaaan!'

I gasp; fall to my knees, my hands grabbing at the dirt underneath them.

'Gareth, NO! NO! Gareth! Don't do that. Think about this,' I call up to him. 'Think about Rosie… your sister, your twin sister; you loved her, didn't you? You didn't want to kill her; *she* made you do that, Gareth. Iris is bad, Gareth, but you, you're good, there's good inside of you, Gareth… reach for it, fight her, don't let her win!' Panic seizes me as I implore him. 'Daisey… Daisey's your friend, Gareth, you don't want to kill her either. I know you don't… don't do this… please don't do this…' I'm begging him, my arms outstretched upwards of the tree. 'You do this and you will never be free of her, of Iris… she will haunt you forever, torment you, make you do more bad things, Gareth…'

I hear the sound of voices, of bodies moving through the woods, drawing closer. Flashes of light hit the tree, illuminating it like someone has switched on a spotlight. In a split second he takes the rope from Daisey's neck and places it around his own.

And then he jumps.

CHAPTER FORTY-SIX

'I should have your badge for this.' Archer glares at me from across her desk; her face is flushed a little pink and her chest is heaving, but even then I can tell she's not nearly as angry as she wants me to believe. 'You went into a dangerous hostile situation, unarmed, alone, unprepared... a hostage situation where you were dealing with a suspect with clearly some serious mental health issues, someone armed, a killer who'd murdered three women, and tried to murder a fourth – twice! You put DS Davis in an unprecedented, untenable and extremely unfair situation, and you did not follow even the basic protocol. You were reckless and unprofessional, you put the lives of the victim and the suspect at risk and you put your own at risk too.'

I let her finish before I look up.

'But she's alive, isn't she?' I say. 'Daisey Garrett is alive and unharmed.'

'That's not the point and you bloody well know it, Dan!' she barks back, though I suspect it's worse than her bite. 'That she is still alive is no real thanks to you; doing what you did, flouting every goddamn rule in the book and steaming in all guns blazing...'

'I was unarmed, ma'am,' I reply, 'remember?'

She fixes me with a steely gaze. 'You know exactly what I mean, Riley, so drop the facetiousness. Woods may have stood for it, but I'm telling you now, I won't. I won't have my officers – senior officers no less – behaving in such a reckless and potentially suicidal way.'

I say nothing, let her carry on, get it out of her system. 'Because of your actions, Gareth Eggerton is in ICU, barely alive, barely conscious… he could've died, Riley; he still could die. It's unlikely he'll ever be fit enough to stand trial.'

'Gareth Eggerton is already dead, ma'am,' I say flatly. 'And he's already in prison,' I say, tapping my temple with a finger, 'in here.'

'Well, I'm sure that will be of enormous comfort to the families of his victims, Riley.' She straightens out her tie with her hand. 'I'm meeting with them after I've finished with you and then I'll be giving a statement to the press, a TV interview – the public wants to know what happened,' she says. 'And they'll be an inquiry, of course.'

'Look, I did what I did because I know… I knew where he was taking her, ma'am. I knew what he was thinking, how he was thinking, and what he was planning to do – to kill Daisey. Eggerton thought, in his mind, that if he killed her then he would be free of his inner torment, of this "other self" inside of him that had plagued him his whole life. There was no time for protocol, no time to think things through. I reacted; I did what I do best, ma'am.'

'And what's that, Riley?'

'Not doing as I'm told, ma'am.'

She snorts then, incredulous, and even begins to laugh a little, her head dropping into her hands.

'Jesus Christ,' she says, turning in her swivel chair. Her desk looks as neat and pristine as ever and, perhaps, churlishly, child-ishly, I take one of the pens that she has placed in perfect alignment with her laptop and place it at an angle while she isn't looking.

'Sometimes you have to go off script, to break the rules in order to get the result you need, ma'am,' I say. 'I did what I thought I had to do at the time. I tried to save both the victim and the suspect. And at the end of the day, ma'am, that's exactly what I did. The suspect is no longer at large, he will never be free to kill again – that's what you wanted wasn't it, what we all wanted? Now you'll be able to go on camera and tell the world how we stopped the Rose Petal Ripper, how the police managed to capture him and that the public can feel safe again.'

She shakes her head, draws breath. 'That's as well as may be, Dan.' She notices the pen suddenly, repositions it immediately. 'And this has *nothing* to do with going on camera at all!' I suspect that's not entirely true though as her hair looks freshly styled and she has applied some lipstick, ready for her close up, her moment of glory in the spotlight. 'It's how you went about doing it that bothers me. It wasn't just their lives at risk, it was your own too, remember.'

'I wasn't thinking along those lines, ma'am, not at the time.' That had come later, the fear and the relief that I had come out of it all unharmed.

'Well, you damn well should've been!' She raises her voice in line with her eyebrows. 'You have a family to think of now, Dan.'

I nod. But the truth was that I *was* thinking about my family all along, about Pip and Fiona and Leo too and that I have throughout this whole case. You see, Fern Lever, Jasmin Godden, Leilani Stewart and Daisey… they were, are, simply ordinary, everyday people, someone's family, someone's daughter, sister, cousin, lover and friend… and I did what I did because they could've been *my* family. I think to explain this to Archer but I'm not sure she'd fully understand, or if I could articulate it well enough to make her.

'I want you to take some time off,' she says stoically, clearing her throat. 'We're arranging for you to have some therapy.'

I raise my own eyebrows.

'You above all people should know that PTSD is a very real condition, Dan, and I need you fighting fit.'

'What for, ma'am?'

'For when you come back,' she says, meeting my eyes. I think I see a twinkle in them.

'Yes, ma'am,' I say, standing.

'Don't pull a stunt like that again,' she says, her tone much softer now, and suddenly I'm struck by the thought that perhaps she hasn't meant a word of anything she's said about protocol and blazing guns and recklessness and that deep down she's nothing more than a kindred spirit who would've done exactly the same as I did in that situation. But it's only a fleeting thought.

'No, ma'am.' I nod. 'And by the way, I thought I should let you know, you have lipstick on your teeth.'

CHAPTER FORTY-SEVEN

'He's gone,' Annabelle Henderson says as she sits down next to me in The Swan and places a Scotch on the rocks on the table for me, giving me a waft of her perfume as she does. 'Whatever was left of Gareth Eggerton is gone, I'm afraid. It appears he has no recollection of that night's events, no memory of trying to hang himself. I suspect that the trauma he's experienced combined with any neurological and spinal damage he suffered due to lack of oxygen to his brain has caused this part of his personality, his dissociative disorder, to trigger self-annihilation.'

I blink at her, throw back a sip of Scotch. Dr Henderson has been one of the professionals tasked with the unenviable job of psychologically assessing Gareth while he lies in hospital, to see if he is fit enough to stand trial. I wasn't holding out much hope.

'Self-annihilation?'

'Right,' she says, 'effectively killing this part of himself off.'

'And Iris?'

Henderson rolls her eyes gently, taps the rim of my glass with her own.

'It's too early to tell but in my opinion, I would say that this part of himself has most likely become *the* self.'

I blink at her blankly again.

'Gareth Eggerton no longer exists inside of him and Iris has taken over,' she explains. 'But I can't be sure. He's not saying anything much; he's not saying anything at all.'

I sigh and try not to close my eyes because every time I do, I see his image, the image of Gareth Eggerton jumping from the tree, hanging by his neck. I suspect it will be a while before it fades from my memory, if it ever does.

Maybe eight minutes had passed before the paramedics had arrived and cut him down. They'd managed to resuscitate him, bring him back to life. But enough time had elapsed to ensure some serious damage had been caused, both to his body and his brain.

'I doubt he will walk again either,' Henderson says. 'Though stranger things have happened.'

Haven't they just, I think to myself.

'In my opinion he's not fit to stand trial, neither physically nor mentally. I've recommended he be housed in a secure psychiatric hospital, in a special unit equipped to deal with his numerous physical and psychiatric needs.'

'No trial…' I say the words aloud and Henderson looks at me with those big green eyes of hers.

'I know it's a disappointment, Dan. I know that you wanted a conviction, a custodial sentence for the families of the victims – for Daisey especially. But you know, even if it had gone to trial, even if it still does, he will plead a mental disorder defence, insanity, diminished responsibility at the very least and they'll send him back to where he is already, where he needs to be, in a secure mental hospital, indefinitely.'

I throw back the rest of my Scotch.

'I know,' I say lightly, 'but try telling that to Archer, and the families… she's right, you know, it's not much in the way of consolation, is it? No trial, no sentence, no… justice.'

She laughs a little; it's a nice sound and it reminds me that I haven't heard one of those in so long.

'Don't worry about Gwen. I think an intelligent man like you has already worked out that she's just playing by the book. She thinks you're a hero really.'

'A hero?' I snort into my glass a little. 'I don't feel much like one of those.'

She smiles, flicks her long hair back off her face.

'You know, justice doesn't always come in the form you think it does, or even should. Sometimes life metes it out in a different way, in its own way.'

'Like karma?' I say, signalling to the barman for another Scotch. Thanks to Archer I'm off duty now so why not?

'Of a sort, perhaps. Arguably you could say that Eggerton was born into a life sentence, an intersex baby, all those operations, his physical disability and the rejection from his mother, living in the shadow of his sister… his complex identity disorder… We'll never truly know what turned him into a killer, but we do know that he lived in a constant state of torment, trapped inside himself, battling between two identities, living in fear and guilt and shame about who he was… what he was… you could, if you wanted to, say that this is far worse than any sentence any judge could hand him.'

'Jesus, you make me feel sorry for him,' I say, the Scotch beginning to rush through my veins and soften my edges.

She touches my hand then, the tips of her fingers resting ever so gently on my own.

'Would that be such a terrible thing, Dan?' she asks.

I shake my head. 'I'll reserve my sympathies for the victims and their families, thanks all the same,' I say as George – the landlord – brings another Scotch to the table and waves his hand to let me know that this one's on the house.

'Of course you do,' she says, meeting my gaze with her own. I can tell that she doesn't quite believe me though and that somehow she knows, once again, what I'm really thinking inside. 'It's OK to feel empathy, Dan, even for a psychiatrically disturbed young man who has committed some awful crimes. To feel empathy is to be human – it's what sets us apart from psychopaths.'

'Yeah, well, I've had enough of those,' I say, standing. 'And' – I swallow my Scotch back in one – 'I've had enough of these too. I've got to go,' I say. 'I'm picking my daughter and… and her mother up from the airport later and I want to stop in on Daisey before I head off, see how she is.'

Fiona, Leo and my Pip are coming home tonight and I want to be there to meet them at the airport, to surprise them. I can't wait to see them – all of them.

She nods, flashes me that Julia Roberts smile.

'It's been great working with you, Dan,' she says, standing herself and shaking my hand. It feels soft in mine. 'I hope one day we can work together again, right?'

'Right,' I say, 'you too, Annabelle. And thanks.'

I begin to walk away but something stops me and I turn back. 'You know that thing you said?'

'What thing?' she says, still smiling.

'About not being able to see something right under your nose because you're looking too closely.'

'Yes?'

'Well, you were right, but sometimes you need distance too; sometimes distance makes you realise what you already knew all along.'

CHAPTER FORTY-EIGHT

'Is that the last of the boxes, love?' Ros asks as the removal men collect the final few things.

'Yep, I think that's it now,' she says, looking around her.

'Great, well I'll meet you back at the house then. Ron's driving us to the airport; he won't take no for an answer so no objections.' She hugs her gently, watches her leave through the open front door.

Sighing, Daisey looks round her empty apartment. Soon it will be someone else's and they will fill it with their own memories. Thoughts flash through her mind, transporting her back to the day they'd moved in together, her and Luke. Suddenly, she sees him in her mind, carrying boxes and huffing, grumbling about the tardiness of the removal men they'd hired, *'incompetent imbeciles… not a brain cell to share between them.'*

She smiles to herself as she recalls the relief they'd both felt when it was all over and they'd closed the front door behind them. They didn't have a sofa to sit on that day; it was on order and hadn't arrived in time. That beautiful deep seaweed-green velvet sofa… they'd drunk fancy wine out of mugs as they'd sat on boxes and looked out of the large double windows at the busy street below, surveying the new neighbourhood, filled with a sense of anticipation, that feeling you have when you're embarking upon something new and exciting, the thrill of the unknown. Memories were strange things; perhaps they are never a true representation of the facts, of things that actually happened, but more a snapshot of what you were feeling at the time – of what you wanted to feel.

She lights a cigarette, looks at her phone. That journalist has called her again, the one who wants to write a book about her, tell her story to the world and 'make her famous'. She claims she already has a lot of interest from publishers; she thinks it will make a great docu-series too, be 'snapped up by Netflix in no time' – she says it will be very lucrative. She'll call her back later.

It was her idea to sell up in the end. Luke had not forced her into it, had even said she could stay in the place 'as long as she wanted to'. But she no longer did. Too much had happened, too many memories.

Charlotte left Luke eventually, aborted his baby and quickly moved on to someone else, a car mechanic by all accounts, a man less educated, less affluent, though perhaps in reality he was simply 'more' in other ways, ways that counted, ways that really meant something. She'd even felt sorry for him when he'd told her. She couldn't help it – we are what we are, she supposed.

She jumps as she hears a knocking sound and sees an outline of someone standing in the doorway. She's still a little jumpy, but her therapist says that this is only to be expected and that in time this will lessen, will fade, along with the dreams she has, of her, of Iris… *Everything fades eventually.*

'Dan!'

'I'm sorry,' he says, greeting her warmly, 'I did knock. I didn't mean to startle you.'

She goes to him and hugs him, puts her arms around him, briefly rests her head on his shoulder. She likes the way he feels, strong and solid yet also soft somehow. He smells good too.

'It's so lovely to see you!'

'You too, Daisey, so,' he says, 'this is it then? You're really off?'

She extinguishes her cigarette in an old mug that used to belong to Luke, one that has 'Keep Calm and Stay Philosophical' emblazoned on the side.

'I fly tonight. Ros is taking me to the airport; she's insisted, though I'm not fond of goodbyes.'

'Goodbye? How long are you going for?'

She pauses, unsure how to answer. 'I'm not sure. A few weeks, months, forever maybe… Mum says I can stay as long as I want to.'

Her mother had insisted that she fly over and had bought her an open-ended plane ticket. 'I need to take care of you, Daisey,' she'd said, 'after everything you've been through, I want to be able to look after you – please come and be with your family; let us help you.'

'Wow… Australia… such a vast country, so many new possibilities.'

He looks at her kindly.

'Mum says a change of scenery is what I need.'

'She's probably right,' he says, adding, 'Mums usually are.'

'She thinks I need to put all those bad memories behind me, only…'

'Only what, Daisey?'

'Only memories remain with you, don't they? I mean, you can travel anywhere in the world – be anywhere, with anyone, doing anything – but your memories travel with you wherever you go.'

'Yes,' he says quietly, 'I suppose they do.' And she likes the fact that he hasn't lied to her, like most people do now, tell her lies in a bid to make her believe that one day she will forget. That one day she will wake up and it won't be there, that none of it ever happened.

'Listen, Daisey,' he says, and his tone suggests he has something to tell her that she might not want to hear. 'There's no easy way to say this, but there's not going to be a trial. Gareth won't be taking the stand. The doctors say he's not mentally or physically fit enough to. But,' he adds quickly, 'he'll remain at a secure psychiatric hospital for the rest of his natural life, what there is of it. He can't walk, can barely talk even. His life is over, and yours is just beginning again; remember that: I want you to know that, to feel safe knowing that he will never ever be able to hurt you or anyone else ever, *ever* again.'

She moves into the kitchen area, opens the fridge.

'Mind if I have a glass?' She holds up a bottle of cheap Prosecco. 'Care to join me in a small one – please?'

He hesitates but acquiesces. She pours them both a measure in some mismatched mugs that she's leaving behind – they were only good for the bin, anyway.

'I sometimes wonder,' she says, 'if things had been different…'

He raises his eyebrows a touch.

'You're not alone in that thought, Daisey,' he says.

'If I'd never gone to the party that night, if Luke hadn't been cheating, if I'd let Tommy White stay over…'

Tommy. They'd finally been out for that Japanese meal she'd promised him on that fateful night and had been surprised by how much she'd enjoyed his company. He'd been different to how she'd remembered him, respectful, polite, chivalrous even, not a lewd remark to be heard.

'It was just an act,' he'd explained when she'd challenged him about it, 'all the banter… just a façade to cover up insecurities and shyness…'

'You! Shy?' She'd laughed at him but then she'd remembered; *maybe we're all two different people at the end of the day*… Anyway, it had been a nice date and she'd promised to stay in touch while she was away in Australia. You never knew… stranger things have happened, she'd thought, and they had, they really had.

'… And maybe, maybe if when Gareth was young, if someone, anyone had listened to his mother… if the doctors had helped

him, recognised there was something wrong and treated him...
maybe his life would've been different... maybe all our lives
would've been.'

'Sometimes,' he says, 'it doesn't pay to overthink things. We
are all a world of "what ifs" when we think about it, our whole
lives and existence, once we start asking those kinds of questions,
where does it end? I guess,' he says, looking at her with those kind
eyes that she's always thought match his smile, 'we just have to
try to live in the moment, to recognise that this moment is the
only moment we can be sure of.'

She feels like crying, but not through sadness, not entirely,
but because she knows he's right. She looks at him, Dan Riley,
her hero, the only man who has ever made a promise to her and
kept it.

'So I guess,' she says, touching his mug with her own, 'that
this moment is goodbye.'

CHAPTER FORTY-NINE

I've always had mixed feelings about airports. For me they're a place of extremes – ecstatic welcomes filled with whoops of joy and hugs, and painful and protracted goodbyes filled with sadness and tears. People behave differently at airports; it's a scientifically proven fact, or at least I think it is; they spend money on things they wouldn't dream of in their usual everyday environment and order gin and tonic for breakfast.

I'm living proof of this as I find myself standing in the arrivals hall with a makeshift sign I'd hastily knocked up ten minutes before leaving for Gatwick – one that seems to be causing quite a stir among the passengers who're coming and going.

I can't explain the sensation that rushes through me as I spot their tired little faces slowly coming into view, Fiona carrying our Juno in her car seat in one hand as Leo pushes the trolley, but it's the closest thing to joy I think I have ever felt, a happiness and sense of relief that somehow lifts me up above the crowds, making me feel weightless, like a balloon set free. For a brief moment I see them before they see me, and I have to wrestle back tears. I'm not an overly sentimental man, not outwardly at least, but those few private seconds where only I can see them are a beautiful epiphany. They're back; *my family.*

They start to wave the moment they see me and I watch as their faces light up, smiling, animated, energised. Leo picks up pace with the trolley as he hurtles towards me through the crowds of weary travellers.

'Dan! Dan! You're here!'

Fiona is a little way behind him, her expression changing into one of total confusion as she gets closer and can read the words I've written on the back of the cornflake packet I'm holding up.

'Well,' I say as she stops in front of me and looks around her at a sea of expectant smiling stranger's faces, looking on. '*Will you?*'

In that moment everything stands still, time even, and no one makes a sound.

'Yes,' she says. And the place erupts.

It's cold in the apartment when we arrive home. I'd left the windows open to air out the smell of paint.

'You painted the walls?' She says this with such incredulity that it makes me laugh out loud. 'You actually managed some DIY in between catching a serial killer and becoming a national hero – pretty impressive.' She raises her thin eyebrows at me.

'Well, you know,' I humour her, 'it's not just women who can multi-task.'

We talk a little about her mum, about the funeral, and how it had been – 'just as she would've wanted – a celebration of her life' – before we settle down on the sofa, Fiona and I with our Pip sandwiched in the middle between us. I'd spent at least ten minutes at the airport just sniffing her, burying my face into the folds of her neck and inhaling deeply – that smell of pure joy. Passers-by probably thought I was trying to eat her, but I didn't care. She'd felt heavier in my arms than I remembered, soft yet strong and warm. I've fed her and changed her nappy, rocked her to sleep in my arms before placing her down in between us on the sofa. I don't want to put her in her crib – I don't want her out of my sight for another moment.

'That was some welcome home, Dan,' Fiona says as we both look down at our sleeping daughter. I stroke her soft tuft of fluffy dark hair; it feels like silk on my fingertips. 'It certainly wasn't the one I was expecting, you, holding a sign up saying, *will you marry me?* I didn't even expect you at the airport.'

'Yes, well, I wanted to surprise you,' I say.

'Well, you sure as hell did that!' She laughs.

I take hold of her hand; it feels small and soft in mine, and she looks at me as if I've suddenly become a different man who she doesn't recognise. I suppose I have.

'We can spend a bit of time together now – you, me, Leo and this little lady here, now that Archer's signed me off for a few weeks.'

She raises her eyebrows again.

'She should be presenting you with an award, a medal for what you did, Dan, not punishing you.' She sniffs.

'It's protocol, just while there's an inquiry,' I say. 'She's just doing her job.'

'No, Dan, *you* were the one just doing your job,' she says, defending me. It's a nice feeling. 'I mean, you saved that girl's life, put your own on the line, for Christ's sake – and you made sure the man responsible can't kill again. You got him, Dan, just like I said you would.' She looks at me with her almond eyes, eyes that always seem to be smiling, even when she's not.

She rests her head on my shoulder.

'What made you make up your mind,' she asks me, 'about us? I mean… marriage, Dan? When I went away, I wasn't fishing for a proposal, or giving you any kind of ultimatum, I just wanted you to think about things – you know, us, about what you wanted…'

'And I did,' I say. 'I have. And what I want is right here,' I say the exact same words to her as she'd said to me before she'd left. 'It always has been.'

She smiles and I kiss her on the lips; let it linger.

'I've got DVDs,' I say, tapping a pile on the coffee table, 'if you're not too tired.'

'DVDs?'

'Yes, well, I realised – while you were gone – that I have no idea what your favourite film is, and that we've never even watched one together, so…'

She picks them up, begins to sort through them until she selects one from the pile.

'Which one?' I ask, intrigued.

'*From Here to Eternity*?' she says, holding it up.

'Well,' I say, 'that's as good a place as any to start.'

A LETTER FROM ANNA-LOU

Dearest Reader,

Huge heartfelt and humble thanks for choosing *The Woman Inside* to add to your reading list – I'm truly honoured. If you want to keep up to date on my new releases, or view my past ones, just click the link below to sign up for my special newsletter.

www.bookouture.com/anna-lou-weatherley

You'll need to give your email but I will never share it with anyone and only contact you when I have a new release, promise.

This book was written in the vortex of a global pandemic and although not too much changed for me personally (I write from home) the world around me did. For this reason it was a tricky book to write, but I feel incredibly grateful that I was lucky enough to be able to and my heart goes out to everyone who has been, and continues to be, affected by Covid-19.

Perhaps as a result of such challenging and unprecedented times, mental health has never been more at the forefront of our social conscience and although I could never have predicted the events of 2020, it does by default make the issues covered in *The Woman Inside* perhaps even more topical. I'm fascinated by the psychology of the mind and how so often people appear to be one thing on the outside and quite another on the inside and I wanted to explore this on a much deeper psychological level for *The Woman Inside*.

I also wanted to explore the concept of the emotional transition from victim to survivor and how human strength and spirit can prevail even in the face of the worst kind of adversity. I'd really love to know what you thought of Daisey's character and how she deals with the emotional aftermath of her ordeal. I hope you enjoyed Dan's continuing story too and how he has grown both as a man and a detective – I have a real soft spot for him!

The subjects touched upon in *The Woman Inside* – personality and identity disorders, mental health and gender – are delicate and often misunderstood issues and I hope I have given them the justice, compassion and understanding that they deserve.

Your comments, feedback and reviews mean absolutely everything to me as an author, so I'd be delighted to know what you thought of *The Woman Inside*. If you enjoyed it, it would mean a lot to me if you would take the time to leave a review letting me and other readers know why.

I often read titles by recommendation from friends and family and vice versa, so if your review encourages others to read one of my novels and enjoy them too then I cannot thank you enough.

Rest assured, whatever the world throws at us, Detective Dan Riley and the gang's story will continue with a new case very soon. Until then…

Stay safe and much love,
Anna-Lou x　.

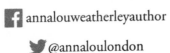 annalouweatherleyauthor

@annaloulondon

ACKNOWLEDGEMENTS

Firstly, I'd like to thank my amazing editor at the wonderful Bookouture, Claire Bord, for her unwavering faith in me while writing this book, for her continued and on-going support and for her invaluable help with editing. It is a genuine pleasure to work with such a professional, kind and lovely person as you. I really cannot thank you enough for everything – you are an inspiration and I'm lucky to have you!

Thank you to my beautiful mummy, another great inspiration and support that I could not be without and whose love of reading and writing she passed on to me – love you.

My sister, Lisa-Jane and brother, Marc and my beautiful boys, Louie and Felix, my friends, Kelly and Sue, and to Liz and Colin – thank you all for your interest, friendship and support (and all the laughs).

Thanks to absolutely everyone at Bookouture, to Kim, Noelle and all the other amazing and supportive authors in the fantastic family. I'm so honoured to be part of such an incredible publishing team. Thanks to the MM Agency and to the anonymous man who kindly took the time to speak to me so candidly about living with dissociative personality disorder – your words will always stay with me.

Thank you to my darling David. It's been an incredibly tough year but we made it through together! I couldn't have done it without your love and support and all the belly laughs. I love you to the moon and back.

Lastly, I want to thank anyone who is suffering with or has suffered from mental health disorder. It's OK not to be OK sometimes and I send you love and strength. In a world where we can all be anything, let's be kind.

CENT 06/11/2021

Lightning Source UK Ltd.
Milton Keynes UK
UKHW010628091021
391930UK00001B/172

9 781800 193574